THE UNRAVELING OF LUNA FORESTER

MARISA NOELLE

Cover art by Fay Lane - https://faylane.com/

FIRST EDITION

www.marisanoelle.com

REVIEWS FOR THE UNRAVELING
OF LUNA FORESTER

"Full of adventure, mystery and heart, with nightmarish creatures lurking at every turn - it kept me guessing to the end!" - Kat Ellis, author of *Wicked Little Deeds*.

"Another tense and twisty ride from none other than Marisa Noelle. I didn't expect anything less!" - Melissa Welliver, author of *The Undying Tower* trilogy.

"Take everything you know about fairytales, then forget it. This twisted tale snatches you in and doesn't let do!" - Hannah Kates, author of middle grade horror.

"A deeply immersive story of eclectic characters with an ending that broke my heart." - G.R. Thomas, author of *Child of Fear and Fire*.

"Noelle's story will make you say aloud...Wow! I didn't see that coming!" - Sue Scott, editor.

"Action-packed fantasy with a huge twist. Marisa's beautiful writing has you emerged into the book and leaves you wanting more!" - Melanie Gee, booktoker.

"Absolutely loved the entire cast of characters! Gah! So sad. But Matthew will always be my favourite." - book blogger.

"I need more of this story! I can't believe it's over!" - ARC reader.

OTHER BOOKS BY MARISA NOELLE

The Shadow Keepers

Plastic

The Mermaid Chronicles Series

Secrets of the Deep

Quest for Atlantis

Fight for Freedom

Ghost Pirates

Vendetta

Denizens of Darkness

Vortex Returns

The Mermaid Chronicles Companion Guide

The Unadjusteds Trilogy

The Unadjusteds

The Rise of The Altereds

The Reckoning

The Unadjusteds Companion Novellas

Silver Melody

Matt Lawson

Joe Rucker

Paige Starling

Hal Small

Erica Swiftfield

Kyle Lewis

Jacob Shea

Sawyer Watson

Addison Shields

President Bear

CONTENT WARNINGS

This book explores mature psychological and emotional themes. It contains depictions and references that some readers may find distressing, including, but not limited to: mental illness, trauma, PTSD, gaslighting, domestic and emotional abuse, suicide ideation, death, self-harm, violence, and manipulation. It also includes strong language and scenes of psychological horror. Reader discretion is advised.

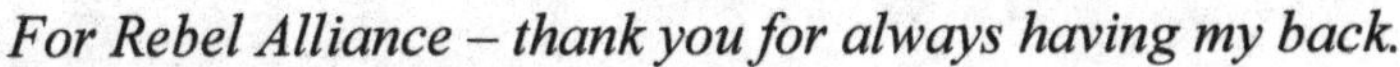

For Rebel Alliance – thank you for always having my back.

*For Team Swag – thank you for navigating the murky waters
with me.*

CAST

Welcome to Matthew & Luna's family.

Luna – A seventeen-year-old who lives in an isolated cabin in an alpine forest. She lives with her father and together they foster their found family.

Matthew – A seventeen-year-old who loves to run. He is Luna's best and oldest friend.

Piper – A fifteen-year-old mute with native ancestry. She is religious and is also adept at natural medicine and healing herbs.

Alessandra – One of the older members of the group, she is prone to wearing long skirts and numerous bangles and is often a voice of reason when the others are bickering.

Faith – A no-nonsense sixteen-year-old who strives to be a professional ballet dancer, even if she does have a smart mouth.

Hope – A fifteen-year-old who suffers from anxiety and panic attacks. To ease her worries she draws in a sketchbook.

Tyler – A seventeen-year-old varsity football player, he thinks of nothing more than the cheers of the crowds.

Kalisa – One of the older members of the group, she follows her own religion which centers on a medallion she wears at her neck. She is wife to Joseph, and mother to Caleb, Jasmine & Nell.

Joseph – A quieter member of the group, he can be easily spotted by his beaded, blond dreadlocks. Husband to Kalisa, and father to Caleb, Jasmine & Nell.

Caleb – A twelve-year-old boy who loves nothing more than to run wild in the woods, building dens and chasing Ulrich. His siblings are Jasmine & Nell. His parents are Kalisa & Joseph.

Jasmine – An eight-year-old girl who loves to play with Ulrich and make stick dolls. Her siblings are Caleb & Nell, her parents are Kalisa & Joseph.

Nell – A one-year-old baby. Her siblings are Caleb & Jasmine, her parents are Kalisa & Joseph.

Kerry – One of the newer members of the group, he is a

mysterious, Irish drifter who takes Luna on fast rides on his motorbike, and smokes constantly.

Ariel – Over four hundred years old, Ariel is the oldest member of the group and is also an angel. She wears white clothing and only offers advice when asked.

Beacon – A supernatural creature in the form of a humanoid light who is without the power of speech.

Obsidian – A black-feathered gryphon.

Ulrich – A telepathic fox, happiest in Luna's or Jasmine's company.

Monty – One of the newest arrivals of the group, brother to Robin. Handy with a shotgun.

Robin – One of the newest members of the group, sister to Monty, mostly interested in Matthew's best interests.

CHAPTER 1

LUNA

THE NIGHTMARE CLAWED at my heels as I ran down the hall. I reached the door and scraped at the handle, desperate for it to turn. Finally, it opened. I peered into the gloomy interior. Caleb slept, his mouth open and his covers kicked off to the floor. Tyler's massive bulk faced the wall. I swiveled my gaze to Matthew. He held a book and a flashlight in his hands. A hardback textbook of some kind. I couldn't make out the title.

He raised his head and smiled. "Couldn't sleep?"

I shook my head and inched into the room. With a trembling hand, I wiped the sweat from my brow. Even the roots of my hair were damp. I shut the door behind me and leaned against it. The smell of dirty trainers and sweaty socks lingered in the air. "I had a nightmare."

Matthew sat straighter, his book falling to the floor with a soft thud. "The same one?"

I nodded.

He held out his hand.

Thank God for Matthew. He never minded me interrupting his nights. He was the only one who could banish the images. I tiptoed across the room and sat on the edge of his bed. He threw an arm around me and gave me a squeeze. A tear leaked out of my eye. All I could see was the blood in my dream. But it wasn't just a dream. It was a memory.

"*Shhh*," Matthew said. "You're whimpering. You'll wake the others."

Tyler stirred. Matthew laid a finger across my lips while we waited to see if Tyler would wake. But he rolled over, his toned bicep covering half his face. I hadn't seen much of him over the summer. He'd been training for weeks, determined to retain his varsity quarter-back position when the school year began. His arms rippled with newly defined muscles. I liked to watch him chop wood on the stump in the yard. Such power. Such strength.

Caleb muttered in his sleep. Sweet Caleb. I longed to reach out and wipe the smudge of dirt from his young cheek. He'd spent all summer building dens in the woods and camouflaging his face with mud. And sometimes terrorizing his little sister with sticks, pretending they were swords.

"Shall we go outside?" Matthew asked. "So we don't wake the others?"

I stood. Matthew went to the sash window and threw it open. He climbed onto the roof and offered me his hand. I scrambled after him. He slid the window down behind us, leaving it open a fraction. The sweet smell of pine trees drifted toward us from the forest and helped to settle my stomach. I inhaled deeply, and my hands ceased to tremble.

I gazed over the yard and forest beyond. The dark pines stretched up to the full moon, almost reaching it. As we settled ourselves on the roof, I shivered. The cold of the slate tiles leached through my pajamas. I lifted my toes so only my heels were in contact with the cold roof. Raising my face skyward, I shivered again.

The stars were out in all their infinite glory. This far up the mountain, their undiluted light shone almost supernaturally. The immense blackness of the sky hinted at what lay beyond; the stretching, never-ending universe. Sometimes I wished I could be among the stars. Maybe things would be easier. I spotted the constellation Orion. My favorite. Orion the hunter who slayed animals and loved the Goddess Dawn.

Obsidian's wings beat against the black night. It took me a moment to locate him, camouflaged against the inky darkness. I followed the path of the blotted-out stars. He flew in high circles, throwing me the occasional squawk. It echoed through the trees, and I wondered why no one else had ever discovered him. A gryphon of midnight black and a wingspan equal to the length of two buses, almost as big as the house itself, one of its kind, hidden away. And then I remembered. No one else would ever know him, because he was all mine. Only mine. I smiled.

"The nights are getting colder," Matthew said. He removed a loose roof tile and brought out a tin. Opening the small box, he took out a pre-rolled joint.

Looking at him, I threaded my arm through his. My chest tightened as I felt a rush of love. He was my favorite. Of course he was. He always would be.

"School starts next week," I said, accepting the joint. I bent my head as he lit it. Inhaling deeply, I felt the headrush and the edges of the nightmare slip away. "SATs soon. They're going to work us hard this year. Are you ready for it?"

Matthew smiled. "I've got pre-season training first."

"You're the fastest person on the track team." I rested my hand on his thigh. His warmth seeped through his sweatpants and into my cold hand. I took another hit on the joint and offered it to him.

He shook his head at the joint. I could never tempt him. He took his training and health seriously. I was slightly envious of his willpower, of the clear lines he lived by. But he never judged. That was one of the things I loved about him.

"You haven't had the dream for a few weeks."

I shifted my gaze to his face. A small frown interrupted his smooth brow. "Six weeks, two days."

"You've had a nice summer. No dramas."

I exhaled a perfect smoke ring toward the sky. The stars wobbled, the effects of the marijuana taking hold.

"It helps, being around all of you. Not seeing the pitying stares at school." I shivered again. In the distance, an animal barked. Or yelped. Maybe it was Ulrich.

"Do the others know?" Matthew touched my hand and a fire flamed under my skin.

I looked through the window. The rest of my convoluted family slept during this dark hour of the night. None of the others had trouble sleeping. Except for Hope. Occasionally.

"About my mother?" I asked.

Matthew shook his head. "No, I meant, about you. And them. And…you know."

I did know. But I didn't like to talk about it. When my father went away to work, Kalisa and Joseph took care of us all. And Alessandra. They were the oldest members of our group. The surrogate parents for kids that didn't belong. I didn't belong. Not really. Not without them. And I didn't like to think about it too much. It magnified my differences. If I could change, I would. If I could get along without them, I would. My throat went dry at the thought. I needed them, especially after what happened to my mother. The blood. So much blood.

I gripped Matthew's hand. "Protect my secrets."

He looked up, concern softening his eyes. "Of course."

"You'll always take care of them, won't you?" I asked, suddenly gripped by the fear that something would happen to them. Us. Me.

The furrow in his brow deepened and his lengthening hair flopped over his eyes. "Take care of them? What do you mean? They're here because of you, not me."

"I know." I tapped my toes against the roof. "I just worry."

"That, I can help you with." He tapped the joint and grinned. "And anyway, that's what the grownups are for, aren't they?"

"I suppose," I replied, taking another drag. But Matthew had different qualities. He knew how to keep them all together. "I think they need you more than you think."

Matthew snorted, then rubbed the accumulating dew from the slate tile with a finger.

I pulled my knees against my chest. "Not everyone likes each other."

"Of course not. Even in a traditional family, that's not unusual."

"And there are seventeen of us."

Matthew smiled. "I wouldn't have it any other way."

Nor me.

"With great power comes great responsibility," I said.

"You're quoting superhero movies at me now?" Matthew laughed.

"You're the only one who likes them as much as I do."

Another yelp peeled through the quiet forest. Farther away.

Maybe Ulrich was hunting. Sometimes he brought me the carcasses of rodents from his night-time hunts. Sometimes he would sit in my lap and let me work out the tangles in his fluffy tail. Other times he would just follow me around.

"I think I'm ready to go back inside." I stubbed out the joint and threw the remains in Matthew's tin.

Without speaking, Matthew took my hand and led me back across the roof to the window. He pushed it up and we crept in, careful not to disturb Caleb and Tyler. Once he shut the window again, I hesitated. His flashlight lay on the floor, illuminating the title of the book: *Abnormal Behavioral Psychology*. I'd forgotten he was studying psychology this year. An extra credit class so he could up his GPA.

Matthew reached for my hand. "Do you want to sleep here?"

I nodded. He lifted the blankets and I crawled into the bed, next to the wall, where I would be sandwiched between it and Matthew and nothing bad could get me. He climbed in after me and placed his warm feet next to my freezing ones.

"Thank you," I murmured, as my eyes drifted closed.

Matthew picked up his book and flashlight and continued to read.

CHAPTER 2
MATTHEW

Smoke billowed along the cabin's upper hallway, obscuring the windows, turning everything hazy.

"Fire!" Matthew yelled.

Luna. He had to get to Luna. He ran down the hallway, pounding on the bedroom doors. The timber frame of the house shook under the power of his violent thumps.

"Fire! Wake up! Fire!" He coughed, struggling for breath, and lifted his T-shirt over his nose and mouth.

A door opened. Piper peered out, sleep gluing her eyes half closed. One look at his face and the smoke billowing behind him and she dashed back inside to wake the others.

Luna. Where was Luna? Matthew threw open her bedroom door, but she wasn't there. Her sheets spilled off her mattress and puddled on the floor. Her curtains blazed a trail of flames, mantling an open window. On the ledge sat a trio of church candles, an incense holder, and a framed picture of her at last year's Homecoming dance; all burning, wilting, fading from existence.

"Luna?" He was tempted to check the closet or under the

bed. But she wasn't in the room, didn't look like she'd been in the room all night. One of her nightmares? He checked his watch. 2 am. She must already be outside.

"Fire!" Matthew called, retreating and closing her bedroom door.

Coughing into his elbow, he kept his shirt over his mouth and nose. He ran back the other way, making sure everyone was up. His eyes watered and stung as he fought his way through the thickening smoke. He attempted to push it away, but it was so dense, almost opaque, like a solid substance, and it quickly filled any gap he temporarily cleared. Scalding door handles burned his palms as he fought entry to each room.

He ran into the nursery and plucked the youngest, Nell, from her cot. She screamed in his ear, her arms and legs as stiff as rolling pins. He looked for the others, doing a count in his head: Nell, Jasmine…where was Caleb? He'd just graduated to the big boys' room, but Matthew hadn't seen him there, and sometimes he crept back here to sleep after his night walks. He gestured for Jasmine to follow. She slipped her shoes on, snatched her denim jacket from the floor, and grabbed a stick doll from her bed.

"We need to go. Where's Caleb?" Matthew raised his voice above the crackle of flames and the cries of his friends. He looked wildly around the small room, hoping Caleb would magically materialize.

"Not here." Jasmine balled her jacket under her arm and clutched the stick doll to her chest. "He hasn't been here all night."

"Outside. Now," Matthew said, pushing the eight-year-old out the door. He glanced once more inside. The windows shook with an unseen vibration. A menacing shriek from beyond the house permeated inside. The noise almost reversed his blood flow. Ulrich? But Ulrich had never made his stomach churn or his jaw clench. The window vibrated again, almost rippled, threatening to implode. They didn't have much time to get outside.

He coughed. Spluttered. It was almost impossible to draw breath. Nell was still screaming in his ear. He stuck his little finger in her mouth. She silenced almost immediately. He glimpsed her winter onesie hanging on a hook behind the door. The one with the arctic foxes chasing after snowflakes. She'd grown so much over the summer, it might not fit anymore, but he didn't have time to delve through wardrobes. He grabbed it and dashed out the door after the others.

With Nell balanced on his hip, Matthew ran down the stairs and joined a melee of terrified people scampering for the back door. He couldn't be completely sure, but it seemed everyone had made it out of the bedrooms. He'd do a head count outside. They scrambled through the small laundry room, grabbing coats and boots and whatever they could reach. Shoving his feet into his boots, he spotted Luna's red coat hanging on a hook and tucked it under his other arm before tumbling outside.

Luna. Where was Luna?

Take care of them, Matthew. How long ago had she said that? Was it only three nights? Did she know this was going to happen?

Of course not, she couldn't have.

Matthew shivered as the night air wound round his limbs. Overhead, the large, round moon smiled benignly, its face beaming down at them. He drew in a deep breath of pine-scented air and coughed the smoke out of his lungs. Retching, he spat dark muck onto the ground. They huddled by the enormous oak which marked the boundary of their unfenced yard. The one with the swing that Hope spent hours in, not swinging, but drawing in her notebook. Now, the swing was empty, swaying in an unseen breeze.

Matthew passed Nell and Luna's coat to one of the others and turned back to the house. Orange flames engulfed the entire right side of their home. Curtains and wood blazing, without forgiveness. It had been a hot summer. No rain for over a month. An unprecedented heatwave. The house was going up like kindling.

"Luna?" he called, his gaze glancing over the tops of heads. But the smoke wasn't done with him. He doubled over in a coughing fit. His eyes stung and his lungs burned. A deep, searing pain ricocheted the length of his old scar. He felt for the risen ridge between his shoulder blades, almost convinced he was alight. There was no fire on his back.

"Luna?" he called again. He stumbled through the crowd, counting heads, but they were all moving about and searching for each other, and he had to keep starting over. Seventeen wasn't that big a number. If they'd just stay still, he'd be able to count them. He didn't see Luna. Where was Luna?

The moon illuminated everything in graphic detail. The kind of detail he didn't want to see. The fire was spreading. Completely swallowing the house. The only house he'd known for the last ten years crumbled before his eyes. The young ones cried. Alessandra shushed them as she used her heavy skirts to wipe the soot from their faces. Alessandra. Thank God for the older woman. Everyone was coughing. Nell began bawling again, her little arms and legs rigid. Alessandra wrestled the small child into her onesie. Her hands and feet stuck comically out of the ends.

"Luna?" Matthew called.

"I haven't seen her," Alessandra replied, glancing over her shoulder. When she looked at him, Matthew rebelled against the level of worry in her eyes.

Luna. She had to be okay.

Matthew turned at the sound of the familiar voice. Caleb stood at his side. The twelve-year-old wore jeans and heavy boots, with a thick goose-down jacket; the only one of them properly dressed. Daytime temperatures wouldn't drop off for another month, but the nights were always cold in the forest.

"Where have you been?" Matthew snapped.

Caleb shrugged. "I couldn't sleep." Twigs and leaves from his recent escapade decorated his brown hair. His impish ears twitched and turned red.

"Help me look for her." Matthew pointed to the far side of the house.

Caleb nodded and dashed around to the front.

"Luna!" Matthew called again. His throat burned every time he spoke.

The noise of the fire hit him. Loud and crackling, like a malevolent voice, taunting him. He could barely hear anything above the hissing and spitting wildness. Nell's crying faded to the background.

"Help me!"

Matthew swiveled toward the voice, expecting to see Luna. Too late, he realized the voice was male. A person trailing a tail of fire shot out of the remains of the house, hurtled across the deck, and ignited a path of pine needles in its wake.

"Tyler?" Matthew stood glued to position for a moment,

watching Tyler turning macabre pirouettes. Kalisa, the mother of the three youngest children, ran after him, patting small flames out with her nightdress.

"Help me!" Tyler screamed again, slapping at the flames on his face with a fiery arm.

Spurred to action, Matthew dashed forward, removing his jacket. Piper rushed forward too, following his motions. Matthew pushed Tyler to the ground. "Hold still!" Tyler's arm and hair blazed with flames. Matthew wrapped his jacket around his burning friend, patting and rolling him. After a few moments, the fire went out.

He turned to Piper. She swept her long fringe out of her eyes and turned her face into a question mark. He knew what she was trying to ask.

"I tried to help him," Kalisa said. Her afro smoked and several burn holes pock-marked her bathrobe. "He still alive?"

Matthew stuck a hand under Tyler's nose. A small, warm, breath tickled his finger. "He's alive," he said. "Just passed out. Help me move him."

Piper, with her long, dark hair in her sleeping braids, gave him another questioning look. She wouldn't speak, hadn't spoken for years, but her looks were strong enough to command attention.

"You know we're not going to be able to stay here. With Luna's father at work. We can't be found here," Matthew said. "Not like this."

Piper nodded and looked at Kalisa.

"S'okay, sweetheart." Kalisa touched one of Piper's braids and pushed it behind her shoulder. "We'll stick together. I'll take care of you." She lifted her spiritual medallion at her neck and kissed it. "The Goddess will keep us healthy." She turned to Matthew, rubbed his arm with her maternal touch. "Do we call for help?"

Matthew shook his head. "We need to protect Luna, we need to…" *protect her secret*. "If the authorities find us all here, it could be bad for her." How much could he say without freaking them all out? Luna had never answered his question the other night. On the roof, after her nightmare. He'd asked her if the others knew. But she hadn't answered. She'd asked him to protect them.

So that's what he must do.

Piper crouched, ready to help lift Tyler. Although she was only fifteen, she was an inch taller than Matthew.

Matthew grabbed Tyler's legs. Piper lifted his arms. Tyler's head lolled awkwardly to the side, but there was nothing they could do. They carried him a few yards into the tree line where he would be hidden from view.

"Find Alessandra," Matthew said. "She'll help you gather the herbs to treat him."

Piper nodded, patted a canvas bag hanging from her shoulder, then dashed off to find the older woman.

Matthew retraced his steps, heading for the inferno. There wasn't much left. The woodland cabin burned fast and hot. It would be no more than a pile of ash in minutes. He didn't know fires could burn so quickly, so completely. If it weren't for the heat of the fire, Matthew might have thought he was watching the first gentle snow of winter. The flakes floated around his head, drifting on the thermals, adding a magical quality to the surreal night. When his fingers went to his face, they came away covered in a thin, gray layer. But it wasn't snow, it was ash, and there was nothing magical about this night.

"Luna!" he called again. His eyes cleared but his throat remained achingly hoarse.

Matthew shuffled backward, double checking the crowd as he headed away from them. Most of the others had gathered near Tyler. Nell was with her mother and quieting down. Alessandra looked to be counting heads, her gold bracelets jangling as she patted peoples' shoulders. Matthew faced the front and walked around the side of the house. Sirens wailed in the distance. They didn't have much time.

He found her by accident. Tripping over something, he landed badly, a stone gashing a cut across the bony part of his knee. Rough pine needles blanketing the forest floor grazed his palms. He looked back at the shape that had caused his fall. Luna. Lying next to the blackberry bush still ripe with berries. Not moving. Breathing?

CHAPTER 3
MATTHEW

MATTHEW CRAWLED to Luna on hands and knees, ignoring the pain that shot through the cut one. He squeezed his eyes shut and breathed deeply, dreading the worse. What would they do if she was dead? *Please, don't be dead.* It would be the end of them all. He almost wept there and then.

Caleb joined him, his eyes widening as he fell to his knees. He held Luna's red coat in his arms. The one with the hood that reminded Matthew of Little Red Riding Hood. "Is she okay?"

Half by the firelight and half by the light of the moon, Matthew saw her chest rise with life's breath.

The relief shuddered out of him and his teeth chattered. "I don't know, Caleb."

He leaned closer to Luna's inert form. What was wrong with her? He swept her dark hair off her face, looking for burns. Checking her over for injuries and fire damage, he found nothing obvious, not a single hole in her blue pajamas.

"Luna?" he whispered. "Luna?"

No response. He watched her chest rise and fall for a

couple of moments. Her eyelids fluttered. There was nothing else to do but to pick her up. "Come on, let's get her away from the fire."

With Caleb trailing him, Matthew carried her into the woods toward the others. It looked as though Piper had found the herbs. She mulched something together and spread it all over Tyler's face and arm.

"What's wrong with Luna?" Hope whispered, clutching her sketch pad to her chest. She wore a nightdress, one of those old-fashioned, high-necked things. Totally unsuitable for the forest. But then, most of them weren't dressed appropriately.

"You okay?" This was the first glimpse he had of Hope since the fire. Her skin was as white as the ermines that roamed the northern forests and her blonde hair hung long and wispy. And although nothing like darker-skinned Jasmine, she probably could have borrowed most of the younger girl's wardrobe. Her eyes were sunken and her breaths came in shallow gasps, like she was on the verge of a panic attack. Her feet were bare, her shoes consisting of a thick layer of mud. He couldn't remember the last time he'd seen her wearing shoes.

She didn't answer. Her trembling body gave him all the answers he needed about her state of mind.

"Remember to breathe, in and out, nice and slow. Cup your hands over your mouth and nose if you need to. Breathe *slow*."

She nodded, and shoving her notebook under one arm, followed his instructions.

He laid Luna down at the base of a tree on a soft blanket of pine needles. Funny, how they were rough when he'd fallen, but now they served a different purpose. Caleb covered her with her red coat. Matthew rescued the scraps of his ruined jacket and helped Hope into it. The hem came down to her knees.

What's wrong with Luna?

Hope had asked the question. He didn't have any answers.

He swept his gaze over Luna, so peaceful, like a fairytale princess. Kneeling, he stroked her hair and her eyes fluttered open and stayed open. Her jet-black eyes focused on him, but she didn't speak, and she didn't acknowledge him. Despite the heat at his back, goosebumps erupted over his skin and a cold sweat pooled on the small of his back.

The others whispered. "What's wrong with Luna? Why won't she talk? Is she mute now like Piper?"

"*Shhh*!" he hissed at them. "Give her a chance."

He turned back to Luna. "Luna? Are you okay?"

Her eyes widened fractionally. But she still didn't speak. Or look at him. The shiver of foreboding that raced down his spine caused goosebumps to break out all over his skin. His heart picked up tempo. Luna was different. Luna was altered. Luna needed help.

"Luna?" he said, so only she would hear. "Are you hurt? Please say something. *Please*."

She blinked. That was all.

"Where do we go, Matthew?" Alessandra laid a hand on his shoulder. Near his scar. It made him jump. Her bracelets jangled in his ear, and the scent of her lavender perfume, mingled with the reeking smoke, swept over him. Sirens wailed in the distance. They were louder, then fainter, zigzagging their way up the mountain road. The fire burned so brightly someone from the village at the bottom of the mountain must have seen the flames and called it in.

"The woods," Matthew replied.

"Yes." Caleb punched an arm into the air. "A real life adventure. Finally. With all of us."

"The woods?" Hope asked around her cupped hands, eyeing the dark forest. "I'm not going in there. Didn't you hear about those campers who went missing over the summer?"

Caleb rolled his eyes. "*Pah.* Just rumors. I've been in the forest countless times, and I've never gone missing."

"That you know of," Matthew muttered, then turned to Hope. "Don't worry about that now. We're all here together, that's the important thing."

Alessandra pointed to the woods with a shaky finger. "You think that's the answer?"

"The only one. But I don't know how we go with Luna like this." Matthew waved a hand in front of Luna's face, trying to make her flinch. He clicked his fingers. Nothing. "How do we get her to move? Can she hear us? Why isn't she talking?" His voice cracked. What was wrong with her?

"We'll help each other," Alessandra said. Her gold hoop earrings caught the light of the flames. "It's what we do."

Hope backed away, dropped her hands from her mouth, edging toward the fire. Her sketchbook fell from her arms. "I don't want to go into the woods."

Matthew approached her, snagged her shoulder, and gave her a hug. "It's going to be okay. There are seventeen of us. Nothing is going to hurt seventeen of us."

Caleb puffed up his chest. "I know the forest like the back of my hand. I'll take care of you, Hope."

Hope smiled at the younger boy, then wound her thin arms around Matthew's back. "Promise? Promise it will be okay?"

"I promise." Matthew pulled away, picked up the sketchbook, and pressed it back into Hope's hands. "We need your help with Luna. Think you can manage that?"

Nodding, she swiped at her cheeks. Her tear tracks glistened in the firelight.

Alessandra turned to Luna and grabbed both her hands. "On your feet now, dear."

Luna allowed herself to be pulled to a standing position. She was able to bear her own weight, but merely stared blankly into the forest. "There we go. We'll be going for a walk now, you'd like that, wouldn't you, Luna?"

"She's not a baby," Matthew said, clenching his jaw.

Alessandra gave him a sharp eyebrow. "She needs to be treated delicately. You of all people know that."

Caleb found a tiny posy of bluebells and tucked them behind Luna's ear. "There you go. All better now." He ran off at the sound of his mother's voice.

"Did you call an ambulance?" Tyler sat up, his eyes darting, his face distorted by the herbs Piper had covered him in.

"*Shhh.* It's okay, Tyler." Alessandra kneeled by his side, using her long skirts as protection from the ground.

Tyler clutched his arm. "It hurts."

"Looks like a second-degree burn," Alessandra said, turning Tyler's face to the side. "Lucky Kalisa found you when she did. Maybe that medallion of hers actually works. Could have been a lot worse."

"Feels a hell of a lot worse than a second-degree burn!" Tyler snapped.

"Hey!" Matthew stomped over to him. "If Alessandra says it's a second-degree burn, then it's a second-degree burn. You're going to live. Hallelujah."

Tyler's dark eyes drilled into him. "Bet you're glad about that."

Alessandra spread her arms between them. "Easy, boys."

Matthew backed off, his mind racing with the things he really wanted to say. Not that Tyler deserved to be burned, of course not, nobody did. But Matthew hoped it would take him down a peg or two. He was a guy who'd preen in front of a mirror for hours a day, flexing his biceps and performing pectoral jigs, who spent longer on his hair than any of the girls, and there was a fraction of a moment when Matthew thought he deserved it.

"Are you sure I don't need a hospital?" Tyler muttered to Alessandra.

"It's going to hurt, but the herbs will kick in soon." Alessandra removed the bright red headscarf that covered her graying roots and dabbed gently at Tyler's cheek. "You're going to be okay."

Matthew watched the beefier boy. All that muscle. Wasted on an arrogant personality. What did Luna ever see in him? But as he took in the heat radiating from his blistered skin, the swelling, and the smell, guilt rushed at him. He'd promised Luna he'd look out for them. That included Tyler.

Tyler's hands roamed over his face and arm. "My face is ruined!"

Matthew bit down on the inside of his cheek. "Think of the story you'll be able to tell the girls."

Tyler's cold glare was filled with fury. "They're not going to come near me if I don't get to a hospital and get this fixed!"

"No hospitals." Matthew stepped close. "You know the rules."

"Rules? *What* rules? I can't live like this!"

Rules. Of course they had rules. To protect Luna. If they didn't protect Luna, none of them would survive. How could Tyler not be aware of that? But now wasn't the time to bring Tyler up to speed.

"You can, and you will. For Luna's sake." Matthew pointed at her. She stood motionless, robotic, waiting instructions. Someone had helped her into her red coat and pulled the hood up. A spark of color in the dark night.

"Screw Luna," Tyler said.

A stony silence swept over the group. Even the children turned to stare. First at Tyler and the curse that had slipped from his lips, and then at Luna, standing impassively, so altered from the person they knew her as.

"I don't want to hear that kind of talk," Alessandra said, walking her hands up her thighs until she was standing again. She re-tied her headscarf, but it barely managed to contain her long, dark curls.

"Just because she turned you down," Matthew added.

Tyler glowered at him.

"Let the herbs work, Tyler," Alessandra said. "You will heal."

"But not completely," he replied.

"We all have our crosses to bear," Alessandra said. "You know you'll heal. Even without the herbs. You always do."

"Matthew?" It was Kalisa, the mother of the children. Her black hair stuck up at all angles and twin moons danced on her ebony cheeks. Her pupils glistened. Nell was bundled in her arms, sound asleep. Finally quiet.

"You okay?" he asked. "We've got to go into the woods."

Kalisa pulled him away from the others. Her eyes darted all

over the forest, looking everywhere but at him. Her hand went to her back as if massaging a tight spot.

"Even with the Goddess's help, I don't move the way I used to." She pointed to the medallion at her neck, a complicated twisted metal figure, vaguely resembling a woman with lots of triangular points. It symbolized the spiritual path she chose to follow. "I'm getting older. But I'll be okay. If that's where we need to go, then that's where we need to go." She drew in a shuddery breath as though the words had exhausted her. She coughed. Smoke inhalation. They were all suffering.

"You're beautiful, Kalisa," he said, and he meant it. But he was glad the others were out of earshot.

She smiled, revealing a wide gap between her front teeth. There was so much warmth in that smile, Matthew barely noticed. "Don't let Joseph hear you talk like that."

"I'd never…that's not what I meant…" A warm flush flooded his neck and cheeks.

"I'm just teasing you," Kalisa said. "Thanks for grabbing Nell." The baby slept soundly, the lighter color of her skin framed by the dark of Kalisa's arm.

"Of course. We're all in this together." Including Tyler. And Kerry, if he ever turned up again.

She glanced at Tyler. Piper was helping him to his feet. He cursed again.

Matthew shook his head. A tug of guilt pulled at his gut. "Tyler will be fine."

Kalisa lowered her voice. "What do we do about Luna?"

It was a good question. Luna was leaning back against the trunk of the oak tree, her hands holding the rope of the swing as if she might go for a midnight ride. Her eyes were open. They moved from side to side, taking in the scene, but

Matthew had a feeling she wasn't really seeing anything. Alessandra and Ariel stood next to her, trying to get her to talk. If anyone could get her to talk, it would be those two.

I don't know. He wanted to say. But he couldn't. He always knew what to do. Either him or Alessandra. Always. Just not now. He couldn't remember the last time he'd seen Luna like this. No, scratch that, he could. But he'd been so young and it was such a frightening experience, he'd shoved it into some dark recess of his mind.

"Don't worry." He attempted a smile. Maintaining it made his cheeks ache. "She'll be fine." *Everyone will be fine.*

Take care of them, Matthew.

"We really have to go in the forest?" she asked, her worried gaze scanning the dark shadows.

"It's safer than waiting for the authorities," Matthew replied.

She looked at him. "I know. I'll do my best."

"You always do, Kalisa." Matthew wanted to say more, to tell her he thought of her like a mother, a real one. That she was one of the best foster mothers around, but he felt time was slipping away.

Kalisa's gaze shifted to the burning house as a large beam fell to the ground and shuddered a small earthquake toward them. It reverberated into the forest and caused a few of the others to scurry deeper inside the tree line. In the silence that followed, Matthew heard the unmistakable beat of giant wings flapping overhead. He raised his eyes to the night sky. By the light of the moon, he could see the large, dark wings. Their undersides were veined with reflective luminescence, making him easier to spot.

"Obsidian," Hope said, her body no longer trembling.

Caleb appeared again, punching a fist into the other palm. "Awesome, maybe he'll finally let me ride him."

"He's been gone awhile." Matthew eyed the enormous gryphon as he flew in circles overhead. *And if he's back now, it can't be good.*

"He never goes far though." Hope shivered inside his jacket and wrapped it around herself more tightly. She shoved her sketchpad in one of the large pockets.

Matthew cocked his head as the sirens wailed again. He waited, breath held, the smoke tightening his chest. Then he blew it out when they faded away again. They had a few more minutes.

Matthew turned to the wings once more. The mammoth gryphon flew in low circles, just grazing the tops of the tall pines, gliding on the mountain thermals. Once in a while he flapped his powerful wings and gained a few yards of height. A couple of times Obsidian glanced down, his large yellow eyes fixed on the chaos below. Then he would squawk and turn his head to the snowy peaks.

Please don't blow out a breath, Matthew pleaded. They'd had enough fire for one night.

"I really need to go to a hospital," Tyler said. He crumpled to the ground, put his elbows on his knees and held his head in his hands. "It hurts!"

Matthew had promised to look out for them, but going to a hospital with Luna like this? It would be the undoing of them all.

"We need to go," Alessandra said. She tucked her baggy shirt into the waist of her skirts and tightened her head scarf.

"Help me with Luna." Matthew whispered to her so the others wouldn't hear. They bent their heads together and observed the group. Luna stared vacantly into the dark forest. Her face slack. Her arms slack. Everything about her was slack. She wouldn't look out of place in one of those old-fashioned mental asylums where they wore tracksuits with elasticized waists and shoes with no laces. Where they drugged them with things like Thorazine until they couldn't close their mouths to stop the drool from dribbling out. Where they ate out of plastic trays with plastic utensils, and where they formed a line every evening to down the meds and start the process all over again. Eat, get drugged, sleep, repeat. The analogy cut a little close to the bone.

"Of course." Alessandra nodded. "She might not be talking, but she seems physically unharmed. She can walk."

"She's only wearing slippers." Matthew looked at the soft fleece of her rabbit slippers. At least she had her red coat on over her pale, blue men's pajamas.

"She's better equipped than many of the others." Alessandra shivered in her oversized shirt.

"We can't be here when the fire trucks arrive."

"I know."

"There's nothing left inside the house." Matthew's gaze fell over the burning inferno.

"What about Luna's father?" Alessandra asked.

Matthew dug a booted toe into the ground, hesitating. Even within the unreality of the situation - the numbed trauma of a devastating experience that would only come to him later, in pieces - he recognized a defining moment. The forest might not contain the authorities, but it wasn't without peril. Hope was right on that account. The darting shadows, the ravens…

As if on cue, a raven squawked above his head. A sliver of

icy fear cut through his bones. He hated ravens. So black, so dark, so evil.

"He won't make it back in time. Not before the fire trucks and police," Matthew said. "I promised him I'd take Luna to Grandmother. If there was ever a problem."

He scanned the woods. Nothing moved. Maybe it would be okay.

"What about Luna?" Alessandra asked. "You've known her the longest, have you ever seen her like this?"

The question took Matthew right back to that moment. The time he'd pushed way down deep, that had just reared its ugly head again, the incident he really didn't want to think about. It was when he'd first met Luna. Right after *it* had happened. The death of her mother. She'd been so affected, so full of trauma and nightmares with that haunted, paralyzed look in her eyes, that he felt like he'd been there with her, witnessing it all. And he didn't want to think about that. Ever. But that was the only other time he could remember Luna being unresponsive.

"Not since…" he trailed off. He wasn't sure if the others knew. Had Luna told them? If they did know, they didn't talk about it. Not once.

"That's what I thought," Alessandra said.

"She needs help. And there's only one place we can get it."

"Grandmother's house." Alessandra bit her lower lip. "But the forest…"

Matthew didn't want to go in the woods either, but they didn't have a choice. "She'll know what to do. She helped her the last time, when the hospitals couldn't."

Alessandra nodded. "Tyler's not going to like it."

Matthew shrugged. "We'll do what we can for him."

Obsidian's wings sent a gust of hot air billowing into the

trees. The fire's stray sparks heated Matthew's cheeks as the gryphon flew by. Obsidian ascended, straight up, like a helicopter, then flew further away, until all Matthew could make out was the feathers of his inky black tail. He was deserting them. Where was he going? His presence had unnerved Matthew, but now that he was leaving, Matthew felt more anxious. He seemed to be heading toward the coast. At least it was the right direction for Grandmother's house, if that's where they were going. There was nowhere else.

"Do you remember the way?" Alessandra asked.

"I know it," Caleb piped up.

Matthew gave the twelve-year-old boy a once over. The pockets of the boy's coats contained a penknife and string and all sorts of other odds and sods, but could he have really made it to Grandmother's house before on his own?

"I sincerely hope you never tell your mother that," Matthew said, and was rewarded with a cheeky grin. "I'm going to need your help, buddy."

"You got it." Caleb threw him a salute and dashed off again.

Alessandra touched his arm gently. "We can't rely on Caleb."

"I know," Matthew replied. "But it will keep him busy. Keep his mind off Luna, the fire…"

"Good idea." Alessandra smiled, then scanned the woods. "Ulrich knows the way."

"Have you seen him?" He was the one member of the group Matthew wasn't worried about. Ulrich always slept outside, usually behind the woodshed or near the log pile, even when there was a foot of snow on the ground.

"I saw him scampering into the woods when I first got out. He'll be around somewhere," Alessandra said.

As they walked back to the others, a robin fluttered nearby and disappeared inside a hole in a gnarly tree. It was better than a raven. He listened to the sounds of the robin's gentle whistles before it fell silent. As silent as Luna. She stood there and stared, barely blinking. Tyler's whines reduced to low murmuring. The others looked at him and Alessandra, knowing they would have instructions.

Alessandra put two fingers in her mouth and let rip a piercing whistle.

The others turned to scan the tree line.

A bark erupted from deep in the woods. Its abrasive sound pierced Matthew's bones and made him shiver, despite the heat of the fire only a few yards away and the thickness of his sweatshirt. But there was something else in the quality of that bark. Something he hadn't heard before, something that made him question whether fleeing into the woods was the right idea.

"It's Ulrich," Jasmine whispered, her lips lifting into a toothless smile. She'd just lost her two front teeth last week.

Matthew noticed the two glowing eyes first. Then the forelegs and the twitching ears. He waved his hand to beckon him over. The fox padded through the crowd, earning himself a pat from Jasmine. He shrugged off her touch, shaking his torso as if emerging from a lake. He walked slowly, never in a hurry, despite the sirens rising in volume. Arriving at Matthew's feet, he sat on his haunches.

"We need to talk," Matthew said.

The red fox just sat there. His haunches tilted to one side, his fluffy tail wrapped around his flank, his narrow nose sniffing at the air and his glinting eyes watching Luna.

"Seriously, Ulrich, we need to talk. We don't have much time."

The fox chuffed and whined. Then his fur began to shimmer, a sign that the fox was ready to use its telepathy. Ulrich gave him a nod with his fox snout.

"There's been a fire," Matthew said,

Ulrich shifted his gaze to the cracking flames. *"I can see that. And smell it. Is everyone okay?"*

Matthew nodded. "Physically."

"Speak for yourself," Tyler said.

Alessandra stepped up to Ulrich and placed a hand on his flank. "Something's wrong with Luna. We need to take her to Grandmother's house. Can you lead the way?"

"Why can't we just stay here? If everyone's okay?" Ulrich asked, his voice penetrating their heads.

"Yes, why can't we just stay here?" Tyler whined.

"We don't have time for this!" Matthew ran his fingers through his hair, gripping the ends tightly. Did no one know about Luna? "We can't be found here. Trust me. We need to leave. Now."

"Grandmother can help?" Ulrich asked.

Matthew nodded.

Ulrich dipped his snout, and his whiskers twitched. *"Okay then."*

The fox jogged over to Luna. She didn't look at him, even when he gently took her hand in his mouth and tugged. Matthew frowned. He'd never seen Luna not respond to Ulrich before. She loved him even more than Jasmine did.

Ulrich lowered his head and dashed a few paces into the woods.

"It's time to go," Matthew called. "To Grandmother's house." He waved them all into the woods.

"I need a hospital!" Tyler said from his position on the ground.

"Suit yourself." Matthew turned on him. "Come with us or stay here. It's up to you."

"You'd like that, wouldn't you?" Tyler snarled, cradling his blistered arm.

"If you're coming with us, keep your distance," Matthew snapped back. "I don't care for the stench of burnt meat."

"Oh, you *little*…"

"Come on now, we can't argue amongst ourselves," Alessandra said. "We need to get Luna the help she needs."

Tyler pushed himself to his feet. "It's all about Luna, isn't it?"

Alessandra turned on her heel, her long skirts swishing. "Would you rather it be about you?"

Tyler didn't reply. He frowned so hard it split his brow in two. But he stumbled after them, his face angrier than the fiery inferno at their backs. Matthew watched him go. The herbs should have been more effective. He should be halfway healed by now. Luna. It was because of Luna. She, and she alone held the power of healing at her fingertips. Merely by willing it. But with her in her current state…

"Is everyone accounted for?" Matthew asked Alessandra as they approached Luna.

"Everyone except Kerry, but that's not unusual. I can't remember the last time he came around," she replied.

"Makes Tyler seem like a saint."

"Don't start."

Matthew held his hands up. "Kidding."

He took Luna's hand and gave it a small tug. She took a couple steps, tripped, her blue fleece slippers digging into the dry dirt and a couple inches of brown pine needles. Matthew tucked her arm in his and guided her through the moonlit woods. At least the sky was clear. They'd be able to use the moonlight for a while, until the trees thickened.

Alessandra flanked her other side. An owl hooted somewhere in the distance. And a raven. Matthew wished he had a slingshot. He'd take that raven out before it could follow them, before it could cause any damage.

Crickets chirped at their feet, falling silent when they walked by. He couldn't smell much beyond the smoke, until they walked a little way. Then the scent of pine needles wound around him, urging him on. And the faintest whiff of Alessandra's lavender perfume. And his own stale sweat.

"This way!" Faith called, twirling through the trees on pointed feet. "I can see Ulrich ahead."

"Hey! I'm in charge!" Caleb called from somewhere ahead.

"Do we know where Kerry was when the fire started?" Matthew asked.

Alessandra paused. She stepped over a bulbous root and helped Matthew to guide Luna over it. "No. No, we don't."

CHAPTER 4
MATTHEW

INTO THE WOODS THEY WENT. They had no choice. Anything was better than facing the authorities.

Hope walked ahead of him. Matthew thought back to the one time he'd peeked in Hope's sketchpad. Her imagination was vivid. Startlingly so. Most of the drawings of fantastical beasts and nightmarish scenarios took place in a hastily sketched forest. But that didn't make them real. That didn't mean *this* forest.

The group spread out through the trees. Faith, with her thick jacket rolled up to her elbows, picked up sticks and hacked at ferns with her typical bad attitude. Her unicorn tattoo flashed with every backhanded slice. Jasmine ran after Ulrich, her long legs stretching to keep up with him. She reached out to touch his tail as it bobbed in the air.

"Fire! Fire!" A scream came from ahead.

Matthew looked over his shoulder expecting to see snaking tendrils of fire chasing them, grabbing at their heels, cornering them into death. He imagined he could still hear the crackling and hissing of the flames, but they were far away from the house. They'd been walking for half an hour, and the light from the inferno which destroyed their home had long since disappeared. Not even any floating flakes of ash. But the acrid scent still inundated his senses. The stench of fire and smoke and tragedy clung to them all.

"Fire!" The voice came from ahead. Others murmured and cast darting glances back the way they'd come. Was a forest fire coming their way?

"Is that Caleb?" Kalisa asked, shushing the baby in her arms. She turned her worried eyes on Matthew. "Please, Matthew, find out what's going on. You're quicker than me."

Matthew dropped Luna's arm. She stood there, not blinking, just staring. Alessandra nodded at him to go ahead. He pushed his way through the others, swinging his head side to side, examining the trees for a heat source. Ulrich ran back to him, growled softly, pleading with him to follow.

"It's coming!"

As they jogged through the woods together, Matthew checked the others over, trying to decipher Caleb's position, if it was him screaming. Joseph, Kalisa's husband and father to the three youngest, followed Jasmine, shouting warnings for her to slow down. Matthew bit down on his lip as he jogged, pointing farther ahead. Had he given Caleb too much responsibility when he'd asked him to help lead?

When Matthew reached Caleb, Ulrich was there, standing guard. Caleb lay on the ground, his arms and legs thrashing, despite Faith holding him down. She swept a muscled leg over him. That worked. Her strength was all in her dancer's legs.

Beacon hovered by Ulrich, a blurry human shape. Although she didn't speak, and was only barely human in the form she presented to them all, she was one of the most calming presences and could dispel a heated argument in a few seconds. Humanoid in shape, her essence was mostly made up of a shimmering golden light. A light that kept the shadows at bay as they trekked through the forest.

Her golden aura leached into the fox's fur and illuminated the immediate area. Matthew's breath plumed on the frigid night air. He hadn't realized it was cold. He'd been thinking about the fire and heat.

"He's having a vision!" Faith exclaimed, receiving a flailing fist to her jaw. She fell back, losing a flip-flop. She refused to wear anything else when she wasn't in her ballet shoes. Her thick, sheepskin coat fell open, revealing short pajama shorts and a spaghetti-strap singlet.

Ulrich barked, once. Matthew dropped to his knees and tried to grab Caleb's arms. The young boy's eyes rolled back into his head and flashed white. Matthew pinned Caleb's arms down on his chest with one knee. Faith recovered her flip-flop and rubbed at her reddening jaw.

"Thanks a lot, C," she muttered.

"It's not his fault," Matthew said.

"Fine time for a vision."

Matthew rolled his eyes.

"At least it wasn't my feet," Faith said, still rubbing her jaw.

"Is he okay?" Joseph slid to his knees beside Matthew, the beads in his blond dreadlocks clattering over his shoulder. Kalisa hovered back, jostling the baby, trying to keep her asleep, but her eyes were trained on her son.

"He's having a vision," Faith said. "And he keeps screaming about fire." The pendant attached to a choker around her neck swung gently. One of Ulrich's milk teeth.

Jasmine had given it to her for her last birthday. She rarely took it off.

"I'm here now, son," Joseph cooed to Caleb. His hand went to the boy's head, smoothing back damp hair from his forehead. "I'm here."

While Joseph hoisted Caleb's torso onto his lap, Matthew grabbed hold of his kicking legs.

"The fire! It's coming back!" The tendons on Caleb's neck protruded and his eyes rolled around in their sockets.

"I'm not sure it's a vision, maybe it's just the aftermath of the fire affecting him now," Matthew said. But a flap of wings above made him doubtful. Obsidian circled the treetops. And that could mean more fire. As Alessandra had said, the forest was dry from a summer of no rain. If the fire crew hadn't gotten the remnants of their house under control, it could spread. Maybe engulf the entire forest, depending on the winds. Matthew performed a quick scan of the area. There was no sign of fire. Not yet.

Caleb stopped thrashing. He opened his eyes and sat up straight. "The fire isn't over." His voice rang clearer than the mountain ice that surrounded their home in winter. "There's more fire to come. There's more…*everything*." His eyes closed and his breathing slowed. Then his head dropped. The visions always took it out of him. Sometimes he'd spend the whole next day in bed, sleeping it off.

"Great," Faith muttered. "Fine time for a nap."

"We really can't stop." Matthew agreed with her for once. "We haven't come far enough from the house. If they search the woods…"

"I know, I know," Joseph said. "You don't have to tell me what's at stake." He lowered his voice. "How *is* Luna?"

Matthew sighed. That was the million-dollar question. Alessandra whispered to her. But she remained frozen, barely blinking, staring at nothing. "We need to get to Grandmother's house."

"Why is that so important? Why can't we just go back and wait for her dad?" Joseph asked, a deep frown cutting across his smooth brow.

"You really don't know?"

Joseph shook his head, making the beads at the end of his blond dreadlocks clatter again.

They really didn't know. Why hadn't Luna told them? Why had she left it all up to him?

Matthew's gaze skittered around the group as he considered an appropriate response. "I promised I'd take care of you all. Luna made me promise. And sometimes that means doing things that don't make sense. But trust me, it's for your own safety. And I'm sorry I can't say more. It's not my secret to tell."

Joseph's round blue eyes locked on him, considering, then he gave a curt little nod. "I trust you, Matthew. But you don't need to do this on your own. Let me help."

Matthew's throat tightened before he could choke out his thanks. His thoughts cycled back to his own childhood, before he'd met Luna. In foster care from birth, he'd never known his real parents. He'd bounced from home to home until Luna's dad had taken him in. She'd just been through her own trauma. She hadn't spoken for months. But she did offer him the odd fragile smile. A smile so beautiful and full of pain that Matthew had fallen in love with her right then and there. And vowed to protect her. From everything. Anything. As long as he could. Ever since then, their lives had become permanently entwined. He was part of her. And she was part of him. Forever.

Take care of them, Matthew.

He closed his eyes and inhaled the centering smell of the pine needles. "We need to stay away from the authorities. Otherwise they'll stick her in the hospital again and pump her full of drugs. That didn't help last time. It just made everything worse. So, we couldn't wait for her dad."

"So, Grandmother's house," Joseph said, peering through Beacon's light at the dark forest.

"Exactly," Matthew replied. "Hopefully her dad will be waiting there for us. I promised him, if there was ever an emergency, that's where we'd go."

"Okay." Joseph hugged his sleeping son. "We better get a move on. The sooner we get there the sooner we can get treatment for everyone who needs it."

A raven cawed and Matthew winced, checked to see if Piper had noticed. But Piper's face was a mask. She was always so good at putting on a brave face. Matthew couldn't tell if she'd heard the raven. But it could just be a normal raven. It didn't have to mean anything.

Matthew returned his attention to the most immediate problem. "What do we do about Caleb?"

"I'll carry him," Joseph said. He tossed his dreadlocks over his shoulder and pulled a limp Caleb into his arms.

"When was the last time you picked him up?" Matthew asked. "He's grown. A lot. And he's wearing all that winter gear."

"He's my son. I'll carry him." Joseph rose to his knees, then stood, pulling Caleb after him. As he threw him over his shoulder in a fireman's lift, his beads clunked together again, rattling Matthew's nerves.

"We're moving?" Faith asked, shivering on the ground.

"We're moving." Matthew blew on his fingers to stop them from turning stiff with the cold.

Faith pushed herself to her feet, wrapped her buttonless coat around her waist and stomped off after Ulrich. Dry twigs cracked under her ridiculous flip-flops. The soles sucked at her heels and marked her presence. She'd been wearing them all summer, the flimsy, plastic kind that were expensive even though there wasn't much material for the money. Yesterday, Matthew had noticed one of the straps was fraying. Those shoes would never make it all the way to Grandmother's house. And Faith was precious about her feet, insisting on monthly foot massages with the money she earned from her Saturday job at the shoe shop in town. With all the bruised toes and cracked toenails, was it really worth it? He stifled his exasperated sigh. Dancers. He would certainly not be carrying her. Why couldn't she have grabbed her hiking boots from the laundry room? Everyone had left that way, it would have been so easy.

Ulrich trotted through the woods once more. Beacon hovered nearby. Her shimmering aura lit the way and illuminated the reflective eyes of night-time animals. Joseph hung back and walked with Matthew and Luna.

Faith stayed close. "I don't suppose anyone has an ice-pack? This is going to swell." She fingered her jaw.

"Do I look like I have an ice-pack on me?" Matthew snapped. He didn't know why he was snapping. Faith didn't deserve that. But the burden of their safety rested heavily on his shoulders.

"I was only asking!"

Matthew needed some peace and quiet to think. "Why don't you go hang out with Tyler, you can compare injuries."

Faith scoffed. "I wouldn't be caught dead with that egotistically-inflated jock!" She stormed off, a curtain of short, dark hair hiding her jaw. She tripped and lost a flip-flop to a root. By the time she had it back on Matthew drew level with her once again. He chuckled. She narrowed her eyes and stormed off again, this time placing her feet more carefully.

"And I'd take a punch to the jaw over a burned face any day," Tyler said. "*Buddy*." He stormed off too, in a different direction.

Matthew took Luna's arm.

Alessandra offered him a wry smile. "It might help if you didn't goad them."

"I know, I just…get sick of it sometimes, you know?"

She put a gentle hand on his arm, a maternal pressure. "I do know. But right now, we need to be strong, and patient."

Strong and patient. Sometimes he was tired of being strong and patient.

"Matthew?"

"Okay, okay." He raised his palms. "I'll be strong and patient."

He saw the look on Jasmine's face every time she glanced at Tyler's scalded flesh. The older ones didn't hide their revulsion much better. And Luna. Everyone was worried about Luna, because if she didn't recover, if it was going to be like last time…no, it didn't bear thinking about. Grandmother would know what to do. They just had to get to Grandmother's house. They had to be strong and patient.

He helped Luna climb over a fallen tree trunk, careful to

brush away the trail of soldiering ants. He could almost pretend they'd snuck out of the house with a bottle of her father's moonshine and were going for a stroll in the woods on a balmy, summer's evening. Almost. Except, if they'd really done that, she would be talking to him, telling him her dreams, what she wanted to do after high school. And she'd be laughing at his stupid jokes. He'd bitch about the others, and she would listen tolerantly with that fragile smile playing on her lips. But she'd never say a bad word about them. She was good that way. Too good. And it wouldn't be so cold, or late, or dark. They wouldn't have ventured this far into the thick forest. Pines and oaks and silver birches whose trunks shone unnaturally in the moonlight.

The raven cawed again. This time he didn't miss Piper's stiffening shoulders.

"Come on, Luna. Talk to me." He squeezed her hand, but she didn't squeeze back. She didn't look at him, didn't blink. Just planted one foot in front of the other as if she were made of parts. *Please, Luna.*

Matthew turned to Alessandra as they guided Luna along a hint of a path. "Do we need to worry about this vision of Caleb's?" Dry leaves crackled under their feet and the smell of pine competed with the smoky scent in his hair and on his clothes. His throat felt drier than a camel's ass and his eyes still stung.

Alessandra shook her head, causing more dark curls to escape her headscarf. "I'm sure it was just the effects of the fire."

"Hmmm." Joseph ducked his lanky frame under a low-hanging branch. "I've come to believe that all of Caleb's visions should be adhered to." He shifted the boy on his shoulder.

"But fire?" Alessandra questioned. "We've just escaped a fire. Surely there won't be another?"

They raised their gazes to the sky. Looking for an enormous gryphon that could expel fire, or ice, depending on the situation. Obsidian was nowhere to be seen, but they all knew he was there. Somewhere. Watching.

"The forest is drier than sand in a desert," Joseph said. "And sand doesn't burn."

"It hasn't rained all summer," Matthew said.

"The quicker we get to the river the better," Alessandra said. "Piper is the only one with a bottle of water. It won't last between us."

Food. Water. At the rate they were moving, with shoeless members of the group and flimsy clothing, it would take over a week to travel to Grandmother's house.

"Come on, Luna." Matthew clenched his teeth. A dull headache knocked at his temples. She'd asked him to take care of the others. That night on the roof, she specifically asked him, as if she knew this was going to happen.

He grabbed her hand and pulled her roughly after him, keeping her on her feet and making her march at a quicker pace. Caleb's vision, Tyler's arm, maybe even the fire. This was all her fault.

"Matthew," Alessandra said gently, quietly. His throat thickened and he struggled to swallow. She gathered her skirts to catch up with him.

"We need to get to Grandmother's house," he said, not interested in any advice, even if well intentioned.

She sighed, but she didn't make him slow his pace. And Joseph managed to keep up too.

"Fire!" Caleb shouted.

Joseph stumbled but maintained his grip on the young boy. Matthew jumped. Luna's body bucked beside him.

"Another vision?" Matthew turned.

"No, he's awake." Joseph placed Caleb on his feet. He kept his hands on Caleb's shoulders, steadying him. Despite the thick, goose-down jacket, Caleb shivered as if he'd spent a week in his underwear climbing Everest.

Kalisa came running, jostling the sleeping Nell, eager to reach and embrace her son.

"Oh, my sweet Caleb," she panted, then coughed.

She pulled him to her side, kissed the top of his head, until he pulled away and wiped the kisses off. "Yuck."

Everyone laughed.

Catching her breath, Kalisa wagged a finger at him. "You can't ever wipe off the power of my kisses. You're branded for life, son."

Caleb rolled his eyes, then looked at Matthew. "What happened?"

Matthew crouched so he was eye-level with the younger boy. "You might have had a night terror."

Caleb shook his head but didn't say anything. His teeth chattered so violently Matthew worried he might chip one. Joseph rubbed his back with swift strokes. A raven cawed. Matthew tried to ignore the menacing sound.

"Was it a vision?" Joseph asked.

"I don't know what it was." Caleb clenched his jaw and his teeth stopped chattering. "It felt so real."

"Do you remember the fire?" Matthew asked. "The real one? The one we just escaped?"

Caleb shook his head. Then nodded. His eyes widened. "I was helping you find Luna." He looked around, spotted her standing with Alessandra near a fallen tree. He frowned. "What's wrong with her?"

"She's fine," Matthew replied quickly. No use getting the kids worried. "We're taking her to Grandmother's house. I'm more worried about you right now."

Caleb doubled over as coughs wracked his prepubescent body. Then he vomited on his shoes. "Sorry," he mumbled, wiping his mouth.

Kalisa swept him into her arms again, laying more gentle kisses on top of his head. This time Caleb didn't wipe them away. She let go of him to cover her mouth as she coughed again. "Can't seem to catch my breath." She patted her chest and handed the baby to Joseph.

"Don't worry about it, buddy." Joseph handed his son a tissue from a deep pocket of his winter jacket. "It's the smoke."

"Sure is," Kalisa said, resting her hands on her thighs.

Caleb shook his head. "I wasn't in the house."

Joseph sighed. "It doesn't matter now."

"It *does* matter." Kalisa arched an unamused eyebrow at him. "You've been told not to go wandering off at night on your own. You know the woods are dangerous. The things Hope draws about—"

"Well, can we talk about it as we walk?" Matthew said. "And after we decide whether it was just a dream or a vision."

"Eyes like fire," Caleb murmured, stumbling into his father. Was he thinking of Obsidian? But Matthew's attention was diverted from the boy's ramblings. Kalisa's breaths grew shallower, her chest rattling with every inhale. Her brown skin turned chalky and sweat beaded over her forehead.

"Kalisa?" Matthew stepped forward. Her eyes glistened and she sucked her cheeks in. "What's the matter?"

"Just dog tired." She curled her lips into a half smile. Although it looked more like a grimace. She waved him away. He glanced at Luna. There was no change in her condition, nothing to indicate what she was thinking.

"Kalisa?" Matthew questioned again. She leaned heavily on the nearest tree. The roots of her hair were damp and shining in the filtered moonlight.

"Kalisa?" Joseph pushed the baby into Matthew's arms and reached for his wife, just as she fell to her knees.

"I'm tired," Kalisa said. "Just tired. I was so worried about the children."

"Kalisa," Matthew said, standing behind her, jiggling the baby. She wore a pink bath robe over the T-shirt and sweatpants she usually slept in. A stain marred the robe beneath her right shoulder blade. Mud? Burned? It bloomed and spread. "Are you hurt?"

He reached out a finger to the widening stain and prodded it gently. Kalisa screamed.

CHAPTER 5
MATTHEW

THE RAVEN CAWED. Matthew spotted its location in a high branch and gave it his best death stare.

"Kalisa!" Joseph yelled, lowering her to the ground.

"Piper!" Matthew called for the healer. "Piper!" Her heavy footfalls sounded.

"It's too late for herbs," Alessandra said, gently. She gave Luna's hand to Piper and told the young girl to watch over her. Piper stood there, a bunch of useless herbs in her hand, her gaze alternating between Kalisa on the ground and Luna standing like a statue. Tears brimmed in her eyes under her long fringe.

"Help her!" Joseph yelled, cradling his wife and shooting desperate looks at the others. "Somebody help her!" The stain on the bathrobe dripped a steady, ominous stream of blood. A puddle formed on the ground. Kalisa's eyelids flickered.

Caleb stood almost as still as Luna, watching his mother bleed out all over the ground. He whimpered, like a trapped kitten in a cardboard box.

Matthew gave the baby to Alessandra, kneeled by Kalisa, and ripped the bathrobe away. Blood soaked her white T-shirt.

"What happened?" Joseph asked, one hand on his wife's head, the other going to his mouth. He bit down on his knuckles. Tears glinted in his eyes. He wouldn't cry in front of the children.

"Burning rafter fell on me," Kalisa answered. "I knew a splinter had pierced me, but most of it glanced off. I didn't think the wound was so bad. Especially when I didn't feel it anymore."

"Adrenaline," Alessandra said. She parted her skirts and kneeled next to Matthew. With the baby tucked on her hip, she used her free hand to lift the sodden T-shirt and inspect the wound. "It stops us feeling pain, when we need to."

"I felt something still inside. So I yanked it out. Just now," Kalisa muttered. "Stupid. Now it's bleeding. I think the Goddess's charm might be running out."

"Oh, Kalisa." Joseph took one of her hands in both of his. Caleb stopped crying and hiccupped.

Kalisa beckoned to him. "You need to take care of your sisters. You're the oldest. Look out for them." She lifted the medallion from around her neck and pressed it into Caleb's hand.

"Don't talk like that," Joseph said, his voice catching. "There must be something we can do." He looked at Alessandra and Piper. They both shook their heads. Piper's sacred medicine notebook lay propped on a rock, depicting complicated drawings of herbs they didn't have. Joseph searched his wife's back, his hands quickly reddening with her blood.

Silent tears spilled down Piper's cheeks. She bowed her

head. Her fingers went to her necklace. A cross, which she lifted to her lips and kissed four times. Ariel, another of the non-human members of the family, appeared and hovered over Kalisa. Her skin shone with a strange inner glow and the halo hovering over her head whirred with light. Strange to others, but familiar to them. Some would call it godly. But not Matthew, he wasn't that gullible. Ariel bowed her head and clasped her hands in prayer.

Matthew scanned the woods for Jasmine, hoping she wouldn't be near, that she would stay away from the death of her mother. He couldn't see her anywhere, so assumed she must be farther ahead with some of the others. Thank God for small miracles.

"Can't you do something?" Matthew asked Ariel. *Something practical*. Clasping hands in prayer over a dying body never saved anyone. Certainly not Luna's mother. Nor his own. Ariel was an angel, she had to be able to do something.

Ariel shook her head. "I cannot bend the will of God." Her lips moved, but her voice seemed to come from all around, like a ventriloquist playing a trick with the trees. She bowed her head once more, rested a hand on Kalisa's head, and whispered a quiet prayer.

Matthew snorted. "We can't lose her. She's the mother." *The mother*. The mother figure. Everyone looked to Kalisa as if she were mother to them all. Especially after the death of Luna's mother. Why did he keep thinking about that? But he knew why. It was because of Luna, how she was then and how she was now.

He marched over to Luna and peered into her unseeing eyes. She alone could put a stop to this. She alone could save Kalisa. She had the power to heal. If she wanted to. Luna wouldn't just let Kalisa die. She loved Kalisa. But why the hell wasn't she doing something?

If she would just say something. Do something. Blink, even. Why was she doing this? He tapped her cheek with a prodding forefinger. Nothing. Anger broiled in his stomach. How dare she leave him to cope with all this on his own. She needed to wake up. Now. Right now. He slapped her face. Hard. Her head snapped sideways. Still nothing.

The raven cawed. Death was coming.

"Luna, please," he whispered. His hands went to her cheek again, gently caressing, stroking the reddening area. He tilted his forehead against hers. "Don't do this. Kalisa needs you. We all need you."

Take care of them, Matthew. Is that what she'd meant? He turned back to Kalisa and kneeled beside her.

"S'okay, Matthew," Kalisa said. "S'just my time."

"I thought your religion…the spirituality…I thought… I thought it would save you," he stuttered.

Kalisa's lips pressed into a thin line. "Everyone's gotta die. Ain't no religion or magic spell that can stop that."

He glared at Ariel. If Luna wasn't able to save Kalisa, surely Ariel should. All the resentment and disbelief that they were actually losing a member of their group powered through in that glare. He could do nothing to stop it. Surely a four-hundred-year angel ought to be able to do something?

"No!" Joseph said, his voice breaking. "Please don't leave us."

"Please don't leave us," Caleb repeated, crouching by his father.

Kalisa rolled onto her side. A ghostly smile formed on her paling lips. She patted her son's hand. "I'm going to a good place. Don't be sad. Look after each other. Love each other. Be kind."

Joseph stifled a sob and shoved his knuckles in his mouth, while Caleb just stared at his mother as if he couldn't understand what was happening.

The murderous raven cawed again, and Matthew clenched his fists and shouted obscenities at the trees.

Beacon arrived, spraying her aura of hope around the desolate scene, easing the tension and fear that had landed between Matthew's shoulder and raced along his old scar.

"We don't need you here," Matthew snapped at her. His vision blurred. He couldn't think straight. "Go keep the others away." She shimmered back the way she'd come.

With one last raggedy intake of breath, Kalisa passed away. Her head lolled to the side and she never exhaled. Her face seemed to crumple in on itself. Matthew held his breath, waiting. Surely, she would come back. She couldn't die. Not like this.

The raven remained silent.

He held his breath and waited. Piper picked up her notebook and crossed herself. Caleb cried. With a dry face, Joseph closed his eyes for a moment and lifted his cheeks to the heavens, whispering silently. After a moment, he let go of his wife's hand and stood.

"No," Matthew said, refusing to accept the situation. He'd been holding his breath all this time.

Joseph chewed on his bottom lip. His eyes could barely contain the brimming tears. "We can't even bury her. There's no time." He pointed to the moon, beginning its downward arc. "We haven't traveled far enough into the woods. If they send someone after us…"

Matthew didn't need to be reminded of the dangers — a catatonic girl with healing powers, a fox that could communicate with telepathy, a gryphon who breathed fire and ice, an angel, an essence of light and a hapless group of children, teens and grownups all living in a house, off the grid - but still he refused. "No. She can't be…" he couldn't say it. *Dead*. It was an unbearable word. A word that should never exist. An ugly word.

Piper was crying. Shaking and crying. It was the closest she'd come to making a noise. A strange, garbled sound came from her throat.

"We'll come back for her." Alessandra closed Kalisa's clouded eyes. She whispered almost to herself. "We'll come back for her."

"We're in the woods. By the time we can come back here the animals…" Matthew trailed off, the image too bitter to contemplate.

Alessandra put her finger across her lips and flicked her eyes at Caleb.

Kalisa. Loving Kalisa who was second mother to them all was going to spend her afterlife being eaten by wild animals and her bones nibbled clean by ants. It was grim. And unfair.

"So, the first one hits the knackers, eh?" Kerry appeared. His soft Irish lilt made his caustic words even more mocking. He leaned against a tree near Piper and lit a cigarette. He took the bottle of water from the canvas bag slung over her shoulder and tipped it into his mouth. "My mouth was drier than Ghandi's flip-flop."

"Easy. That's all we've got," Matthew said.

"You do know there hasn't been rain for several weeks? And Caleb has been having visions of fire?" Alessandra eyed his cigarette. Even she couldn't keep the edge from her tone when Kerry was around. "Where have you been?"

Kerry shrugged and blew a puff of smoke at Alessandra. She waved it away and glowered at him. "The baby doesn't need to inhale your second-hand smoke."

"I knew when the fire started that something like this would happen." Kerry kicked the heel of a black-studded boot against the tree, causing a mini avalanche of dried bark to crumble away. The resulting dust made Matthew sneeze.

"Something like what?" Alessandra asked.

"Where were you when the fire started?" Matthew turned on him, fists at his side. To match Kerry's black boots were black, skinny jeans, his trademark black leather jacket and a black T-shirt underneath. "I can see you weren't caught unawares."

"Are you accusing me of something, Matthew?" Kerry picked some invisible scrap from his front teeth with a thumbnail.

"Did you start the fire?" Matthew asked, closing the gap between them. "Is that clear enough for you?"

"Just come right out with it, why don't you?" Kerry grinned. The grin lit a fire in Matthew's stomach. "And careful there, wouldn't want the precious Matthew to get a lungful of cigarette smoke."

"You didn't answer my question." Rage filled his veins and seethed through his limbs. "Because, if you did start that fire, Kalisa's death is on your hands."

"Aye, she got a bad dose of something."

Red flooded Matthew's vision. "Did you kill Kalisa?"

Kerry smirked. "Why would I kill Kalisa?"

Matthew could never tell when Kerry was lying, so it was

best to assume everything that came out of his mouth was a bunch of bullshit.

Matthew clenched his fists. "You still haven't answered the question."

"Oh, quit your bletherin'," Kerry replied, taking another drag. "No need to make a holy show of yourself." A pause. "I might not be into holding hands and singing Kumbaya, but I certainly didn't ax Kalisa."

Joseph inhaled sharply, then let the exhale out in a long, shuddery breath.

"Come on, Caleb. Let's find the others," Joseph said, taking his son's hand and leading him away from Kerry. He cradled Nell close to his chest. For a few seconds the only sound was the rattle of Joseph's beads. Maybe he was wise to walk away. But Matthew believed in justice. And that people should be held accountable.

"How dare you speak about Kalisa like that! When her body's not even cold! All she ever did was worry about you on that damn motorcycle of yours!" Matthew raised one of his fists and plowed it into Kerry's jaw. Kerry dropped the cigarette. Alessandra stamped it out. Matthew cradled his skinned knuckles in the palm of his other hand.

Take care of them, Matthew.

Kerry narrowed his eyes. "You better watch it, *boy*." He raised his fists and took a swing at Matthew. Matthew ducked out of the way. Kerry may have been the James Dean of every schoolgirl's dream, but he smoked and was unfit. Matthew ran cross country. Four times a week with meets on Saturdays.

Matthew swung again, but his blow glanced off Kerry's shoulder. Kerry grabbed him by his collar and hoisted him off his feet. Kerry might have been unfit, but he was still taller.

Matthew swung his fists and kicked his legs, feeling the ache in his cut knee. He managed a direct hit to Kerry's stomach. Kerry dropped him. Matthew stumbled backward as Kerry came for him, a malicious glint in his eyes. They rolled over Kalisa's body.

"Stop!" Alessandra yelled.

They wrestled just next to Kalisa, occasionally rolling into her or hitting her face with a flailing fist. *Take care of them, Matthew.* Kalisa shuddered violently when Matthew slammed into her side. Her eyelids snapped open and stared at them disapprovingly. Matthew caught glimpses of her dead body; the stained white T-shirt, the smoothness of her calf where the moonlight shone on her through filtered branches, a stick of black hair, her hand curled around a pinecone. It was distracting, but fueled his anger. Kerry had had it coming for a long time.

Kerry straddled him and punched his face. Blood poured out of his nose.

"Stop!" Alessandra called.

"Oh, don't stop." Faith appeared, opening her palms for a slow clap. "I do like a good fight."

Alessandra stepped between them, lowering herself to the ground. But it was just as Matthew swung, and instead of his fist connecting with Kerry's jaw, he punched Alessandra in the neck. Both her hands went to her throat as she tumbled sideways, gasping for air.

Take care of them, Matthew.

"I'm so sorry, Alessandra!" Matthew wiggled out from under Kerry and went to her side. She held up a hand, indicating she just needed a minute, but managed to frown at him too.

Kerry got to his feet, brushed himself off, and flicked his dark hair back in place. He lit another cigarette. "And all I wanted was a wee drop of water."

"This is your fault!" Matthew poked a finger into his chest.

"Let's not start again." Alessandra gained her voice and her feet.

"Oh, let's!" Faith clapped again, obviously over her own punch to the jaw.

"Faith!" Alessandra exclaimed.

"I think I've had enough excitement for one day," Kerry said. "You need to spend some time in the gym, Matthew, you're turning into a skittery whelp, so it is."

"A what?" Faith questioned. Sometimes they needed a translator for Kerry's Irishisms, but not now, Matthew didn't need to be told it was an insult.

"You're not looking so hot yourself, *buster*." Matthew cringed as soon as the lame retort shot out of his mouth. Kerry offered him a wide, sly smile, then turned his back. "Wait! Don't you dare go disappearing again." Matthew stomped after him. "Luna needs help. You may not give a shit about the rest of us, but I know you care for her."

Take care of them, Matthew. He wasn't doing a very good job so far.

"Aye. That may be true." Kerry glanced at her, his eyes drifting over her face. "She knows I'm here."

"No, she doesn't!" Matthew snapped. "She doesn't know any of us are here."

Kerry hesitated a moment but carried on walking, his usual swagger diminished. The small light on the end of his cigarette shone brightly for a moment as he sucked deep. The cigarette smoke reached Matthew's nose. It reminded him of the fire. He coughed. His lungs burned.

"Kerry!" Alessandra called, her voice cracking.

"Let him go," Matthew said. "We don't need him."

"I wish I could be as confident in that fact as you," she replied. "He's just walked away with the only water we have."

CHAPTER 6
MATTHEW

"Kalisa is dead."

"Kalisa is dead."

"Kalisa is dead."

Kalisa is dead.

The deathly whisper spread around the group like the fire that had destroyed their house. Even the trees seemed to hold their breath. The leaves murmured, ever so softly, the word 'dead' shifting through their cracked veins.

"Kalisa is dead."

"Don't be silly." Jasmine clutched her stick doll to her chest. "Kalisa wouldn't leave us."

"Jasmine." Joseph crouched by his eight-year-old daughter. But his voice caught. He looked away.

Jasmine frowned. She looked at Ariel and Beacon. Ariel, being an angel older than time, and Beacon, well, being just what her namesake implied, were the more benign and honest beings in their group. But neither were able to offer her solace.

"She can't be dead!" Jasmine stamped her foot, sending

Ulrich skittering away from her side. Her dark, wild hair shook with indignation.

Caleb slid an arm around his sister and shushed her like they'd all seen Kalisa do a thousand times. She used to call them into the yard for dinner and send Ulrich after the more adventurous ones who'd ventured into the forest. This forest. It was only a few nights ago that Matthew had sat on the roof with Luna, and she'd commented on the smell of the pine trees. Matthew sniffed. He could only smell smoke. And earth. And fear. He could smell his own fear where it coated his armpits. *Take care of them, Matthew.* Epic fail.

Matthew approached Jasmine, trying to think of the words as he went. He pulled at the neck of his shirt. There was no denying the truth. Kalisa should be here with them. And she wasn't. It's not like they wouldn't notice. Especially when Nell started crying for milk. She was down to one feed a day, but there'd be hell to pay, sooner or later.

"Jasmine." Matthew crouched down to her level. Her copious curls fanned out around her face. The stick doll hung from two dirty fingers. Her blue leggings were ripped on one knee. "Kalisa's gone. She's not coming back. I'm so sorry." He squeezed her shoulder, but it didn't stop the tears streaming down her face.

Joseph took a deep breath. "It's true. But the rest of us are still here. We need to stick together. We need to get Luna to Grandmother's house."

Jasmine cocked her head and glanced at the motionless Luna, eyeing her suspiciously. "What's so special about her?"

Caleb took the stick doll from Jasmine and fiddled with its coarse, yellow hair. Then he grabbed her hand and laced his fingers through hers, the whole time staring at his boots, shooting furtive glances at Luna.

"She doesn't understand yet," Alessandra said.

Matthew's stomach twitched. He didn't feel like talking about *it*. Luna's real power. Or when he'd first met her. When any of them had first met Luna. He just couldn't. Not out loud. Hearing those words spoken aloud…*no*.

"Well?" Jasmine demanded, throwing a hand on her hip, imitating an annoyed Kalisa perfectly. The image brought a stab of pain.

"It's complicated," Matthew sighed. "And you're only eight. It's…*complicated*." Eight. A similar age to when Luna lost her mother.

"I'm scared, Matthew," Hope said. She clasped her notebook to her chest, hiding the secrets she spent many midnight hours drawing. Her blond hair hung in dirty clumps and her bony shoulders were hunched up around her ears.

"We're all scared," Matthew replied, more shortly than he'd intended. Hope was only fifteen. And fragile. Of all of them, she was the one he worried about the most. Besides Luna.

Hope shook her head, clutching her notebook with white knuckles. "I can't breathe…"

"It's the smoke, everyone's struggling." Matthrew wrapped his arms around her, hugged her tight. "Breathe deep, breathe slow."

She shook her head into his chest, her tears dampening his sweatshirt. "I can't."

He pulled away, holding both her thin wrists. "You can. Do it with me."

He inhaled an exaggerated breath, waiting for her to join him. His nose throbbed where Kerry had punched him.

She wiped at her tears, then sucked in her own ragged breath.

Matthew held his, counted to three in his head, then let it out gently and slowly. He coughed, the effects of the smoke still tickling his lungs. Hope exhaled and coughed too.

They smiled at each other. "Keep going."

She nodded, then tugged on his arm. "I'm thirsty too. My throat is so dry."

"We need to find water," Alessandra said.

"And I need something for this pain." Tyler held his blistered arm in front of his body.

Piper dug into her canvas bag. It never left her side. Matthew wondered if she slept with the damn thing. But it housed all her herbs. She rifled through it now. Then approached Tyler with a handful of something. He didn't protest as she smothered a mixture of herbs all over his arm and cheek, but groaned with relief.

"Ulrich says there's a stream ahead." Jasmine pointed through the trees then dug her hand deep into the fox's fur. The other hand held the stick doll. Straw for its hair and clothes. The lone survivor of the house fire.

"Thank God!" Faith rushed by. "I'm parched. Lead the way, fox!"

Yes, *thank God*, Matthew thought, giving Ariel a cursory look. Maybe that's all Luna needed, to be rehydrated. Then she would return to herself, talking of a wild dream she'd had. She'd give him that smile. And everything would be okay again. They could go home. Except they couldn't. Their home had burned to the ground and one of them might be responsible.

"Aye. Grand idea. I could use a wee drink about now." Kerry reappeared, tapping the empty bottle against his palm. "And I'm not talking about getting fluthered."

Piper rushed over and snatched the bottle out of his hand, shaking her finger at him as she marched away.

"Was it something I said?" Kerry laughed. "Don't be putting any of yer freaky-deaky spells on me."

Piper shook her fist at Kerry.

"You ran off with the only water we have." Matthew jabbed a finger at his chest. The action made his nose throb, right where Kerry had punched it. "And you weren't even in the fire. Do you ever think of anyone besides yourself? You utter dick."

"You given' out, are ye?" Kerry feigned a dagger to the heart. "Sticks and stones and all that." He flicked imaginary dirt from his leather jacket. He had the audacity to light up another cigarette. The small circle of heat served as a hostile reminder of what they were fleeing.

"You disgust me." Matthew pivoted on his foot and grabbed Luna's hand, and without a second thought, guided her through the trees.

Nell began to cry. Her piercing, needy sob echoed a hundred yards away. The breath catching in her throat. The subsequent irregular hiccups. Faith took a turn carrying her. She jostled her up and down, cooed into her ear, and patted her back, almost violently, unwilling to the task.

"Shut up!" Faith muttered into the one-year old's face, holding her at arm's length. Nell cried louder, her pudgy face turning red and tears streaming out of the corner of her eyes. Snot soon followed. "Gross."

"Here." Alessandra took her. "She's hungry." She stuck her little finger in Nell's mouth, but she wasn't fooled for long, and began to cry again after a few seconds.

Looking through the thick branches, Matthew checked the sky. A dusting of bruised, gray light made its way from the east and the worst of the cold leached from his bones. It must be around 5 o'clock. Nell woke at 5 o'clock every morning for the dozy feed that Kalisa hadn't been able to wean her from. This time, there was nothing they could do.

Joseph took his daughter from Alessandra. He propped her over his shoulder and began to sing. "Hush little baby, don't say a word. Papa's gonna buy you a mockingbird."

Jasmine took up the song too, waving her stick doll in Nell's face. "And if that mockingbird won't sing, Jasmine's gonna buy you a diamond ring." Her voice carried over the forest. A softness that belied the awkward angles of her growing limbs. At eight, she retained the pureness of a child's voice. So innocent. So perfect. Angelic. But as different from Ariel as you could get. Matthew closed his eyes for a moment and imagined they were all in Ariel's Heaven. What did it look like? Could they stand on the white, fluffy clouds? Did angels play harps on strings spun from gold? Could they eat as much cake as they wanted and never get fat? Would there be a running track that never tired him? Or was it all foolishness? Was God even there? Because if He was, how would He explain how much suffering He'd put them all through?

"And if that diamond ring turns brass, Caleb's gonna buy you a looking glass," Caleb chimed in.

"And if that looking glass gets broke, Hope's gonna buy you a Billy goat." Hope came close to the small child and stroked her fly-away hair, her gentle voice floating over the rustling leaves.

"And if that Billy goat won't pull, Papa's gonna buy you a cart and bull," Joseph sang. Nell quieted. They began to walk again. A slow march through the woods. Purposeful.

"And if that cart and bull turn over, Faith's gonna buy you a dog named Rover." No one could resist the charm of Nell's chubby cheeks and cocoa bean eyes.

Matthew shot Faith a surprised eyebrow.

"What? I like dogs. And Nell. She's cute," Faith said. "When she's not snotting all over me."

"And if that dog named Rover won't bark. Alessandra's gonna buy you a horse and cart." They all chuckled at the length of her name, throwing the song off. Jasmine handed Nell the stick doll. Nell wrapped a chubby fist around the primitive toy and clutched it to her chest.

"And if that horse and cart fall down, you'll still be the sweetest baby in town." Matthew couldn't help it, even though he couldn't sing worth a dime, but it was one of those moments.

They smiled at each other and began the song all over again. All of them joining in. Even Ariel with her weird synthetic voice. Her semi-translucent skin glowed, a radiant luminescence that Matthew had always twinned with peace. At that moment, they were at peace, all of them. Even Kalisa.

Matthew grabbed Luna's hand. He noted, with guilt, the red mark on her cheek where he'd slapped her. *I'm sorry. But please wake up. Please.*

As dawn brightened the sky, Beacon's inner light faded in

and out of view. Only her humanoid outline shimmered between the trees. Beyond her, movement drew Matthew's eyes. A doe. Standing still, watching them, its nose twitching with their scent. Only a few yards away, unnoticed by the others, half hidden behind a clump of ferns. He was reminded of the time a young fawn came into the front yard to nibble the leaves on the apple tree. But this one was different. Older. And hurt. A deep gash ran the length of its side and down her flank. Actually, three deep gashes. Like claw marks. The three long lines were spaced at least two inches apart. No animal in this forest had claws that could make marks like that. Before he could analyze it further, the deer turned and crept away. He watched her go, until he couldn't see her anymore. It felt like he'd been shown a secret. It had just been him and the doe. No one else.

He listened for a raven among the waking birds, but nothing cawed. Then he made a quick scan of the forest. It was a large, vast woodland, the type of place that people got lost in if they didn't know the way. But they knew the way, and there were seventeen of them. No, sixteen now. Surely there was nothing in the woods that could cause such a large group any problems?

Joseph approached. "Matthew?"

"How are you? You okay?" Matthew asked Joseph as he came near. "Jeez, don't answer that. Stupid question. Of course you're not okay."

Joseph laid a hand on Matthew's shoulder. A brief squeeze. "You really loved her."

Matthew thought of how Kalisa had made him blush, only a few hours ago. He blinked away the sting of tears. He hadn't cried. He'd been so pissed at Kerry. And now his mind was focused on getting Luna to Grandmother's house. Maybe he could avoid the whole grief thing if he concentrated hard enough on just surviving. "Yeah, she was kind of a mother to all of us. And a friend. Maybe a sister. I don't know…"

They walked in silence for a few moments, both contemplating a well-loved woman and their recent loss.

"Maybe it's better this way," Joseph said, throwing a glance over his shoulder. He cradled Nell close, but she was too young to understand his words.

"Maybe what's better?"

"Kalisa had cancer."

Cancer? CANCER? Kalisa had cancer? "Huh?"

"I know, it's a shock."

"How did I not know that?" Matthew stumbled, stood still, started walking again, in a zigzag, as if he'd been drinking. As if he were riding an uneven skateboard, one set of wheels on a higher plane than the other, always just about to fall off. He knew everything about everyone. How Faith was secretly in love with one of her fellow dancers in her company, that she swung both ways; that Tyler was in love with Luna; how Piper had once taken a car out, even though she was too young to drive, just to find some rare and powerful herb; how Hope screamed in the night about monsters that plagued her dreams but acted as if everything was fine during the day and hid the evidence of her fears by volunteering for laundry duty. And of course, there was Luna's secret, which wasn't his to tell, and he wasn't even sure if he understood the entirety of it anymore, anyway. But this. Kalisa having cancer. It was bigger than all of it. And he'd never caught a whiff of it.

"We didn't tell anyone," Joseph said. "Not even the kids." Nell murmured in her sleep. Joseph patted her back in a rhythmic pattern, lulling her deeper. "I think that's why she went after Tyler."

"She felt as if the risk was worth it." Typical Kalisa.

"Exactly."

"What? Where? How long?" Matthew didn't know what to ask first. His cycle of thoughts was like the revolving colors of a carousel. "Don't tell me you've been relying on magic? Talismans and amulets are one thing. But you don't take a knife to a gunfight."

Joseph shook his head. "No magic. Well, not just magic."

"I'm sorry, you probably don't want to talk about this."

"It's okay. I've had time to get used to it. Time to prepare. But...I just didn't expect...anyway...she was diagnosed a year ago. We tried treatments. But it became so advanced. There were a couple of clinical trials. It was a long shot. Kalisa wanted to spend the time with her family instead. She may have had another four months in her." The beads in his hair clicked as he walked. It was the exact same sound the abacus made that Matthew had played with as a child. The ornamental one he wasn't supposed to touch and took prize position in the middle of the front window. He would lay it on its side and click the beads up and down. Up and down. Listening to their small music while he waited for Luna's father to come home.

"Joseph, I'm so incredibly sorry." The world slowed down as he tried to picture Kalisa, in a hospital gown with needles in her arm, receiving treatment. "I really wish I'd known sooner." He closed his eyes and breathed deeply. The fresh scent of a new day arrived. And the familiar aroma of pine remained constant, comforting. And Nell. That milk smell that always followed her.

"It wouldn't have changed anything. It's not what Kalisa

wanted. She didn't want to be a burden, or an object of pity." He patted Nell's back and murmured to her.

"But didn't the rest of us deserve the chance to say good-bye?" Matthew trudged on, watched the others picking their way through the various overgrown pathways, all littered with inches of brittle leaves and pine needles. The sun angled through the branches and touched the top of moss-covered rocks, making them seem on fire. He ducked under a cloud of whirling midges. "I'm sorry. That was selfish. I just…I just…I can't believe I didn't know."

"Luna tells you her deepest secrets," Joseph said. He kissed Nell on her slack, chubby cheek. "And we're glad she confides in you. But Kalisa had me, and so she leaned on me. As it should be. You had enough on your plate."

"That's not fair. We're a family. All of us. If there was anything I could have done…"

"That's just it, Matthew, there was nothing you could have done. Kalisa wanted to save you from that pain for as long as possible."

Matthew rubbed at the back of his grimy neck, pushing at the mounting tension. "That's why she kept hanging those little parcels of herbs in my room. Trying to keep me distracted."

"She cared about you."

Matthew watched his feet trudge along the forest floor. The sun was high now and the humidity closed in on them. Sweat pooled on the small of his back. Joseph was right. But still, it burned a bit that he hadn't known. If he could have comforted her in some way. Maybe he could have found a way to tell the others. But most of all, he had to admit to himself, it was the being kept in the dark. That Joseph and Kalisa had a secret. An awful secret, but a secret nonetheless. It made him wonder if he knew everything he thought he did.

"Matthew?" Joseph said.

Matthew lifted his head and met the older man's eyes.

"It doesn't matter anymore," Joseph said. "None of the others need to know."

And so Kalisa's cancer would stay a secret. Why not?

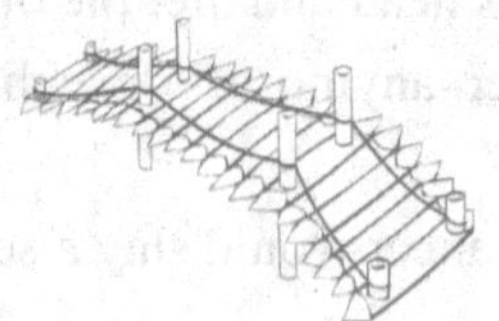

CHAPTER 7
MATTHEW

MATTHEW LISTENED to the birds chatter over his head, trying to pick out the whoosh of Obsidian's wings or the caw of a raven.

Tyler called from ahead. "I see a stream."

Matthew and Joseph traded an anxious look. Matthew jogged up to Luna and helped Alessandra rush her forward. Piper ran toward them, communicating in charades, her fingers a pair of scissors slicing across her neck. Then her hands cycled so fast in her sign language that Matthew couldn't keep up with it. She veered off in the direction of the stream, her hands already diving into her bag, waving at anyone who chanced to look her way.

"Tyler!" Matthew called. "Wait!"

But it was too late. By the time they got to the stream Tyler had stripped off the clothes that weren't melded to his body and crawled into the water. It was just deep enough to be immersed in. He groaned and sighed. It was hard to deny him the relief. Even when Piper was signaling with impossibly fast hands for him to get out.

Despite the state of his arm and chin, Tyler's toned muscles stood out. He was the star quarterback for the varsity team. Of course they would stand out. Chiseled. That's how Luna had described him. Chiseled! Did girls really like 'chiseled?' Matthew was an athlete too. He ran. He was toned. In a nice, understated, unintimidating way. Chiseled might not be a word he used to describe himself, but he didn't think Tyler was *all that* either. And Tyler hadn't been around long. Not as long as he had. He hadn't been around when Luna had lost her mother. Or when her healing power developed. Matthew had helped her come to terms with that and learn to wield it effectively. They'd almost lost Sampson. Permanently. Matthew had been there for it all. Not that Sampson was around much these days. He'd moved on. His choice.

Hope and Faith cupped water into their mouths, drinking greedily. Ulrich sniffed at the water and whined, all four legs shifting nervously.

"He says it's poisonous." Jasmine stared at the fox.

Matthew swiveled to face a noise at his back. Kerry retreated into the woods. He'd obviously heard the devastating news and didn't wait to be around for the consequences. Selfish bastard.

"It's *what*?" Faith leapt backward, losing both her flip-flops.

"Poisonous," Jasmine said, this time loud enough for everyone to hear.

Piper rushed toward Faith and Hope. She held a handful of something putrid smelling and dogshit brown.

Faith wrinkled her nose. "What am I supposed to do with that?"

Piper pointed at her mouth.

"You're kidding, right?" Faith took a step backward.

"Just do as she says," Matthew said.

"Well she's hardly 'saying,' is she?" Faith crossed her arms over her chest.

"Don't be smart." Alessandra nudged Piper toward Faith.

Hope stepped forward, emitting a waft of suffocating smoke from the jacket he'd lent her. She leaned over Piper's outstretched palm and took a mouthful. She chewed and swallowed it down without a single grimace.

With her arms crossed tightly over her body, Faith followed suit, retching and gagging as she swallowed. She took deep breaths to keep it down.

"Will they still get sick?" Matthew asked Piper.

She shrugged and wiggled a flat palm. *Maybe*.

"They just won't die," Alessandra said.

Joseph ran up and down by a patch of the stream, pulling the kids away, yelling at them not to drink.

"We need to get Tyler out of the water," Matthew said. "Piper, you got more of that stuff?"

She nodded. Another shrug. A flurry of sign language. She had more, but it might not be enough.

"Tyler!" Matthew called.

"It feels so good!" Tyler groaned, rolling in circles, slathering the water on his blistered limb like it was a magic balm.

"I know, buddy, I know." Matthew checked his hands for cuts and grazes. Scratch marks lined his palms from when he'd fallen over Luna back at the house. As if someone had tried to slash him a new lifeline. Bruises decorated his fist. The one he'd used to punch Kerry.

"Give me some of that mulch, will you, Piper?" he called over his shoulder as he submerged his hands in the water and grabbed Tyler's collar. He pulled. But Tyler was a football player. He was big. And completely soaked.

"I'll help." Alessandra squatted next to him.

Piper crouched by Matthew's side and fed him the mulch from her palm. He gagged and choked. Piper covered his mouth with her hand so he couldn't spit it out. He couldn't breathe. Tree bark. That's what it tasted like. And felt like. Rough and coarse and maybe he'd cut his throat open just swallowing it. But not just tree bark. Something gelatinous. Squidgy. He looked at Piper with one eye, wondering where she'd gone when she'd taken the car. The docks? The image of a rubbery squid flashed across his mind as he chewed. Maybe a tentacle. Squid mixed with tree bark. With his eyes beginning to stream, he blocked any more analysis of the mulch and gulped it down.

"Jesus!" he gasped, feeling a new admiration for Hope and Faith. Piper crossed herself at his blasphemy.

Matthew refocused his efforts on heaving Tyler out of the stream. This time he managed to pull Tyler's top half out of the water and drag him onto dry land. The stream bubbled and hissed at him, as if annoyed. Weird.

"Hey!" Tyler exclaimed, trying to bat Matthew away. His efforts were weak and ineffective, as if the water had drugged him.

As Matthew dragged the rest of him out of the stream, his stomach heaved. Too soon. The poison wouldn't have worked itself into his system yet. He needed to keep the mulch inside, for now.

He swallowed back bile and squid/bark-tasting mulch. He held his breath and pinched his sore nose, waiting for the nausea to pass. When he opened his eyes again, Piper grinned at him and clapped her hands. Then she dug a jar of paste out of her bag, smothered it on his knuckles and wrapped them tight with a bandana. It showed a repeating pattern of an owl and a cougar. Sacred animals in her belief system.

"Let's keep going," Alessandra said, helping Tyler dress again. "We'll find a place to rest once we're past the stream."

Matthew hadn't drunk any of the water, and while it had been tantalizingly close and his throat had almost closed up from not drinking, at least he'd got to feel it, to touch it, and let it soothe his sore knuckles. Even if it was infected. Infected with what?

And then he saw it. A dog? No, not a dog. But not a wolf either. The dead carcass lay half in the water upstream and was larger than both animals combined. He'd never seen anything like it. Not even in those fantasy books Hope sometimes left lying around. No wonder she had bad dreams.

He glanced at Ariel. She wasn't human. Did she know what this unrecognizable beast was? Was it something she knew from her time above? With Piper as her only ally, she'd not yet been able to convince Matthew that God was more than a myth and religion, more than an excuse to start a war. She'd never met God herself, being a guardian angel tasked with looking after humans on earth. Matthew thought it was a flimsy excuse. But her number one mission was to look after Luna, so he had to give her that.

She'd been introduced to the group when Luna needed protection the most. A couple years after her mother's death, when she was having bad dreams and couldn't shake the idea something bad was going to happen again, despite Matthew's reassurances. No one deserved that kind of bad luck twice. Ariel was soft and gentle, sometimes stern, and didn't speak often, but her other-worldly presence often calmed the group. Though taller than Kerry and thinner than any of the girls, Luna loved to fold herself into those long limbs and touch her luminescent skin. Ariel would sing, her voice like bells, and stroke Luna's hair until she calmed, until the nightmares receded, and she soaked up the painful memories with her comforting presence. If Matthew had to use one word to sum Ariel up, it would be *patient*. And not just with Luna.

Other non-human beings existed within their group. He wasn't sure where Beacon was, but knew she wouldn't stray far. She was one of the newer additions to the group. Luna had never shaken her fear of the darkness, of the night, because of what had happened, and when she reached a certain age, her father denied her, her childish nightlight. The sliver of light that pressed against the crack in the closed bedroom door wasn't enough to chase the monsters from her dreams. Beacon entered their world as a softness, bringing not only light but the sense of hope too, the sense that fear could be conquered, permanently.

Ulrich sat by the stream, between the water and the kids, preventing them from going too close. A fox. With telepathic powers. It was obvious he represented strength and cunning.

Matthew first met the red fox when Luna turned thirteen. She'd been fascinated by the vampire and werewolf culture that swept the country. Of course she wanted her own magical animal. But Ulrich wasn't anything that had ever existed before. He wasn't a storybook character or a cliché. His aloofness defined him, spending most of his time alone in the shadows of the woods. Sometimes they didn't see him for weeks. But he would eat right out of Luna's hand.

Ulrich, Ariel, Beacon, and Obsidian were Luna's creatures.

Creatures that had been accepted into their human group so subtly and naturally. Supernatural creatures denied in the real world. Special and real to only them. They were all lovely, in their own way. Powerful, but merciful. Individuals, but all kind. Luna would never befriend anything devastating. Not like the dead creature lying in the stream that Matthew couldn't classify. Nothing with all that matted fur streaked with blood, and fangs bigger than a man's fingers, and claws that could slice through fully grown tree trunks. Not Luna.

So where had it come from?

The creature's stomach had been ripped open and its black intestines trailed into the stream. The carcass buzzed with insect life, loud like a raging river. A thick, black substance oozed from its ruined insides and snaked into the water, where it was washed downstream. Matthew followed the trail to where Tyler had been lying. The tacky substance crept up the other side of the small bank. Black tendrils of inky malevolence spread in every direction. A burgeoning growth of black moss on an insidious rampage through the forest. He looked over his shoulder. The blackness clung to the path they'd walked on. It wasn't just in the water. It was all around them, sneaking along the ground, climbing up trees, swaddling thorny bushes, making everything look dark and dismal despite the sun in the sky.

"Luna?" he questioned, as Piper slathered fresh balm on Tyler's burns. He chewed on the mulch, then spat it out.

"Keep it in," Matthew said. "You took a swim in an infected cesspit."

"Cesspit or not, the water tasted better than this crap."

"Keep it in." Matthew clapped him on his good shoulder, then turned back to Luna. She seemed to be staring at the terrible, dead creature. But she didn't say a word. Did she know what it was?

Jasmine pulled on his hand. "Matthew? I'm hungry."

"Well," he said, turning to her. "Let's go find some food. Your Mom taught you how to pick berries?" His throat caught at the mention of Kalisa. But Jasmine nodded. "Let's go find some."

"Are we going to make a pie?" Jasmine asked.

Matthew smiled, removing a leaf from her curls. It didn't have the black moss on it. "Maybe. If we can find enough. We can bake it at Grandmother's house."

"Will there be enough for everyone?"

"It's your job to make sure."

Jasmine grinned and dashed away to find the berries, calling to Caleb for help.

"Come on, Tyler, time to go." Matthew offered him a hand.

"I think I'd rather stay here and rest a while," he said. "I don't feel so good." The mulch Piper had spread over his arm and face gave off a stench like rotting cabbage, boiled eggs, and God knew what else. Red veins lined the whites of his eyes, and he rubbed at his head as if a headache was building.

"You'd get no argument from me, but I think the others would crucify me if I left you behind. So, up and at it."

Tyler sighed and gripped the offered hand, clenching his teeth as he was righted.

"We're on a mission to find food," Matthew said. "Enough for all of us. And don't go picking any mushrooms."

"Who died and crowned you king?" Tyler muttered. But the comment stilled both of them. They turned and looked at Luna. "What's wrong with her? I've never seen her like this."

"No, you wouldn't have."

"Still won't talk about it, huh? The big secret? What happened to her way back when? Why she can heal any of us with just a glance? She can't hear you. You can tell us. It's not like you were there."

"You don't know she can't hear us!" Matthew rounded on him, but he didn't have the energy for another fight, not with his skinned knuckles and his stomach roiling. He lowered his voice. "I might as well have been. It felt like I was."

Tyler raised his hands and stepped away. "Have it your way."

"Find some food, Tyler. Can you do that?" Matthew asked, tucking Luna's arm into his once more.

"Whatever." Tyler threw him a back-handed wave and walked away. At least the putrid stench was gone.

"Look, Matthew!" Jasmine ran back to him. She'd already found a handful of ripe berries and the purple juice dripped over her palm and stained her white pajama top. One drip ran down her blue leggings and into a laceless boot. Piper removed a net bag from her pack and handed it to her. After checking they were clear of black moss, Matthew helped her tip the berries into the bag, then she licked her fingers clean.

"Eat some as you go," he told her.

"I want to save them for the pie."

"There'll be plenty more. And give some to your brother."

Jasmine ran off to find Caleb. He lost sight of her as she caught up with Ulrich in the lead position. He ran a hand through his hair. Flakes of ash tumbled loose and the scent of smoke hung close.

They walked for an hour. Mosquitos whined in his ear and insects buzzed near his feet. The scent of pine carried on the air, reminding Matthew of the candle they lit every Christmas that filled the house with the smell of fir trees and cranberries. They lit it every day from the first of December, taking turns with the matches, the older ones helping the younger ones when it was their turn. It remained lit all day and into the evening, only blown out when the last person went to bed. That smell aroused a certain excitement. Christmas, Santa Claus, family. It was his favorite time of year. And now he could smell a trace of it on the pine needles surrounding them. Then, like now, they were all together. That was the important thing.

Matthew spoke to Luna as they walked, a constant level of conversation intended to coax her out, despite his throat feeling as though he'd just eaten a packet of dry crackers. He described the forest, what had happened to the house, where they were going. He didn't mention the creepy black moss. It was everywhere, snaking and weaving through undergrowth and shrubs, up tree trunks, and veining leaves with darkness. He would have run through the woods if he could, but with the kids, a faster pace was impossible. Luna gave no sign she'd heard or understood. But she continued to walk. She was in there somewhere, he just had to find a way of reaching her.

The group paused ahead. He couldn't see over Joseph's and Alessandra's heads, but a faint groaning reached his ears. No doubt Tyler would be complaining again and moaning about going to a hospital.

But when he reached the scene, the filtered sun revealed Hope doubled over, puking her guts onto the forest floor. There wasn't much. The carrots from last night's lasagna dinner. But she was expelling all her precious liquid.

CHAPTER 8
MATTHEW

HOPE COLLAPSED TO THE GROUND, her sketchbook falling out of her hands and landing in a pile of dry pine needles. Ariel held her hair back as peristaltic shudders wracked Hope's body.

"What's going on?" Matthew asked.

"It's the water she drank," Alessandra said in his ear. A quick scan of the forest revealed several tendrils of the moss had followed them and stretched out in all directions. Maybe they'd been there already. It must be the cause of the infected water. What else could it be?

"I'm okay." Hope used a tree trunk to right herself and gave Ariel an appreciative nod. "I feel better now." Black moss covered the base of the tree. Matthew kneeled to inspect it. He put his nose inches from the blackness. No odor. Just tree bark and earth. He watched it for a moment. He swore he could see it moving. Snaking its way further up the tree. Maybe he should touch it, see if it was tacky or smooth. But an inner voice told him not to. He pulled his hand away.

"You sure?" Matthew turned back to Hope. Her skin was

pale under her long wispy hair. The dampened roots adhered to her scalp. Her eyes seemed sunken. She was dehydrated.

She clutched her stomach. "I could use some water."

"We all could." Matthew looked ahead to see if there were any signs of life's liquid. His first hit of real panic trembled down his spine. It grabbed the back of his knees and shot up to the roof of his mouth, making it even drier. He was the one who'd suggested they go to Grandmother's house. He was the one guiding them. He was the one steering Luna and trying to coax her to talk. *If she would just talk!* And he was the one who'd left the house with none of the basic items needed to stay alive. He was going to be the death of them all.

Take care of them, Matthew.

Hope planted an unsteady foot. Her calf trembled. Worse than before.

She shrugged off his arm. "I can make it."

"You know we have to carry on?" Matthew asked her.

"I could stay with her." Tyler chimed in. "I haven't got much in me. We could stay here together."

"Tyler, you know we have to stick together," Joseph said, saving Matthew the trouble.

Tyler shrugged, then cradled his arm. "Worth a shot."

Surely it was almost healed by now. How he managed match after match on Friday evenings, throwing himself at the opponent, ramming his body into a pileup with a whiny attitude like that. Matthew shook his head. Luna always indulged Tyler by making a footbath for him with steaming hot water and Epsom bath salts. Sometimes she rubbed his calf muscles, loosening the tension. A tendril of envy spread through Matthew's veins like a sinister whisper. She never did that for him after a track meet. But Matthew could rub his own damn calf muscles and pour his own Epsom salts foot bath. Not that he ever did.

"I'll be okay," Hope said, shoving her notebook back into her pocket. There was a steely determination in her watery blue eyes.

Matthew stepped forward and fastened the zip on his jacket that she wore. "Stay warm."

"Wait!" Joseph called.

"What is it now?" Matthew questioned.

"Daddy?" Jasmine walked into the center of the group. Ulrich was on the ground, his forepaws stretched out, but his haunches raised. He raised his lips and emitted a high-pitched yowl.

Jasmine paused in the center of the group. A brave smile wobbled on her lips. She was definitely Kalisa's daughter; never wanting to upset the balance. But now her dark face drained of color and she looked in danger of passing out. Ulrich padded over and sniffed at her clothes, her face.

"What is it, Jasmine?" Joseph said, jostling a sleeping Nell on his shoulder.

She still had the collection bag in her hand. Purple juice stained both palms and the front of her shirt. Smudges dotted her lips, making her paling face look almost vampiric. Ulrich whined.

"Did you eat all the blackberries?" Matthew asked.

Jasmine nodded and clutched her stomach, a new stick doll falling from under her arm. The net bag slipped from her grip and landed in a pile of the strange black moss.

"There weren't that many." Faith frowned. "We only ate about six each."

"That shouldn't make her sick," Alessandra said.

"Did you eat anything else?" Joseph kneeled in front of his daughter, rubbing at the blood-red juice on her cheeks. Alessandra took the baby from him.

Jasmine nodded sleepily. "Mushrooms." Her eyelids fluttered. "I remembered them from the salad we ate last week."

"I told you not to eat those!" Faith said, as Jasmine fainted into her father's arms.

Matthew grabbed Faith's arm. "Where did she get the mushrooms?"

Piper crouched next to Jasmine, feeling her forehead, and then dug through her bag.

"Kerry," Faith replied. "Kerry gave her mushrooms. But I told her they were poisonous."

"She was so hungry," Hope said. "We all are."

Piper held something under Jasmine's nose that made her eyes pop open and sit up straight. She gasped, leaned over, and puked all over Joseph. Piper smiled. Ulrich chuffed and pressed his snout into Jasmine's chest until he elicited a weak smile.

"Will she be okay?" Matthew asked.

Piper nodded, signing they'd caught it in time.

"Alessandra, if you can carry Nell, I'll carry Jasmine," Joseph said. The older woman nodded, her gold, hoop earrings swinging as she repositioned Nell.

But the group didn't move more than five yards before Faith threw up too, and Tyler fainted dead away.

"Great," Matthew muttered.

"We're all tired," Alessandra said. "And ill. They need to rest."

"We don't have time to rest. And we need water."

"I know." Alessandra placed a hand on his arm. "But

there's nothing we can do about it now. There's that old cave up ahead. Let's shelter in there for a few hours and let them rest.

"Damn Kerry, damn the fire, damn the infected water, and damn these forsaken woods!" Matthew's voice rose as he stomped through the trees, pulling Luna after him. "And damn you!" He said to her impassive face. If she would just wake up, she could heal them all.

As he stormed on, he stepped in a puddle of the black moss. He stumbled, tried to wipe his boot clean on the leafy floor, and fell over into Kerry, who stood in the middle of the path, counting matches in their little box.

"What are you trying to do, Kerry? Kill us all off?" Matthew got up in his face. "Did you kill Kalisa?"

"I wasn't even there," Kerry replied, unruffled. "I've nothing against Kalisa."

"Just piss off, will you?"

"Thought I could lend a hand, carrying Tyler."

"You want to help now? What's it going to cost us? Besides, not sure a skinny Irish bloke like you could carry anything heavier than Nell."

"Then let me carry Nell."

"Nope. No way," Matthew said. No way was he letting Kerry near an innocent child.

"I just want a share o' yer food and water." Kerry walked abreast as Matthew began steering Luna again.

"Oh! That's what it comes down to. You figured out you *need* us."

"Well, I wouldn't put it like that. I'd call it more of a symbiotic relationship."

"I think you'll find it's parasitic when one organism takes

and doesn't give anything back," Matthew snapped. "And if you're going to stick around, go help with Tyler."

Kerry sauntered away. Matthew didn't care if it was away for good or to find Tyler and help. As long as he was out of his eyeline, maybe his blood pressure would return to a healthier level.

A few minutes later, they arrived at the cave. The group came to a whispering stop outside the gaping entrance. A leafy floor extended a few yards into the mouth, but overall, it looked like some dark, gaping maw about to swallow them whole. He shuddered. What was wrong with him? He assumed the effect of the fire, lack of sleep, and no water were toying with his mind. The scratch marks on his knuckles were starting to heal, but a worrying white line laced the top of the wound. He tried to wipe it off on his shirt, but it made the cuts sting like a bitch.

Ulrich stood closest to the entrance. He released one long, low warning cry, declaring the cave his territory. Rumbling barks and yowls returned in response. It had been a long time since Matthew had been this deep in the woods. He knew there were other animals around – other foxes, wolves, mountain lions - real animals that weren't part of their family. And he'd never feared them. He was grown. An adult male. The forest animals wouldn't usually make an attempt on an adult male. It wasn't even the thought of wild animals roaming this forest, but that low rumbling growl hadn't sounded like an animal at all. Animal-*like*, yet entirely different at the same time. What was that beast by the stream? Its decayed status had made it hard to tell. And Matthew didn't believe in yetis or bigfoot or other such nonsense. But it was huge. Ten times the size of Ulrich, and if he'd imagined how it sounded, it would have been something like that responding grumbling yowl. His heart stuttered. It hadn't occurred to him that there might be more than one of those dreadful...*beasts*.

"Beacon?" Matthew called. His heart stilled and the stinging in his knuckles abated. She was nearby. "We'll need you to light the way." Her path could only be followed by the gentle disruption of the leaves on the forest floor and the almost indiscernible shimmer of light, until she reached the mouth of the cave. Then it lit up. Jutting stone, low ceilings, stalactites, and stalagmites greeted them. A few joined together in some eternal expression of yearning love. A waft of damp stone. The smell of ancientness.

The group, almost as one, walked forward, following Beacon's light deeper into the cave. Matthew tugged on Luna's hand. She followed without question. Then squeezed his hand. He stopped, looked at her, waiting for another sign. He watched her fingers, willing them to squeeze again. But with each passing second, he became more convinced the small gesture had been a reflex, or the product of wishful thinking. Her blank gaze never wavered, never blinked. Her breathing was slow and measured. She never flinched or made any reflexive actions.

"Please, Luna," he whispered, squeezing her hand, hoping for a boomerang effect. He waited five minutes. The others grew impatient. Time to move on.

He ducked under the lip of the cave and turned to help her. Too late, she was about to hit her head.

"Duck!" he warned.

Luna ducked, then remained still in an awkward hunched position. So, she *could* hear him. Maybe she really had squeezed his hand. She was in there somewhere. Ignoring them. When they needed her. Anger flamed on his cheeks.

"Walk," he commanded, pushing her forward.

The drop in temperature cooled the sweat on his forehead and small of his back. His hairline prickled as it dried. After a few minutes, Beacon led them into a wide chamber. He couldn't make out the limit of the roof, but the girth was wide enough for them to stretch out and rest. The immediate ground consisted of soft, loamy earth, perfect for sleeping on, before it hardened into limestone and began sprouting interesting structures. Beacon sat in the middle of the cavern. The rest gathered around her in a loose circle, comforted by her guiding light. It was almost as if they were campers gathered around a fire to roast marshmallows and tell stories. But there were no stories now. Or marshmallows. The thought made his mouth water. *Water*.

Jasmine fell asleep in her father's lap, the stick doll nestled under one arm. Caleb sat with them, weaving dandelions through the stick doll's head to make hair. Hope and Faith huddled together, arms flung over each other, their contrasting hair colors like misshapen pieces on a checkers board. Hope lay still, but Faith snored, the sound punctuating the few murmured conversations. They seemed okay for now. The coolness of the cave refreshed him after the humidity of the forest. Fewer insects bothered them.

"How's Jasmine?" Matthew asked Joseph, scratching at a mosquito bite on his left wrist.

"She's hot." He laid a hand on her forehead. "The sleep will help."

"I'll go look for water." With effort, Matthew pushed himself to his feet.

"You need to rest too, Matthew," Alessandra said.

"I'm fine." He helped Luna to the floor, but she seemed to be pulling him after her.

"Tyler's asleep. Nell's asleep. Everyone's resting. There's nothing you can do right now," Alessandra said.

"Kerry?"

"He helped with Tyler, then took off."

"We need to make tools, to hunt. We need water. We need…"

"*Shhh*." Alessandra placed her hand on his. "*Shhh* now. All that can wait."

It really couldn't wait, but Matthew lost the will to argue. He sat and dropped his chin to his chest. The weight of his limbs dragged him to the ground. He was tired. Exhausted. Maybe he'd sleep for a few minutes. He rubbed at his eyes with the backs of his hands. "Okay." He settled on the ground next to Luna and let his eyes close and his breaths deepen.

A growl rumbled in the distance, somewhere beyond the cave. He snapped his eyes open and cocked his head. Several growls. Something else was out there. It would be foolish to go looking for water alone now. He was safe in the cave, with the others, away from the dead beast and creepy black moss. And the menacing growls. Whatever they were.

Luna curled her body around his and laid her head on his chest. A tendril of hope fluttered in his stomach. He held his breath, waiting for more. There were little responses. Maybe she would be okay. Maybe she didn't need Grandmother. Maybe she needed only him.

He touched her hair. He began to stroke, feeling the softness between his fingers. His chest swelled with the love he felt for his friend. "I'll help you," he whispered to her. "I promise." He kissed the top of her head. As his eyes closed and his brain let go, he could hear a drip of water in the distance. Probably dripping from a stalactite. How his throat craved that miniscule relief. But he didn't have the energy to move.

Someone coughed. Faith continued to snore. Nell hiccupped in her sleep. Beacon's warm light glowed over them all, keeping watch. She and Ariel never slept. Matthew let go and the world went mercifully blank for a little while. But not long enough. Because his dreams were filled with heat and fire, and then they took him back to that other time. When he heard Luna's screams and almost felt her memories.

CHAPTER 9
MATTHEW

MATTHEW WOKE WITH A START. Sat straight up like a starting gun had been triggered at the start of a meet. He tried to swing his legs out of bed to the floor, but he was already on the floor. Had he fallen out of bed? Then Matthew remembered. The fire. The journey through the woods. Grandmother's house. Luna. He needed to save Luna.

Sweat beaded on his forehead and dampened the hair under his arms, his shirt stuck to the small of his back. Panic constricted his airway. He placed a hand on his pounding heart and tried to take deep breaths. The others slept. Beacon remained among them. Her light glowed brighter for a moment and chased the panic away.

He rubbed the grainy exhaustion from his eyes. His limbs felt weighted, as though he was filled with lead. So heavy. So easy to give into the feeling. He couldn't have been asleep long. Something had woken him. He checked his watch. Almost 6pm. But he wasn't sure what time he'd laid down.

Then he heard it. A soft fluttering. A gentle noise, like a butterfly's delicate wings. Perhaps Obsidian had returned. But his wings whooshed with slow, powerful, deliberate strokes. Maybe he flew high above, his sounds coming to them like the engine on an airplane when directly overhead. But something told him Obsidian hadn't returned.

Another flutter. More than one. Several. All at once. He looked around, using Beacon's light, checking the depths of the shadows. Nothing moved. He squinted, narrowing his gaze, straining his eyes to see more.

More fluttering. Getting louder. Growing to some kind of crescendo. He jumped to his feet, fists held high, waiting. About to shout to the others. His pulse pounded in his ears. He held his breath, listening.

"What is it?" Faith muttered sleepily.

"Not sure," Matthew replied. "You feeling okay?"

She nodded. "Better."

His fists ached. His knuckles oozed with a substance he couldn't see. He avoided looking at them; there was nothing he could do about an infection now, and it was best not to scare himself.

Faith cocked her head, a curtain of hair falling over her cheek. Her nose ring glinted in Beacon's glow. Smudged mascara ringed her eyes, and a deep, purple bruise spread along her jaw where Caleb had hit her during his vision. She got to her feet and came to stand next to him. "What is that?"

Matthew frowned. The sound could no longer be called fluttering. It was more like a hoard of cicadas, chirping and calling to each other in their summer mating rituals. But cicadas didn't live in caves. A faint smell of excrement hit him. He looked at the ground where he'd been sleeping. Soft, loamy earth. Except it wasn't. His frown deepened. The ground consisted of uniformly sized pellets.

"I think we need to get out of here," Matthew said, resisting the urge to turn and flee.

Faith pointed above. "Beacon, could you go up and shine a light on what's going on?"

"No!" Matthew shouted, disturbing some of the others. But it was too late. Beacon was already directing her light upwards. The whirring insect noise increased to a deafening discord of ear-covering cacophony. Faith wrapped her arms around her head. Matthew didn't waste any time. "Up! Everyone up! Bats!"

As soon as he said the word, a wave of the ugly animals dropped from the dark roof of the cave, covering Beacon, almost extinguishing her light, and surged toward them like miniature vampires with murder on their minds.

Faith screamed, crouching low, covering her ears with her hands. Matthew dived under the stream of flying bats. He caught the odd glimpse of hairy faces and elongated ears. Pig snouts and fanged teeth. They were the ugliest animals he'd ever laid eyes on. Apart from the dead thing in the water maybe.

The others were awake. Ducking and rolling out the way. The cavern filled with their yells and the noise of the bats. Matthew wasn't sure if the bats were trying to find their way out of the cave or looking to exact their vengeance on being disturbed from their sleep.

Only Luna remained calm. Sitting with her arms folded on her knees, staring at the mouth of the cave and the sliver of moonlight that illuminated the torrent of flying rodents on their exit. They took Beacon in the next wave, her light sucked away by the dark creatures. She hurtled toward the exit and fell to the ground out in the open. Matthew lost sight of her.

In the semi-darkness, he crawled his way to Luna as the others rushed past. Luna sat and watched the bats around her, not moving her head or her eyes, but they flickered as the bats streamed past her, as if taking in the unreal experience to digest at a later, calmer time. The stream of flying rodents turned more aggressive as they veered closer and knocked into her. She didn't seem to notice. Her eyes never registered. There was no reflexive cowering. Matthew crawled along the cave floor to avoid the buffeting stream. One got tangled in Luna's hair. Its wings flapped and it entwined itself further. Still Luna didn't react.

The worst of the torrent passed. With the others outside, Matthew knelt in front of Luna and examined the tangled bat. It wouldn't be still. Its wings beat and its mouth opened and closed, chirping almost inaudibly, perhaps calling for reinforcements. He needed to work quickly to avoid its mate's rescue attempt. Which meant he had to touch the bat and avoid being bitten by carnivorous teeth.

Dammit, Luna!

At least, for once, her stillness worked in his favor. But the bat might turn on her and try to bite its way free. With one more hesitant breath, he gripped the terrified animal with two hands, near its neck, trying to avoid its teeth, and attempted to haul it out of Luna's hair. Nothing happened. He tugged again. A shadow of a wince crossed Luna's face. Well and truly entangled, the bat snapped its teeth all over the place. Matthew's wounded knuckles throbbed with the effort. The wings beat against his scabs, opening them.

"Shit!" Matthew muttered as he took his hand away.

Kerry chuckled. "Looks like you've got a wee bit of bother on your hands."

Now where the hell had he come from?

"No shit, Sherlock."

Kerry leaned against the cave wall, picking his fingernails clean with a hunting knife.

"Care to toss me the knife?" Matthew hated the needful tone in his voice.

"Nope. Not going let ye get yer hands on me knife." But he stepped forward and cut the bat loose from Luna's hair.

It flew away, screeching with all its might, Luna's dark hair tangled in its claws. Matthew checked over her face. She seemed unharmed.

"You're welcome," Kerry said, turned his back, and walked out of the cave.

"Yeah, well, it's not like you'd get far without Luna anyway," Matthew hurled at his back. What a douchebag. "And we could use your knife to get some food!"

Matthew got to his feet, then helped Luna to hers. Her blue, rabbit slippers looked decidedly gray. She'd had them for over seven years. Matthew remembered the trip to town. Her feet had grown, and she kept getting splinters from the worn, wooded floor of the timber house. They'd ridden in the back of her father's red pick-up together, just the two of them, none of the others. On old cushions, sitting thigh to thigh, with the wind blasting their hair and the sun caressing their faces, like they were beginning a journey. Maybe they didn't need to go back to the house in the woods, maybe it could just be the two of them, forever.

"I want these!" Luna had said in the shoe shop, a delighted smile spreading across her lips as she dug her fingers into the soft fleece of the rabbit slippers.

"Hardly practical," her father had chuckled. "They don't even have a hard sole to wear outside."

"Please?" Luna had begged, her hands together, hope shining in her eyes.

Her father couldn't deny the look on her face. Neither could Matthew.

"I suppose it'll be okay. It's summer after all, and we'll only be back in six months getting the next pair. You're growing so much," her father had said.

Matthew had nodded his encouragement. But neither of them had realized that her feet stopped growing that summer. She was stuck with the blue, rabbit slippers. By the next summer Luna professed to hate them and thought they were childish. But Matthew still loved them. They symbolized that glorious day when it was just the two of them for a few hours.

Outside the cave, the others huddled in a tight group. Faith sported a long scratch above her swollen jaw. Piper administered herbs.

"It stinks!" Faith complained.

Piper frowned at her and continued rubbing the reeking paste onto her jaw.

Jasmine whimpered as she inspected an array of small, but bleeding cuts on the backs of her hands. Ulrich licked them clean. She was next in line for Piper's healing herbs. The others seemed unharmed. Terrified, but unharmed.

"I don't know if I've been bitten!" Tyler said. "Through my burns and the pain, it's hard to tell! I don't want rabies."

"There's a cure for it now," Matthew said.

Tyler glowered at him.

Take care of them, Matthew. He reigned in his irritation. He'd never had to spend this kind of time with Tyler before.

They avoided each other. And now he was supposed to take care of him? A long sigh escaped his lips.

"Has anyone seen Kerry?" Matthew asked.

"A few minutes ago." Alessandra pointed. "That way."

"At least he's going the right way," Matthew said. "And hopefully has the good sense to hunt for food."

"Kerry?" Faith snorted. Piper was done rubbing in the paste and had moved on to Jasmine. "The only thing he uses that knife for is picking the motor oil out from under his fingernails."

"I wouldn't be so sure about that," Hope said, coming to stand by Matthew. "We haven't known him that long. Think of the mushrooms he gave Jasmine. You okay now, sweetheart?" she asked the younger girl, her tone softening.

Jasmine nodded and patted her stomach. Ulrich slid in beside her so his head rested under her hand.

Faith frowned and tilted her head. "We haven't known you that long either."

Hope shrugged. "Just saying."

"Hope might have a point," Matthew said. "None of us really know him that well. He hasn't been friends with Luna that long."

Faith pointed at Hope, suggesting the same of the girl a year her junior.

"Hope didn't come with a knife," Matthew said. "Or a brooding attitude and a motorcycle."

"No, she's all rainbows and unicorns." Faith gesticulated wildly, flashing the unicorn tattoo on her left wrist.

"We've known Kerry for less than a year." Alessandra twiddled one of her gold hoop earrings.

"He's dangerous," Hope said, shivering inside Matthew's jacket.

"He's just a mysterious biker, a drifter," Faith said, a dreamy look in her eyes as if she might be undressing Kerry in her mind. It was attitudes like hers that had welcomed Kerry into the fold. But Matthew had sensed there was something wrong with him from the start. The way he looked at Luna, like she was a mouse to be played with. And the way Luna jumped on the back of that motorcycle, no helmet, at the mere hint of a suggestion. It made his blood curdle.

"He's a prick." Tyler scoffed at Faith. "He can just drift off."

"For once, I agree with you," Matthew said.

"He's what Luna needed." Ariel joined the conversation, her synthetic voice echoing oddly off the trees. She stood with a ramrod-straight back, her silver hair shifting ethereally even though there was no breeze. Countless silver necklaces of many lengths caught the light of the waxing moon.

The chatter stopped. It was unlike the angel to offer an opinion in such matters.

"How does she need someone to take her out on a motorcycle, on dangerous, winding roads, to bars, drinking, smoking, when she's underage?" Matthew's fists clenched involuntarily, making his knuckles sting.

"I didn't say it was good for her," Ariel replied, her calmness diffusing some of his anger. "I said it was what she needed."

"Hell yeah," Faith exclaimed. "It's what I need too. If only I'd met him first."

Hope laughed. "You're too young for him."

Faith frowned. "He's twenty-one!"

"Exactly," Hope said. "And you're sixteen."

"Well, you're only fifteen." Faith kicked her foot and a flip-flop went flying.

"But I don't have a crush on a dangerous drifter who may or may not be homicidal."

"Kerry's not homicidal." Faith snorted. "And no, you'd never get on his bike, you barely leave the house. Always drawing in that stupid sketchpad. Maybe it's time to show us what you've been drawing."

"That's private!" Frowning, Hope hunched her shoulders and dug her hand into the pocket where her sketchpad was hidden. "And at least I have the good sense not to dance on my feet when they're bleeding."

"That's because you can't dance," Faith snapped back.

"Girls, please," Alessandra said. "This isn't the time."

"Does anyone know how the fire started?" Matthew asked, breaking up their argument with the one question that had been on his mind. "Do you think someone started it on purpose?"

Faith gave a piercing stare. "If you're implying it was Kerry, we don't know that."

"Can you prove that?" Hope asked.

Faith turned on her. "Can you?"

"Kids, please. Please, don't fight," Alessandra said. "We don't know how the fire started. There's been no rain all summer. The forest is dry. The house was dry. Besides, we have more pressing matters to deal with."

Faith bristled. "I'm not a kid."

"Then don't act like it," Alessandra snapped. She never snapped. "We need food and water. It's been almost twenty-four hours since any of us had a drink. Now that those who were ill seem recovered, this is our priority."

"I'm not recovered," Tyler said. "The herbs aren't working."

"There's no hospital around here." Matthew gestured to the trees, the ferns, the pine-needle floor, and the creepy black moss. Which, now that he'd noticed it again, seemed to be shifting. If he recorded it for a day and watched it on fast forward, what secrets would its growth reveal? Scratch that. Maybe it would be best not to know. At least until they'd arrived at Grandmother's house.

"We need to walk at night. We lost time during the day sleeping in the cave. And we need to find water. I suggest we split up into small groups, keeping each other in sight," Alessandra said.

Matthew nodded and began dividing them into groups.

"I want to lead a group!" Caleb said.

"Yeah, well, as long as I'm in it, Squirt," Joseph replied. "We'll take Beacon too."

"This isn't football where you get to pick the best ones." Faith retrieved her flip-flop and slipped it back on her foot.

Matthew ignored her and put Tyler in the group farthest away from him. With Faith. They could keep each other happy. With Tyler, Hope, and Jasmine walking again, Joseph was free to carry Nell. Matthew walked with Luna. He'd never let her out of his sight.

As they walked, he glanced over his bruised and cracked knuckles. He couldn't be sure in the pale light of the moon, but the hint of blackness showed deep in the cuts. He told himself it was just dried blood. But his quickened pulse and fluttering stomach believed differently. Every time he thought about the black moss or the diseased beast, he looked around the woods and would see the snaking tendrils stretching through the forest. Slithering under fallen leaves, stretching up stalks of ferns, hugging the bases of the tree trunks, deepening, darkening. *Taking over*. But it was just moss, black moss. And just because there had been black moss in the stream, it didn't mean it was the moss that had infected the water. It might be harmless. The infection source was most likely the dead beast. Festering germs, leaching into the water. But Matthew knew in the pit of his stomach. There was something wrong with the black moss. Not just wrong. *Evil*.

"We need to make tools," Matthew said.

"I know," Alessandra replied.

"We need food, something more substantial than berries. With the kids along, it's going to take a while to reach Grandmother's house. Maybe more than a week." He snapped off a branch from a tree, intending to whittle it into a spear when they stopped for a rest. But he'd need Kerry's knife for that. As much as he hated to admit it, they did need him. Well, maybe not *him*, but what he was carrying.

"I know, Matthew."

"So, what's the plan?" He tried not to sound exasperated. It was always up to him, and for once, he really wanted someone else to take the lead. To make a decision. To bear the responsibility.

Take care of them, Matthew.

"We do the best we can," she replied.

"Alessandra! That's not a plan."

She shrugged, causing her earrings to dance. She glanced at the following moon and lowered her voice. Her breath puffed out in front of her, and she wrapped her arms around her waist. "We do the best we can."

"And if we lose people along the way? Like Kalisa?" He

winced. Luna was probably listening. Well, maybe not listening, per se, but hearing.

"Then we lose people. We don't have control over this situation. Trying to take control would be fruitless. Control is an illusion. You've yet to learn that, Matthew. We help when we can help, and we do the—"

"—best we can." Matthew threw his hands in the air.

They walked for a few more minutes. Alessandra rubbed her hands together and blew into them. The middle of the night coldness chilled him to the core. Made him stick his hands in his armpits and contemplate peeing on them. Just to feel a bit of warmth. Or for a drink. Could they drink their own urine? He seemed to remember learning it was possible. Hopefully it wouldn't come to that.

"Maybe we should go back," Matthew said.

Alessandra shook her head. Her bracelets jangled along her arm. "We can't. You know that. You were right to make us leave."

"I didn't have time to think," Matthew said. "I totally panicked."

"We all panicked." Alessandra rubbed a hand over his back, near his scar. "We were all terrified. And we appreciate your leadership. Even when we don't show it."

"You, maybe," Matthew said. "But some of the others… not so much."

Alessandra let out a gentle chuckle. "Don't mind Tyler. He's all bluster. And he's jealous."

"Jealous?"

A scream interrupted Alessandra's reply. A scream so loud and full of pain. Blinding terror. Like a woman being attacked. Luna's mother. Matthew didn't pause to think. He pumped his legs and ignored the weeping liquid oozing over his skinned knuckles and the burn in his smoke-affected lungs.

"Run, Matthew!" Alessandra called at his back.

He left Luna and ran. Just like when he raced at a meet. But there had been no starting gun, no breeze cooling the nervous sweat at the back of his neck, and no time to tie his laces. He ran through the woods, jumping over fallen trees, stumbling over jutting roots, skidding along patches of black moss, startling a racoon ambling through the undergrowth. The moon came in and out of the scudding clouds, making visibility perilous. He fell to a knee once but was quickly back on his feet. He could feel Coach barking in his ear. Could imagine the mistakes he would highlight on the training videos. It made him run faster. Over a stream. A stream! Water! His throat ached to be quenched. But he couldn't stop. He had to find the source of that bloodcurdling scream.

He heard Ulrich. The fox's terrifying cries whipped through the forest, startling sleeping birds from their nests and setting off a series of responsive barks, howls, yowls, and yaps from other animals. The desperation in the fox's voice grew until it felt as though the forest was filled with an entire skulk of foxes yowling in unison. It was beautiful and creepy. And entirely unnerving.

Matthew hurdled another fallen tree, dreading the worst. He could see the fox now, sitting on his haunches, his muzzle aimed at the moon. The cry built and released. Built and released. Again and again. Ulrich's jaw quivered each time he gathered himself, and his hackles trembled when each cry tore into the night.

As Matthew neared, the fox's thoughts came at him in a scattered onslaught. The moonlight glinted off his fur, lending a spectral impression to his form. The cry cut off abruptly. Ulrich laid on the ground, his head resting on his paws, tears running down his furry snout.

Matthew skidded to a stop. Nell sat abandoned on the ground. Awake and crawling off in the wrong direction. A patch of the treacherous black moss was in her path. He plucked her from the ground and set her next to Ulrich.

Joseph kneeled on the ground, cradling something. Matthew pushed past him to see. Caleb. Dear, sweet Caleb. Lying so still.

A raven cawed.

CHAPTER 10
MATTHEW

MATTHEW HELD HIS BREATH. Ulrich sobbed as if his own cub had been taken from him.

"*Noooo!*" Joseph roared, his face hunched over Caleb. "*Why?*"

"What's going on?" Matthew asked, wondering if he really wanted to know, if he could bear another tragedy. He looked at Joseph and realized how much worse it was for him. He'd already lost his wife.

"Animal trap," Joseph spluttered.

Matthew leaned down. The metal teeth of a rusted and highly illegal animal trap imprisoned Caleb's right leg. These woods were protected. It wasn't even hunting season. And none of those points really mattered right now.

Matthew tried to pull the teeth apart with his bare hands, opening the wounds on his knuckles and creating new ones on his palms. But the iron jaws wouldn't budge and dug painfully into the meat of his hands.

Caleb lay with his eyes closed. His face, like the pale and indifferent moon, was both colorless and devoid of expression.

His calf lay ripped open. Blood soaked the forest floor. Insects buzzed around the rich source of food. A protrusion of white bone, broken, severed in two, poked out from his flesh at an unnatural angle. The smell of blood rushed up Matthew's nose, a smell so strong not even the pine trees could mask it.

They were in the middle of the woods. They had no phone, even if they could garner a signal from a distant mast. Would any ambulance find them in time? It was pointless to even go down that line of thought. They were on their own.

Matthew removed the owl and cougar bandana from around his knuckles. He wrapped it around Caleb's leg, just below the knee, and tied it tight. It was the only thing he could think to do. No amount of Piper's herbs was going to cure this. As he worked, his old wound between his shoulder blades throbbed in time with his heartbeat.

Take care of them, Matthew.

"I can't lose him! I can't lose another member of my family!" Joseph's pallor matched his son's. His lips trembled and deep furrows lined his forehead. He cradled his son's head in his lap and lifted his face to the unsmiling moon, pleading, begging, muttering prayers under his breath.

"I know, Joseph. I know." How the hell was he going to keep Caleb alive? They had at least another five nights in these woods before they got to Grandmother's house. Maybe they should turn back. Facing what lay behind was surely a better risk for them all. But the others would never agree. Not if they knew the truth. The real truth. About who they all really were. About why Luna could heal them. Why wasn't she healing Caleb?

Some of the others caught up to the devastating scene. Jasmine gasped, turned, and heaved into the bushes. Hope muttered; "Oh, my God. Oh, my God," over and over again. Matthew checked for a pulse in Caleb's wrist. He spotted a faint twitch in Caleb's neck. The blood loss was slowing. Maybe it wasn't too late.

Alessandra crouched next to him, Matthew's grim expression reflected in her dark pupils.

Caleb's eyes fluttered open. He looked at the moon, then at the group surrounding him. He smiled. "Is it my birthday, or something?" His breath plumed upwards, visible in the cold. He shivered. His teeth chattered like a ventriloquist's possessed dummy.

"Or something." Matthew took one of the boy's hands. Joseph held the other, his free hand tucked into his mouth, biting on his knuckles.

Whimpering, Jasmine crept closer to Caleb. Beacon's light showed the severity of his wounds; the blood on the ground, the jutting bone, the leg bent at an unnatural angle. No one spoke. Reality dawned on them. Caleb would go no further. To move him would cause excruciating pain.

Ariel stood over the injured boy, her hands clasped in prayer, her unearthly glow basking him in an eerie light. Matthew frowned at her hard enough to make her look in his direction. But she only shook her head.

A raven cawed and Matthew punched the ground with his injured knuckles, not caring about the new spasm of pain.

"Caleb!" Jasmine threw herself at her brother.

"Ow!" Caleb screamed.

Jasmine backed away, on hands and feet, like a crab, her eyes wide. Hope took her hand and pulled her to her feet. She smoothed Jasmine's hair away from her eyes and wrapped her arms around her, pressing the young girl's face into her chest so she couldn't see.

"I didn't mean to hurt him," Jasmine mumbled.

"It's okay, Jasmine," Caleb mumbled. "Come back." Sweat beaded on his brow. He struggled to suck in each short, shallow breath. Matthew released his hand so Jasmine could hold it.

"Please don't die," she whispered. Matthew's lips formed the same plea, silently. A hopeless prayer.

"It's okay." Caleb patted her hand, an echo of Kalisa's death.

Matthew smiled at the boy, seeing in his prepubescent features the man he would soon become. If he lived. He imagined, once Caleb had grown a few years, they would be great friends, have more in common, share the brunt of the back-breaking chores around the cabin. If a task involved an ax, or a chainsaw, or any other tool perceived to need brute strength, Caleb was first in line. Always wanting to help chop the logs into firewood. He'd been ready a few months now, but Luna hadn't wanted him near the ax. Instead, Caleb read to Jasmine after her bath. He chased Nell around the living room floor and made her giggle with delight. He was a good kid. A good big brother.

Caleb's voice became a whisper. "I was going to die anyway."

"What are you talking about?" Matthew asked.

"The fire," Caleb replied. "I was going to die in the fire."

"But we escaped the fire," Matthew said. He must be delusional. Hallucinating.

Caleb didn't speak again. His eyes closed. He exhaled one last, tremulous breath. And then he was gone. *Gone.* Just like that. A boy of twelve, taken from them mercilessly. A useless and unnecessary death. Matthew's jaw ached with the injustice of it.

Joseph wept. Great, heaving sobs wracked his body and shuddered his shoulders.

"*It's all my fault.*" Ulrich's voice in his head. "*It's all my fault.*"

"*Shhh.* It's nobody's fault." Alessandra stroked the fox.

"I promise." Matthew put a hand on Joseph's trembling shoulder, "no one else is going to die. I'll get you all to Grandmother's house." He simply wouldn't allow any more death.

Mockingly, the raven cawed once more.

Take care of them, Matthew. Why had she asked him to protect them? *Why, Luna? Why?*

"*It's all my fault,*" Ulrich spoke with his telepathy again. "*That trap was meant for me.*" He paced a few steps away. He threw one last screeching yowl at the moon and scampered deep into the woods.

"Now, now, Matthew." Kerry crouched next to him, examining Caleb and prodding the exposed bones. Caleb's body twitched under his touch. Matthew smelled the cigarettes on his breath. "Can ye really make such promises?"

White hot anger flashed through Matthew's veins, threatening to burn him from the inside out. He wanted to renege on his promise right now and punch the smug smile off Kerry's face until he was nothing more than a bloodied corpse. Instead, he swatted Kerry's hand away from Caleb's leg.

"As you're here," Matthew said, through clenched teeth, "care to hand over your knife so I can whittle a spear?"

"Why would ye need a thing like that?" Kerry asked. "We aren't cavemen."

"We. Need. Food. You know that."

Kerry pointed to the ground, at Caleb. It took Matthew a moment to understand the implication. And then he couldn't speak. A red mist exploded in front of his eyes. And he went for him.

"We. Do. Not. Eat. Each. Other." Matthew's fist flew through the air. But Joseph caught it in his palm. And then Alessandra and Ariel were between them. The three of them had to hold him back. He strained against them. Sweat beaded on his upper lip, and a rage so intense swam through him he thought he might explode. He swung his fists and kicked anywhere he could, not caring that he caught Alessandra on the shin or Joseph's arm.

Take care of them, Matthew. If only he could.

"I wish it was you!" he screamed at Kerry.

"I bet ye do." Kerry narrowed his eyes. He stood straight, sweeping his hair back into place, then pulled out a cigarette and tapped it against the box, repeatedly. "You've not been sure about Luna's affections since I've been around, have ye?"

"What the hell is that supposed to mean?" Matthew yelled.

Kerry ignored him, plucked the plastic water bottle from Piper's hand, walked over to the stream – black moss free - that had reappeared a few yards away, and lowered the bottle into the bubbling liquid. He took several, long sips, draining half the bottle. He refilled it, then gave it back to Piper. He walked away, but not before handing his hunting knife to Joseph, hilt first.

"Screw you!" Matthew yelled against his restraints.

When he could no longer see Kerry, the others released him. He collapsed to the ground, tears threatening to seep through his tightly closed eyes. Caleb's inert body lay right in front of him. It wasn't fair. None of it was goddamn fair. He felt like he was about to crack in two.

Take care of them, Matthew. He couldn't take care of them. He couldn't do anything.

"Drink, Matthew." Hope held the bottle to his lips. He was glad it was her. He would have decked anyone else.

He drank. And the water soothed his parched, burnt throat, making its way to his belly where it satisfied some of his hunger cravings. When Hope removed the bottle, he wiped his wet lips on the back of his arm. He felt much better. Which he hated. Because Caleb would never feel better again.

"I need to bury him," Joseph said. "I can't leave him here to be picked apart by wild animals."

Matthew nodded.

"I'll understand if you need to carry on. Just take the children with you."

"Don't leave, Daddy," Jasmine said, clutching her stick doll tight. The one with the dandelions for hair that Caleb had picked for her.

Were they all feeling as frightened as Matthew? Did the children sense their whole world was crumbling apart? If only Luna would wake up and heal them. Would she be able to bring Kalisa and Caleb back from the dead too? Matthew remembered the first time she'd healed him. He'd been twelve and chopping wood with the ax. The heavy ax was too much for him to handle. He'd split the skin between his shoulder blades and blood had poured. Luna had screamed and come rushing toward him. Crying, she'd hugged him tightly. He'd tensed against the pain. But then it was gone. The pain, and the blood. Just a scar remained. He'd always known she was special, but healing him like that was on a whole other level.

"We won't leave you," Matthew said. "We'll all help."

The others murmured their agreement.

"I'd like to help. But there's not much I can do." Tyler indicated his burnt arm. "I liked Caleb. He had a good throwing arm."

"Sit down and rest," Matthew said. "Piper can put more herbs on your burns. And wash them first. In the stream."

Take care of them, Matthew. He was trying. Goddamn it, he was trying.

Piper nodded and set to work, leading Tyler to the stream and digging the relevant herbs out of her bag. Once the group sated their thirst, they set about digging a hole. It wouldn't be deep, considering they had nothing more than a knife and bare hands to dig with. Joseph quickly abandoned the tool in favor of his fingers. But it would be deep enough that wild animals wouldn't unearth him easily. They took turns sitting with Luna, dribbling water into her mouth and making sure she swallowed.

It took three hours. And when they finished, the night was only half over. Matthew sat by the edge of the hole and rested a moment. Tyler found a thick branch and managed to pry the trap apart. Once the jaws were gaping wide, the whole thing fell apart with an awkward clanging of rusted springing hinges and missiling pins.

Matthew reached for Caleb.

"I'll do it." Joseph lifted his son into his arms. He walked the few feet to the open grave and gently lowered him in.

"I promise," Matthew said. *I promise to keep you all alive*.

Joseph nodded and reached a hand to his son's head. He touched his forehead and smoothed away his unruly hair. He stayed that way for a moment. Jasmine came and took her father's hand. Putting his arm around her, he drew her in close. He choked out a garbled sob, swallowed, and hugged his remaining children tighter.

"Who's going to steal the cookies from the pantry for me?" Jasmine gasped.

"I will," Matthew said.

Jasmine shook her head. "I don't want to be the oldest."

"Don't worry about that," Joseph said. "We're a family. We're all together."

One, lone tear fell out of Jasmine's eye, ran down her cheek, and dripped off her chin. "I'll try to be brave."

"You don't need to be brave," Matthew said. "You just need to be you."

"Rest well, my brave son, for you may have only lived a short life, but it was a full one, a loved one, and you will be missed." Ariel stood at the foot of the makeshift grave. Piper made the sign of the cross while her lips moved in silent prayer.

"He was the best big brother anyone could ask for," Jasmine said.

"And son," Joseph added. "His insatiable curiosity was both irritating and enthralling." His statement earned a couple of hesitant smiles.

"I'll never forget when he asked me how to beatbox," Tyler said. "Like I knew."

"And me, how to kiss a girl." Faith tucked her arm into Hope's. "And that's something I could tell him about."

"He asked me how to draw," Hope said, fiddling with the hem of her white nightdress.

"We always talked about what was beyond the stars," Ariel

said. "Although I had the feeling my answers were never satisfactory."

Nope. Not in a million years.

"We talked about medicine, herbs, and healing," Alessandra said. Piper signed that she'd been involved in those discussions too.

"We talked about Luna," Matthew said. "Caleb loved her."

"We all love her," Jasmine piped up, receiving a handful of responsive smiles.

Ariel bowed her head. "Rest well my weary traveler."

Filling in the hole took far less time. The entire group got down on their hands and knees and pushed the dirt over Caleb's composed face. Like it was a ritual, or something. When it was done, they patted it down with their hands. Many shed tears into the earth over his body. Piper collected wildflowers and planted them to mark the grave. Some bright red flower that Matthew couldn't name. Then she added some pungent branches of holly and pine. He was thankful he could no longer smell the blood, instead the smell of freshly dug earth filled the air.

A raven cawed in a branch just over their heads. Caleb was gone. Their journey beckoned. Would they ever find their way back here?

"I think we should stick closer together from now on," Joseph said. The man looked pale and withered. His hair was lank. Even the beads in his dreadlocks refused to clatter.

"Agreed," Matthew said.

Matthew took Luna's hand again, wondering if she was aware of the tragedy. He guided her over exposed roots. But this time he felt a tremor of anxiety. As he looked at her emotionless face, he felt a tiny bit afraid of her. The last time she'd been this way had been nine years ago. Just after he'd met her. She'd been terrifying in her grief and fear then too. And just as unpredictable. In recent years, they'd fallen into a comfortable pattern. They didn't all get along, but they managed. New friends were welcomed, but they never went away. Not like now.

As Ulrich had disappeared, dealing with his guilt somewhere else, Beacon led the way. Matthew felt a surge of disproportionate anger toward her. For all her light and feelings of hope, what good did she ever actually do? She wasn't capable of saving people. Kalisa and Caleb were dead. And all she did was shine a light on that fact. Illuminate faces that would never smile again. Perhaps they'd be better off in the dark, feeling their way without her.

CHAPTER 11
MATTHEW

THEY LEFT Caleb's grave behind and moved through the whispering trees. No one spoke. With two deaths among their group in such a short space of time, Matthew couldn't blame them for their silence.

The woods were cold, the sun had not yet risen, and half of them weren't dressed appropriately for the weeklong trek to Grandmother's house. Holding Nell in his arms, Joseph kept his eyes on his shoes, and whispered to Jasmine as they walked.

Jasmine frowned, scanning the tree line. "Where's Ulrich?"

Matthew followed her gaze, searching for a hint of movement. "He's upset about Caleb. Give him some time."

Jasmine's frown deepened, two little furrows above her nose that never left an imprint. Berry juice stained her chin. "He was my brother." No accusation. Just a statement.

Matthew leaned down to her level and placed a finger under her chin. "Everyone deals with things differently. In their own way. He just needs some time."

"I can't believe he would leave me." Her voice was only a whisper, but Matthew caught the note of hurt.

"He'll be back," Matthew said. The truth was, he was running out of platitudes, and with Ulrich gone, he was on his own leading the group to Grandmother's. He'd been on this journey once before, but he had no confidence he knew the way. Not with young children heading in directionless circles, or towering pines obscuring the pattern of constellations, or the snaking black moss that made everything look different. Ulrich had fled. Ditched them when they needed him. Matthew was pissed too.

"He'll come back?"

"Yes." Matthew hoped it wasn't a lie.

Jasmine walked with her father, plucking wildflowers from the undergrowth. Keeping her eyes low, she pressed her nose into the growing posy. The others remained quiet as they continued their journey. The pace was slow. Slower than a herd o' turtles, as Kerry would say. Only a few droplets sloshed in Piper's water bottle.

Take care of them, Matthew.

He'd tried. But it wasn't working. His shoulders sagged. He kept replaying it all in his mind. Could they have acted any differently? Could it have been avoided? Could they have saved Caleb? Should it have been Ulrich?

The last was spiteful, perhaps, but he was running out of kindness. Kindness didn't make the kids walk quicker. Kindness didn't get them to Grandmother's house any faster. Kindness didn't find water or food. Kindness didn't stop Kerry from disappearing or being a total dick. And kindness didn't take the nightmares away. The ones he and Luna both had in the middle of the night. That gut-wrenching, all-encompassing terror like they were living through it all over again. But with more adult eyes, able to understand what they were watching. What the red of the blood actually meant. And it made it all the worse.

But when she had nightmares, Luna would crawl into his bed, or he into hers, and they would whisper together. While the others slept, they could talk about it without fear of eavesdropping. It had been nine years. When would the nightmares stop?

But there were new nightmares now. Caleb. And Kalisa. Jasmine slipped her arm around her father's leg as he carried Nell and watched where she put her feet. Every time he looked at her, her eyes glistened.

"Matthew." Alessandra approached. "Are you sure of the way? Without Ulrich…"

Matthew glanced at Luna. A low branch swept in front of her face. She didn't even flinch as the pine needles scratched her cheek, drawing a thin line of blood. She was getting worse.

"I think so. It's been a long time since I've walked it. But I think so." *I hope so.*

Alessandra nodded. She didn't pass judgement. There was nothing else they could do. But she cleared her throat and smoothed her skirts and looked anywhere but at him.

The sky lightened and melted the cold of the night. The forest lay under a thin layer of dew he couldn't remember forming. Birds woke from their hidden nests and greeted the day with song. Thankfully, there were no ravens. But the cacophonous chirping only added to Matthew's building headache. Both temples throbbed in time with his heartbeat.

"Water!" Faith cupped an ear, rushing forward, leaving both her flip-flops behind.

Matthew eyed the waking birds. Could he take one out with a well-placed pebble? Would he be fast enough?

"I hear it, too," Hope exclaimed, color flooding her cheeks for the first time since the fire.

The girls rushed forward to the edge of something. Ulrich was there. A heavy relief swarmed Matthew's chest. Jasmine saw the red fox and threw herself at him.

"Don't you ever leave me again," Jasmine said. He opened his mouth and released a few twigs into her hand. No doubt to be weaved into a stick doll. A peace offering of sorts. Jasmine immediately set to work and used the stems of the yellow wildflowers to hold the new doll together. She used the petals for hair. Matthew marveled at its primitive beauty.

The fox barked and whined.

Ulrich's voice floated into his head. *I was trying to get to Grandmother's house quicker, but couldn't find a place to cross the river.*

"Appreciated," Matthew said. "But can you just stick with us from now on?"

The fox snorted, which Matthew took for assent.

Matthew scanned the area. The trees thinned and bushes shrank. A wide blue sky framed the rising sun. There was a clearing of some kind. A wide clearing that dropped off to nothing. A gap in the land. Loud, rushing water filled his ears. A raging torrent.

Faith and Hope hovered at the edge of a deep canyon. Three hundred feet. Maybe more. The river ran at the bottom. White and frothing, water surged over jutting boulders as if they were mere pebbles. The rocks lined the banks like a monster's gaping jaw. There was no way they could reach its source.

"Step back," Matthew warned. It was a death drop. And he'd promised no more death.

"How do we get across?" Faith asked, retrieving her flip-flops.

"There was a bridge…" Matthew looked up and down the canyon for the slatted, wooden bridge. Last time he'd run halfway across and started jumping up and down, swaying it precariously. He'd scared the hell out of Luna. She'd cried and insisted he come back.

Even without Ulrich's help, he thought he'd been zeroing in on the location of the bridge.

"You mean that bridge?" Tyler pointed across the canyon as he lowered himself to the ground.

Squinting against the sun, Matthew followed his finger. The bridge dangled by two ropes on the other side of the canyon. There was no way they could reach it. No way they could pull it back. Even if they could, most of the wooden planks had rotted and fallen away. His heart sank. In the cave, yesterday, Luna had squeezed his hand. Now she didn't even react when a branch whacked her in the face. Whatever was happening to her was getting worse. They didn't have time for broken bridges.

Jasmine tugged on his hand. "Ulrich says the next bridge is fifty miles away." The stick doll lay completed on the ground, the crown of yellow flowers offering a sweetness to the air. Now she had two to carry.

"I know," Matthew replied through his clenched teeth. *I know*.

Matthew tried to judge the distance across. He didn't know why he was bothering, because it wasn't like they'd be able to jump it. But it was something to do. The others waited for him to make a decision. Why did he always have to make the decisions? And what decision could they possibly make?

Take care of them, Matthew.

Go back? To the fire? And to everyone that would be looking for Luna? Everything would be revealed. The police would be looking for them. For Luna. Because of her history. The forest was no place for a damaged seventeen-year-old. Not alone. But she wasn't alone. She had him, and the others.

Find another bridge? Fifty miles downriver? With children, that would take at least another four days. And what if it was further? Or what if that bridge was broken too? Even if it wasn't, they'd have to trek back the fifty miles on the other side. Impossible.

Please wake up, Luna! He stared at his best friend, wishing, willing. He placed his hand on her shoulder. She averted her head. Blinked in slow motion. His chin dropped, and he focused on her bunny slippers. *Please, Luna.*

Go back?

Find another bridge?

Go back.

Find another bridge.

His eyes stung. He squeezed his lids against the tears. If he cried, he'd never live it down.

"I had me a gander upstream. There's a fallen tree trunk a few hundred yards upriver." Kerry's voice reached him. Then the strike of a match, the sharp inhale of breath. The repressive smell of smoke reached his nose.

"It's a forest, Kerry," Matthew snapped. "There's a lot of fallen tree trunks."

"Well, you're a sandwich short of a picnic." Kerry took

another drag, inhaled deeply, then exhaled in Matthew's direction. "You're missing me point, so it is."

"Would you care to elaborate?" Matthew refused to wave the smoke away.

Kerry kept him waiting, took another couple drags.

"Kerry?" Alessandra questioned. At least he wasn't the only one Kerry aggravated.

Kerry nodded upstream. "A tree's fallen across the canyon. It stretches right to the other side. You've got your bridge. Let's not make a bags of it now."

A flicker of hope. If the trunk was big enough. Maybe. Just maybe.

"Show me."

"Thank you, Kerry," Kerry said, not moving.

Matthew stared him down, but Kerry wasn't going to budge. He sighed. "*Thank you, Kerry.*"

Take care of them, Matthew. Did that include Kerry?

Kerry dropped his cigarette and ground it out under a heavy, black boot. He turned and led the way along the ridge of the canyon. The high banks consisted of an orange-brown sand. Clumps of struggling grass grew between the trunks of the thinner trees. Pockets of white and yellow flowers swept between the ferns. Tying his sweatshirt around his waist, Matthew ducked under a cloud of midges and pulled his collar up to protect his neck from the relentless sun. The sound of the rushing water rose up to meet them, tantalizing their parched throats. Matthew's throat felt like it was going to close in on itself. Maybe he should jump into the water and let the refreshing liquid rush over his head. Drink and drink and drink until he was full. Maybe he'd stay there for a while, just floating on the current. Maybe he'd even let the water fill his mouth, his nose…

He looked again over the edge. Matthew knew the boulders lining the river were giant-sized, but right now, they looked no bigger than the palm of his hand. He *could* jump. But that would be certain death.

Kerry hovered inside the tree line by the fallen trunk. It was a massive oak. The diameter at its base must have been three feet, narrowing to one on the other side, if Matthew judged the distance correctly. Oaks were sturdy. It looked as though it had fallen some time ago, dug into the ground, and could be quite stable.

But if it had been there for some time, it could be rotten, exposed to the elements, dead inside. One wrong foot would be disastrous.

"It looks okay," Tyler said. He'd stepped onto the base of the tree and volleyed his weight from one foot to the other, testing its durability. His blistered arm dangled uselessly by his side.

"We don't know what it's like on the other side," Matthew said.

"Don't be such a wuss." Kerry smirked. "Ye wanted a bridge, I gave ye a bridge."

"And how do you propose the children get across?"

"Not me problem."

"You keep wandering off, Kerry. Why don't you just stay away?"

"Call it a morbid curiosity. I'm interested to see what happens to ye all."

Matthew glared at him. If they fought again now, one of

them could easily go over the edge. And it could be Kerry. It would be so easy. But it might be him.

As if sensing his thoughts, Kerry backed away from the edge of the canyon.

"Ulrich says he'll go across first." Jasmine stood next to the fox with her hand wrapped around the two stick dolls.

"How do we get the kids across?" Matthew asked.

"I'll carry Nell," Joseph said. "It's fine. But I need help with Jasmine."

"I can do it," Jasmine said, stepping onto the trunk and raising one leg. She balanced for three seconds before she wobbled and fell to the ground. "I can do it."

"I know," Matthew said. He crouched to face her. "You know what. I haven't told anyone this, but I'm a bit afraid of heights. Think I could go with you? Think you could help me?"

Jasmine nodded, and grinned.

"Everyone else okay with this plan?" Matthew turned to survey the group.

"What about Luna?" Hope asked.

Jesus. He'd almost forgotten about Luna. How could he have forgotten about Luna? That's why they were here. But she wasn't talking. Barely moving. She was so quiet. It was easy to forget she was there, even with the block of color her bright red coat offered.

Matthew's eyes stung for a second time as he looked at his best friend. He had a memory of last year's dance. She'd worn a dress of dark-blue satin that complimented her midnight eyes. Her hair piled on top of her head. It was the first time he'd seen her in that way. She was beautiful. And she hadn't stopped talking while she got herself ready. Babbling with nerves. Matthew had loved just sitting on the edge of her bed and listening to her voice. She had a lovely voice. How could he have forgotten what it sounded like?

Could he trust Jasmine with someone else? Could he trust Luna with someone else? Matthew didn't want to let either of them go. He'd promised, no more death.

Take care of them, Matthew.

Piper came up and grabbed Luna's hand, her intention explicit. Although Piper didn't speak, she was physically strong and, out of all of them, the most at home with nature. Besides Ulrich.

Matthew and Jasmine stood by the stump of the oak. He cursed the water raging below. He couldn't even muster a drop of saliva.

Ulrich jumped lightly onto its trunk. He gave them one backward look and then picked his way carefully across. The black moss followed. Or had it already been there? It ran across the length of the tree and spread out on the other side. It was everywhere. Matthew turned in a slow circle. There wasn't a single angle where he couldn't see the black moss. He had a feeling it would continue to grow up the tree trunks, past the canopy, stretch straight up, into space, until it strangled the sun.

On the other side of the river, the fox yapped once then paced back and forth.

"It's okay," Jasmine said, tucking her hair behind her ears. It sprung back immediately. "Ulrich says it's okay."

"You can hear him from that far away?" Matthew murmured. The fox's gentle voice was never that clear to him.

Jasmine nodded and smiled at the fox.

"Can you just sit still?" Tyler called to Ulrich. "You're making me nervous."

"Thought you didn't get nervous?" Faith slapped her flip-flops together near Tyler's face. He jumped. Then scowled at her.

"Everyone gets nervous, Faith. It's what you do with it that counts."

"Quit whining about your arm then," Faith said, tucking her flip-flops into the waistband of her shorts.

"Nerves and pain are two entirely different things." Tyler glowered. "Now if you don't mind, I have a tree to cross. I'm not interested in petty arguments from a prima donna ballet dancer."

Faith scoffed, but didn't retort.

"Shame we don't have a ball," Hope said to Tyler as he mounted the trunk. "If we threw it, you'd run right across the tree after it, no problem."

"Thanks, kid." Tyler tousled her long hair.

On the other side, Ulrich sat on his haunches, then lowered himself to the ground and stuck his head on his forepaws, his eyes keen.

Tyler inched his way along, sideways, keeping his right foot going first. A football move in slow motion. He held his hands out and kept his eyes focused on his feet. Matthew held his breath.

"You can do it, Tyler!" Hope called out.

Tyler wobbled. Frowned. Re-gained his balance.

"*Shhh*." Matthew put a hand on her shoulder and gave it a gentle squeeze.

He followed Tyler's progress. But his attention was drawn to his injured arm. It was dark. Which wasn't surprising considering he'd been trapped in a fire. Had only just managed to escape. Second-degree burns ran the length of his right arm and most of his right cheek and jaw. He looked like he'd been transported to some b-rate horror flick where cannibals roasted humans on a spit. And all that dark, green mulch that Piper kept spreading all over it only deepened the effect. But there was a quality to the skin that concerned Matthew. A depthless inkiness that had him frowning and narrowing his eyes to get a better look.

Second-degree burns didn't char, but a blackness spread beyond the burn areas to the back of Tyler's neck. And on his face, it stretched down his chin and over his nose into the tip of his right nostril. Inside? It was like he'd pressed through a thicket of jungle vines and had forgotten to shake himself loose. But Matthew knew the blackness wasn't anything to do with the burns or the trek through the woods. It was the black moss. The infected stream. The black moss was growing on Tyler, spreading. Tyler was infected.

Tyler reached the other side of the trunk and jumped to the ground with a satisfied smile. He waved and beckoned them across.

Faith held Hope's hand as they approached the trunk.

"I can't do this," Hope said, her gaze glued to the raging river below.

"Yes, you can." Faith tugged her along.

Hope turned back to look at Matthew. "Matthew, please, I can't do this." Her breaths came in shallow gasps, a panic attack on its way.

Matthew approached the two girls, both not much younger than he and Luna. He put his hands on Hope's shoulders. "You can do this. It's a bridge. And a river. And once we get to the other side, we're one step closer to Grandmother's house."

"But I——"

"Hope?"

She looked at him.

"We don't have a choice," Matthew said.

Her lips puckered and she looked like she might cry, but she gave him a curt nod of acceptance.

"When we're both on the other side, I'll give you the biggest hug ever," Matthew said.

A ghost of a smile curled Hope's lips. "I'll hold you to that."

"I can balance on one toe for an hour," Faith said, stepping on to the trunk. "You're in good hands with me."

They mounted the enormous trunk. Faith positioned Hope in front of her and pushed her down on her hands and knees.

"Don't look down." Matthew helped Faith balance on the trunk.

She nodded. Then crawled after Hope.

"Not on your hands and knees!" Matthew called. "Straddle it to give you balance!"

But it was too late. Hope was already two feet past the line of the ridge. Any change in position now would be detrimental. Faith crawled after her, biting her lower lip in concentration. Her knees were already skinned and bleeding.

Matthew's heartrate kicked up a couple notches. Crossing on hands and knees was potentially the most precarious position to attempt this, with all those knotty lumps and uneven surfaces, protruding twigs and gnarled crevices. And the black moss. Was it slippery? Sticky?

Matthew's breath caught in his throat. He examined Hope's

knees. Already scratched to smithereens. But she seemed to be looking straight down. Matthew was about to call out. But he didn't want to startle her. Then he realized she wasn't looking past the trunk to the smashing river three hundred yards below, but at the trunk itself, and the progress of her hands. And the line of black moss that traversed the other side. She kept getting it on her palms and trying to wipe it off on her clothes.

"It's just tree moss," Matthew called softly.

"It's sticky!" Hope complained. Seeming to forget she was three hundred yards above ground, she continued to examine the tacky substance adhered to her palm.

"You can wash it off on the other side," Faith said. "Keep moving."

Matthew's chest tightened. He held onto the long branch he'd carried with him, the one he'd finally whittled into a spear with Kerry's knife. Piper carried the knife in her bag now and had been using it to slice off shoots of interesting plants to add to her herb collection. She'd wrapped each one carefully in a square of white cloth before placing them in individual baggies.

"Aww, naw." Kerry's eyes glittered like lumps of coal. "Would be a shame to lose one so young."

Watching the wobbling duo, Matthew squeezed the shaft of his spear until his knuckles ached.

All eyes watched Hope as she made slow progress, inch by agonizing inch. And that's why nobody noticed when Faith came to a complete standstill halfway along the trunk. It was only as Hope neared the end that Matthew's attention snapped to Faith.

She was still on her hands and knees, both of which spilled

thin rivulets of blood. Tears dripped out of her tightly closed eyes. Her entire body trembled.

"Hold on, Faith," he called, softly.

Jasmine's hand was still tucked in his. He'd have to leave her here. He didn't want to leave her here.

"You can do this!" he called.

"I can't! I'm going to fall!"

"Open your eyes! Your balance is better with your eyes open!"

"I don't want to see what's down there."

Her right knee slipped off the trunk and she screamed. Her eyes flew open and panic contorted her features. She slipped sideways, her arms going to the trunk, reaching around, hugging it to her chest. Now she was lying stomach-down on the large trunk, legs and arms wrapped around. But she wasn't directly on top. She was off to one side. She wouldn't be able to maintain that position long.

Matthew leaped onto the tree. "I'm coming!"

"Hurry!" she yelled.

He turned to Jasmine. "I have to go now. One of the others will take you across."

CHAPTER 12
MATTHEW

AGAINST HIS BETTER INSTINCTS, Matthew left Jasmine behind and positioned himself on the trunk. He straddled the enormous tree and placed his hands on the rough bark of the oak, pulling his butt along.

"Don't look down," he reminded himself.

One foot. Two feet. Three feet. He reached the sticky trail of black moss. It had widened, almost encapsulating the entire tree. Sticky and slick. It made it difficult to find a secure handhold. A line of red soldier ants marched beside him. One of them crawled onto his hand and stung his little finger. Right on his sore knuckle.

The water below deafened him. A vicious contest between foaming white water and protruding rocks. The river swirled and burbled, trying to loosen the rocks that held fast to its bed. Eventually it would. Eventually the river would win and pound those rocks into nothing more dangerous than grains of sand.

"Help me!" Faith yelled.

She was only a few feet away. But Matthew didn't dare

quicken his pace. He could hear her accelerated breathing and knew her heart would be pounding as fast as his.

"Hang on, Faith!"

Watching her struggle, he misplaced a hand and came face to face with the angry torrent of water. He still gripped the trunk with his other hand, and he managed to pull himself back up. But now he couldn't take his eyes from the water. It contained a deathly, mesmerizing power.

The cacophonous roar quieted, softening to a whisper. Whispers that were tempting, alluring, like a siren, and wanted Matthew to come closer. He was so thirsty. His throat was damaged from the fire. And his knuckles ached with the desire to be immersed in healing water.

Come closer.

It was a long drop. He might make it. All he had to do was release his hands. He could be on his own. Leave the others behind. Even Luna. He couldn't remember the last time he'd been alone. Solitude. Not something he'd thought much about. But right then, he craved it.

"Matthew!"

Faith's scream snapped his head up. She hung upside down from a thick branch, her head arched over the raging water, her eyes wide with the knowledge of imminent death.

"Shit!"

He shuffled faster.

One foot. Two feet. Almost there.

Matthew climbed over Faith's crossed ankles. With his left hand firmly wrapped into a gnarly hole, he leaned down to one side and offered her his right hand.

"I can't let go," Faith whispered.

"You can." Her ankles were crossed tight. Her flip-flops

gone. "You could hang on by just your legs. You're strong enough."

"Everything's shaking."

"Give me your hand," he said.

"Please, don't let me die."

"I won't."

Take care of them, Matthew.

She released her hand and shoved it toward him. The black moss surrounded them. Not just on the trunk itself, but coating the back of Faith's calves.

Her fingertips grazed his, but missed, and she fell, hanging upside down by her crossed legs.

"I don't want to die!"

"You have to swing up to me!" He lowered himself as far as he dared, so that when she rose her hand would meet his.

She swung herself up. After the first three practice attempts, she engaged her core and swung her torso toward Matthew. Her fingers grasped his, and then slipped again.

She hung down again, letting her arms dangle and released a desperate cry.

"You can do it, Faith! One more time! I'll get you this time. Try. Try again. *Please*."

She swung. He felt the tips of her fingers. He pulled, pulled her up, gripped her arm.

Ulrich yowled from the other side.

"Matthew!" Faith yelled. "Don't let go!"

The crashing of the water below disorientated him. The white foam swirled and frothed around jagged rocks, sweeping away everything in its path. If you weren't smashed by the rocks in the fall, you'd be drowned in seconds by the violence of the water. Water. It had seemed so harmless just yesterday;

used for bathing and washing. But during their time in the woods, the word had taken on new meaning; primarily their lack of it had turned it into the ultimate challenge for survival. A beast that needed to be conquered. Now the raging water was a different personification. And equally formidable.

Matthew held onto Faith's hand. He had a firm grip on her now. But her ankles began to slip. It wouldn't be long before her entire weight hung from his injured right hand. She was good at watching her weight. But she was a dancer. She had muscles. She was heavier than she looked.

"Matthew!" Jasmine screamed.

He sensed, rather than saw the movement. He let go of the gnarled crevice he was gripping onto with his left hand and squeezed the trunk between his thighs, ignoring the way the black moss crawled onto his jeans. He dangled over the side, struggling for breath and strength.

Take care of them, Matthew.

His raw knuckles burned with pain. Sweat dripped from his brow and ran down the crevice of his back. Soon his hands would turn slick. Very soon.

"Shit!" he muttered.

"I'm coming!" Tyler called from the bank, pumping his legs to action.

The trunk groaned.

"Stay there!" Matthew called. "The trunk's not strong enough!"

"Matthew!" Faith called.

A menacing growl rumbled from behind him, back where the others waited. Close by. But he didn't have time to think about the implications. He needed to save Faith.

"You have to crawl up my arm."

Her bottom lip quivered, but she climbed. She was a good climber, always climbing the large oak marking the border of their property. She pulled herself up his arm, then dug the heel of her foot between his shoulder blades, right on top of his ancient injury. It screamed at him with a memory of pain. Faith collapsed on top of the log, panting for breath, eyes squeezed closed, hands gripping the rough bark.

"Climb across. Now," he said.

She did as she was told. Tyler and Ulrich waited for her on the other side.

With their eyes locked on the far bank, they shuffled along the trunk. Matthew didn't stop until Tyler's hand was on his shoulder and solid ground cradled his butt. Faith collapsed on top of him.

He wrapped his arms around her. "I told you I wouldn't let you die."

She punched his shoulder. "You didn't have to make it so close." She hiccupped. Her eyes welled with new tears.

Five of them were safely across. That left nine more. Matthew would have to stand by the edge of the canyon and watch as the rest of them made the attempt. Nell. Joseph. Luna. Alessandra. Jasmine. Piper. Ariel. Beacon. Even Kerry, who was still standing there smoking with his foot propped on the trunk. All of them. He'd have to watch all of them gamble their way across. Luna. But especially Luna.

The black moss snaked out before him in all directions, as far as he could see, already claiming whatever path they might choose. Matthew grabbed leaves from nearby shrubs and wiped down his jeans and his hands. His knuckles worried him. Black specks dotted the wounds. Could be dried blood.

Could be something else. He poked at them with the stem of a leaf, but they began to bleed.

He glanced at Tyler. The thick tendril of black moss he thought he'd glimpsed snaking into his nostril had disappeared. Had he imagined it? Had Tyler cleaned himself up? The arm and cheek remained dark. Could just be the newly forming scabs from the burns. *Please just be the burns.*

Joseph, Nell, and Jasmine came across the makeshift bridge. It was an uneventful crossing with the baby tucked between Joseph's legs as they shuffled across. As they crawled off the trunk, another growl rumbled from the undergrowth on the other side. The ferns shifted. A cloud of insects hovered nearby.

"Quick!" Matthew called. Something was out there. Something was close. Something wanted them. "Hurry!"

Piper and Luna stepped onto the trunk. Piper tried to push Luna down to straddle the tree, but Luna stood rigid. Piper raised her panicked face toward Matthew. Another growl. The group on the other side edged closer to the trunk, all of them climbing onto it. The sunlit water continued to seethe beneath them.

"If she won't sit down, you're just going to have to walk," Matthew called.

Piper nodded. She hesitated for a moment, then nudged Luna. Luna picked her way along the trunk with little difficulty, never looking down, not at the surging river or where she placed her feet along the gnarled tree. Matthew's rushing blood boomed in his ears. When she finally placed a foot on solid ground, he resisted the urge to hug her and never let go. He smiled at Piper and offered her a high-five. She dipped her hand into her bag. With her fingers covered in something tacky and purple, she rubbed the new paste over the developing sunburn on his neck and cheeks.

A clump of dense ferns on the other side shifted. They parted in the middle, a heavy weight tunneling a path through them. Kerry was the closest and he looked over his shoulder. Yellow eyes appeared. There were no pupils, no irises, just yellow sockets filled with burning, yellow fire. Something from a horror movie. Matthew couldn't make out the rest of it, but he could sense its enormity and its murderous intentions. The eyes disappeared, as if their owner had shut its eyelids to prepare for an ambush.

Alessandra quickly removed one of her skirt layers and left it on the ground, keeping her gaze trained on the flattened ferns. She stepped onto the trunk, gathered the material of her remaining skirts between her legs and shuffled across. Beacon and Ariel followed her. The three of them looked like scuttling crabs. They split their attention between the trunk, the safety of where Matthew stood, and the bush where the yellow eyes had appeared.

"Come on, come on," Tyler muttered. He scratched at his ear, then rubbed his nose. His arm hung loosely, dark scabs forming around the white blisters.

Kerry stepped onto the trunk. A nonchalant smile shifted onto his lips. A cigarette danced between thumb and forefinger, and he held Matthew's spear. The yellow eyes appeared again. Several sets of the inhuman, yellow, flame-filled sockets. Emerging from the undergrowth. Followed by enormous bodies of black and brown fur. Needle-like teeth and scythe-like claws. Not dog, nor wolf, nor bull, nor any other animal. But a combination of all, or something entirely different. Their size was intimidating, their claws and teeth terrifying, but it was their eyes which stilled the blood in Matthew's veins. They transmitted one purpose, one desire; blood, death.

"Run, Kerry!" Matthew screamed.

The beasts leaped. High into the air, jaws open, claws slicing.

Kerry risked a backward glance. The cigarette fell from his fingers, bounced off the tree, and helicoptered to the river below. He swung the spear, almost losing his balance.

Faith screamed, her hands cupping her mouth.

"Alessandra, take the children and start running," Matthew instructed.

There was no time for shuffling and safety. Kerry ran. No longer looking backward, pumping his arms and legs, a wild look in his eye Matthew had never noticed when he'd seen him riding his motorcycle. The beasts snapped at his back, their jaws chomping, their claws tearing at the trunk, their yellow eyes fixed on Kerry. Matthew was sure Kerry could feel their breath on the back of his neck.

A dark shape blotted out the sun and the sound of powerful wings interrupted the roar of the beasts. Obsidian flew down from the sky, his beak open. As one of the beasts snapped at Kerry, Obsidian plucked the awful creature from the air and squeezed him between his beak. The beast wailed, spurting unnatural, yellow blood all over Kerry. The other beasts stopped, stared at Obsidian, and slowly backed away. Kerry ran, across the trunk, pumping his arms and legs like he'd challenged Matthew to a race.

Obsidian flew back to the sky, still swallowing the carcass of the great beast, as if he were part pelican. The other beasts retreated, returning to the undergrowth, growling complaints and portraying threats with their yellow eyes.

Kerry landed on their side in a heap, panting, holding the spear aloft. He rolled over and looked back the way he'd come. "What the fuck was that?"

"I have no freaking idea!" Tyler replied.

"We can't let them follow us, whatever they are," Matthew said. He squinted at the shadows on the other side. The small of his back was damp. A combination of sun and fear. "We need to get rid of the trunk."

Before anyone could speak, the black moss on the trunk shifted and magnified, glistening under the strong sun. Large movements. Not the subtle shifting Matthew had spied during their trek. Much, much bigger. Jagged. Abrupt. The moss grew upwards from the middle of the trunk, gathering itself into a column, accumulating mass. Within seconds it became the height of a human male. And then it took on its shape, the blackness undulating as if constructed of skittering insects. A humanoid figure. Standing. Gathering itself. Becoming. Becoming what?

"Holy…" someone muttered.

"What is that?" Tyler whispered.

No one moved. Or spoke. They were transfixed. Until the black shape shifted. Placed one leg in front of the other. Slowly at first. Then advanced along the trunk. It mimicked Kerry, pumping its arms and legs, and ran across the trunk. As it ran, it gathered more of the black moss, until it became bigger than any human.

They all shuffled backward. Matthew grabbed Luna. How far would it run? What would it do when it reached them?

"Run!" Kerry screamed, getting back to his feet.

But as they turned to flee, the black shape dissolved. It fell back onto the ground and spread out under their feet. Stretching, spreading, searching for their footsteps.

"I don't know what that is, but it's not good," Tyler said, trying to find a patch of ground devoid of black moss.

"Quick. Help me with the tree," Matthew said, as the blackness that constituted the humanoid shape leached into the ground and disappeared. But there was more black moss. Growing. Everywhere.

"If we move the tree, how are we going to get back?" Tyler asked, circling back.

"We don't need to go back," Kerry said. "Ever. Didn't ye see what just happened?"

"But our home…" Tyler trailed off as he followed Matthew to the trunk.

"Is destroyed," Matthew said.

The three of them found handholds on the moss-encrusted trunk and lifted. It took a few attempts, but finally they rolled it along the ridge until it fell into the river. A thunderous crash echoed up the ravine as the trunk disintegrated into splinters and slivers of wood. The bulk of it floated downstream and snagged itself on an outcrop of rocks.

"At least those animals won't be able to follow us," Tyler said.

"As long as they're not also made o' that dodgy black stuff," Kerry said, lighting another cigarette. "Because that followed us across. And it's everywhere. Smells bad enough to gag a maggot."

Matthew followed his gaze. Some of the others stood in a clump a few hundred yards away. But a snaking black trail led directly to them. The black moss grew up tree trunks, over rocks and boulders, it slithered through patches of grass, and dripped from the leaves of shrubs. It was everywhere.

CHAPTER 13
MATTHEW

HOLDING HIS SPEAR, Matthew stared at the raging river.

"Reckon we should just burn the whole thing." Kerry flicked his silver lighter and swept it around in a circle, indicating the puddles of black moss that seemed to pulsate with life.

"Do you have some kind of death wish?" Tyler said, veering away from the small flame.

"Jesus, Mary and wee Alex Driver, I just ran for me life. 'Course I don't have a death wish," Kerry replied. "But this black stuff. It's totally Tara. It needs to burn."

Matthew shook his head. "The forest is dry. It will go up instantly. And we'll be stuck in the middle of it."

"I'm not going to fight another fire," Tyler said. "Have you not seen my arm?"

"Might be better than the alternatives," Kerry muttered.

"Kerry, you're not helping anyone," Matthew said. "You're scaring the kids. Our only alternative is to get to Grandmother's house. No one asked you to come. You can just go your own way."

139

"That trunk is tatters. Think I'll be sticking around," Kerry said.

Great.

"Let's go," Matthew said. He passed a hand by the back of his neck, massaging tense muscles. He could still feel the weight of Faith. His arms felt six inches longer and his shoulder sockets stretched as though he'd been tied to a rack.

The group began walking. Away from the ridge and the fallen tree. Away from the yellow eyes and terrifying beasts. How many were there? In all the confusion, it had been hard to tell. But they operated like a pack. Those flickering eyes everywhere. Eyes of actual fire. Had they started the fire at the house? No. Impossible. Ridiculous.

Matthew prayed the beasts wouldn't find another way across. There were other bridges. Miles away. If the beasts were determined, they could find them again.

"Glad to see you're back with us," Matthew said, as he passed a hand over the fox's head. He leaned down and whispered in his ear. "It wasn't your fault." Ulrich sniffed and turned his snout away.

Jasmine called out. "Matthew? What were those things?" She walked next to Ulrich. Her hands gripped the fur at his neck, and she carried the stick dolls tucked under an arm, its yellow petals beginning to wilt.

To lie, or not to lie. But he couldn't hold the truth from the others forever. "I don't know."

Jasmine nodded, a short little nod that told him she was trying to be brave. "I didn't know anything like that existed."

"Me, neither." He kept pace with Jasmine and held a branch out of her way as she ducked underneath.

Faith veered close. Now that she'd lost her flip-flops, she

picked her way carefully over the forest floor. Dirt clung to the underside of her feet. Or was it the black moss? A hint of it still clung to her bare calves. "It reminds me of that drawing of Hope's from last summer."

"What drawing?" Matthew asked.

"It's in her notebook," Jasmine said. "She showed it to me once, because we both like to draw. But I didn't get through more than a few pages. They were filled with monsters."

He afforded Hope a sidelong glance, remembering the brief glimpse he had of her sketchpad. The things in there were so terrifying he'd never been tempted to look again. Hope walked a little distance away with Alessandra and Piper, talking to them both.

"Yeah," Faith said. "She's always reading those hefty fantasy books. She draws the monsters in her mind. Among other things. But she's really private about it. I snuck a look one day…"

"Faith…" But he couldn't reprimand her, he'd done the same thing.

"What?" She spread her hands. "She hasn't been around that long. She's quiet. And so pale it's like she's never seen the sun. Or heard of self-tanning lotion. I just didn't get what Luna saw in her. I was curious."

"Me too," Matthew said.

Faith smiled. "The great Matthew has committed sin, ladies and gentlemen."

Matthew nudged her. "*Shhh.*"

Truth was, they *didn't* know Hope that well. But still, she was no Kerry. Luna had brought her home one day, and no one knew where she'd come from. They'd bonded over their disdain for quadratic equations. But it was more than that. How could Luna ever turn down a girl named 'Hope?'

Faith lowered her voice and checked over her shoulder. "Her drawing was just like those beasts. A massive dog-bull-wolf-weird thing."

"So articulate." Matthew grinned. She threw him a gentle punch.

"Anyway, it was the eyes that got to me the most. Just yellow. With striations of orange. Like fire. It freaked me out. Slept in the nursery that night," she said sheepishly. "Thought I might have to spend more than one night there."

"How could Hope know about a beast we were going to meet a year later?"

Faith shrugged. "Thought you were the figure-outer."

"Sometimes I think my head's going to explode with all the figuring out required in this family."

"It's going to be dark soon." Alessandra strolled toward them. "Piper has found a stream. I think we should make camp for the night."

Matthew followed her to a small clearing. A stream trickled by the edge of a grassy bank. He leaned down to inspect it. It was beautifully clear. He risked entering a finger-tip, and then couldn't stop himself. He immersed his whole head and drank. After he was sated and the urge to throw up threatened his esophagus, he submerged his hands and rubbed at the blackness on his knuckles. He scrubbed with leaves and stones. The wounds opened again, but he didn't care, the black dots were gone. Tyler sat next to him. Matthew tried to inspect his burns without appearing too conspicuous. Scabs or black moss? Hard to tell.

Piper approached and spread something soothing over his knuckles. Then she bathed Tyler's arm and did the same.

Matthew walked back to the group. Joseph slept, his mouth open, crumpled against a tree, mercifully clear of the black moss. Jasmine and Nell followed the example, draped over him like ornaments on a Christmas tree.

Alessandra brought Luna to him. He helped her to the ground, and she curled up into his side. With her eyes closed, he could almost imagine she was normal again. Not that she'd ever been normal, in the truest sense of the word, but who was? It was almost cool to be different these days. As long as you didn't flaunt it.

Matthew put an arm around Luna's shoulders and watched patchwork shapes reflected by the moon as it rose into the sky. It would be cold soon. Another hour and their breath would start pluming and Matthew would wrestle with the regret he felt in giving his jacket to Hope. The chirp of courting crickets drifted around their small area, reminding him of lazy summer nights sitting on the double swing. All that seemed like a lifetime ago.

Beacon took position in the middle, her gentle glow melting into them, easing preoccupied and harried minds and draining the tension out of fatigued muscles. Tyler sat opposite Matthew. Kerry stood off to the side, the ubiquitous cigarette dangling from his lips, reading the back of his matchbox by the light of the moon.

"I was havin' a thought," Kerry said.

"Uh-oh, that'll be dangerous," Tyler replied.

Kerry lifted the corner of his lips into an ugly sneer. "Shut yer bucket hole."

"Don't get your knickers in a twist!" Tyler held up his good hand in a mock apology.

Kerry gave him one long glare. "Anyway, it's like a fairy-tale, so it is."

"What is?" Faith asked, rubbing her bare feet with quick strokes. Beacon's light warmed and strengthened as it seeped over her feet.

"This Luna situation," he replied.

"How so?" Matthew asked, his eyelids drooping, half wanting to be asleep before it got too cold.

"She's in some kind o' freaked-out, zombie state. Like Sleeping Beauty or Snow White – and yes, I know about Disney stories. I had a ma. So, maybe she just needs to be awakened with a kiss."

"It's true love's kiss, you idiot." Tyler threw a pebble at Kerry, which he easily dodged.

A blush warmed Matthew's cheeks, and he hoped, in the muted darkness, none of the others noticed. He felt eyes on him. Alessandra stared at him, her eyebrows twitching. His scalp prickled as she continued to stare.

"It might be worth a shot," Alessandra said.

"I asked her to the formal at the end of the year, she shot me down, remember?" Tyler said, his lips puckering.

A strained silence fell over the group. Kerry sniffed. Alessandra shifted her skirts. Faith picked at the dirt on her toes. Tyler played with a few twigs lying at his feet, building them into a haphazard tower as if they were pick-up-sticks.

"Ah, bless ye, Tyler," Kerry said. "Looks like you came up in the lagoon in a bubble."

"What?" Tyler shifted his gaze between Kerry and Alessandra. "What does that mean?"

"Can't see what's right in front o' you," Kerry replied.

"What are you talking about?" Tyler pushed himself to his feet, kicking the little pile of twigs.

"You're not Luna's true love," Kerry said.

"I'm pretty sure I just said I knew that." Tyler picked up a large stick and smacked it against the ground.

"That doesn't mean she don't have one," Kerry said.

Tyler stuttered and looked at Luna. The weight of Matthew's arm around her shoulder intensified, until it was the only part of his body he could feel. Tyler's mouth fell open.

Kerry smirked. "Is that a beamer you're wearing now, Matthew?"

"You?" Tyler stepped forward, waving the stick.

Matthew removed his arm. Shook his head. "No. Not me. Luna doesn't feel that way about me."

"But how do *you* feel about *her*?" Tyler demanded.

"Easy, boys," Alessandra said.

"Not now, Alessandra." Tyler turned back to Matthew and used his stick to emphasize each word. "Matthew? Do you have anything to say?"

"I care about Luna, we all do. You know that," Matthew said, getting to his feet. He resisted the urge to pick up a stick too. He glanced at Luna, alone in the crevice of a tree, her dark hair touched by the moonlight, her wide, expressive eyes, unblinking. Love clenched his heart.

"That's not what I'm asking, and you know it!" Tyler jabbed the stick again.

"Here it comes," Kerry said, beating a rhythm with his fingers. "We're having a craic now."

"I... I..." Words failed Matthew.

"You *like* her." Tyler marched over, so close Matthew

smelled the smoke and sweat on his clothes. And the faintest whiff of his aftershave. Something heavy and musky. "You *like* her. Even when you knew *I* liked her."

"I didn't do anything." Matthew raised his hands like he was already condemned.

"But you wanted to."

Matthew nodded. His fingertips tingled. "Maybe." His ears burned beneath everyone's stares.

Faith giggled. "Well, I'll be…"

"How long?" Tyler asked.

"Nothing's been going on," Matthew said. "Luna's never given me any suggestion that she feels the same." He shoved his hands in his front pockets.

"All those late nights sitting on the roof," Kerry said. "And don't think I didn't notice the nights when she slipped into your bed."

Tyler's eyes looked ready to pop out of his head.

"Nothing happened!" Matthew said. "It was the nightmares. She only comes to me because I've been with her since the beginning. Almost."

"You love her," Tyler said. It wasn't an accusation. More a dawning realization.

Matthew looked at Luna again. She hadn't moved. Hadn't flinched. He wondered if she even needed to breathe anymore. She was so incredibly beautiful. He'd give anything for another night on the roof with her, talking about life, about the world, about themselves. He did love her. Very, very much.

"I love her," he told the group. "I do." It was out there now. They could do what they wanted with it.

"And she might love you," Alessandra said.

Matthew shrugged, but his heart beat painfully against his ribs.

"I can't believe I'm saying this," Hope said. "But maybe Kerry is right."

Tyler blanched. "What do you mean?"

"Maybe Matthew should kiss her. Maybe she'll wake up," Hope replied.

Matthew snorted a laugh, but the others didn't join him.

"Oh, come on!" Faith flicked her wrist dismissively.

Hope burned in his chest. He turned to Luna and stared upon the face he'd loved for more than a thousand moons. The pale lips he could never stop watching when she spoke, wondering what it would be like to kiss them. Would she taste of her coconut lip balm, or would he get a sense of her true essence? The dark hair she sometimes let him stroke and was the softest thing he'd ever touched. And those midnight eyes that always stared directly into his soul and understood what he was thinking, feeling, without him having to speak.

"Matthew," Alessandra said. "It might be worth a try."

"This is ridiculous!" Faith laughed.

Matthew's heart beat a staccato rhythm. He looked from Kerry's indifferent pose to his curious eyes, to Tyler's fuming stance, to Alessandra's hopeful face. Faith and Hope watched, interests piqued. Ariel and Beacon. Silent Piper nodded at him encouragingly. She kissed the silver cross that dangled at her neck and made its sign over her chest.

To kiss Luna. How he'd longed to. But now? In front of everyone?

Hope stood and gingerly picked her way over. She touched his elbow. "You're not the only one who loves her, Matthew. Please try. For all of us. None of us like seeing her this way."

Matthew swallowed and made his way to Luna. Kerry offered him a slow clap, which he tried to ignore, but made his heart beat faster. On trembling legs, he kneeled. Her eyes were open. Where was she looking? What was she thinking? He wasn't sure if she was looking at him, or beyond him, or seeing something not there at all.

"Luna?" No reaction. "Luna? I do love you." He leaned forward and pressed his lips against hers. He forgot about everyone else. He heard her heart beating, solid and steady. And he could feel her soft lips under his. How he'd always imagined it. Better. No trace of coconut. He kissed her, wondering how deep to take it. But her lips never parted, never responded, and he pulled away. His heart rattled an unnatural rhythm. His ears flamed. His chest ached.

"Not her true love then, eh?" Kerry said as Matthew leaned back on his heels. "So it is."

"See," Faith said. "It was a stupid idea."

The pain was brutal. A physical blow to his chest. Drawing breath became almost impossible. Grabbing his spear, he launched himself to his feet and stomped into the woods. Tyler's mocking laugh trailed after him. Fumbling through ferns and tripping over roots, he pushed forward, off balance. He had to get away from them. From her. From everything.

"Don't go!" Hope called.

"Matthew!" Alessandra called too.

"Matthew!" This was Faith. "We need you!"

They didn't need him. He couldn't even awaken Luna. He'd known her the longest. They looked to him to know what to do. But he had no idea. He stormed through the forest, letting branches flick back into place behind him, kicking at exposed roots on the ground, feeling the shame burn his ears and set his heart on fire. He loved Luna. But she didn't love him. Not like that.

Take care of them, Matthew. They could take care of themselves.

"Matthew!" The others continued to call. But he wasn't going back. Not now. Maybe not ever.

He ran, aimlessly, not caring what else was in the forest, just needing to get away. Beacon followed, lighting his path until he told her to disappear. And not very politely.

He ran. Like at a track meet. But this time there was no starting gun or finish line. He ran to feel the blood pump through his veins, to feel his breath rush into his lungs, to feel the shame wash out of his heart. He ran. And ran. And he never looked back.

He fell. Landed face first in a shallow puddle. He didn't move. Exhaustion chained him to the ground. He was so tired. Tired from the fire. Tired of running. Tired of worrying about everyone else. Beacon's glow eased his mind, but he still didn't want to move. He didn't tell her to go away this time, but allowed her glowing touch to stroke the back of his head. And he slept.

CHAPTER 14
PIPER

PIPER SCANNED THE GROUP, wondering if she had enough herbs, the powerful ones to stem the building anxiety. If only she'd held onto her grandfather's pipe. Hope always appeared more fragile, but she knew it was Faith who worried more. And Kerry. If anything ever happened to Luna, Kerry would throw himself under the wheels of his own motorbike.

"What if he doesn't come back?" Hope asked.

"He'll come back," Alessandra replied. She removed her headscarf, spat on it, and wiped at the dirt streaked across Hope's pale cheeks.

"But what if he doesn't?" Faith chucked a stone at a tree. It rebounded with a *plonk*.

Sometimes their bickering gave Piper a headache. Then she would mix some white willow bark and orange blossom into a paste and rub it on her temples.

"He will," Alessandra said.

"Who cares if he comes back?" Tyler said. Faith threw a pinecone at him. "Seriously. He's always telling us what to do. How to be. What's best for Luna. I'm sick of it."

"Would you rather have the job?" Alessandra asked him. "Matthew never asked for this. But he's known her the longest. He met her right after it happened…"

"But what is '*it*'?" Tyler snapped. "We all know Luna's mother died. But none of us know how. Luna won't speak of it. Matthew won't tell us. Don't we have a right to know?"

"Maybe ye should all just mind yer own beeswax," Kerry said.

Faith glared at him. "No one asked you."

Alessandra sighed. Maybe she would need the most herbs. Sitting next to Luna, Piper rummaged through the multiple bundles of cloth, mixing a recipe in her mind, carefully unfolding the parcels. She'd already tried so many things on Luna. But she remained unresponsive. Even her most sacred ground cedar hadn't worked. Piper wasn't even sure if Luna could hear them. And if she couldn't, and remained looking this close to a deathly image, the Raven Mocker might come. Again.

Piper shuddered and crossed herself four times. Once for each direction. Four was a sacred number. If she abided by traditions, she might avoid a meeting with a Raven Mocker. She'd only heard stories, but she'd seen terrifying pictures. Thankfully she'd never seen one in real life. But with Caleb and Kalisa dead, she knew one of the killer witches might be around. She'd heard that raven caw just before Kalisa died, and then again after Caleb's death. One of the signs. But it wasn't enough of a warning. Raven Mockers were invisible forces that ate people's hearts as they died. How could any of them go up against something like that?

Alessandra beckoned them all close. Piper leaned into the group. She knew of Luna's trauma. She knew all of it. And she wished she hadn't. She hadn't spoken ever since. She would never tell anyone else. You can't undo knowledge like that. Did Tyler know what he was asking? She tried to warn him. She laid her hand on his good arm and shook her head at him. But he just frowned and shrugged her off.

Piper blew her fringe out of her eyes and retied her plaits. Maybe they should know. No more secrets. But what would happen?

Alessandra spoke softly, her eyes darting between Luna and the others. "It's a horrific story."

"How did she die?" Faith asked.

"She was murdered. Violently. In front of Luna," Alessandra replied. "That's all I know. Neither Luna nor Matthew will speak of it. It's almost as if he was there. He seems just as traumatized. So, you need to give him a break."

Tyler snorted. Kerry blew a smoke ring. Alessandra raised a disproving eyebrow at them. Piper massaged her temples.

"Poor Luna," Hope said.

"I can't even begin to imagine what that felt like," Alessandra said. "What she must have seen."

"So, what do we do now?" Faith asked.

"It's the middle of the night," Alessandra replied, tucking loose strands of hair into her headscarf. "Get some sleep. Mathew will be back in the morning."

WHEN HE WOKE, Beacon was no longer there. Or perhaps the daylight hours made her impossible to see. It didn't matter. He was essentially alone. Alone. He couldn't remember the last time he'd been alone. They all lived in the house together.

There was always someone around to annoy him. Apart from Luna. She could never annoy him. He remembered the kiss and the embarrassment flowed over him once again. No. He wasn't going back. Not to be mocked and humiliated by Tyler and Kerry. Alessandra would give him her kind, understanding eyes. And Luna would do absolutely nothing. He couldn't face all that. No. He was done with them.

Take care of them, Matthew.

His memories cycled through his mind. Of everything he was leaving behind. He remembered the time when the apples had dropped early. He and Luna had gathered them before the birds and deer arrived, piling them into a worn-out wicker basket. They'd spent the afternoon in the kitchen, just the two of them. Flour coated the counter and their noses and made white trails on the tiled floor. Luna had rolled out the pie crust. Matthew made the lattice markings and stabbed it with a fork to let it breathe. They'd sliced the apples, piled them in and slid the overflowing dish inside the oven. That night, they'd eaten apple pie for dinner. Just apple pie. Nothing else.

Take care of them, Matthew.

No, thank you. He couldn't take care of them anymore. Maybe he never could. Why had she ever trusted him?

CHAPTER 15

LUNA

MY MEMORIES CYCLED FASTER and faster. Or maybe they weren't memories. Maybe they were thoughts. Or images. Or dreams. Or wishes. Or a combination.

Animals and lights and angels. Ballet shoes and fantasy books and running. Riding fast and hard with the wind in my hair. A unicorn tattoo. A painting. A sketch. A stick doll. Blood. So much blood. And a knife. Where did it all come from? Was it real?

It had to be real. I could barely remember anything else. The blood dominated my thoughts. And the heat. A fire. Crackling and spitting and turning everything I loved to ash. Who started the fire?

Matthew saved them all. Just like I asked.

Take care of them, Matthew.

But it was getting hard for him. Had I asked too much of him? Was it even fair?

The memories pressed against my skull. Knocking. Insistent. But there were too many of them. My mind couldn't contain them all. I must relieve the pressure. Somehow. I could do this. If I tried. If I tried hard enough, I could relieve the pain. On my own. Maybe I didn't need Matthew. Maybe I could do it on my own.

Could I take care of myself? I had to try.

CHAPTER 16
PIPER

PIPER COULDN'T SLEEP. How could she when Matthew was away and Luna was in the state she was in?

"We have no food." Mascara smudged the skin under Faith's eyes, barely covering the deep purple bruises of exhaustion.

"We're going to starve to death." Hope clutched her stomach. Blackness encircled her eyes too.

Piper watched through her long fringe. Leaning back against a tree, her eyelids drooped, and the noonday sun made her burst out in sweat patches. Her stomach growled. She hugged her canvas pack protectively.

Nell was crying. Not just crying, screaming with all her little might. She wouldn't be mollified with a finger in her mouth, or the juice of a blackberry. Jasmine had found a ton of them earlier, but it wasn't enough to sate twelve or more hungry bellies.

"Where did Matthew go?" Faith asked.

"Do we care?" Tyler retorted. "We don't need Matthew."

Alessandra crushed berries in her palm and dripped them

into Nell's searching mouth. Joseph held her head steady. She gulped the mush greedily.

"We do. You know that," Joseph said. "Luna trusts him."

"I'm not sure Luna trusts anyone right now." Hope curled into a ball and closed her eyes.

Luna slept. Well, at least her eyes were closed. Her head rested on Matthew's burnt jacket which Hope had balled into a pillow for her. Piper searched through her bag for anything she could substitute for food. They could eat the herbs, but they didn't taste great and they wouldn't fill their bellies for long. With Luna so affected, unable to heal them, they could get into serious trouble if one of them became injured or sick. They needed the medicinal herbs for their true purpose.

The whole time they'd been walking, Piper had searched for edible mushrooms and fungus. She'd almost suggested scraping off tree bark, but every time she got close to a trunk, whether an oak or a silver birch or the more prevalent pine, she noted the presence of the black moss. It quivered slightly. As if alive. Well, all plants were alive, but she detected something beyond a mere plant brain. She'd poked it and black spores released into the air. Definitely not good for eating. Definitely. Even if they boiled it. But that would involve water, which they didn't have, and a pot, which they also didn't possess.

"What are we supposed to do?" Faith asked. "Matthew's gone. Luna is…well doing whatever it is she's doing. Caleb's dead. Kalisa's dead. What the hell are we supposed to do?" She paced in circles in front of the group, stepped on something and cried out.

Hope frowned. "You could start off by being a little less blunt."

"We go to Grandmother's house," Alessandra said, helping

Faith to sit down. She plucked a splinter out of the meat of Faith's heel.

Piper straightened her back and shook her head vigorously, so they could all see. They couldn't leave without Matthew. They couldn't go anywhere without Matthew. Didn't they know that? He was the glue.

"I can't walk to Grandmother's house, I have no shoes!" Faith examined her feet, picking away clinging dirt and muck. "And how am I supposed to get back to the dance studio if my feet are ruined!"

"Don't you get it?" Tyler said. He kept his bad arm close to his body, cradling it. "We're not going back."

"Of course we're going back," Jasmine said. "We have school next week."

A strained silence turned the air viscous enough to cut with a knife. No number of herbs could dissolve that tension. Piper watched. None of them looked to her; she couldn't speak. They often overlooked her. But she knew stuff. For instance, they had to wait for Matthew.

"Jasmine," Joseph said gently. "Our house burned down. We have nowhere to go back to."

Piper's chest ached. It was the only home she'd ever known. The only one she cared to remember. No one had said the words aloud until now. Now they were out there, claimed by the air and the forest and the moss.

Hope uncurled and sat cross-legged on the ground. "The important thing is we're all together."

"I do love these touching, Hallmark moments. Gives me all the feels," Kerry said.

"Shut up, Kerry." Tyler jutted his chin at him.

Piper lifted her necklace to her lips and kissed it for the

thousandth time since they'd been trekking through the woods. She glanced at Ariel. The angel sat on a stump with her long arms crossed over her knees, watching, her face impassive. How did she feel when they fought? Piper, for one, hated it. They were supposed to be friends. A family. They were supposed to love each other, warts and all.

"Matthew had a plan. To go to Grandmother's house. It was a good plan. We should stick to it," Alessandra said.

Not long ago the crow's feet around Alessandra's eyes appeared as delicate as a Spanish fan, but in the last couple of days the lines had become more like plowed furrows. But it didn't alter her natural beauty, and in fact, actually added to it. Piper stood and approached the older woman. She shook her head again and signed her message. They couldn't go without Matthew. They had to wait. Everything would fall apart if they went without Matthew.

"I know you're worried about Luna. And Matthew," Alessandra said. "But we can't just sit around and wait to see if he comes back. What if he doesn't come back?"

Piper shook her head, her bottom lip trembled. The thought never occurred to her. Of course Matthew would come back. He just needed a moment. How could they all doubt him? The salt from her developing tears stung her eyes. Even though the fire had been awful, and Tyler's burns, and Caleb's bloody death, and Kalisa...even though they'd gone through all of that, she hadn't yet cried. Not properly. There had been too much to do. Too much at stake to let grief overwhelm her. But without Matthew, it would all fall apart. More of them would be in danger. That certainty swam in her guts.

She turned her back on the group, kissed the cross at her neck that Luna had given her for her last birthday, and whispered a silent prayer to God. Was He watching? Did He know all they had been through? All they were yet to face? Was He going to help? In her bag, she fingered Kalisa's medallion. She didn't remember putting it in there. But it brought her comfort.

She wished she had her rosary. Then she would sit on her knees and whisper all her prayers, like every night before she went to sleep. Seven times. Seven was another sacred number. Even though she couldn't speak, Luna had liked to watch her lips move.

Luna. *Please wake up, Luna.* Her heart clenched as Piper remembered the devastating truth that had tumbled from Luna's lips. Luna had spoken of blood. Great rivers of blood. Like a vampiric Charlie's chocolate factory where the chocolate river was replaced with blood and the gobstoppers were human teeth and the jelly was brains. Everywhere. Piper had pictured the worst kind of grisly death. And it had been grisly, the murder of Luna's mother. For weeks she only saw the color red. But the worst part, the one thing that had choked the words on her lips, was the fact that a seven-year-old Luna had witnessed it all. And seven was supposed to be a sacred number.

And now the group were thinking of leaving without Matthew. The one other person Luna had trusted with her terrible truth. Piper could help with her herbs. She could offer a hug. And prayers. She was useful. But they *needed* Matthew. They couldn't go on without Matthew. Didn't they know he was everything? The pin that held them together? Perhaps more so than Luna. Maybe even more important.

As the group prepared to leave and walk on for the day, Piper slipped away. No one ever noticed her anyway. She went to find Matthew.

She walked through the woods, the chatter of the group fading to the background, until they could no longer be heard. Beacon followed her. She saw her light in the darker shadows, always just ahead, leading the way. Beacon never spoke either. Maybe she couldn't. She wasn't exactly human. A light in a vaguely humanoid shape. A light that could ebb and flow and change intensity of brightness and color. Her limbs were undefined and often blurred, but Piper always noticed the full lips, and the wide, round eyes. Colorless of course. Or the color of light. And hair, she had hair that cascaded past her hips and trailed to the back of her knees. But mostly, she wore it piled on the top of her head. So, a light, in a humanoid shape. Beautiful. Serene. She brought a sense of order and calm whenever her light ebbed close.

Now, Piper sensed something in the quality of her light. Perhaps she agreed with Piper and was willing to help find Matthew.

After an hour, Piper grew weary. The breezeless forest offered a haven to insects and humidity. She lifted her fringe off her forehead and wiped at the sweat there. A small, winding stream offered refreshment and Piper dabbed water on the back of her neck. Her stomach heaved. So hungry. She caught sight of her reflection in the water. Something was wrong with her face. Smudges of black on her cheeks distorted her features. It was hard to tell in the rippling surface, but it was most likely just dirt from the trek through the woods. She scooped the water between cupped hands and splashed it over her face. A hard ridge running from her ear, across her cheek and into her left nostril offended her fingertips. She prodded it. It was hard, yet malleable, clinging to her cheek tighter than the vines of a climbing ivy. She picked at it with her finger-nails. A raven cawed.

The Raven Mocker.

Finally, it began to loosen. Small fragments fell from her cheek into her palm. It looked like black moss. No one had mentioned the black moss, or the beasts, or the strange humanoid shape that had materialized on the trunk, since Matthew had left. No one. It was easy to pretend everything was okay when it wasn't right in front of you. Explain it away with crazy imaginations, lack of sleep, food and water, fire damage. Any number of things could cause mass hallucina-tions. Even herbs.

Being alone forced her to be truthful with herself. Piper could no longer blame this creepy black substance on a mass hallucination. Besides, she'd seen the look on Matthew's face when he thought she wasn't looking, when he was inspecting Tyler's arm, or his raw knuckles, or the dead beast in the stream. She'd seen the infected beast. Everyone had. But no one had named it. They lived with Obsidian after all. But there was something about these particular creatures with yellow eyes. And the shadow man that had appeared and dissolved. At the time, she'd thought that's all he was, made of shadows. Like the mischievous Little People who helped lost kids. Why weren't they helping them? Maybe she'd angered them. Maybe she'd stared at one without realizing. They were prone to muddling minds if you gave them too much attention.

But these were nothing like the Little People. These shadows were made of nightmares and worst dreams. Now, she knew better. Now, with Matthew's absence and the black frag-ments in her palm, she knew it was something insidious.

As Piper surveyed the woods, Beacon's weak light showed

the black moss growing on every surface. Up the tree trunks to higher branches, creating dripping vines back down to the ground as if they were in a jungle, not a temperate zone. The veined leaves looked to be full of bursting, black blood. Sneaking trails and puddles of blackness covered the ground. Unaware she'd been kneeling in a patch, she jumped to her feet. Her stomach rolled again. She inspected her face once more. A hot flush covered her skin. Her knees buckled and she fell into the puddle of black moss. She tried to get to her feet, tried to push herself up to hands and knees, at least. But she was so tired. And not hungry anymore. Her limbs quivered. She no longer possessed the will to move.

She could rest for a moment. And then find Matthew. Just for a moment. As her eyelids closed, Beacon's presence hovered nearby, but it failed to soothe her. Piper liked to think of Beacon as being like a lighthouse, representing that glimmer of hope to lost ships on tumultuous seas. Beacon was the same for them. She often sat with the children when they were ill, and they recovered much quicker. Piper was always drawn to her during the day. Even when she couldn't really see her, she would instinctively be pulled toward Beacon, her glow like a magnet for those needing reassurance.

Now, her golden glow flickered around Piper, pulling at her heels, intensifying in her eyes. An insistent fly of discordant light. But Piper was so tired. She couldn't even shoo her away. She would rest. Find Matthew. Reunite him with the others. Then everything would be okay.

As her head hit the forest floor, Piper's vision filled with beasts with yellow eyes and screaming children. The raven cawed again.

CHAPTER 17
MATTHEW

MATTHEW WOKE to the gentle light of a caressing moon on his face. He thought he was back at the house, in his bed, still ignorant of the fire and pivotal decisions. The weight of a presence lingered nearby and he wondered if Luna had crawled into his bed again. With the thought of her, everything came rushing back. The kiss. Humiliation burned his cheeks all over again.

That was why he was out here in the middle of the night on his own. He'd left the others behind. He'd left Luna. Actually left her. Something painful twanged in his chest.

Rolling over, he found a wet patch on his shirt. Scanning the area, he spotted the puddle he'd fallen in. He vaguely remembered crawling to a shady crevice when the sun came out. How many nights had he been gone? Guilt and thirst clamped his throat tight. He crawled to the puddle and drank, not bothering to scoop the water with a hand, just immersing his face and sucking with his lips.

Beacon shimmered out from behind a tree and kneeled next

to him. Her golden hair cascaded to the ground, surrounding her like a cloak. A comforting hand caressed the back of his neck, his head, his shoulders. But he didn't want comfort right now. He wanted to be alone.

Take care of them, Matthew.

The lie he told himself rang hollow in his stomach and made his glands swell. The thought of never seeing Luna again. He could barely swallow. He missed her. Already. Maybe even some of the others.

Matthew looked at Beacon and took in all her radiant serenity, the assurance she offered. "I love her." Inside, his heart died a little.

Beacon nodded. She knew. They probably all did. Were they laughing at him?

"And she doesn't love me," he said.

This time Beacon shook her head.

"She doesn't," Matthew insisted. "Not like that. Not the way I love her."

Beacon plucked Matthew's primitive spear from the ground and drew a large heart in the dirt. Inside, she wrote; 'Matthew & Luna.'

"She didn't kiss me back," Matthew said.

Beacon scrawled a new word. *Time.*

Matthew sighed. Time. It would take time? He would get over it in time? Did it even matter? He'd abandoned them. He had no right to be upset.

Beacon touched him again. He pushed her hand away. Couldn't she see he wanted to be alone with his humiliation? But she shook the spear and wrote quickly in the dirt. *Go* and an arrow.

Beacon rose to her feet and jabbed at his shoulder with the stick. Placing her hands under his armpits, she tried to pull him up.

"Just a minute!" he snapped, flinging his arm at her.

She stepped back, waiting, her glowing outline ebbing and flowing. Then she stepped forward and grabbed him again. She tried to pull him. And she was surprisingly strong for a semi-insubstantial creature. She pulled and pulled on his arm, back the way he'd come. He stumbled after her.

"What?" he asked. "What's wrong?"

She shook her head and pointed. Then indicated for him to hurry.

Something was wrong. Luna. Oh God, please let Luna be okay. He loved her. So much. He'd die a million miserable deaths to spare her. If anything happened to her...

He ran. Following Beacon through the scattered trees. But as they approached last night's camp, she veered off in a new direction. Had they left without him? Would they do that? Could he blame them?

Take care of them, Matthew.

He hurdled fallen trees and dodged puddles of black moss. A growl at his back made him run faster. Ulrich? A beast? Something else? He stumbled and landed on a knee, and wasted no time pushing himself back up. Ignoring the burn in his lungs, he pretended he was at a meet. This was training. If he ever could get back. He wanted to go back. He wanted to run again. But that depended on Luna.

He wasn't paying attention, lost in thoughts and memories, and skidded straight through Beacon. He'd only done that once before and it wasn't a pleasant experience. Like a nasty electric shock. He was left breathless and his thoughts felt scattered, like a million rolling marbles. She shimmered, her essence reforming. She used the spear in her hand to point. The others were nowhere to be seen. Then he looked down. Piper lay at an awkward angle half hidden by a bush. Her top half was visible. He almost missed her, concealed by leaves and pine needles and black moss.

Matthew took a reflexive step back. The black moss twisted across the ground and snaked over Piper's body, trailing over her hands, her cheeks, her torso. One tendril entered a nostril.

Revulsion rose in the back of his throat. He coughed and tried to swallow it back down. His hand went to his mouth and nose, but there was no stench.

Beacon hovered over Piper's inert body. Piper's chest rose with a weak breath. She was alive. But maybe not for long. Frozen with indecision, Matthew stood and stared, thinking. Thinking what it would be like without her. Without any of them. If he did nothing, she would die. The black moss would enter her body and suffocate her from the inside out. If he did nothing.

Beacon nudged him with the stick. Hard.

Take care of them, Matthew.

Matthew forced himself to his knees beside her, and by Beacon's light, brushed the black moss from her face and torso. Some of it was soft and wiped away easily, smearing across her skin. Other tendrils had hardened and he had to chip them away with his fingernails.

Thicker, vine-like tendrils tied her to the ground. Her canvas bag was still slung around a shoulder. Opening its flap, he delved inside. Past the vials of herbs and other unidentifiable objects, Matthew's hand closed around the hilt of Kerry's knife.

He attacked the vines entangling Piper, slashing wildly, and when she was free, her eyes flew open and she sat up, coughing black muck out of her lungs.

Beacon's light glowed on her back, easing her pain.

"There you go, you're okay now," Matthew said, rubbing her back and bringing the girl in close. He could have just stood there and watched her die.

She looked at him and her lips moved in silent thanks. He helped her stand and handed her bag back. Although free of the black moss, her eyes appeared sunken and her cheeks sallow, and leaves were tangled in her braids. He probably didn't look much better. She gulped water from the plastic bottle then offered him a sip. It soothed his throat. And then his throat clamped up. The others needed water. Piper had their only water source with her. If the others died of thirst…

With unspoken agreement, Beacon and Piper walked on. Matthew hesitated. He could retreat again. He could be alone. Or he could follow them to the others. Why did he need to take care of the others? Because Luna had asked him to. But he wasn't sure he should. The truth of their strange, interconnected relationship felt hazy and elusive. Was he forgetting something?

Piper offered him a fragile half smile. Beacon's light shimmered with unearthly beauty. He couldn't leave them any more than he could hack off his own foot. It had been foolish to try. Not that returning would be easy. But really, there was no other choice. *Save Luna.*

He jogged to catch up and the three of them carried on. When you wanted solitude, Piper and Beacon were the best ones to be with, as they never spoke. And they didn't judge much either. Maybe, by not speaking, they observed more than the average person. Did they know more about Luna than he'd given them credit for? There was something to be said for standing along the sidelines, rather than in the thick of it. Their gentle silence might encourage Luna to talk, to open up. But had she divulged everything? Those hazy secrets that clawed at the corner of his mind?

Now, they smiled at him encouragingly and shot him side-long glances, making sure he stuck with them. He attached Kerry's knife to his belt and found himself holding Piper's hand. He'd just saved her life. She would have died without his intervention. And there he'd been lamenting over Luna's rejection. *Piper could have died! And you almost let her!* He felt the weight of responsibility for her life from this moment on. For all their lives. He might not care for all of them, but he didn't want them to die. Not even Kerry. Not really. He had his uses. Matthew had never asked for the responsibility, he'd never wanted to be in charge, if that's what he was, but Luna had always relied on him, and he could never refuse her when she set those midnight eyes on him.

As they approached the area where Matthew last saw the others, a new dawn brightened the sky. Beacon's light faded and the spear walked on, somewhat disembodied.

Not a single soul occupied the temporary campsite. Matthew picked out the shallow depressions where bodies had slept during the night. He detected a thin river of red raspberry juice splattered across a tree trunk. Piper frowned, her thick eyebrows becoming one angry line. She gesticulated wildly. Her hands moved too fast to follow. He turned in a slow circle, searching. The forest waited, unmoving, holding its breath.

The panic in Piper's face depicted a startling truth; the group had continued without them. The realization surprised him. Matthew, neither arrogant nor selfish, believed his position in the group to be integral. He brought order and logic to their chaos. Like planets, they orbited around Luna, but Matthew reflected Luna's magnificent light like the moon reflected the sun. They completed each other. Everyone knew that. And yet, their absence proved otherwise. Perhaps he ought to re-evaluate his place in Luna's life. *Luna.* The thought he might not see her again grabbed hold and sent him running through the woods, searching bushes, and peering round trees. *Luna.* He loved her. She may not love him, but he still wanted her in his life. Correction. *Needed* her in his life.

A pained yowl echoed through the trees, chilling the sweat on Matthew's back and rooting him to the spot. Piper and Beacon hovered at his side. Another yowl and then a drawn-out shriek, followed by a series of whimpers. The last time he'd heard a yowl like that Caleb had died.

They sprinted toward the whimpering, which didn't seem far away. As he ran, Mathew removed the knife from his belt. He ran so fast, so blindly, so desperately to get to Luna, that he stumbled into the middle of the scene.

He skidded past Ulrich, who stood on three legs, the fourth raised and bleeding. Blood dripped from the fox's flank, and he whimpered miserably.

"Thank God you're back!" Hope declared, hovering behind Ulrich.

Matthew's eyes settled on Luna. She stood next to Faith, her status unchanged. Tension leached out of his chest as he exhaled long and slow. But when he looked to the others, his limbs tightened in preparation to flee. Each stood motionless, their pupils large inky spots, widening, and pressing him with silent warnings.

As he turned to face the unseen, the threat he'd missed emerged.

A peeling squeal broke the strained moment. No, it was much more than a squeal. So much more. A screech filled with venom and hatred. So loud Matthew was sure trees would fall with its vibrating echo. The all-encompassing noise rattled his teeth. He tightened his grip on the knife.

He came face to face with a wild boar. He'd never seen one in the woods before. He knew they roamed the forest, he sometimes heard them from a distance of a few miles, across the woods, through an open window. But not like this. Less than three feet away its ungodly noise loosened his sphincter. Sweat slickened his grip on the knife. He examined the boar. So much bigger than he'd ever imagined. Solid muscle coated with thick, brown fur. Ugly. Everything about it was ugly. The beast, the bats, this boar…why was everything in this forest so damn ugly? A reeking stench rose from its lice-infested fur.

He locked eyes with Piper for a fleeting moment. Her horrified face said it all. Ulrich barked a warning. The boar squealed again. This time Matthew noticed it wasn't an ordinary boar. While it exhibited the usual brown fur and protruding tusks, this boar's eyes contained nothing but yellow fire. Just like the beasts.

Matthew couldn't move. Equally terrified and mesmerized, he stared into those yellow flames and heard nothing but screams. With his breath shallow in his chest, he watched the yellow eyes flickering. Burning. Crackling. Hypnotized into some sort of weird trance, he stepped forward. The eyes drew him closer. Someone whispered. *Luna*. The screams changed into something less devastating, something enticing, alluring. Something he craved. Soft and warm, like a lover's caress. As he stared into those yellow mirrors of fire, he could see himself with Luna, in the embrace he longed for. Was it possible? He took another step forward. He needed to know.

"Matthew!" Alessandra's voice was muffled beneath Ulrich's yapping and all the squealing. The sound of his own heart was all he registered. And Luna's. He could hear Luna. He'd promised no more death.

The boar squealed once more. A challenge. The illusion presented in its fiery pupils shattered. As the forest whispered Luna's name once again, Matthew saw the flaming eyes for what they were and shivered at how close he'd come to letting it all go. *Luna*.

The boar charged. Keeping its head low, diving in with its tusks, its yellow eyes focused on Matthew.

Beacon threw the spear. It glanced off the boar's flank and rolled away. Matthew's legs flew out from under him. He somersaulted in the air and landed in a heap by Piper's feet. A flare of agony ignited in his chest. He lay on the ground, winded. Stars flooded his vision and darkness clouded his mind.

"Get up, Matthew!" someone yelled.

"Give me the knife, Matthew!" Kerry called.

But Matthew couldn't move. He could only watch helplessly as he tried to draw breath. Dirt caked his eyes and nostrils. Pain lanced through his muscles.

The boar charged Ulrich. The fox leaped and twisted into the air, narrowly avoiding the gouging tusks, but landed heavily on his wounded leg and collapsed with a single, plaintive whimper.

It took all of Matthew's energy to roll to the side, just as the boar charged at him again. Hope screamed, and for a moment, it drowned out the whispering leaves.

"Get up, Matthew!"

"Where's the spear?"

"Kill it!"

"Run and hide!"

"*Luna*," the trees whispered.

Everyone was yelling. Matthew gripped the knife until his fingers ached.

The boar charged again. Its breath swept over him. Matthew closed his eyes and listened to Luna's whispering voice. He blocked out the screams, the leaves, the yells and the squeals. He concentrated on only her.

"*Now, Matthew*," the silent words reached his soul.

Turning, he thrust the knife upwards. Warmth gushed over his hand and wrist, and rushed down his arm. The boar squealed with wretched whines. Matthew opened his eyes. His hand was buried wrist-deep in the boar's stomach, still holding the hilt of the knife. He looked into the animal's face. The yellow pupils faded and turned black. The boar spasmed, once, twice, three times, before laying still, dead, diminished. The leaves ceased their insidious threats and the mysterious breeze that carried their words died away.

Panting, Matthew pulled the knife out of the boar's guts. He rolled over and retched onto a clump of weeds. But only fluid came out, tinged with black.

"Well, at least that solves the food problem." Kerry strode closer. "I'm about ready to eat a nun's arse through a convent gate." He took the blade from Matthew and wiped it on a patch of the boar's fur. He sliced into the animal, severing chunks of flesh. When he slit the stomach and pulled out the intestines, Matthew averted his head. "Someone start a fire."

Matthew crawled to Luna. He climbed up her legs until his face drew level with her stomach. He wrapped his bloody arms around her waist and wept into her red coat, emptying all his love into her. "I'm sorry I left you. I'll never leave you again."

He'd made her promises before. But this time, he meant it.

CHAPTER 18
MATTHEW

A GENTLE HAND cupped Matthew's elbow and urged him to his feet. Alessandra's face softened and her eyes moistened. "You're back with us now, that's all that matters."

She guided him away from the dead boar and set him in front of a circle of thick branches. Faith and Joseph had built a ring to keep a fire contained. Piper arranged the kindling in a continuous circular pattern to honor her sacred native legends. Then she sat next to a bleeding and unconscious Ulrich. From her bag, she produced a needle and thread and began to stitch his wounds. He woke and yelped and whimpered, pain dancing in his pupils. Jasmine sat beside him and stroked him where it didn't hurt.

"You're okay. You're okay. You're okay," Jasmine whispered the words into Ulrich's floppy ear as tears streamed down her dirt-marked cheeks. When Piper finished sewing, she uncapped a vial from her bag and dribbled it into Ulrich's mouth. His eyes rolled back in his head and he fell into a deep sleep.

Luna settled beside Matthew and Hope sat on her other

side. Someone threw a match on the kindling. Nothing happened. Not at first. After an unusually long delay, the fire erupted, greedily consuming the dry sticks. But it wasn't an ordinary fire. The flames were black. Just for an instant. Just long enough to register something was wrong. And then they changed to the familiar flickering orange. Matthew frowned at the dancing flames.

The first sizzle of meat had his stomach growling, even if it had come from a questionable source. The enticing aroma of roasting meat filled the air and had them all gorging before it was truly done. They sat silently, filling their starving bellies, manners and etiquette forgotten. Joseph chewed the meat into a pulpy mess for Nell. Matthew slid thin slivers of the most tender parts into Luna's mouth. His bloody hands had stained her clothes. But they were all stained. With blood and dirt and weird black moss. Is that why the fire had started black? He wasn't sure anymore.

"So, where did ye go, Matthew?" Kerry asked, wiping his hands on an unidentified rag. "Thought you might have legged it for good."

Matthew ignored him. He didn't owe Kerry anything. He watched the others eat around the fire. Every once in a while, he thought he caught sight of a shadow deeper in the woods. A darting figure, darker than the shadows. A presence that seeped from the surrounding trees and embodied itself in the shape of man. But when he tried to catch it, it would disappear, or dart off in a new direction. He had the impression of a humanoid shape. The black moss man from the river crossing? But he couldn't be sure. He was tired. Injured. Worried about Luna. His mind was most likely playing tricks on him. But he didn't stop watching for the shadow man all the same.

"Are you going to stay?" Jasmine asked him, her pupils blazing.

The growing lump in his throat threatened to silence his reply, but he owed them an explanation.

"Aye, spill it, Matthew," Kerry said, wiping his hands clean of meat and blood. "Are ye all planning on sticking around this time? You were acting like a right maggot, disappearing like that."

"Piss off, Kerry!" Matthew growled. To his surprise, Kerry stood and walked off into the night without another word. But he wasn't *gone*, gone. He always came back.

He turned to Jasmine. "I needed a moment. I'm sorry." He faced the others. "I won't leave you again."

"Like Ulrich?" Jasmine asked.

"Yes, like Ulrich."

She nodded, smiled, and pulled out a stick doll. But when he looked at the others, one by one, trying to impart a silent promise, their faces were sterner, their lips tight, their eyes less trusting.

"Perhaps if you shared your burden, we could help you carry the weight of it," Joseph said. "That is what we're here for, after all."

"Because you and Kalisa were so good at sharing yours?" Matthew snapped. Pity shone in Joseph's eyes, and Matthew hated himself a bit. "Sorry. I didn't mean that."

"It's okay," Joseph said. "We're all trying to cope."

"Some things you can't take back. Once you know, you can't unknow it. I wouldn't wish that on any of you," Matthew said.

"I want to know." Faith narrowed her eyes. "I think we deserve to know how Luna's mother died, why you're pulling a disappearing act, what's got you so twisted. As Joseph said, we're all in this together, so let's be in it together."

"That's a lot of questions," Matthew said.

Faith's narrowed eyes didn't shift. "So answer them."

Matthew surveyed the group. Silent tears cascaded down Piper's cheeks. Did she know? The haunting darkness of her pupils suggested she did. How many of the others knew secrets that Matthew thought he carried alone? How many of them carried their own secrets, only to whisper to another in the dead of the night, or when Matthew was running?

"It's not a juicy piece of high school gossip," Matthew said. Smoke from the fire drifted up in lazy circles, heating the already humid air. Insects buzzed around the bush where Kerry had hidden the boar's carcass. Sticks snapped and popped as the fire caught them. Sparks jumped out of the circle. Alessandra chased down each one.

"Matthew," Alessandra said. "Considering what we've been through in the last couple of days, I think it's time."

It's time. For them to learn about Luna's mother. But not anything else. But what else was there? He wasn't sure he remembered anymore. Only that he and Luna were inexplicably linked. Because he'd promised to protect her. But what about the others? Did they promise her that too?

Take care of them, Matthew.

A gentle breeze dried the tears on Matthew's damp cheeks that he hadn't even noticed he'd shed. He looked at Luna, his Luna, nestled next to Piper, seemingly oblivious of her surroundings. Piper took one of her hands and held it in her lap. She nodded at Matthew to start.

"Luna's mother was murdered. When she was seven. Right in front of her. Not more than three feet." Matthew choked and coughed. He felt strangled from the inside out. He'd been with Luna through all the nightmares. He knew she still remembered every second of that devastating ordeal. Now, sitting on her haunches, she rocked her body back and forth. On some level, she could hear his words. Was she seeing it again in her mind? Was she stuck there? Stuck with all the blood? Piper put a hand on Luna's shoulder. Matthew longed to touch her, to wrap his fingers in her hair and kiss her fluttering eyelids.

"Luna was tied to a chair, gagged, and made to watch. Her mother was raped first. But the murder...." His voice caught on the word. "She was stabbed over sixty times. The murderer was skilled. He didn't want her to die right away. Only the last stab wound was fatal. He wanted her to feel pain, for as long as possible. When the police found her body, lying not two feet from Luna's chair, she was unrecognizable. Luna was sitting in the chair still, bound and gagged, staring at her mother. She was covered with her mother's blood. Completely red," Matthew finished. That was it. It was out. The terrifying truth. What he protected Luna from. That was why she was how she was. And why Matthew was terrified to see her this way again. He got to his feet, his legs trembling, and made his way to Luna's side. He sat beside her rocking body and wrapped his arms tightly around her.

"Did they catch him?" Hope broke the painful silence.

"Eventually," Matthew replied. "After he killed another fifteen women. He killed himself."

Faith's face drained of color. "I had no idea..."

Tyler punched his good fist into the ground. "That's one twisted mother..."

They all stared at Luna. Matthew smoothed her hair from

her face and pulled her into his lap. She stilled her rocking and blinked rapidly, not focusing on anything.

"And you met her just after?" Alessandra asked.

Matthew nodded. "After, they pumped her full of drugs and stuck her in a hospital. For six months. It did nothing. Grandmother pulled her out, took her home, and over the summer brought her out of herself. She moved into the area, and we met when her father took me in. She refused to talk to anyone, except me. She told me about all of it. She saw every-thing, but I was the only one she ever told."

"Christ," Joseph muttered. "No wonder…"

"That's why we have to go to her," Alessandra said. "Grandmother can help her. The authorities will stick her in a hospital again."

"Poor Luna," Faith said, tracing the outline of her unicorn tattoo.

"But Kalisa and Caleb are gone," Hope said. She held a small bundle of kindling in her lap and used a twig to empha-size her point. "What does that mean? For Luna? For all of us?"

"It doesn't mean anything," Tyler said. "There was a fire. And there was an animal trap."

"We're together," Joseph said, his voice gruff. "The rest of us are still together. We'll help each other, and we'll help Luna. That's what's important."

"But it has to mean something," Hope said, snapping one of the twigs in her lap.

"Mean something? Like what?" Tyler asked. "It's just death. It will happen to us all, one way or another."

"Tyler, the kids." Alessandra glanced at the younger children.

"It's part of life," Tyler said, scowling. "They need to know."

"You think Grandmother can help her again?" Joseph asked.

Matthew nodded. "She's the one who got through to her last time. She's the one who got her talking again. It's our best hope."

"Hope?" Tyler muttered. "Jesus, H! And what if it doesn't? We need more than a wing and a prayer."

No one replied. Piper made the sign of the cross and kissed her necklace four times.

With Luna in his lap, closer than she'd been for a long time, Matthew buried his face in her hair, breathing her in, whispering into her ear, begging her to talk, to respond, to come out of it. He told her he was there for her, just like last time. If only she would let him help.

With full stomachs and the truth now told, some of the others fell asleep. No one felt like talking. The group needed time to digest the devastating truth. Even though they should probably be walking during daylight, nobody had it in them to get up and carry on. They needed to rest. Be together.

Piper smiled at him, clearly pleased that he'd returned and divulged the secret. Would she still be smiling if she knew he'd almost let her die? *Take care of them, Matthew.*

But he did feel lighter for sharing it. It was no longer just his secret to keep. Piper pointed to the empty carcass of the dead boar and stuck her thumb up. The boar was now only a shell of the terror it had recently been. Those yellow eyes. He shuddered.

As his eyelids drooped, he turned back to Piper. But her wide smile and encouraging eyes were gone. Instead, her skull grinned manically back at him. Yellow flames filled her eye sockets. Out of her mouth dripped a steady stream of black gunk. It poured from her nostrils, out of her ears. Her fiery pupils danced with demonic intent.

A raven cawed.

Matthew rose to a crouch, doubting his eyes, fumbling for Kerry's knife, not remembering where it had ended up. Piper's head tilted to the side, inquisitive, watching him. But all he saw was her skull and black moss consuming her. Like a mass of scurrying ants marching to a certain death in those lava-like sockets. Was this some weird native spell of hers? None of the others had noticed anything. She continued to grin at him. Matthew's mouth went dry and he reached for the spear at his knees. Could he kill her? If it came to that? He'd just saved her life.

The shadows in the trees moved and flickered, drawing his eyes, whirling with impossible speed until he was sure he was going plain old crazy. The leaves began whispering again. *Luna. Luna.* Fleetingly, he wondered where Obsidian was. The gryphon hadn't made an appearance since he'd saved Kerry from the terrifying beast. He stood, clenching the spear.

"What is it, Matthew?" Alessandra whispered, her eyes flitting between the bowing leaves.

He tightened his grip on the spear. "I'm not sure."

He looked at Piper. No skull. No yellow eyes of fire. No inky blackness oozing from her face. It was just Piper. Her chin rested on her chest. Lowering eyelids indicated she was falling asleep. Had he removed all the black moss from her body?

"Maybe nothing," he said, sitting back down. But it didn't feel like nothing. His accelerated heart rate continued to rush in his ears. Something was out there, something in the woods. Something that meant them harm. More than one something. The beasts with eyes of yellow fire. The trailing black moss infecting everything in its wake. The black moss man. Could he protect them all from these ungodly threats with one whittled spear?

CHAPTER 19
MATTHEW

"WE NEED TO GO," Matthew said, getting to his feet. "We can't sit around here all day." In truth, he didn't want to be anywhere near the carcass of the boar now that the flies had come and the smell of death percolated, staining the air. The stench assaulted his nostrils and made his stomach heave. The others might think he was capable, that nothing ruffled his calm, exterior feathers, but they'd be wrong. He'd never been around anything dead before. Nothing this big. And nothing since he'd met Luna.

The shadows continued to bother him. Big time. He saw them - whatever they were – darting among the trees, running at the periphery of his vision, flanking them. Their black eyes glowed with supernatural eeriness. And hearing Luna's name on the rustling leaves, it was a preternatural omen that made his spine feel like it was jacked into electricity. He wanted to put as much distance between them and this small clearing as possible. His gut told him time was a factor. They were running out of it. *Fast.*

"I don't have any shoes," Faith said. "My feet...I can't... they're insured, but...Matthew, I really want to dance again."

Matthew sighed. They needed to go, but really his body yearned to lay down and sleep for a hundred years. Sleeping Beauty style. If only it were that simple. The thought of Sleeping Beauty and her curse being broken by an adoring prince's kiss sent a new wave of humiliation burning through him. He could still feel Luna's unresponsive lips on his. Softer than he'd anticipated, but impassive. A bitter-sweet memory. No, not a memory, it was too recent for that. It was a painful present.

Glad of a practical task to approach, he pulled some leaves from nearby trees and wound them round Faith's feet. He fastened them with the veins of green ferns, mercifully clear of black moss. "That's the best I can do. And with Ulrich injured, we'll be going much slower anyway."

Faith nodded. She knew there was no use complaining. For once. She'd shed tears during the story of Luna, and now her smudged mascara made her unrecognizable from the girl she'd been a few days ago. A strange beauty softened the angle of her chin, lending her dark eyes a new depth of emotion, and added fullness to her lips. Matthew took her in, with her dirty face and bruised jaw, her shoeless feet and ragged sheepskin coat. A warrior in the making.

He remembered when he'd first met her. What an unlikely addition she'd been to the group. Although she'd already been taken in by Luna's father, Matthew didn't spy the new family member until school the next day. He'd been sitting with Luna in the lunch hall. One look at new-student Faith, with her trayful of unrecognizable canteen food, had been all Luna needed to beckon her over. The nose ring and multiple ear piercings and the - admittedly - delicate tattoo of a unicorn on the inside of her left wrist, was everything Luna wasn't. But Luna had insisted they invite her over. Faith had smiled. Who knew girls like that could smile?

"Where are you from?" Matthew had asked.

"Is it that obvious I'm new?" Faith had replied, placing her tray on the table and sliding onto a stool. Her denim hot pants and baggy band T-shirt - not any Matthew had heard of - were incongruous to the slight tremor in her voice.

Luna shrugged. "It's a small town."

"Great," Faith muttered, forking a wilting lettuce leaf.

"Food's not great here." Matthew said, showing his brown lunch bag.

"You figure?" A curtain of dark hair fell over her perfectly made-up cheek. Luna nudged him. Faith wasn't all she seemed. She was more. And less. She needed help. Matthew sighed. This would be another of Luna's projects. Most left as soon as they found their 'own' people, swayed by the rigid demographics of school social groups. Everyone was trying to find themselves. Find themselves in a group where everyone appears the same. But Luna and Faith had become fast friends, and with Faith being taken in by Luna's father, there was no way she was leaving. He didn't try to understand the inner workings of Luna's mind and who she invited in. Faith was a year younger and came to them when he and Luna were thirteen. He put it down to puberty and girls and approaching high school and all the other weird female vices. Sometimes he joined them, sometimes he left them to it. Especially when they wanted to paint his toenails in a rainbow of colors. Who did they think he was? He might not play football, but he was still an athlete, still someone to be respected. Experimentation had to happen behind closed, secret doors.

Faith surprised Matthew and stuck around. Not all the foster kids did. She escorted Luna to the winter formal that year. Matthew had gone with them, and even then, he'd yearned for her. Privately. Remorsefully. He'd watched from the side lines as Luna had met Tyler that night. He didn't like the look in his eyes when he stared at her. Nor the one in Luna's. Matthew had been biding his time, waiting to make a move, longing from the sidelines. But time was running out. He couldn't compete with a football player. Could he? What was it about bashing your brain cells out?

He glanced at Tyler now. Even with his arm and half his face still blistered, he exuded natural good looks – if that was okay for a guy to admit. Built. A football player. A jock. Popular. Good looking. The typical cliché. Not that Matthew wasn't any of those things, but he wasn't all those things either. Even with his scabbing skin and damaged face, Tyler radiated *something*. He represented strength. Brute, physical strength. Was that really what females craved? Was that what they wanted?

Matthew wasn't a nerd. He wasn't the high-flying academic that could woo a female over a tutoring session, nor the bodybuilder spotting the oversized weights on the bench. He knew those guys. And he didn't. It wasn't an unfamiliar story. In fact, it was everyone's story. Wasn't everyone's school existence filled with trying to fit in? Trying to find your place, no matter who you were? He was part of it, and he wasn't. Most of the time he didn't care. He had Luna. And he had track. His teammates. But she insisted on bringing all these others into their lives. It forced him to take stock. It forced him to re-examine who he was, who she was, and who they all were. She was always surprising him.

Take care of them, Matthew.

Matthew took his position beside Luna and guided her through the tangled trees. They grew in dense clumps, and he had to make sure she ducked her head under low-hanging branches and raised her bunny-clad feet over exposed roots. Not long after they started, the ground slanted away. Their path steered them downhill, which the kids found much easier. Jasmine even began to skip. After another hour, with the sun just touching the tops of the trees, the clearings grew larger and the trees smaller and thinner.

He heard water half an hour before they came across the swollen river. Angry and loud, and just as Matthew had pictured it on the approach to the steep banks. It was also impossibly wide with precariously deep stepping stones. Another obstacle. ANOTHER OBSTACLE! But they couldn't go back.

He'd forgotten there was another river. He'd only made this trip once before.

They didn't have much time to cross before nightfall. Pain glinted in Ulrich's gray irises. A long, jagged wound ran down his flank. It was tinged with black.

"I can take Nell across on my shoulders. But Jasmine..." Joseph trailed off, his face pinched and his eyes trained on the roaring water.

"We'll figure it out," Matthew said, though he didn't believe it. He'd promised no more death. But the raging river threatened to break his vow. In the pit of his stomach, he blamed Luna for not waking up and healing them. But there was nothing she could do about a river. Or black moss men. Or wild beasts. Was there?

Alessandra eyed the river. "We'll make a human rope with our hands. We'll all be joined. We'll space out the strongest and the weakest."

Matthew nodded. It was an obvious plan. But it didn't mean it would work.

"Form a line!" Tyler called, taking advantage of Matthew's moment of numbed inaction.

Matthew held tight to Luna's hand. There was no way he'd let anyone else near her. Piper took her other hand. He was okay with that.

With Nell tucked under his right arm, Joseph led the wary procession, holding fast to Alessandra's hand. She laced her fingers through Jasmine's and Jasmine grabbed Tyler with a white-knuckle grip. Ulrich dashed over the rocks with ease. Then the trio of Matthew, Luna, and Piper. Reluctantly, he placed his whittled spear on the bank. Hope, Beacon, and Ariel were last. There was no sign of Kerry, but Matthew had no doubt he was nearby, watching. Laughing at them.

"You can do this," Matthew said to Luna as Joseph approached the bank. "You can do this." He whispered it again and again, like a mantra, perhaps trying to convince himself.

Joseph placed a wary foot on the first stepping stone. It jutted an inch out of the water and was a confident beginning. The next stood an inch below the water. But it was no contest for Joseph's heavy boots. The water ran over his laces. Nell made a noise. It could have been a laugh or a cry. She pointed at the water with a chubby finger. Joseph kissed her cheek and shushed her. She wriggled in his arms, her tiny feet kicking out. Joseph tightened his grip around her. He stepped onto the third rock. With little surface area, he had to wedge his boot into an angled gap. At the same time, Alessandra rested on stone two and Jasmine stepped onto stone one. So far so good.

Take care of them, Matthew.

Joseph moved onto stone four. A large, flat rock that should have been easy. But the gap between it and stone three stretched more than two feet across. And it sat three inches under the rushing water level. Joseph jumped. Nell let out a wail. He jiggled her under his arm. The movement dragged Alessandra across to stone three. Her soft pumps proving a disastrous choice, she teetered and stretched her arms over the wide gap to Joseph.

"Keep moving!" Matthew called. They just had to go for it. No more thinking about it, or they'd all be pulled into the river.

The all moved forward, rock by rock. Tyler stood on stone one. He squeezed his lips together and a muscle twitched in his neck. He must be in pain. But it was too late to change it all now. They were moving. Fast. Too fast. Joseph was halfway across. The line tugged forward.

It was Matthew's turn to step onto the first stone. He gasped. The ice of the water through his boots paralyzed his toes. And the sound. So much louder than when he'd been standing on the bank. The angry gurgling of rushing water unbalanced him.

Careful with the way he held Tyler's injured hand, Matthew stepped onto the second stone, no longer able to keep eyes on the line ahead. He moved just as Joseph tugged the line forward. He pulled Luna onto the first stone. The river drenched her bunny slippers instantly. Then he was balancing on the third, angled rock, watching Luna, making sure she placed her feet carefully. Her eyes stayed on some unseen horizon. In order to keep his eyes on Luna, Matthew crossed almost backward, as much as Tyler's grip would allow. Miraculously, each step she took seemed perfectly planted and without hesitation. Maybe they'd get through this after all.

Nell began to cry. The raging water almost drowned out the sound of Joseph's gentle cajoling. White foam surrounded Matthew. His feet turned to icy blocks. Then the bottom of his jeans, all the way up to his calves. The water pulled at him, quick and insistent, licking greedily at his legs.

A shout. Tyler? More shouts. Curses. Exclamations. Tyler teetered, stumbled, and fell. Into the water. Pulling them all with him. Swept downstream, Matthew still held Luna's hand. But not Tyler's. Tyler's head bobbed along, going under far too often to catch a decent breath. Joseph ran alongside the opposite bank with Nell jiggling in his arms. Too slow. Way too slow. The river was a machine, faster than any human could run, faster even than him. But Joseph didn't give up. He kept running. Matthew lost sight of Tyler.

His head went under. He couldn't see much through the swirling, white foam. He caught a glimpse of Luna's dark hair and her red coat. She was under the water too. Icy water slammed against his chest and his head ached with the coldness. Something soft swept by his hand. His fingers closed around one of Luna's bunny slippers. With all his strength, perhaps with the last of it, he pushed her to the surface. And didn't let go. It was his one thought. *Save Luna*.

As his head broke the surface, his lungs spasmed and his

frozen chest contorted. Luna was still with him. Others were nearby, shouting, screaming. But he couldn't make out a word.

The water spun Mathew in a circle. Slammed his back against a jutting boulder in the middle of the river. But he managed to anchor himself there. He held Luna close, her chest pressed against his. Everything slowed down. With the sun almost gone, he held on to Luna and he held on to life. He sucked in a strangled breath and glanced upwards. The moon hovered in the darkening sky between a pair of purple clouds. The stars were more beautiful than he'd ever seen. Why was he noticing this now?

"Matthew!" A voice screamed nearby.

He swiveled his head. Piper zoomed straight at him. Was it her who had yelled? He'd never heard her talk before. But there was no one else around. He held out his free hand as she came level with him and pulled her onto their rocky outcrop. The three of them climbed out of the water and onto the megalithic boulder. Out of the river, at last. But they were stranded in the middle of it.

Matthew's teeth chattered. With the diminished light, the cold set in quickly. They were soaked. Hypothermia became a real possibility. A probability. Something caught his eye rushing through the water. A light. Several inches under the surface. An unnatural light. Beacon. Matthew dropped flat on the rock and dug his hand into the water. His fingers brushed against a coarse material, and he yanked. He pulled Beacon out of the water by her golden, luminescent hair. As he did, another mass streamed by. A black, dark mass. As equally unnatural as Beacon but devastatingly menacing. As it rushed past them, the water around them turned black. Blacker than ink. Blacker than Obsidian's wings. Blacker than the blackest of black thoughts. *Black*.

There were four of them now, crowded on the rock. Luna shivered. He tore off her waterlogged coat and threw it on the rocks. Piper's teeth hammered a skeletal dance, reminding Matthew of the vision he'd had of her empty skull. Freezing tremors swept through his body, but maybe they weren't because of the cold. He rubbed his hands up and down Luna's arms, fast, trying to bring some warmth back into her body. Then he barked out a laugh. The situation was absurd. He was stranded on a rock with three people who didn't speak. He laughed, and laughed, and continued to laugh hysterically until he almost felt warm again.

Piper arched an eyebrow. "The others?"

"Oh, you're going to start talking, now?" Matthew continued to laugh. It just made the situation funnier. If he'd known that was all it took to get Piper to speak…well, he'd have axed a couple of them, taken them on a dangerous trek, introduced them to impossible, fantastic beasts, and tried to drown them all in the river months ago. Oh, and not to mention the creepy black moss and whatever that was doing.

"It seems as if now I can," Piper replied. "So, any suggestions on how we get off this awful rock?"

Matthew laughed.

"Matthew?"

Matthew continued to laugh. Maybe he was losing it. Maybe it was hypothermia. Maybe it was all he could do. *Save Luna*. Why did he even think he was capable of it? She was supposed to save *them*.

But he had saved her. He'd pulled her from the river. She was alive. So, there was still hope. Hope. *Hope*. The others.

The thought sobered him. He knew Joseph and Nell were still alive, he'd seen them running along the bank. But the others? Alessandra. Jasmine. Tyler. Hope. Ariel. They couldn't all be gone. Could they?

"We need to get off this damn rock," Matthew said, echoing Piper's words.

Piper clapped her hands. "That's my boy."

"Before we freeze to death," he said.

Beacon stepped in between them. Her light glowed brighter and Matthew felt a flicker of warmth. It radiated into waves of heat and in moments they were dry. He noticed Luna had, unbelievably, retained one of her bunny slippers. The left one.

"I didn't know you could do that," Matthew said to Beacon.

Her light dimmed and the heat dissipated. They were no longer cold or wet, but they were still stranded on the damn rock. Before Matthew could ask Beacon to dry Luna's discarded coat, the river pulled at its hem and tugged it into the river. It sailed downstream, a bright red swatch of color among all the green and brown. Watching it go, he felt a significant loss. A superstitious anticipation. Luna had lost her red coat. The coat that reminded them both of her favorite fairytale. She wasn't supposed to lose her coat. She was supposed to make it all the way to Grandmother's house wearing it. But now it was gone, and Matthew wondered if something worse than a big bad wolf would cross their path. It already had.

He tugged off his dry sweatshirt and Piper helped him put it on Luna. He was left with only a long-sleeved shirt, but it would have to do.

"We need a plan," Piper said.

Beacon's light glowed brightly one more time, rising from

her golden head. Matthew followed the trail of shimmering luminescence. A branch hung over their heads. Connected to a tree. All they had to do was get to that branch, some three feet above their heads. Maybe there was a way out of this after all. One more ridiculous giggle escaped his lungs. And then he prepared himself to continue. It wasn't over yet.

"Piper? I'll give you a boost," he said.

Piper nodded. Matthew laced his fingers together and bent, waiting to receive Piper's foot. She was barefoot, as many of them were now, but she seemed at ease with it, as if she had never put on a pair of shoes. Maybe she hadn't. Matthew couldn't remember.

She placed her hands on his shoulders and stepped into his makeshift step. Matthew lifted his hands, higher, higher, until his back quivered and the old wound between his shoulder blades ached. At last Piper circled her hands around the sturdy branch. More graceful than a varsity gymnast, she swiveled herself on top of the branch and laced her ankles together. She could give Faith a run for her money. Piper reached her arm down, her fingers probing. Matthew placed Luna's hand in Piper's and then he lifted the girl he loved most in the world as high as he could, until all his muscles trembled. The bunny slipper slid past his face and Piper pulled her onto the branch.

Piper helped Luna shuffle down the branch to the safety of the trunk and then the ground. She held Luna's hand so she wouldn't wander off. Matthew nodded to Beacon. It was her turn for a boost. Beacon was much lighter and Matthew pushed her up easily. Once she sat astride the branch she reached down for Matthew's hand. He grasped it firmly. With her legs wrapped around the branch, and his one hand grasped between both of hers, she pulled him up. Easily. Her strength was surprising. Matthew noted the glowing light closing around his hand, illuminating the invading blackness in his scabbed knuckles. It was more than old, dried blood. Much more. The blackness was far too deep, too permanent, too rich. It gave him a moment of hesitation. More than one moment of fear.

But then he was on the branch and climbing down to the bank. His relief that they were safe overshadowed any over-thinking of mysterious, black moss.

"We need to find the others," Piper said.

He couldn't get used to hearing her speak. Her voice didn't fit with the way he imagined it in his head. Piper was gentle and helpful and caring. But her voice was deep and gravely. Maybe from being silent for so long.

"Up or down stream?" Matthew asked, taking Luna's hand. It was warm and reminded him of the first time he'd taken her hand. So many years ago. But the memory pierced his mind clearer than a looking glass. He could feel it, just as he did now; warm, soft, welcoming. But most of all, natural, as if they'd been made for each other. Why hadn't she returned his kiss?

"Downstream," Piper replied.

They walked. Silently. Matthew was thankful for Beacon's light. At least he wasn't in complete silence. Piper was talking. To Luna. Constantly. Describing every tree they passed and every weed they stomped on. Or rather, Matthew stomped on them while Piper edged around them, sometimes unearthing one to add to her bag. Her words droned like busy bees, deafening his thoughts. And he needed to think. About where the others might be. All he cared about, now that Luna was safe, was finding the others.

Take care of them, Matthew.

The screaming could be heard over the raging water. Loud. Tortured. Pitiful. Matthew prayed it didn't belong to a member of their group. But in his heart, he knew the truth. The tortured sounds weren't even words. The victim had given up on making sense. Matthew recognized the agony of approaching death. So familiar now.

Moments later they stumbled upon the scene. Tyler. He'd washed up along a stretch of shallow bank. His legs lay in the water where the current tugged at them, sucking him in.

It didn't take a genius to see the problem. The scalded skin on Tyler's arm and face was no longer there. It had been sloughed away by the river. Leaving behind raw, unprotected muscle. But that wasn't even the worst of it. Underneath his missing skin, Tyler's arm and cheek were completely black. And the black moved. A seething mass that was difficult to distinguish. It surged and seethed and skittered all over his arm and face. It was unnatural...*alien*. Tyler would never survive this. *No more death.* So many of them were still unaccounted for.

A surge of revulsion swam up Matthew's throat. He coughed up a mouthful of river water.

A raven cawed.

Tyler screamed. He shrieked out curse words and pleas for mercy. Constantly. His screams echoed through the still, moonlit night, until Luna began to rock again. Tyler wasn't going to survive. *No more death.* Maybe Matthew wouldn't survive either. Should they just walk away? He couldn't do that. He couldn't leave anyone in so much pain.

"Help me!" Tyler gurgled. The dancing pain in his pupils dominated everything else. The blackness surged, trying to swarm to the other side of his face. Tyler continued to writhe on the ground, lacking the strength to pull himself out of the water, but yet, somehow…twisting and thrashing in parody of a possessed marionette.

"Hmmm. How long is it going to take for ye to put him out o' his misery?" Kerry asked. He wore his leather jacket and fondled a dry pack of cigarettes. Dry, he was completely dry. Where the hell had he been?

A white-hot rage seethed through Matthew. Like jet fuel steaming through his veins. Of all the times to turn up. Of all the things to say. The anger energized him, but not enough. He didn't have enough in him to go at Kerry again. And, as much as Mathew didn't want to admit it, he was right. *Jesus*. How could he even think that?

Tyler was going to die. Tyler *was* dying. Painfully. Slowly. Was it right to let him suffer?

"Please…" Tyler begged. The blackness crawled into his mouth. A parasite? What would Tyler become? His eyes found Matthew's. They locked gazes. They exchanged understanding and misery.

"Please…Matthew…"

Any pet would have been put down way before this stage. Why was it so different for humans? Because they had consciousness? Money? Intelligent ideas? A soul? Matthew didn't pretend to know the answers. Maybe he'd ask Ariel when he saw her again. *If* he saw her again. But he did know suffering wasn't right. But ending it? The act of ending someone else's suffering? Let's call a spade a spade: murder was still murder.

"Matthew! Do something!" Piper yelled. Tyler's flailing arms batted her out of the way.

"Look who's talking!" Kerry clapped his hands near Piper's face. She raised her middle finger at him.

Kerry turned, his voice high and sing-songy. "What are ye going to do, Matthew?"

Before he could think any more, feel anymore, or ask for consensus, Matthew crouched and pinched Tyler's nose between his thumb and forefinger. Tyler gasped. Locked his eyes on him once more. Another unspoken thought passed between them, an understanding. Tyler calmed, closed his eyes, but they snapped open when Matthew covered his mouth with the other hand.

"Aye. That'll do it," Kerry said, the light of his match sparking in the dark.

Tyler struggled with more resistance than Matthew thought him capable. So much so, Matthew second guessed his decision. But now wasn't a time for thought or careful deliberations. Tyler was dying. Matthew's only duty was to see it was as easy as possible. If that was even a concept.

He pinched Tyler's nose harder. He planted a knee on his heaving chest. Tears ran down his cheeks. He averted his head. Tyler struggled a few moments more. Matthew received several blows to his jaw. Kerry didn't bother to lend a hand. Then Tyler fell limp. Tyler's last exhale snuck between Matthew's murderous forefinger and thumb.

"Well, well." Kerry's cigarette glowed brightly. "Didn't think ye had the balls."

"Fuck you, Kerry," Matthew screamed. He stood, fists clenched, but Kerry was no longer there. He'd taken off, again.

"I really hoped no one else was going to die," Piper sobbed. "I believed it. But the ravens…"

Matthew looked over Tyler's inert body. The blackness

scurried away. Had it even been there to start with? Tyler's face and arm were raw and pink. The river lapped at his submerged legs.

"Me too," Matthew fell to his knees. "I promised. But I was wrong. And I'm terrified I'll be wrong again." *No more death*. He looked into Luna's inscrutable face. No more death. *Please, Luna*.

CHAPTER 20
PIPER

TYLER WAS DEAD. For all the time Piper had spent learning about her herbs, understanding natural medicine, she hadn't been able to do anything. The Raven Mocker, it was following them.

"Matthew?" Piper hesitated, worried her voice might disappear as suddenly as it had come. She held onto Luna's hand. Beacon hovered a little way off, maybe giving him the darkness he needed.

Matthew sat. Silently. His hunched shoulders the only sign he was stressed out. He sat in a puddle of the weird, black… weirdness - she still had no idea how to classify it - a few yards from Tyler's body. She was sure it was moving. The moss, not Tyler's body.

"Matthew?" Piper sighed. He didn't respond. She couldn't blame him. This journey through the woods, supposed to solve all their problems, not just Luna's, was proving deadlier than they'd anticipated.

"Matthew! Get out of the black moss!" She hated to yell, but didn't know how else to make him hear. She dropped

Luna's hand, stormed over to him, and dragged him backward. There. At least he was free of the crawling blackness. "And you know what? I need a minute too!"

She connected Luna's hand with Beacon and walked away from the river, into the direction of the trees. Where had Kerry disappeared too? Why did he keep disappearing? What good were motorcycles and cigarettes? What had Luna ever seen in him? He was such a cliché. The rebellious teen who'd left home – probably escaping an alcoholic mother, or abusive father, or small town where he was invisible, no matter how hard he tried or how loudly he gunned his engine - and drifted from town to town. He had a knife. He exuded danger. But was he really dangerous? He was never around. Probably more aloof than anything else. She could see why Luna was attracted to that. Considering.

Piper walked further into the tree line. Somewhere in the distance, a raven cawed. Her mind filled with images of the Raven Mocker, images she couldn't shake away no matter how tightly she squeezed her eyes shut.

She stumbled forward a bit further and knew she'd gone far enough when she could no longer see Beacon's light. Maybe aloof would work for her too. She sat on the ground. The cold of the sunless earth immediately seeped into her. Shivering, she lifted the silver cross hanging at her neck and kissed it. She whispered a silent prayer. Twice. Three times. Four. Was God listening? She had to assume He was. But they were a large group. *Save Luna*. He couldn't save them all. She understood that much about God and religion and faith, even if she was only fifteen. But wasn't it during your teenage years you decided who you were, what you believed in, which paths to follow? *Save Luna*.

Hot tears ran down Piper's cheeks. She swiped them away. She had to have faith. This was not the time to doubt. But how could she not? No, she couldn't think like that. *Faith*. Where *was* Faith?

With clasped hands, she offered more prayers. She didn't know how many or for how long, but it wasn't enough. Or maybe it was. She was praying for Luna, not herself.

Exhaustion pulled at her eyelids and made her head swim with fatigue. Her stomach heaved. She coughed up a mouthful of water. She wasn't entirely sure, but she thought it looked completely black. It didn't sink into the ground as water should. It remained on the surface, bubbling as if on a stove. The bubbles connected, climbing over one another until a surging tower of black water formed over a foot high.

She coughed again. Retched again. More black water spewed from her throat. She opened her mouth to call for help. But her voice deserted her. She was vomiting so much she could barely catch her breath. Where was it all coming from?

Twelve small pillars of frothing bubbles wobbled by her feet. They hissed and spat and became something else entirely. They moved close to each other, merging. To become something else. Something insidious. A personification of evil. She could sense it. It was all *wrong*. In the most profound sense of the word.

"Hel…" Her voice refused to obey her will.

She tried to turn her head. Could just make out Beacon's light. She thrust her right hand in the air to wave. Her hand flailed vigorously from side to side, desperately, almost unconnected from her body. But she would never be seen. Too dark. Too far away. Too silent.

A raven fluttered down and hovered near her feet. It looked at her with midnight eyes. Then opened its beak and cawed.

Something strangled her from the inside. That's what it felt like, if she'd known what being strangled felt like. The water became viscous, then solid, and filled her throat like cement. Her left hand went to her throat. Her right dug into her bag for the knife. Kerry's knife. Maybe he was useful after all. Where was the knife? A sharp pain sliced across her throat. Warmth spilled through her clutching hand. Oh. *Oh.*

"*Shhh,*" someone said behind her. She couldn't see. She couldn't move. The Raven Mocker.

Both hands on her throat now. The warmth was too much to hold. She couldn't put it back in.

She tried to breathe.

Couldn't.

Tried to speak.

Couldn't.

Tried to live.

Couldn't.

THANK GOD FOR PIPER. Otherwise, Matthew might have sat in that puddle of black moss and let it have its way with him. How many times was he going to renege on his promises? But how many more were going to die and make him second guess…everything?

He pushed himself to his feet. "I'm going to look for Piper," he told Beacon. "Look after Luna." Luna was already curled up by Beacon's side. Beacon's light brightened, signaling her understanding.

Matthew climbed the bank. Immediately, the darkness swallowed Beacon's light and left him deserted. For a moment, it felt like he was alone in the world. Maybe longer than a moment, and not just from an existential point of view like they'd discussed in ethics class. Ethics. That thought took him on another tangent. The word was so distorted, so overused, so *mis*used. No, that wasn't it. Actually, it was totally ignored. Meaningless. No one cared about anyone anymore. Apart from Luna's group. Matthew's stomach contracted. That might not be true either. They'd scattered like dandelion seeds on a spring breeze. Maybe the river was to blame. Maybe it wasn't.

Matthew walked on. He tripped and fell over. Something large. Most likely a fallen tree or exposed root. But instinct told him otherwise. He remembered the night of the fire. So long ago now. That's how he'd found Luna. His legs turned to liquid. He closed his eyes, but he knew what he was going to find.

He felt his way along the near-pitch ground. His hands squelched through something wet and cold. Thick. The black moss? He recoiled, spewing whatever it was behind him.

The moon was no longer full, but the cloudless night gave homage to the countless stars. Matthew took a moment to trace constellations. The big dipper. His favorite. His memories took him back to the times when he and Luna had sat on the roof. He never smoked the illegal substances with her, but he kept the weed in his tin, away from the eyes of her father. He would have liked to try it, but considering his place on the track team and the threat of expulsion, it wasn't a risk worth taking. On those nights when Luna smoked, Matthew stared at the sky and watched the stars shimmer and twinkle. He inhaled some of her secondhand smoke and the resulting mind fog softened the hard edges of his worries. He loved the closeness he felt to Luna. There were conversations he barely remembered, but sentiments that deepened their friendship which words couldn't describe. No regrets. He fell in love with her sitting on the roof one night. It wasn't one thing. One conversation. One look. It was the sum total of all of those things. Thinking of it now stretched his heart to breaking point. Looking at the stars now reminded him of those nights.

Removing his gaze from the starry blackness, he turned his attention to the ground. A body. Unmistakable. Dead. Piper.

Pity burned in his chest. Grief slammed against his throat. Anger made his scalp prickle and his hands fist. He felt his way over her cold corpse, searching for a pulse, until he happened on her slit throat. The knife was in her hand. He reeled backward and screamed at the indifferent stars. Piper wasn't suicidal. Not Piper. It was against everything she believed. So, if not Piper, then who?

The names cycled through his head like a hamster wheel gone crazy. For all he knew Luna and Beacon were the only survivors of the devastating river crossing. Apart from Kerry. The douchebag had made the success of his crossing known. And it was his knife. If he saw him again, Matthew would kill him.

Take care of them, Matthew.

Matthew closed Piper's staring eyes, and even though it wasn't his thing, he whispered a prayer over her and folded her arms over her chest. He hoped wherever she was, she was at peace, and that the monstrous Raven Mocker she'd shown him pictures of hadn't stolen her heart. *Jesus.* She wasn't at peace. She was nowhere. He was never going to be able to delude himself into thinking there was something else.

"I'm so sorry, Piper," he whispered. He forced it out of his mouth. More than once. Countless times. It needed to be spoken. She deserved it to be heard.

He stood. Picked up the knife and her canvas bag. Turning, he spotted Beacon's light. So close. She'd died so close.

"*Noooo*!" Matthew yelled at the stupid stars. Beacon's light wavered. Another figure walked up the bank with long skirts and a loose shirt. Alessandra. Her headscarf was missing and wet hair trailed down her back. He dashed along the riverbank and wrapped his arms around the older woman. She was still soaking wet. He led her to Beacon, whose warm light dried her in moments.

"Thank God you're here," he said in her ear.

She looked upon the small group. "Surely, this can't be all?"

The guilt weighed heavily on Matthew's shoulders. He'd failed them so many times. "Kerry's around somewhere. And Piper's just over the bank."

"She's okay?" Alessandra asked.

Matthew shook his head and the hope died on her face. "It wasn't the river. Her throat was slashed. The knife was in her hand. *Kerry's* knife."

"What are you saying, Matthew?"

He shrugged. Wasn't it obvious? "Just relaying what I know."

"We need to look for the others," Alessandra said.

"Tyler's dead." Matthew pointed with his chin. "A little ways downstream."

Alessandra brought her fingers to her lips. "Oh, no."

"We need to wait until morning to look for the others. They could be anywhere."

"We'll rest here for the night. Then search."

Matthew and Alessandra sat near the others. He rummaged through Piper's bag and found a few morsels of smoked boar wrapped in white cloth. He divided it up and helped Luna eat. She blinked a few times. She swallowed the food, reflexively.

"Luna?" he whispered. "Luna? Come back. We need you."

Nothing.

"Luna? Look at the stars. I can see the big dipper and the seven sisters tonight. And Orion. That's your favorite, right?"

Nothing.

"Luna. You know we're all here to help."

Still nothing.

"Luna? How much longer are you going to keep this up?" A sliver of anger crept into his voice. If she would just speak. Just say something. Just tell him how they could help her.

"Luna, *please*."

She chewed methodically, blinked rhythmically as if connected to a metronome, and remained passive. She was no more than a living doll.

"I should never have…" Matthew said under his breath.

"Never have what?" Alessandra moved beside him. "You were the one that found her after the fire, right?"

"It's not that."

"Then, what?"

"Sometimes, I just wonder…" Could he voice the thought aloud? He'd barely begun to think it.

Alessandra held his hand. "We're all in this together, Matthew."

"Are we?"

"Yes." The answer was unequivocal. But he'd been beginning to doubt.

"Sometimes I wonder if…she would have been better off without me." The words fell out of his mouth as delicate as broken glass under bare feet. He wasn't sure how he felt about them.

"How can you say that?" Alessandra asked. There was no hint of reprimand in her voice.

"Because she's been through so much. And I'm not sure I helped. I might have even caused more damage."

"*Pfff.*"

"I met her right after her mother was murdered."

"We all met her after an incident in her life," Alessandra said. "You and Obsidian came along at the same time."

Matthew rolled his eyes. "He's a gryphon, who lives in the sky and sets the occasional thing on fire, or freezes things, depending on his mood."

"Then there was me," Alessandra said.

"Yes. I'll give you that one."

She offered him a warm smile. It reached all the way to her eyes.

"She befriended Caleb when she found him being picked on at school. Then his whole family came."

"But how did that help? Luna was the one with a shadow around her. The mysterious death no one ever talked about. Actually, no. The kids whispered about it all the time. Sometimes even to her face."

"She recognized a kindred spirit. An equally damaged soul."

"Caleb wasn't damaged. He had a rough time with a couple of buddies. That's not the same as having your mother raped and murdered in front of you."

"No. But Luna was looking for a way to shift attention away from herself."

"And then came Piper," Matthew said.

"Sometimes I think she's the most grounded of us all. Practical. Using nature's plants to cure, well, almost anything."

"Not anymore," Matthew said, unable to look beyond his feet.

"No, not anymore," Alessandra said, squeezing his hand. "Ariel."

"How does she help? She's an angel, apparently."

"She *is* an angel."

"But what good is that? If you can't perform miracles, or roll back time, or bend God's ear? What good is it?" Matthew propped his elbows on his knees and looked up at the starry night. His breath plumed, but he didn't feel the cold anymore. He could barely feel anything.

"Because of what she represents."

"Musical harps and golden halos?"

"Matthew!" Alessandra wagged a finger. "She's so much more than that. She represents all of the intrinsic goodness in the universe."

"But how has she helped? On a practical level?"

"Being practical is a skill. But it isn't the only skill," Alessandra replied. "Tyler."

"Don't," Matthew said. "I don't need a who's who of Luna's friends. Especially the ones who've died. I failed them. It's as simple as that."

"You haven't failed anyone."

"I needed Luna. And she needed me. Maybe too much. Definitely too much. If we hadn't relied on each other so much...I don't know, maybe we would have learned to go it alone a bit better."

Alessandra frowned. "But why should you have to go it alone? Matthew, that's what friends are for; to help each other through."

"I still think Luna would have been stronger without me." *Maybe I would be stronger without her.*

"She isn't weak."

"I didn't mean that." Matthew swept a hand through his hair and left it at the back of his neck. "But look at her now."

"When are you going to get it? Not talking doesn't make you weak. It's just her way of processing. She'll come back to us."

"Processing what? The fire? And now four of us have died," Matthew hissed. "That's never happened before."

"We've never had a fire destroy the house, either. She's been through a trauma. More than one. Give her time."

"We may not have time."

The sun crept over the horizon to bloom in the sky in a kaleidoscope of pastel colors Matthew thought would have been impossible if he hadn't seen it with his own eyes.

"We need to find the others," he said, tearing his eyes away from the soothing sunrise. "And then hopefully Grandmother will be able to help."

"Matthew! Matthew!" His name sounded abrasive in the first light of dawn. Birds took to the air. Small animals scurried into hiding. It even seemed the fish dove deeper.

Faith appeared over the edge of the bank, face streaked with dirt and bare feet cut to ribbons. "Thank God!" she panted. She doubled over and collapsed on the ground. "I can't do it anymore," she mumbled when Matthew kneeled in front of her.

"Yes, you can." He grabbed her arm and pulled her to her feet. She winced and fell against him.

"No, Matthew. It's all gone to shit." Her words fell out, her hot breath like darts in his chest.

"Have you seen anyone else?" he asked.

She shook her head. Then nodded. Matthew tensed for the worst. "Hope was with me. And Ulrich and Jasmine. I lost them."

"When did you last see them?"

"Climbing out of the river when I went sailing by. They tried to help. But it happened so fast."

Matthew sighed with relief. They were alive. They hadn't drowned. That just left Joseph, Nell, and Ariel unaccounted for.

"You're okay now," he said in her ear. He brought her face to his chest and stroked the back of her damp hair. "We'll find them."

Faith shook her head. "Ulrich. He wasn't in good shape. Bleeding. And covered in something black. At first, I thought it was reeds from the river...I went by so fast, it was hard to tell...maybe it was reeds."

"Reeds. Definitely," Matthew said. "What else would it have been?"

"Yeah. That water was moving so fast who knows what it churned up from the riverbed," Faith said. Then she gulped.

Matthew shushed her again. Reeds. Riverbed sediment. Totally. Nothing to do with the creepy black moss and the weird man made of blackness running around.

"We should get moving," Alessandra said. "There's enough light to search now."

"Up or down stream?" Matthew questioned.

The two of them looked up and down. The river roared, scolding them for their indecision. Rocks lined both sides and made a slalom course of the middle. It was a kayaker's wet dream. There was a small, sandy bank on their side that led to a few feet of sharp incline.

"Down," Faith said. "If Hope, Jasmine, and Ulrich are okay, they'll find us eventually. It's the others we need to worry about."

Alessandra gathered her skirts. Matthew grabbed Luna's hand and pulled her to her feet. Together, in a loose clump, the five of them began to walk. Beacon's light was barely visible against the climbing sun, but Matthew felt her presence like a hummingbird, flicking from one person to the next, offering caressing touches.

It wasn't long before they found Joseph and Nell curled up on the beach. They looked like they were sleeping. But Matthew knew they weren't, even without a raven cawing. There was something about the position they were lying in: Joseph's body half covering Nell's. She was so still. She was never that still.

Joseph lay mostly face-down, his mouth gaping open, his eyes wide. But they weren't staring. They were filled with blackness. How? When they'd crossed the river to safety? He must have been trying to save someone else, fallen in, been swept away.

The group approached. No one spoke. Even the roaring river seemed muted for a moment. Matthew nudged Joseph's torso with the tip of his boot. Black steam erupted from his pores. Visible one moment, dissolved the next. The group took a collective step back.

A devastating sadness gripped Matthew's heart. Nell was so young. What right did anyone have to take her from them?

"We need to see if she's alive," Alessandra said.

"I'm not sure I can." All he could see of her was a swath of brown hair. Her face was averted. She still wore her artic-patterned onesie.

"I'll do it," Faith said, gritting her teeth.

Matthew grabbed her arm and pulled her back. "No. Let's do it together."

Faith nodded and repositioned his hand in hers. Together, they took the couple of necessary steps forward. They kneeled in the sand and pushed Joseph's body off the baby. Her mouth hung open in a terrified scream. She stared upwards. Blackness filled her eye sockets.

CHAPTER 21
MATTHEW

MATTHEW STARED at the two dead bodies, trying to make sense of it all.

"You bitch!" Faith lowered her head and ran at Luna. Her head slammed into Luna's stomach and they toppled to the ground. But it was a pointless fight. Luna wouldn't engage.

"Say something!" Faith straddled her and grabbed her by the collar of Matthew's sweatshirt, shaking her hard.

Luna's head snapped back. Matthew jumped forward and yanked Faith off. "That's not going to help."

Faith struggled against him, kicking her legs out. "It's all her fault!" He wrapped his arms around her waist, restraining her, ignoring the pain in his knuckles as she tried to scratch herself free. Alessandra went to Luna, helped her to her feet and led her away.

"Faith!" Matthew yelled in her ear. "Calm down!"

"I don't want to calm down!" She wriggled in his grip, turning to face him. She pummeled his chest with her fists. Tears brimmed in her eyes and streaked down her cheeks, washing the dirt away. Matthew let her hit him, again and again, until she sagged against him and soaked his shirt with her tears.

"I don't want to die." Her hot breath heated his chest.

Take care of them, Matthew.

"You're not going to die," Matthew said, daring to place a hand on the back of her head. She'd never been the most affectionate of people.

"How can you say that? Kalisa, Caleb, Tyler, Piper, Joseph, Nell…we're all dying."

He took her by the shoulders and made her look at him. "But *you're* not going to."

"Don't say 'I promise,'" she said. "Don't. It's a jinx. You can't possibly know what's going to happen."

"I don't," Matthew admitted. "But I know we have to keep going to Grandmother's house. We don't have a choice."

Faith sighed. Her brow wrinkled. "I'm afraid she'll send us all away."

Matthew shook his head. "We're Luna's friends. We don't leave her. Ever." *We can't leave her.* It was impossible. Or we'd die. But he couldn't remember why.

She clung to his shirt. "I'm scared."

"You need to have faith, Faith," he attempted a joke.

"In what?" she questioned. "You? Grandmother? Luna?"

"Yes, all of us."

All the fight sagged out of her. She blew her fringe out of her face. "I'm scared," she said again.

Me too.

He offered her his hand. "We can do this."

After a moment's hesitation, she took it.

A sudden wind almost blew them both off their feet. They reached for each other. Obsidian.

He flew close, his wingtip almost grazing their cheeks. Matthew had never seen him in broad daylight. He was always just black against a blacker sky. But now, as Obsidian landed a few feet away, between the river and the trees, he was able to observe the massive beast. Black. Blacker than the midnight sky, blacker than the end of a cave, blacker than space itself. But there was depth to Obsidian's color. A certain radiance that gave definition to his powerful limbs and torso. Matthew shrank a little as he realized Obsidian would be able to hold both him and Faith in one massive paw.

Obsidian rested his head on his forepaws. Little sparks of flame erupted from his nostrils as he exhaled. His enormous eyes blinked and opened, blinked and opened, revealing a large yellow iris that fixed on them.

Faith took a step forward, her hand out like meeting a new dog.

"Faith," Matthew said. "You don't know what kind of mood he's in. He's no Teddy Bear."

She took another step. "He looks cuddly enough."

Matthew eyed the deep-breathing gryphon. With a wickedly sharp beak and claws longer than a T-rex's teeth, there was nothing cute about him. "Faith, seriously…"

"Relax, Matthew. Obsidian wouldn't hurt us." She drew level with his eye. Obsidian watched her, his pupil following her actions. She placed a hand on his paw. He closed his eyes, as if the touch brought him relief. Matthew dared to take a couple steps closer.

Faith stroked him, the muscle of his foreleg and the feathers around his neck. "He's softer than he looks," she said, with child-like awe.

"Still…be careful." Matthew stood next to her.

Faith pulled her hand away. It was completely black. "Matthew? What is that?" She stepped away, holding her hand away like Lady Macbeth.

"It's the black moss."

She wiped her hand on the ground, repeatedly, until the tacky blackness disappeared.

"He's covered in it," Matthew said, walking the length of the gryphon.

"But what *is* it?" Faith asked.

"I don't know. But it's nothing good. We need to get it off him." He ran to the nearest tree and ripped leaves from branches, as large as he could find. "Alessandra!" he called for back-up.

Faith grabbed her own armful of leaves. They each took a paw and began to rub. There was so much of it. The black moss covering Obsidian was at least an inch thick. As they rubbed, they managed to reveal the glistening black scales on his legs.

"It's going to take a whole forest to clean him," Faith said.

Alessandra drew near. "What's the problem?"

"Obsidian. He's covered in that weird black stuff. Help us," Matthew said.

Alessandra grabbed some of the leaves and set to work on Obsidian's right wing. "It's not coming off. I think it's hardened."

Matthew jogged over. When he couldn't remove the calcified layer with a leaf, he prodded it with a fingertip. It reminded him of chipping away at the tendrils covering Piper. He did the same now. But it was so much stronger. He planted a foot against the gryphon and pulled. Obsidian opened his mouth and exhaled. Tiny particles of ice flew into the air and rained down on them, dusting them with moisture. Matthew stumbled backward as a fragment of black moss gave way and came apart. Obsidian raised his head and roared, ice shooting from his mouth and landing on a tree a mile away, freezing it. He roared again and the tree shattered into a million tinkling pieces of ice.

"Don't do that again," Faith said.

"How are we supposed to get it off?" Mathew asked.

Obsidian returned his head to his paws and closed his eyes. Slow and labored breaths gusted irregularly from his nostrils. The black moss was suffocating him.

The answer came from Obsidian himself. He opened his mouth, but instead of ice, flames licked out of his beak. They heated Matthew's face as they licked by, covering Obsidian's body, burning the moss away.

In the distance, a fox shrieked. Ulrich? Closer, a shot rang out. Obsidian opened his eyes, unfurled his wings and took to the sky, leaving only a flurry of rustling leaves and fiery sparks to mark his presence.

"What was that?" Alessandra asked, stamping out the embers on the ground.

Matthew turned a complete circle. Shadows lurked in all directions. Moving shadows? Yes. They ran at the periphery of his vision.

Another shot. Much closer this time.

A new voice called out. "Duck!"

Matthew ducked. They all did, as a third shot rang out and scored a direct hit. The bullet entered the forehead of a black moss man. Tendrils of black moss exploded from its forehead, reaching for the sky, the ground, the trees, everything. Like taut elastic, stretching and reaching, in slow motion, as if trying to make its eventual reincarnation more poignant and terrifying. But the black tendrils didn't snap back to the main host body as Matthew was expecting. They fell to the ground like dead snakes. The body, now almost headless, collapsed. The shape remained still, but Matthew didn't trust it not to reanimate.

"There's more than one of those, isn't there?" Faith questioned, standing at the edge of the black shape. She lifted a foot, as if contemplating stomping on it, but took a step away.

"I think so," Matthew said.

"Sorry about that, didn't want to shoot you by mistake," the new voice said. "Whiskey, Tango, Foxtrot." A boy spoke into a walkie clipped at his shoulder. "Suspect down and out." The line hissed and crackled. There was no response, but the boy seemed satisfied with his message.

Standing only a couple of feet away, the newcomer extended a hand in greeting. Matthew swept his eyes over him and a girl beside him. The boy wore army combat clothes and heavy boots laced up to his calves. He'd slung the killing rifle over his shoulder with a strap. There was even a finger swipe of mud under each eye. His hair was the color of corn and his eyes expressed a wisdom beyond his years. Matthew put him at seventeen or eighteen. The girl appeared slightly younger. She wore riding trousers and boots. A no-nonsense ponytail of brown hair trailed to the hem of her fitted, tweed jacket. She held a handgun. A big, black, powerful looking weapon. A machete was attached to her belt.

"Who are you?" Matthew asked, not quite ready to take the offered hand.

The walkie hissed. Matthew wasn't sure if he detected a voice or not. The boy pressed his lips to the speaker. "Whisky,

Tango, Foxtrot." He waited for a reply, but none came. He sighed. "Must be out of range." He turned back to Matthew. "Monty. My name is Monty. And this is my sister, Robin." The girl nodded. Her hand remained on the butt of the gun, but at least it was pointing at the ground.

"And what was that you just shot?" Faith asked, pointing at the black shape.

Monty cocked an eyebrow. "The lurchers? You haven't seen one before?" Suddenly, he let the rifle drop from its strap, took it up in both hands, dropped to one knee and pointed the rifle into the woods. His trigger finger twitched. Matthew held his breath and scanned the trees. He didn't see anything, but he was beginning to lose faith in his own mind and eyes.

"You killed it," Robin said, resting a hand on her brother's shoulder. "It's okay." Monty took one last look through his scope before he stood again, but kept the rifle in easy reach. He let out a long whistle, as if they'd escaped a close call.

"We've seen one before," Matthew said. He shivered as the sky clouded over and rain began to pour. Within seconds, it washed the remains of the black moss man away, but Matthew had a feeling they hadn't seen the last of them. The rain drilled into the ground at their feet and into his skin. He was soaked again. "Can we move into the trees? Might be a bit drier?"

Monty and Robin surveyed the tree line and shook their heads. "More lurchers in there," Robin said, with a jut of her pointed chin.

"The lurchers? What are they?" Faith asked, her feet sinking into a muddy puddle. She pulled her coat tight. Lifting the collar as high as she could.

"Well, now, that's an entirely different question. All we know is they started turning up in the backyard a few days ago.

Seem to be made of the earth itself. They run with the shadows and then they lurch at you when they're close enough. It's not pretty. Their depthless eyes suck the life right out of you," Monty said.

"You've seen this?" Matthew asked.

The walkie crackled. "Whisky, Tango, Foxtrot," Monty said. He waited. Still nothing.

Whisky, Tango, Foxtrot. WTF?

Robin screwed her lips up, displaying a haunted smile that was trying to be brave. "Our father."

"I'm sorry," Matthew said. Hunching his shoulders to stop the raindrops running down his neck, he swiped at the drips running down his nose.

Robin gave another of her curt nods, casting a sidelong glance at her brother. "He hasn't quite accepted it."

"We have a mission." Monty frowned, oblivious of the rain soaking him through. "The Whiskey, Tango, Foxtrot mission. Take 'em all down."

"Who's on the other side of that walkie?" Matthew directed the question at Robin, sensing Monty might not be up to questions.

"Our father," Robin said, her voice just above a whisper. Monty scanned the trees with his scope again. "It was our father's code...before."

Monty let loose a shot. Faith stifled a scream. Matthew swiveled to face the threat, his hand going to the knife at his belt.

"Thought I saw something." Monty shrugged.

"Appreciate the assist," Matthew said, offering his own hand. Maybe Monty just needed a friendly face. And it would help if he didn't get shot any time soon. Monty shook it, pumping it up and down at least ten times.

"Before we got here…was that a…did we just see a…" Monty seemed unable to finish the question.

"A gryphon," Robin finished for him. "A big-ass black gryphon with a twenty-foot wingspan, at least." She looked at Matthew expectantly. She'd bared her secrets. Now it was his turn.

Matthew hesitated. Obsidian was their best kept secret. Well, maybe not the best, but one of them. Robin and Monty had weapons. Weapons that could take out these strange lurchers. Their numbers were dwindling. Faith didn't want to die. Neither did Matthew. Robin and Monty could come in useful.

Take care of them, Matthew.

"Obsidian," Matthew said. "He's our friend."

"But gryphons are mythical creatures—" Robin blurted.

Faith laughed, a real throw-your-head-back-to-the-sky laugh.

"——known for guarding treasure and precious possessions," Robin continued.

"I assure you, Obsidian is real," Matthew said.

"And he's guarding you," Robin said, her eyebrows lifting and her lips curving into an impressed smile. "All of you."

"Something like that," Matthew said.

"Who's she?" Robin tilted her head at Luna. In the dismal light, Beacon glowed beside her. Matthew wasn't sure who Robin was referring to.

"Luna's our friend." Faith stepped out of the puddle and stood in front of Robin and Monty, blocking their view of the others. Most of them hovered around Luna and tried to protect themselves from the rain. "She's had an accident and we're taking her to her Grandmother's house."

"You need to call 911?" Monty asked, hand going to the walkie. Matthew doubted it was actually connected to anything.

Matthew shook his head. "Not that kind of accident."

Robin tapped an impatient rhythm on the butt of her gun. The rain continued to drench them. Matthew's shirt stuck to his skin. He blinked raindrops out of his eyes. Squelchy mud sucked at his boots. He offered no explanations.

Robin narrowed her eyes. "I guess we'll see you around."

Matthew hesitated. "Things aren't what they seem here, but we're friendly. We could use your help." He nodded at their weapons.

"The lurchers," Robin said.

"Among other things," Matthew replied.

Brother and sister shared a look. That's all they seemed to need to communicate.

"We'll help," Monty said. "The Whiskey, Tango, Foxtrot mission team is always willing to lend a hand. Operation *Save Luna* is a go. Especially when you have such a nice light to lead the way." He nodded at Beacon.

"That's Beacon," Matthew said.

Robin winked. "Appropriate name."

"We need to go through the forest to get Luna to her grand-mother. Is that going to be a problem?" Matthew asked.

Monty shrugged. "Should be okay while it's raining. The lurchers can't stand rain, unless they've calcified, then they're a real problem." He ran to a nearby tree, pressed his back against it, and slowly peered around its girth. "All clear!" All might be clear in the woods, but it certainly wasn't in Monty's head.

"First we need to find everyone else," Alessandra said.

"There are more of you?" Robin asked, wiping a river of rain from her cheeks. Her boots were in the mud up to her ankles, but she didn't seem to care.

"Yes," Matthew replied. "Ariel, Jasmine and Ulrich are missing. We got separated crossing the river."

"And Kerry," Faith added.

"We don't need to wait around for Kerry," Matthew said.

"We can't wait around for the others, either," Faith said. "They could be anywhere. And that's *if* they survived."

As if to enunciate the point, a long, abrasive shriek split the air.

Matthew cocked his head. "Ulrich?"

"Who knows?" Faith said. "Could be one of those other things."

"If they're alive, they'll be okay. Ulrich can lead the others," Matthew said.

Alessandra's face pinched tight. "You sure?"

Matthew nodded. But he wasn't sure about anything.

Take care of them, Matthew.

Monty beckoned them closer. He pressed two fingers to his eyes, then pointed them at Matthew and the others. *I'm watching you.* He pressed them back to his eyes, and then circled the two fingers in the air. *I'm watching everything.* The rain had smudged the mud under his eyes. He looked entirely unhinged.

CHAPTER 22
MATTHEW

THEY HEADED for the tree line with their new friends. Matthew thought the term was rather loose, considering, but they'd play along for now. Another shriek broke through the noise of the pounding rain. Further away this time.

They picked their way through deepening puddles. Monty scampered from one tree to the next, like on some secret military mission. Only once he'd hugged each tree with his back and peered around both sides of its trunk, did he declare it safe to move on. Nobody paid him any attention, and he didn't seem to mind. But it didn't stop his strange behavior. Occasionally he'd fire his rifle, making them all jump.

"He's...struggling," Robin said. "With the death of our father."

"And you?"

The rain pelted the canopy. Thunderous. Then dripped onto his head.

Robin lifted a shoulder. "I'm okay." She fiddled with the safety on her gun. "I'm okay."

226

Matthew nodded. As strange as he found Monty's behavior, he wasn't one to judge. He couldn't imagine what they looked like to Monty and Robin. Half of them bare foot, a catatonic girl, a humanoid figure that shined as bright as the moon, and a gryphon. Matthew's group won the weird stakes hands down.

Ponds and lakes filled rapidly. It was the first rain the forest had seen in weeks. Matthew walked with his mouth hanging open, soaking up the liquid. Beacon led the way. Robin and Monty were close on her heels, Monty doing his little dashing dancing maneuvers, Robin with her handgun ready, safety off, but not threateningly. The weapons should have made Matthew more at ease, but instead, his head swiveled, scanning for more of those black moss creatures.

Luna's hand felt slick in his grip. He thought it was just the rain, but heat radiated from her palm. He stopped. She was three inches deep in a puddle, the hem of her blue pajamas disappearing into the muddy water. The one remaining bunny slipper drowning. Red-rimmed eyes hinted at another problem. He reached for her forehead. She was burning up. This was not good. *Understatement, Matthew.*

During their trek, with all the obstacles, all the death, Matthew had never considered Luna's physical health. He knew she was in danger, that the catatonia needed attention, that she might lose herself again. But he'd never worried about her physical health. Not Luna's. But she'd been through so much; the fire, the lack of food and water. Only God knew if a bat had bitten her in that cave. The black moss, the infected water, the beasts. More recently the river crossing and freezing rain.

Take care of them, Matthew.

That's what he'd been doing; he'd been taking care of them, as best he could.

Monty and Robin wore cheap ponchos, but the rain ran down their hair and necks, drenching them. Monty's lips were pressed tight together. Faith's sheepskin jacket only added a sodden weight. With arms crossed over her chest she picked her way over the puddles. Her pupils were dilated. Lacerations crisscrossed the soles of her feet. Matthew couldn't let her go on walking like that. Not if she was going to dance again. He wanted to watch her dance again.

Take care of them, Matthew.

He was trying, God dammit.

The rain flattened Alessandra's wavy hair. It made her look…less somehow. Her skirts clung tightly to her legs. Matthew's feet were soaked, even through his boots. They were all…struggling. Only Beacon seemed unaffected.

The gray sky darkened as the twilight hours arrived. The rain continued. Luna shivered, a feverish juddering. Matthew rubbed his hands along her arms, trying to ease her suffering.

"We need shelter," Matthew said.

"There's an old hunting cabin ahead," Monty said, using some complicated hand gesture that Matthew assumed was army related but didn't understand. "Half a mile. Can she make it?"

Luna's knees buckled on cue, and she fell. Matthew caught her before she hit the ground and scooped her up. Half a mile. He would carry her. "Lead the way."

Take care of them, Matthew.

No, Luna, I'm going to take care of you.

He picked up the pace. He needed momentum to carry Luna's weight. Otherwise he might collapse and never get up again. He tried not to think about the rain. On one level, it solved their recurring water issues. But the icy coldness leached through his clothes, eliciting images of skeletal fingers scraping their way out of a freshly filled grave. Cold. Dank. Dark. The grasping fingers in his mind beckoned him to a scary place populated by strange shadowy men made of moss and other things he'd rather not witness. Or think about. Like why Luna was the way she was. And what he really meant to her. She meant the world to him. Everyone knew that. But they didn't know everything else.

He pressed forward, following Beacon, sloshing through puddles and mud, blinking rain out of his eyes. He almost slammed right into Robin's back. She trained her gun, aiming with the sight. She pulled the trigger. Matthew winced as the noise of the expended bullet ricocheted through the trees. A black moss man collapsed fifty yards away, its glowing eyes going out. It crumpled into no more than a puddle. Which was connected to the water he was standing in. His toes itched.

"Keep moving!" He charged ahead.

The square shape of the cabin soon came into sight. The front door hung off its hinges, and there was a small hole in the roof. But it would do. They could light a fire in the stove and get warm, shelter from the rain and hopefully the moss men.

He stepped over the threshold, spotted an old cot strewn with a couple of moth-eaten blankets, and laid Luna down. He stripped off the sweatshirt and her blue pajamas and wrapped the blankets around her tightly. She was still shivering.

Monty lit a fire in the stove. It roared to life immediately. Faith sat in front of it, almost too close, but Matthew didn't have the heart to caution her. They were all tired and wet. She stripped out of her jacket and laid it on the floor in front of the stove. Her hands went to her feet, massaging. Monty and Robin shrugged out of their wet outer layers. Robin went through her bag and re-packed items with military precision. No one said a word. They sat and listened to the crackle of the fire and waited for the puddles of water they'd dripped in with them to evaporate. A bucket in the corner caught drips from the hole in the roof, producing a metallic clinking sound. The steady rhythm comforted him.

Matthew sat next to Luna. The fever consumed her. Monty stood at the door with his rifle trained on the darkness outside. Robin urged him inside and closed the broken door as best she could. Could moss men open doors?

"What do we do?" Matthew asked Alessandra.

Alessandra left Faith by the fire and sat on the edge of the cot. "Check Piper's bag."

"Who's bag?" He couldn't think straight. What with the rain and the heat of Luna's fever under his palm, and the worry. Oh, the worry.

"The one you put on the floor." Alessandra pointed. "Piper's bag of herbs."

Although Matthew had kept Kerry's knife firmly attached to his belt, he hadn't remembered carrying the bag or putting it in the corner. The canvas dripped as he picked it up. He opened the sodden flap and rummaged inside. Thank God for Piper's foresight; each herb was wrapped in individual water-proof wrapping. Even the boar's meat survived. He handed out the strips of meat. Monty and Robin provided their own rations; trail mix, beef jerky, and a bar of chocolate.

"What am I looking for?" Matthew laid the items on a small table next to the bed.

"Yarrow, it's a dried green herb," Alessandra replied.

"Robin, would you put a pot of water on? We're going to need it."

Robin found a pot on a shelf near the stove and filled it with water from a plastic water bottle.

"They're all dried and green," Matthew muttered as he rummaged through the herbs.

Alessandra moved his hands out the way and grabbed the packet of yarrow. "Add a tablespoon of this." She gave the packet to Robin.

"How is this going to help?" Matthew asked.

"It will make her sweat it out," Alessandra replied.

"She's already sweating," Matthew said. "Look at her!"

Luna had her eyes closed. Beads of sweat sprinkled her face and exposed shoulders. Her hair remained damp even though the rest of them had begun to dry out. Occasionally, she shivered, sending small convulsions through her body.

"Where's Monty?" Matthew asked, looking around the small, dilapidated cabin.

"Monty?" Robin questioned.

The front door slammed shut, well, as well as it could on bent hinges, and Monty reappeared. He'd refilled all the water canisters.

"There you are," Matthew said.

"There he is," Robin echoed.

The walkie hissed.

"Whiskey, Tango, Foxtrot," Monty said.

"Anything out there?" Matthew asked.

Monty shook his head. "My father is waiting for me."

"Monty…" Robin circled close to her brother.

Alessandra clicked her fingers. "You." She pointed at

Faith. "Keep an eye on that child." She dug through the canvas bag. "Where is that yarrow?"

Faith frowned. "What child?"

"We already have the yarrow." Robin held the baggie up.

Matthew frowned. Something wasn't right.

The cabin walls suddenly shook with earthquake intensity. Sweeping beams of light blinked through the broken windows. A dark-haired girl sitting in front of the stove curled her hands into fists and pounded the rotting floor.

"Hurry up with that tea," Alessandra said. "Where's the yarrow?" She rummaged through the canvas bag again.

Matthew stood and grabbed the pot out of Robin's hands. It had just begun to boil. Good enough. He poured it into a metal cup and brought it to Luna. The cabin walls continued to shake as if built on a malicious fault line determined to rip their forest in two. The piercing lights swept over the cabin. Had they been found? By who? An alien spaceship? He'd believe anything at this point. Growls rumbled from beyond the broken doors.

"Whiskey, Tango, Foxtrot," Monty said, looking through the front window in the cabin. "Enemy detected." He reloaded his rifle.

"What the hell is going on?" The dark-haired girl with a unicorn tattoo sat on the floor with her hands over her ears.

"Drink, Luna." Matthew kneeled at her side. Alessandra lifted her head. Matthew blew across the top of the yarrow tea and placed the lip of the cup at Luna's mouth. She licked her lips, then accepted the healing brew. She drank greedily, until the last drop was gone.

Robin checked the bullets in her handgun. The weight of the knife at his belt pressed into him. He might need it soon.

The dark-haired girl tucked her head into her arms. Alessandra placed the herbs back in the bag. Monty stood still, staring out the window into the dark forest, muttering. "Whiskey, tango, foxtrot." Again and again.

The shaking ceased abruptly. As did the invading lights and menacing growls. It all stilled as if someone pressed pause. Matthew tensed, waiting, but it didn't come back. Faith stood and sat on a wooden chair, resting her head against the wall.

"Whiskey, Tango, Foxtrot," Monty said. "Enemy departed. Operation *Save Luna* still a go."

"Now what?" Matthew asked, his thoughts clearing, his brain no longer fogged.

"Now we wait," Alessandra replied.

Matthew sat on the floor with his back against the bed. He raised a knee and propped an elbow on top. He flicked the nail of his thumb and forefinger against each other. "Maybe I should go on ahead," he said. "With Luna not well, and Faith with no shoes, I could go on ahead. I could get help."

"We can't split up, Matthew," Alessandra said.

"I don't want to, but how long is it going to take to get there?" He kept his voice low so the others couldn't hear. They'd begun to fall asleep, draped throughout the cabin like abandoned rags. The rain had let up too. No longer pinging into the metal bucket. "With these lurchers infecting every-thing in their wake. Those beasts that almost killed Kerry. What else might be out there?"

"Matthew, we can't lose you."

"You won't lose me. I'd be getting help."

"Or maybe you would lose all of us," Alessandra said. She

stroked Luna's hair. Sweat still decorated her brow, but at least she was asleep.

"I don't know what else to do," Matthew said. "I might be able to find the others."

"Or you might get killed out there on your own."

"Thanks for the vote of confidence," he mumbled.

Alessandra put a hand on his shoulder. "I do have confidence in you. You're one of the stronger ones. We need you. We need you to stay with us."

Matthew nodded. "Alright. But we'll have to figure out what to do about clothes and shoes when the sun comes up. If Luna's better."

"She will be," Alessandra said.

CHAPTER 23
MATTHEW

MATTHEW SAT on the floor of the dilapidated cabin, his butt numb, his eyelids refusing to close. Night pressed in at the single window. Forest noises wound their way in through cracks in the aged walls. The smell of damp and wet earth hung in the air. He placed a couple of logs in the stove. The fire sprang to life again. He tugged Faith's jacket off the hook nearby. It was dry now. Stretching out on the floor next to Luna, he rolled the jacket under his head.

"Caleb said there was going to be a fire," Alessandra whispered.

He hadn't realized she was awake. She sat on the cot near Luna's head. Her shirt and skirts were rumpled, and her eyes portrayed a deep level of fatigue. Faith was still in the chair. Robin and Monty were curled on the floor by the stove, using their packs as pillows. Beacon was outside, sitting on what passed for a porch. She often stayed outside at night, as her light sometimes prevented people sleeping.

"There already was a fire." Matthew tried to picture the young boy's face. Why couldn't he picture his face? He hadn't been dead long. They'd spent so many Sundays together doing chores around the yard. Matthew frowned, straining to bring the boy's features to mind, and when he couldn't with a satisfactory level of detail, gave up, putting it down to fatigue. "How's Luna?"

"The same." Alessandra used the edge of the wool blanket to wipe moisture from Luna's brow. Luna murmured in her sleep. It was the first time Matthew had heard her voice in a week and the soft sound made his heart lurch. She was in there somewhere.

"Caleb said there was going to be a fire," Alessandra said again.

"There was a fire," Matthew replied. He placed his hands on his stomach, willing sleep to take him to oblivion for a few hours. "Back at the house. We escaped."

"I think he meant another fire."

Matthew tilted his head to the window. "Maybe I would have believed that yesterday, but now, with the rain, not a chance. We're going to need an ark."

"Caleb was rarely wrong," Alessandra said.

Matthew thought of the lurchers and the beasts with their flamed-filled eyes. "*Rarely* being the operative word. There were margins for error. His visions were open to interpretation. And as much as I loved the kid, he's not here anymore to explain it."

"I'm just…worried."

Matthew rested his head on a bent elbow so he could see Alessandra. Her hooped earrings danced in the light of the stove. "We've been through a lot. And we're not out the other side yet."

"That's what I mean," Alessandra said.

"I think you can safely cross 'fire' off your list of things to worry about," Matthew said, finally feeling his eyelids droop.

Alessandra didn't reply, and he let the crackle of the flames from the stove carry him off to sleep.

The warm snout in his armpit followed by a rough tongue working over his face was enough to raise him from a fretful dream. Matthew woke to find Ulrich sniffing and licking him, yipping and yapping.

"You're back!" Matthew gave the fox a brief pat before looking for the others. The group he'd arrived with were still asleep. Outside, dawn was a hint on the horizon. Hope and Jasmine stood in the doorway. Ariel was beyond them. Jasmine came inside and stood next to Ulrich, her hand burrowing deep in the fur of his neck. They were all okay. *They were all okay.* His chest tightened as he watched Jasmine, thinking of the news he would have to give her.

"Come in, come in." Matthew beckoned them inside and gestured for them to warm themselves by the stove.

"Are you all okay?" Matthew handed them cups of water. He reached for the baggie of meat and doled out the last of it. They devoured it with filthy fingers.

"We're okay," Hope replied, wringing out her long hair and shrugging out of his jacket. "Just wet and hungry."

"Did you see anything out there?" Matthew asked.

Hope warmed her hands in front of the stove. "What, like Kerry?"

"He means the monsters," Jasmine said. Her voice was clipped, her delivery perfunctory.

"Oh, yeah, the horrible black man-shaped creatures with glowing black eyes intent on killing us all? Them? Yup, saw a couple of them," Hope said. She'd never been sarcastic with him before. But then they'd never been chased through the woods by horrible beasts.

Hope ripped off a piece of meat with her fingers and chewed. Matthew glanced around the cabin. Everyone else slept. He hoped they wouldn't wake to shaking walls and piercing lights and muddled thoughts. Not like before.

"But you're okay, right?" Matthew had to make sure.

"Ulrich killed one. We got away," Jasmine said. Her fingers wound into her pajama top. There was no stick doll in sight. "Just."

"I'm sorry," Matthew said. He hadn't been able to protect them. Thank God Ulrich had been there.

Take care of them, Matthew.

"It's not your fault." Jasmine glared at Luna. "What's wrong with her? And who are they?" She jutted her chin at Monty and Robin.

"Luna has a fever. Monty and Robin saved us from a moss man."

"So, it's all out in the open then." Hope stared at him. She took another bite of meat. Chewed. Swallowed. "We're actually talking about the impossible monsters no one has dared mention?"

"That's not true," Matthew said. He looked to Alessandra for help, but she was just waking up. Faith stirred in the chair and opened her eyes.

"I might only be fifteen, but it's only two years younger than you, and it's old enough to see what's going on," Hope said, squaring her small shoulders.

"Hope, don't be like that," Matthew said. "I wasn't trying to keep anything from you."

"Stop picking a fight," Faith said. "Yes, we all saw the

goddamn creatures. No, we didn't talk about it. We were, and are, all scared shitless."

"Faith!" Matthew said.

She narrowed her eyes.

"Fair enough," he sighed.

Faith turned back to Hope. She wasn't done. "I'm the sarcastic one. That's my role. Stay out of it. You go back to your wishy-washy day-dreaming and candle lighting to reduce negative ions, or whatever it is you do."

"Faith!" Matthew stepped forward, gesturing for her to stop.

Hope frowned. "It's a Himalayan salt lamp."

Faith shrugged. *Whatever*.

"I'm not playing a role," Hope said.

"Matthew is the reason we've got this far," Faith said, pointing at him as though he were nothing more than an enslaved guard.

Matthew's ears burned. Everyone had woken and now they all stared at him. Fine when he was running, but here, in the middle of the group, he never liked being the center of attention. That was Luna's job. She was the glue. Faith and Hope continued to argue over his head, as if he didn't exist. He stood there, with his hands on his hips, and waited for a lull in the conversation.

Faith paused for breath and glared across the room at Hope. Hope didn't respond, but her scowl matched Faith's in severity and scorn. Before they could go at each other with scratching and hair pulling, Matthew turned to Alessandra. "How is Luna?"

"The fever has broken, but she's weak. She needs food."

Hope jabbed a finger into his chest. "So, you're just going

to avoid it? Again? Not talk about monsters from hell stalking our every move?"

He swiveled toward her. "What would you like me to say? That lion-like beasts with fiery eyes almost killed Kerry and are still out there somewhere? That they may have found a way to cross the river? That the black moss men are something out of a nightmare and I don't know how many there are? Where they came from? That at least they can be killed with a gunshot? That the black moss is everywhere and could infect any one of us, might be inside us all already? Hope? Tell me what you want me to say?"

That silenced her. She turned her back and slid closer to the stove, holding her hands out to the warmth. Her shoulders trembled. Kalisa's medallion hung around her neck, catching the light of the fire. He hadn't realized she'd taken it. Caleb had been the last one to wear it.

"I'm sorry," Matthew sighed. She was fifteen. Only fifteen. She thought she could handle it, but she couldn't.

"So, what do we do now?" Hope whispered, still with her back turned.

"I think we should hole up here for another day," Alessandra said. "Luna is still weak, and she needs a proper meal."

Monty shook his head. "Not safe. Mission Whiskey-Tango-Foxtrot could be in jeopardy. These walls aren't as solid as they look." To prove his point, he wrapped his fingers around a section of plywood wall and pulled it away, leaving a gap that looked out into the forest. The scent of steaming soil and pine rushed in. And something else. Something fresh and earthy, but unnatural.

"We need food," Matthew said. "So, I suggest we let Luna

rest up here while some of us go foraging." He poked his head outside the broken door. Water steamed off the ground under the rising sun. Humidity pressed into the cabin. Alessandra was right, the forest would be bone dry in a couple of hours.

"*Oooo*, goodie." Monty cackled, checking the bullets in his rifle.

"Maybe you should be one of the ones to stay here and guard the cabin," Matthew said.

Monty offered him a salute. "Aye, aye captain. Operation *Save Luna* in progress." He waltzed out the door and scampered from tree to tree, aiming his rifle, but this time, mercifully, not firing.

"I'll stay here," Hope said, her voice bitter, still nursing her wounded pride at not being told the truth. "I'm not much use out there."

Matthew decided not to engage with her. Another argument wouldn't help anyone, and now wasn't the time for self-esteem building.

Robin approached Hope. "I have a change of clothes you can use."

Hope had been one of the least prepared to flee into the woods. In just a nightshirt that was no longer white. No shoes at all. And Matthew's jacket. But her feet were in better shape than Faith's. Robin pulled a pair of black cargo trousers and a black, long-sleeved shirt from her backpack and offered them to the blonde girl.

"Thank you," Hope said.

"I'm sorry I don't have any shoes," Robin said.

"This is enough." Hope slipped the trousers on under her nightdress. When she was changed, she handed Matthew back his jacket, taking the sketchpad out of its pocket. She didn't express gratitude or make eye contact. Matthew threw the jacket to Alessandra. Luna could use it.

"Where's my father? And Nell?" Jasmine's voice cut through the humid air.

At the commotion of the group arriving and then the bickering with Hope, Matthew had almost forgotten that Jasmine had now lost both parents and both siblings.

No one said anything. Matthew tried to keep his face neutral. Jasmine's face crumpled. He'd never been a good liar.

"I'm sorry, Jasmine," Matthew said.

Jasmine stared at her feet. "I'm an orphan." She turned her back and an anguished sob ripped from her throat. Ulrich emitted a long, warbling yowl that chilled the back of Matthew's spine.

"You're not an orphan," Matthew said. "You have all of us." But that wasn't really the point.

"Like Jim Hawkins?" Jasmine's wild hair frizzed out in all directions, pain etched on her face. "It hurts."

Matthew kneeled in front of her. How he wished there were words to take away her pain.

"Your daddy and Nell are in Heaven, watching you. They don't want you to hurt," Matthew said, praying, not for the first time, such a place existed. He glanced at Ariel. She nodded. This was really her domain, yet she offered no words.

Jasmine tipped her head to face the ceiling, as if she could see Heaven's outline in the cotton-ball clouds through the hole in the roof. Tears streamed down her face. "I hate Heaven!" She yelled and dashed for the door.

"Jasmine!" Matthew called as she ran. "We'll take care of you. All of us. We're your family." He tried to grab her hand, but she shrugged him off and slipped out the door.

"I'll go," Hope said, trailing after the younger girl.

Matthew kneeled there for a moment. But a moment was almost too long. Because his thoughts whirred again. Which always led back to figuring out what the hell was going on. And that just gave him a headache and a trembling fear he didn't want to acknowledge.

Why *was* Luna so special? He loved her, he knew that much. But beyond that, why did they need to protect her, why did they need to get her to Grandmother's house? The reasons were illusive. But the urgency remained.

Matthew pushed himself to his feet and looked out the doorway. Hope and Jasmine sat on the step of the small porch. Hope put her arm around the younger girl and whispered to her. Occasionally, Jasmine would nod and squeeze Hope's hand. Ulrich lay on her other side, his head resting in her lap, his mournful eyes intent on her face.

Matthew turned his attention back inside the cabin. The others moved around. Conversations had started. Normalcy was returning, as much as anything was normal these days. They still needed food and water. Life continued. Survival.

Take care of them, Matthew.

"I'll take Robin and Ulrich to find food." He looked at the fox. The animal sauntered inside and yapped his assent. "The rest of you stay here, stay warm, and look after…each other." He'd been going to say; 'look after Luna,' but they all knew that was the mandate, and they could all use a little leaning on shoulders right now.

When Matthew stepped outside, filtered sunlight splayed through the tree limbs. The rain had stopped. He shifted his gaze nervously, looking for black moss men. When he couldn't detect any ominous movement, he stepped off the dilapidated porch and into the woods. Butterflies flew, flitting between clumps of ferns. Thick vines hugged a few of the oak trees, winding around their branches. Green moss blanketed the forest floor, creeping up the trunks, smothering the wildflowers. Green moss. Tinged black.

Ulrich and Robin flanked him. He carried Piper's bag and inside were a few spare baggies. They could collect berries. If they weren't infected.

They walked away from the cabin until Matthew was a little unsure how to find his way back. But Ulrich could help with that. Despite the shade of the staggered trees, sweat pooled on Matthew's lower back. After an hour of walking, they had half-finished the water canteen Robin carried. Every twenty minutes or so, she would pull back the hammer of her handgun and check the bullets, as if they might have magically discharged. Well, why not? It would fit with the other strange experiences.

Finally, Matthew caught sight of a raspberry bush. He beckoned the other two over. Matthew and Robin plucked the ripe berries and placed them in one of the plastic bags.

Ulrich surveyed the area. *"I'll keep a lookout."*

"What the…" Robin exclaimed. "Who said that?"

The group didn't spend much time in the presence of outsiders. Matthew had forgotten what was normal and what was not, what needed explanation and nerve-settling.

Ulrich grinned sheepishly. *"I did."*

"You can communicate telepathically?" Robin checked out his furry head and alert ears.

"Correct. When I choose to," Ulrich said.

"Wow. A fox that can communicate with humans," Robin said, regaining her composure and gathering more raspberries.

"You'd be surprised how many animals can communicate, if you take the time to listen," Ulrich said. *"I met a very nice spider the other day—"*

"A spider?" Robin laughed.

Ulrich bristled. *"Indeed."*

Matthew chuckled, licking the juice on his hands. As his eyes traced a particularly large drop traversing the back of his hand, he realized his mistake. The trail of the juice was black. He spat, once, twice, three times. He grabbed the water canteen from Robin and emptied it into his mouth, swirling and spitting, swirling and spitting. Would it be like a snake bite where he could suck out the venom?

"What's wrong?" Robin asked.

Matthew looked at the bag in his hand. How had he not noticed it before? Black veins lined each berry. Matthew pointed. Robin shuddered. Ulrich nibbled away a small branch from the bush and held it up for examination. Each berry, each leaf, each segmented twig was lined and coated in thin black moss.

He dropped the plastic bag.

"We're going to starve," Robin said.

Something shifted within the bush. The black deepened and moved.

Matthew slid his hand to the knife. Robin brought her gun up. It seemed to happen in slow motion. One minute the berries had seemed fine and ripe and juicy, and the next they were lined with shifting blackness. Now the shifting blackness formed into something else and stretched toward them.

A black head rose from the bush. Black eyelids opened to reveal eyes of glowing coal. Matthew raised the knife. A black torso emerged. He brought the blade down. Then twisted his wrist and sliced. Robin pulled the trigger. A hole appeared in the middle of the black forehead. But it continued to rise, gathering mass from the blackness coating the bush, the veins that snaked across the forest floor, and God knew where else the network extended. Matthew slashed a deep gash across its neck, expecting some sort of weird blood to flow. But no cascade of bodily fluids occurred. The black moss from its torso simply rose up and took its place, filling in the gap. Alarmingly quickly.

Robin fired a second time. One dark pupil exploded. A third shot blew out the other. Matthew sliced again, this time dismembering an arm. But the stump began to regrow. Ulrich yowled. Then bit and chomped at the advancing moss man.

"Run," Robin said, as she fired a fourth shot.

Matthew didn't need to be told twice. They turned and fled from the raspberry bush that housed a terrible black moss man. Robin fired shots behind as they ran.

With the knife still in his right hand and his arms pumping, Matthew ran. He could feel Ulrich at his heels, could hear Robin's breath as she turned and fired.

"Got it!" she yelled.

Matthew risked a glance behind in time to see the black moss man explode in a thousand directions.

"They're getting harder to kill," Robin said, as they slowed to a jog. She held the gun by her side, finger resting on the trigger.

Matthew threw another look behind them. The black moss resembled the splattered blood at a violent crime scene; sprayed all over the raspberry bush and nearby trees. But he didn't think it would stay inert for long.

Ulrich raised his snout and sniffed the air.

"We need to get back to the others, we need to move," Matthew said.

"Others?" Robin questioned.

"Luna, Monty," Matthew replied.

"Who's Monty?"

Matthew almost stumbled over his own boots. "Monty? Your brother?"

"Oh, of course," Robin said. Matthew's stomach turned to rock, like before a meet when he was trying to deal with his nerves. Something was wrong. Like in the cabin when the shaking happened and he couldn't think straight.

Ulrich sat on the ground. His snout twitched.

"What do you smell?" Robin asked him.

"*Food*," Ulrich replied.

"We need food," Robin said, reloading her handgun.

His instincts told him to return to the cabin. But he couldn't let the others starve. "Okay, Ulrich, lead the way."

They picked up their pace, trying to keep up with the fox, zigging and zagging among the trees. Looking for the black moss men as they ran. Matthew prayed Robin's gun wouldn't go off accidentally.

As Matthew's lungs seized and lactic acid burned in his calves, Ulrich stopped running. He dropped down to his belly and narrowed his eyes. Matthew dived behind a nearby bush, pulling Robin with him, understanding they were close to their prey and their human presence could ruin the whole take down.

Matthew placed his finger across his lips as Robin began to question him. She squatted next to him and caught her breath. While they waited, she smoothed stray strands of hair away from her face, tucking them back into her ponytail and then readied her gun.

Ulrich inched forward on his belly, keeping his head low, his snout twitching. Occasionally he would shift his position and move in a new angle.

Matthew heard it before he saw it. A rustle of bushes made by something stronger than the wind. Something approaching. The ground started to rumble. Matthew put a hand on the ground to steady his squatted position. Loose grains of dirt leapt an inch or so into the air. Whatever Ulrich had smelled, it was big. Maybe another boar.

Ulrich's tongue swept around his snout in preparation for the ambush. Matthew spotted it. A doe. Running for its life, its eyes wide with terror, stumbling over bushes, the most inelegant sample of the species he'd ever seen. Ulrich prepared to leap. The trembling ground increased, shaking them onto their butts. Matthew frowned. Then he saw it. But it was too late.

CHAPTER 24
MATTHEW

IN A TWISTING DISPLAY of strength and muscle, Ulrich leaped at the deer. But another flash of stealthy movement pulled Matthew's attention. A beast, closing in on both the deer and Ulrich, legs pummeling the ground as it ran, about to make its play.

Matthew crept around the bush, wanting to flee, knowing he couldn't leave his friend. "Robin!" he cried. "Get ready!"

The knife felt like a toy against the beast thundering at them. Lion-like. No. Bigger. Much, much bigger. Like an elephant. Larger than the dead one they'd found by the stream. Larger still than the one that had almost killed Kerry. And while it was the size of an elephant, it had the agility of a cat. Its fur was jet black, its snout canine, housing hundreds of needle-thin and wickedly sharp teeth, with two protruding fangs similar to an extinct Sabretooth. It wore a shaggy mane around its neck, like a male lion, which, as it neared, Matthew could tell was matted with dried blood.

"Ulrich!" Matthew screamed. Ulrich and the deer were on a trajectory for collision, but the beast stormed from behind.

Ulrich leaped into the air, his jaws open, his eyes focused on the deer.

The deer mimicked Ulrich's jump from the other direction, with much more elegance and precision, twisting its body away. But it was out of maneuvering room.

The beast crouched, readying itself, and sprang. An inhuman machine of power and sharp instruments. Its fiery eyes set on twin objects of prey.

"Ulrich!" Matthew screamed, squeezing the hilt of the knife, preparing himself to dash into the fray. Robin rolled over her shoulder, came up on one knee with the handgun held in two hands. She closed one eye.

Ulrich and the deer collided in the air. Matthew flinched. Ulrich clamped his jaw on the deer's flank. The deer tried to twist and wrench out of his grip. As they started to descend, the beast barreled into them. The deer catapulted over the beast's back. The impact flung Ulrich higher, above the tree line. As he came down, silently, Matthew noted the white fur on his left side was now red.

With blood-red fangs, the beast reared back and readied itself for another charge. It watched the tumbling fox.

Matthew fell to his knees, momentarily defeated. The crack of Robin's gun spurred him back to his feet and lifted the fog from his devastated vision.

Within seconds, Robin emptied her clip into the beast's flank. It didn't move. It didn't die. It didn't seem to flinch. It stood only a few yards away, alive and blinking. Ulrich landed on the ground with a heavy *thump*. He didn't move or make another sound.

"Shit." Robin fumbled for a new clip in her pocket.

The beast turned and pierced Matthew with its fiery eyes. Right from the core of whatever he was made from.

Take care of them, Matthew.

Ulrich.

"Robin." He raised a hand, cautionary, and took a slow step backward.

"Almost there," she said, her attention on her gun.

The beast snorted like a vexed bull who'd been foiled at a rodeo. It pawed the ground, then twisted its head to examine them. Without warning, it launched a second attack.

"Robin!" Matthew yelled. He grabbed her shoulder, hoisting her to her feet, backward, stumbling backward. But not fast enough. The beast snorted, and its hot breath swept over Matthew's face like the fiery winds of Hell. The hardness of the knife in his palm reminded him he had a chance.

The beast looked at him squarely. The smell of copper and blood permeated the air. He released Robin's shoulder and pushed her out of the way. The beast advanced. Almost upon them. It was no wild boar.

Adrenaline surged through Matthew. He ran at the beast, a suicide mission, but hoping he might get lucky. The beast's fangs were at eye level. Red and glistening. Matthew jumped. He raised the knife high, aiming at those fiery eye sockets, hoping it would lead to the creature's brain.

He didn't hear the shots, but he felt the bullets whizz by his cheek and ear. As he descended on the downward arc, he struggled to get the knife in the right position for one of those lava-like eyes. He didn't have much time to recalculate before he'd be torn in two by its enormous tusks.

The first bullet pierced between its eyes. The second glanced off the beast's fang, chipping it. The third grazed

Matthew's ear. Before the fourth bullet found a mark, Matthew landed on the beast's head, driving the knife into its skull. The impact made little damage, but it gave Matthew something to hold onto while the animal tried to shake him off. A rodeo show gone wrong. Very wrong.

Bullet number four slammed straight into one of the fiery pupils and bullet number five ended up in the beast's hind flank. They did nothing to stop the beast, who shook his body like a wet dog in an attempt to rid himself of a troublesome Matthew.

Matthew grabbed a fistful of mane and squeezed his legs around the creature's neck. He held onto the knife while the creature shook and bucked. It smelt awful. Of blood and death and everything wrong with the world. He held his breath and pulled the knife from the beast's head, releasing a satisfying stream of blood. So, it did bleed. It could be killed.

Bullet six disappeared somewhere in the beast's mane, and bullet seven passed by Matthew's right calf in a flame of heat and found purchase in the beast's belly.

Matthew took a breath and drove the knife into the beast's neck. Most animals were vulnerable there. Maybe this abomination of nature was too. He jammed the blade to the hilt, and then some, pressing with both hands until they were covered with thick, warm blood. Bullet eight slammed into the beast's shoulder.

Everything went silent. Robin was out of bullets. The beast had yet to react to its new porous status. Blood spilled, painting the ground.

As Matthew gripped the hilt, a great trembling rose from the soles of his feet, all the way up his squeezing legs. At first, he thought it was his own panicked heartbeat. But then the beast raised its head, opened its mouth, and let forth a tremendous roar. Much more than a roar, but Matthew could think of nothing else in nature to compare it to. He thought of all fearsome creatures; dragons, lions, elephants, bears, howler monkeys and even gorillas. This roar was different. Or perhaps some combination of all these. But most bizarre was the human quality. The beast's roar portrayed anger, fear, and pain.

The sound cut off. The neck wound leaked around his hands, faster than a pressured shower. The beast collapsed to its knees. Robin's gun was reloaded and ready. Liquid lava fell from the creature's eyes, igniting stray pine needles on the floor before snuffing out. The beast rolled to its side. Matthew jumped to the ground, just before his leg would have been crushed.

The creature slammed into the ground, shaking a thousand insects into the air. The beast's eyes dimmed, the liquid pools of fire turning the color of coal, then ash, until finally, they were lifeless and not nearly as terrifying.

"I thought we were goners," Robin said.

"Me too." Matthew reached up and over the beast, felt for his knife, and yanked it out. A new stream of blood gurgled into its fur. "We need to find Ulrich." He wiped the sweat from his brow with the sleeve of his shirt.

It didn't take long. The battle had commenced in tight quarters. Ulrich had been flung up, not away. The fox lay crumpled by the spiny trunk of a silver birch. It looked as though he was just resting. But there was no breath. No rise and fall of his ribs. No flicker of whiskers along his snout. Matthew turned him over. A deep wound revealed the truth.

"Shit." Jasmine was going to kill him.

"It's not your fault," Robin said. A gentle hand found his

shoulder. He liked the feel of it. But he didn't deserve sympathy and her touch began to burn. A terrible taste flooded his mouth. Like fresh blood. Coppery. A pool of nausea in his stomach threatened his clenched teeth. He closed his eyes and sucked in a few shuddery breaths. "Really. It's not your fault."

"I promised no more death," Matthew said.

Robin's lips twisted with exaggerated patience. "Matthew, that's not a promise you can make."

With a heavy heart, Matthew stood. He punched the tree, but it only succeeded in opening his barely-healed wound. But for a second, it was all he could feel, and that release from guilt and shame and responsibility brought him a moment of reprieve. It didn't last as he stared down at Ulrich's body.

"I never asked to be in charge," Matthew said. In speaking those words aloud, he finally admitted that he was. "I don't know why everyone looks to me."

Take care of them, Matthew.

"Don't you?" Robin asked. They'd only just met, but looking into her eyes, Matthew could swear she had all the answers. That she knew something about him, about all of them, that he hadn't yet figured out for himself.

Matthew shook his head. She took his hand and led him away from Ulrich's dead body.

"Because Luna wanted you to," she said, as if it was the most obvious answer.

Matthew sighed. "But I couldn't do it without Alessandra. Faith. She's tough. And even Tyler, I didn't like him much, but he was useful."

"You're a team," Robin said. "Together, you are one."

Matthew nodded. "We are. Which is why it's so hard, when one of us...*dies*. And I know they all blame me. They think

I'm capable of more than I am. I keep letting them down. Did you hear what Hope said..."

"So let them down. Walk away. You don't have to stay with them. You don't owe them anything."

Matthew looked at his worn boots. A hole on the side of the seam revealed his dingy sock. His left foot was still damp. "I could never do that. I could never...No....no...I *can't*."

"*Shhh*." Robin placed a hand on his cheek, stroking gently. "You don't need to carry the whole world on your shoulders."

"I can't do it on my own. I can't keep everyone safe. I..I... just want..." but Matthew didn't know what he wanted. For Luna to wake up. For her to love him back. For everyone to just fuck off and leave him alone. To be alone. How he craved to be alone sometimes.

"*Shhh*." Robin continued to stroke his face. She followed the path of his eyebrows, the stubble on his jaw. She even pulled on the lobes of his ears. It felt...nice.

"Meeting you and Monty was great, I mean, the weapons. We needed that. But I don't know how far away we are now, I don't even know where the cabin is. Ulrich was going to lead us back. And Kerry just keeps popping up when it suits him, and I just have no fucking idea anymore. I'm done. Expectation level reset to zero. Done. Done with demands." He wiped at the blood on his knuckles. They were beginning to swell. Funny. He couldn't feel the pain anymore.

"That's right," Robin cooed. "Get it all out."

She raised herself to tiptoes and pressed her lips against his.

Matthew startled. "I can't..."

Robin looked at him with big brown eyes. "You can't...what?"

"Luna…"

"Luna isn't here." Robin touched his hand, her fingertips playing over his skin. It felt…wonderful.

"You don't understand, I love Luna." He blushed, not because he was afraid to admit it, but because it was a dead end. Would he always be trapped in his love for Luna?

Robin cupped his cheek. "And where is she right now?"

Stepping away, Matthew shook his head. "It's not her fault. You don't understand. You're new. You don't know how it works yet. We're supposed to protect her, not—"

"That's not why I'm here," Robin said. "I'm here for *you*."

Matthew's thoughts cycled. What the hell was she talking about? "You don't understand—"

"I wouldn't be here if Luna didn't want you to be happy."

His head ached as he struggled through his convoluted thoughts. "I don't know what you're talking about."

Robin stepped away, tightened her jacket. "Maybe it's too soon." A fragile smile wobbled on her enticing lips. "Always coming second, aren't you?"

Matthew shrugged. "She's my best friend."

"So, are ye going to bring this tender venison back to the group, or what?" Kerry spoke from the trees. The carcass of the deer was draped over his shoulders.

Robin cocked an eyebrow.

"Robin, meet Kerry – one of the less likeable characters of our group. Kerry, meet Robin – she saved us from trouble with a capital T."

"Ye have very little threshold, Matthew." Kerry approached and turned to Robin. "Pleased to meet you." He held out a hand awkwardly from beneath the legs of the dead deer. After a moment's hesitation, Robin shook it.

Kerry picked his way around the dead beast. "Looks like something fell out o' the ugly tree." He gave the creature a sidelong glance. "Mighty happy to see me knife is useful. Everything is grand now, so it is." He marched around the beast, shifting the deer on his shoulders.

"You know where you're going?" Matthew asked, jogging to catch up.

Kerry grinned. A sly grin. He knew Matthew needed him. "That way." He pointed.

Before they left, Matthew picked up Ulrich's limp body and made a shallow grave. Robin helped cover him over. *Take care of them, Matthew.*

When he finished, he stood and rested his hands on his thighs. Exhaustion had crept into his muscles. He ached everywhere. "Lead the way." Matthew sighed, relenting to having Kerry in his life for the next few hours.

He and Robin walked a little ways behind Kerry. Not long into the journey, Kerry started talking. "What were you two blatherin' about under the trees anyway?"

"None of your business," Matthew snapped.

"Aye, well, keep your hair on."

"Ignore him," Robin said. "He's only trying to get a rise out of you."

"Yeah, well, he does it really well," Matthew muttered.

Matthew plucked a few twigs from the ground, a handful of ferns, to make a stick doll for Jasmine. Not that it was going to numb her pain, but it was the least he could do. His ruined fingers proved useless at winding the stems around the twigs, let alone turning the thing into a vaguely humanoid shape. *I tried.* He shoved the whole mess into his pocket.

CHAPTER 25
MATTHEW

Forty-five minutes later Kerry released the deer from his shoulders, letting it fall in front of the rotting porch. "There ye go." He wiped his hands together, as if his part was finished. It probably was.

The 'thank you' died in the back of Matthew's throat.

"I'll do it," Robin said, kneeling by the deer and holding out her hand for the knife. Matthew handed it to her. Kerry nodded, as if a debate had already been settled, then disappeared back into the trees. It was probably better that way. Matthew pushed through the broken front door. Through the window he spotted Monty outside, still hiding behind trees.

"Where is everyone?" he asked Alessandra. She held an old metal cup to Luna's lips, who sipped willingly. They were the only two in the room.

"Hope, Faith, and Jasmine found a small lake. They're swimming," Alessandra replied. "Did you find food?"

Matthew nodded. "A deer. Robin's dealing with it now. But Ulrich…" He shook his head, he couldn't speak. It would be too final.

Alessandra's gaze slipped to her lap. She inspected her fingernails.

"Don't you have anything to say?" Matthew asked, bracing himself for accusations.

"What would you like me to say?" Her eyes lifted but didn't quite meet his.

What else *was* there to say? Ulrich was gone. "Don't you want to know how it happened?"

Alessandra shook her head. "I assume it was violent. So, no. I don't want to know how it happened."

They seemed to have nothing else to talk about, so Matthew switched his gaze to Luna. Color bloomed in her cheeks, and the roots of her hair were no longer damp with fever. She looked better. But also the same. That same blank stare. Hollow. Empty. As if she was just a husk.

Come on, Luna.

Robin came inside with an armful of raw meat and put it on the stove.

"I'll get the others," Matthew said, pushing out the back door. It fell off its hinges. He picked it up and leaned it against the wall.

He heard them before he saw them. And froze. They were laughing. The sound almost brought a smile to his lips. Then he remembered what he had to tell Jasmine.

He walked on to the lake. It was a mercifully clear lake, seemingly devoid of any black entities. Not large, maybe fifty yards across. Enough to have some fun. Hope, Faith, and Jasmine swam near the middle, spraying water at each other. Ariel sat on the bank, watching. Matthew thought he detected the odd glimmer of Beacon's light, but it was hard to tell during the day.

He sat next to Ariel and watched the others play. He glanced at the angel. Her angular chin rested in her hands, and a wistful smile played across her lips as the others splashed and yelled. She was at peace. With everything. How could she be?

"What is it, Matthew?" she asked, perhaps sensing the emotions boiling under the surface of his tightly held constraint.

He kept his voice low. "Ulrich is dead."

Her pupils and skin dimmed. "Jasmine will be sad."

"*Jasmine will be sad*? Is that all you can say?"

Ariel faced him. "Are we going to have the conversation now, Matthew?"

"What conversation?" He couldn't keep the petulant whine out of his voice.

"The one where you question God's plan and I tell you it's not for us to question him."

"God's plan?" Matthew spluttered. "Does He have one? Because right now it doesn't seem like it. Unless it involves killing us all off."

Ariel smiled, as if he were a young child after having a toy snatched away. "Of course he has a plan."

Matthew waited for the explanation. The magic word or phrase that would connect the dots, fill in the blanks, and enlighten him. But Ariel offered nothing else.

"Would you care to tell me what it is?"

"I don't know what His plan is," Ariel said. "Only that there is one. There's a bigger picture. There's always a bigger picture, and sometimes we get caught up in the details."

"What details?" Matthew's jaw tightened and tension gripped his limbs like a coiled snake. "Like surviving? Finding food? Water? Trying to stay alive? Are those just 'details?' How does that help the ones who've died?"

"The ones who've died don't mind," Ariel said, waving at Jasmine as she swam toward them. "They're at peace now."

"I think they minded when they were dying," Matthew said. "I just don't get how your God can do this to us."

"*Our* God, Matthew. *Our* God."

Hope glanced at Matthew, her face an open question mark, her hand rubbing her stomach, signaling she was starving. He offered her a thumbs up.

"Matthew," Ariel said. "Maybe it has nothing to do with God."

"That's what I mean," he replied. "There is no God. No greater plan. No…*help*. And don't give me that 'those who help themselves' bullshit." He frowned, then pushed himself to his feet and waited to greet the others as they swam to shore. Ariel didn't reply to his comments, and he had the sense he'd missed her point entirely. "Do you know?" He turned back to her, a fragment of an idea forming in the back of his mind. He tried to pull on it, but it was delicate and wouldn't reveal itself. Before the fire, his thoughts were much clearer. Now, everything was muddled.

"I know everything," Ariel said. Her pupils bright, her smile half-hearted.

"Then you *know*." Matthew pulled at the elusive knowledge in his mind. But to be honest, he wasn't entirely sure what it was she knew. Did he know?

"Take care of Luna," Ariel said. *Take care of Luna*. Wasn't that what he was doing? She was his best friend. Of course he'd take care of her.

"I found food," Matthew said as Faith and Jasmine clambered onto the small sandy beach. Hope remained, sloshing through the shallows. For a moment he felt like an ancient warrior come home to feed his starving tribe. And all warriors lost men along the way. It was normal. Sad, but normal. Except there was nothing normal about their situation.

Jasmine swiveled her eyes to him. She was looking for Ulrich. He kept his face a mask, giving no indication as to the fox's fate. He found the mess of the stick doll inside his pocket. It would never be enough.

"Bacon?" Faith asked hopefully.

"Even better," Matthew called. "Venison."

Faith stretched and shook out her hair. "You should jump in. It's so nice. Refreshing."

"Another time." Matthew looked at his bloody hands. He walked to the edge of the lake and took a knee, splashing water over his hands.

"I'm starving," Faith said.

"I've never had venison before," Jasmine said, wringing out her hair.

"Me neither, but right now I could eat my own arm off," Faith replied.

Grinning, Hope kicked water at them, then splashed away. The medallion swung low around her neck. It had failed both Kalisa and Caleb. But maybe it would save the rest of them.

Matthew was gentle with his right hand, where he'd reopened his wound. It stung like a bitch when he submerged it. But at least it would be clean. As he watched his family enjoy themselves around the lake, he could almost believe they'd just headed into the woods for a picnic and there'd never been a fire. Luna. He looked back at the cabin. He could just make out the edges of it.

"Matthew...?" Hope's voice pulled him out of his thoughts. She stared at her submerged legs, blinking rapidly, her mouth forming a perfect little 'o'. She stood in water that came past her hips.

"What's wrong?"

"Something's holding my ankles." Her voice remained calm, but tremors shook her body.

Matthew popped to his feet. "Don't move."

Matthew and Ariel leaped at the same time. Ariel wasn't close enough and Matthew felt Hope's wispy hair slip through his fingers. She wobbled, slipped, and her head went under. A raven cawed.

"Shit!" Matthew charged into the water.

The water turned dark and murky. The shallows were full of reeds and the sun chose that moment to disappear behind a cloud. Matthew felt around blindly.

Jasmine dashed past him. She dove into the water, closer to the center. Matthew took a couple of steps after her. Maybe she'd seen Hope. Then Beacon was in the water too. He could see her light better in the dark water. The two of them swam to the middle. Freestyle. Matthew stood in water up to his shoulders. Waiting, still searching with his hands in case Hope was nearby, separating weeds with a fevered despair, hoping the next soft thing his hand brushed against would be Hope's hair.

Jasmine dove deep, her toes the last to disappear. Beacon dove with her and illuminated her path.

"There! She's there!" Faith shouted from the shore.

Matthew caught sight of Hope's head, rising from the depths. Her head popped above the surface, followed by Jasmine's and Beacon's. Matthew's limbs loosened with relief. Hope cried as soon as she gasped a breath of air.

"Thank God!" Faith exclaimed.

Jasmine smiled, punching the air. She was only eight. But she was a hero. Abruptly, the smile fell from her lips. Black liquid leaked out of her nose. Then her eyes, her ears, darkening her light-brown skin. Then she was yanked under the surface.

"Jasmine!" Mathew yelled, charging until the cold water reached his chin. A current tugged at his ankles. In a lake? He took a step backward. Something tried to drag him under, pulling at his ankles, working their way up his legs, the back of his knees, growing in force and insistence.

Beacon dove after Jasmine. Matthew followed Beacon's progress. Jasmine struggled for the surface, bubbles erupting from her nose and mouth, panic twisting her face. She kicked out below, fighting something. Something dark and black that Matthew couldn't determine the shape of. Until Beacon reached Jasmine. Then he saw the black moss man. More than one. Several. An armies' worth. All holding onto Jasmine's ankles, pulling her down. He remembered Monty saying they could calcify and become water resistant.

"Matthew! Do something!" Faith screamed.

Do something. Do something. What?

The force pulled roughly at his own ankles. It took everything he had just to stay upright. He scrambled backward, holding on to the reeds to pull himself out of their clutches. Once he had scrambled ashore, he turned back to the center of the lake. Hope splashed toward him and he pushed her up the bank, away from the grabbing black hands.

Beacon was half light and half dark. The black moss wrapped itself around her torso, flooded her mouth and nose. She bucked and writhed, but couldn't wrestle free.

Matthew closed his eyes. He didn't want to see this. Then Faith scampered to his side, holding on to him, squeezing his arm tight with digging fingernails. He forced his eyes open.

Beacon's light dimmed in the way night swallows the sun, fast and sudden. Jasmine stilled, a floating statue haloed by a crown of undulating hair. Legs that would never kick again, arms that would never mold a stick doll. The bubbles no longer streamed from her nose and mouth. She was motionless, but still the black moss men didn't release her. Beacon's light dimmed to the wattage of a match, then went out altogether.

Matthew couldn't see either of them now. Just the surface of the calm, blue lake.

"No," Faith shouted. "No, no, no. *Noooo.*"

Hope collapsed on the bank. Dripping wet, she didn't wipe the streaming water from her face. She sat and stared at the lake. Her entire body shook. Matthew feared she would shake herself apart. He put his arm around her and drew her to his side.

CHAPTER 26
MATTHEW

Jasmine and Beacon were gone. There was nothing Matthew could have done.

Take care of them. Matthew.

How? How was he supposed to defend his family against supernatural beasts intent on killing them all? How?

"*Nooooo.*" Faith's yelling dulled to a low whimpering. She squatted on the ground, her arms wrapped around herself.

Hope wrestled free of Matthew's grip and sprinted in the direction of the cabin.

"Ariel, can you go after her?" Matthew asked.

Ariel didn't move. She sat on the ground in her white clothes that were now brown with dirt. Her legs splayed and her chin dipped, like an inanimate doll, she seemed incapable of moving. Her feet met the edge of the water. Even her halo refused to shine. "And move your feet."

"No, no, no, no, *nooooo,*" Faith whimpered. She fell onto her side and curled up into the fetal position.

"Ariel?" Matthew questioned, taking a couple of steps

closer. "Is this God's bigger picture?" She had the good sense to look guilty. But she didn't respond. Didn't even meet his gaze.

"That's mighty bad luck, so it is," Kerry said. "At least ye don't have to tell Jasmine about Ulrich."

Matthew braced himself against the voice. Kerry sucked on a cigarette. He raised his chin and exhaled the smoke skywards, the sun beating down on him like a physical force.

"You. Fucking. Dick." Matthew charged. "The others might think we need you, but Kerry, just go fuck off and die." He slammed his fist into Kerry's face, hopefully giving him another black eye, not caring that he might permanently damage his already swollen knuckles. He could still run with a damaged hand. Whatever.

Kerry stood there with an insane smile on his face and blood dripping from a fresh cut above his eye. Matthew's satisfaction was short lived. But this wasn't about satisfaction.

"Did you hear me?" Matthew raised his fist for a second go.

"Aye. I reckon I heard ye alright," Kerry replied, taking another drag. Somehow, he'd managed to hold onto the damn cigarette. But now he let it drop and smooshed it out with his boot. "It's just not up to me." He didn't even wipe the blood from his eye.

"I could go and get your knife back from Robin, I'd be happy to put you out of your misery," Matthew yelled, his spittle flying into Kerry's face and mingling with the blood. Kerry didn't wipe that away either. He lit another cigarette, opened his mouth, and roared with laughter.

The anger that raged along his spine was so intense

Matthew didn't think his body would be able to contain it. It snaked through his veins, clenched his chest, and slammed his jaw shut.

A primal scream came from the depths of his soul as he charged at Kerry. He bent, going in low, like a football player, despite never playing a single game of football in his life. At the last moment, he closed his eyes. He planned to drill into the sonofabitch until he was dead.

When Matthew's shoulder slammed into a tree he opened his eyes, rubbing at the piercing pain. Kerry had disappeared. Again. How did he do that?

With no outlet for his anger, he marched back to Faith, plucked her from the ground, hoisted her over his shoulder and carried her to the cabin.

Inside the cabin he plonked Faith down in a chair, told Robin to feed her, and stormed back to the lake to find Ariel. But Matthew couldn't see her anywhere. He couldn't believe she'd moved; she seemed as rooted as the perfectly flawed marble angels on headstones.

Maybe she'd gone to reason with her God, to contemplate her faith. Maybe she'd come back with a more kick-ass attitude. Or maybe she'd climbed up the stairway to Heaven to knock on the pearly white gates and give God a 'what for.' Or she'd come back with answers, a plan, maybe even their dead friends brought back to life, if God was doing what He should be doing and finally proving to the world what He was capable of. No more doubts. No more mystery. Why the mystery? Surely, He'd have a bigger following if He just proved himself. But wasn't that always Ariel's point? And Piper's? They needed to have faith. *Faith*. Like it was a physical thing you could cling to in the dark when the going got tough. Well, he might have a friend called Faith, but his *faith* was dwindling.

With his hands on his hips, he frowned, scanning the woods for Ariel. They didn't have time to wait. The black moss men might rise out of the water. They needed to eat and go. Ariel would be with them, or she wouldn't. God would look after her. Or he wouldn't.

While he was out there, alone, he took a moment. If Kerry came back he would kill him. It didn't matter anymore that Luna had chosen him to be a part of their group. Sometimes Luna made bad choices.

Kerry didn't fit in and was pissing everyone off. But for now, he needed to expel the anger. How do you expel anger? How do you wake up your best friend? How do you make her safe? Protect her? Make her love you the way you love her? Matthew didn't have the answers. All he could do was keep on going. Grandmother's house. Save Luna. Both directives were beginning to slip away. Did it even matter anymore?

Matthew's stomach growled as he walked back to the cabin, the scent of the venison reaching him. He fingered the primitive stickman in his pocket and threw the mess of twigs in the stove. There was no use for it now.

Robin handed him a plateful of meat, which he devoured with two fingers in seconds. "She won't eat." She nodded to Faith.

Faith hadn't moved from her precarious position half draped across a rickety wooden chair. Her body spilling out of it as if devoid of bones. He walked behind her and heaved her into a more normal position, then kneeled before her.

"*Noooo,*" she continued to whimper. She wrapped her arms

so tightly around her waist she left marks. Gently, Matthew took her hands in his. She glanced at him, not seeing. Matthew held his breath, thinking they might have another Luna on their hands, but Faith finally locked eyes with him.

"You need to eat, Faith." He offered her a piece of meat. "Luna's eating. She would want you to eat."

Faith frowned. But at least she stopped saying; "*Nooooo*."

"Faith, we have to go soon. The moss men..." he trailed off. She didn't need to be reminded of what had just happened at the lake.

"I'll just stay here," she whispered.

"You can't stay here," Matthew said. Robin handed him another plateful of food. He ate a sliver and held another out for Faith.

"Operation *Save Luna*. Mission Whiskey-Tango-Foxtrot." Monty giggled. He stood on the porch staring through a pair of binoculars.

"Faith?" Matthew questioned. She took the meat, but didn't put it in her mouth. Matthew glanced at Alessandra. She held a morsel of meat to Luna's mouth.

"I don't want to go out there. Bad things happen out there," Faith said, ignoring the drips of fat landing on her knee.

"You can't stay here on your own, we need to stick togeth-er," Matthew said, echoing the conversation he'd had with Alessandra. It felt like a lifetime ago instead of last night. When he'd nearly felt like giving up too. That feeling still sat inside, close and heavy. But now, the balance had shifted, they'd lost too much not to carry on.

"Why not?"

Why not? Indeed, Matthew had asked himself that same

question. "Because we need to save Luna. And we can't do it without you."

Faith's frown deepened. She glanced from the meat in her hand to Matthew's face. She shook her head. "Luna doesn't need me."

"*I* need you."

A ghost of a smile. Then the frown again.

"You're stronger than me," Faith said. "You can do it without me."

He was out of words. He leaned his head against her knees. He couldn't do it without her, she was wrong about that.

"Faith, I need you to help me with Hope," he said, when he leaned back on his heels. "She's fragile. She needs you."

A flicker of response behind her dimmed pupils.

"I can't deal with any more death." She watched the straight line of Robin's back where she stood on the porch.

"Neither can I." This time he didn't make any promises. He wasn't that foolish anymore.

"So, I think I'll just stay here," she said, sliding the piece of meat between her lips.

Matthew stood and paced the few steps to the porch. He took a gulp of water from the canteen Robin offered. "She won't come."

Robin shrugged. "You can't force her. If she wants to stay, let her stay."

Monty soldier-crawled on the ground in front of the porch, looking through his binoculars.

"That's not how we work," Matthew said. He scanned the trees for danger. "Don't you see? We help each other."

"There are different ways of helping each other," Robin

replied. "Maybe you need to change the way you're looking at the situation."

"Change the way I'm looking at the situation?" Matthew questioned. "I want to save Luna and I don't want anyone else to die. Is there any other way to look at it?" The anger hovered beneath the surface, thickening his throat.

"Matthew, you can't take responsibility for everyone. You just can't."

"Faith is in shock. She's not capable of making the right decision. And what a friend does, a good friend, is help her make the right one."

"For you," Robin said. "Faith coming is the right decision *for you*."

"I can't leave her alone to die at the hands of the moss men, or the lurchers, or whatever it is you call them! That's insane."

"She's more capable than you think."

"I know she's capable!" Matthew threw his hands in the air. His swollen knuckles ached. "But we're a team. We stick together."

"You may not have a choice," Robin said.

"That's what I'm afraid of." He let his hands rest on the rickety handrail that lined the porch. "What would you do if Monty wanted to stay? Or if his mission Whiskey-Tango-Foxtrot took him off in a new direction?"

"Monty's different. You know that," she replied. "We came to help you, Matthew. I can give you advice. I can be there for you. That's all I can do. But to answer your question, I could never leave my brother."

"And I'd never leave Faith." He pivoted on his heel and stomped into the house to work on her again.

"We need to go," Alessandra said. "Luna's eaten. If we want to put any kind of distance between this cabin and us before nightfall, we need to go." She stood and shook out her skirts.

Matthew checked his watch. It was already after 3pm. That gave them about five hours of daylight left. But he had to convince Faith first. Which, by the look of her slumped in the wooden chair, was going to be no easy task.

"Or we wait until morning," Matthew said.

Alessandra's eyes flicked to the back door as if the moss men might storm the cabin right this minute.

"We have shelter here."

"We lost three today," Alessandra said.

Four, if Ariel didn't come back. Five, if Kerry didn't come back. Matthew prayed for the latter.

"I'm not leaving without Faith," he said.

"I'm not suggesting we do," Alessandra said. "I'm on your side, Matthew. We're all on the same side."

Matthew's shoulders sagged. "It doesn't feel like it lately."

"I know. But we're still a family."

"Even Kerry?" Matthew asked, feeling a wave of guilt about wanting to murder him. Not much had changed.

"I know you and Kerry don't always see eye to eye—"

Matthew snorted.

Alessandra raised a placating hand. "But he serves a purpose."

"Which is?" Matthew asked.

"To help Luna take risks. So she doesn't bottle everything up. He encourages her to be more daring."

"Reckless, you mean," Matthew said.

"Call it what you will, but since he's been in her life, she's become freer, more open about her past. For a while, before the fire, I thought she was going to open up to everyone about her mother."

"You knew?" Matthew said.

Alessandra pulled at one of her hoop earrings. "I've always known."

Matthew's head jerked and his hand flew to his chest. He'd thought he was the only one Luna had confided in. Because he'd known her the longest. Because he was her best friend, and she his. Because they told each other their secrets, and no one else. As he stood there looking at Luna sitting on the bed, the axis of his world shifted. Everything he thought he knew was different, altered, tainted. Did Luna not care for him as deeply as he cared for her? Well, he knew the answer, the unrequited kiss was a big, fat, neon sign. And why couldn't she confide in the others? Why did it have to be their secret? They were all a family, after all. And Alessandra was older, maternal. Of course Luna would seek her confidence. But the knowledge that he was not as special to her, that their most intimate conversations had not been held as tenderly by her as by him, hurt. A lot.

"You could have helped her with all of that." Matthew could hear the whine in his voice, accusing. It made him cringe.

She cocked her head. "You're her oldest friend."

"Friend," Matthew muttered.

They looked at Luna. Inert. Motionless. Wide eyes locked on folded hands, not seeing, not hearing, just being, but barely. What was it going to take to wake her? For her to come back? Kerry may have released her from some shackled burden Matthew hadn't been aware of, but what was he doing now?

Disappearing. *Not* helping. Making outrageous remarks that angered the group. No, he would never understand Kerry's existence in their group.

"If we're going to stay here another night, we need to make the cabin safe," Alessandra said.

Matthew nodded. He started a search of the rickety kitchen drawers for tools, carrying around his new hurt as a hard ball in his chest, trying not to feel it, thinking avoidance might be a good strategy. But how do you swallow when there's a lump in your throat? How do you eat when your stomach is an acidic cesspit of emotion?

He opened and slammed drawers, scoring himself a few splinters, breaking a few flimsy panels, wondering how to fit this altered image of himself into his plans for the future, and how it might affect his relationship with Luna. Mostly, wondering how she saw him, but not wanting to dwell on it, because he suspected it wasn't how he wanted to be seen. Then back to avoidance and teeth gritting. Around and around he went. The tension coiled so tightly around his body that the old wound between his shoulders pulsed, and the scrapes on his knuckles throbbed with his heartbeat.

As luck would have it he found a hammer and a few rusty four-inch nails. He decided to fix the back door first. When he stepped out onto the porch, he found Hope huddled by the corner of the cabin holding onto one of the termite-ridden handrail posts for support.

"You okay?"

She shook her head. Tears trailed down her cheeks. "Did you see what happened? Beacon and Jasmine…just gone."

"I know." He crouched beside her. "I know." What else

could he say? "I could use your help fixing the door. We need to spend another night here. Will you help me?"

Hope nodded. He held out a hand and pulled her to her feet. Despite her lithe appearance she had enough strength to hold the door in place while Matthew nailed it shut. It was a futile act. If black moss could find its way into nostrils, ears, and mouths, it would certainly find a pathway through the gaps of a rotted, wooden door. But the illusion of safety was comforting. When they finished fixing the door, they gathered the others inside and did the same with the front.

Sitting around the cabin, dwelling on death, made the day drag on. When the sun lowered its rays into the front window, Matthew had an excuse to shut his eyes and hide from questioning looks.

Monty peered out the window with his binoculars, blocking the last of the light from entering the cabin. "We should leave first thing in the morning, if Operation *Save Luna* and Mission Whiskey-Tango-Foxtrot are to be successful."

"Agreed," Matthew replied. If they survived the night. He held no hope they'd make it through. How quickly Beacon and Jasmine had been sucked under the water. How quickly the struggle had ended. How quickly the cavities in their bodies had filled with black moss. Cavities. What an ugly word. A nerve twitched on his lower lip and a cold sweat formed under his arms.

"You're coming, right, Faith?" Hope asked, breathing heavily. Was she on the verge of a panic attack? "Because I'm not going without you. And neither will Matthew. And if we stay here, we'll die. We'll all die. You don't want that, do you, Faith?"

"You can't put all of that on me," Faith said, accepting another plate of meat from Robin.

"I'm not putting anything on you," Hope replied, taking a moment to breathe through cupped hands. "But I need you. There, I said it. I know we don't have a lot in common, but Goddammit, Faith, I need you."

Faith frowned down her nose. "You don't need me."

Hope took a step forward. "We need each other. No one snaps me out of a panic attack like you. And quite frankly, no one takes you down a peg like me."

Faith chuckled. "Ain't that the truth."

"Please, Faith." Hope tugged on her arm.

"No more death," Faith said.

Matthew opened his eyes when he felt her stare. "I'm not making any promises. There are black moss men out there, intent on killing us. As well as extraordinary beasts with eyes of lava. One killed Ulrich today. No more promises."

Take care of them, Matthew.

Faith clutched her knees to her chest. "I don't want to die."

"Neither do I," Matthew said.

"None of us do." Hope clutched her sketchpad as if it was the last cup of water on earth.

Robin packed the leftover meat into Piper's baggies. "Your chances aren't any better if you stay here."

"Don't you want to dance again?" Matthew asked. He took one of Faith's lacerated feet in both his hands, circled his thumb under the meaty pad of her sole. "You've been practicing so hard for that recital."

Faith's lips curved into a small smile. She shrugged. "My feet are ruined." She inspected them absently, pulling a hangnail from her big toe.

"They'll heal," Matthew said. "Everything heals with time." Well, maybe not everything. But definitely Faith's feet. Maybe even her soul.

"To be honest," Hope leaned on the small, wobbly table, "I've always been a bit jealous of your dancing. The way you can balance en pointe. On one foot. Those pirouettes." She shook her head.

"But you can draw!" Faith exclaimed, pointing at the sketchbook. "I've seen inside."

Hope blanched, then blushed. "There's no keeping secrets in our house is there? I think it's ruined. It got wet in the river..."

"You can get a new one," Faith said. "Hell, I'll buy you a new one with the prize money from the recital."

"So, you're going to dance again?" Matthew said.

"If you can get us out of here." Faith sighed. "It's in my soul."

"I'll do my best," Matthew said.

"You know that means you have to come with us." Hope grinned, flicking her long hair over her shoulder.

Faith swallowed. "Okay."

"That's my girl." Hope chucked Faith on her shoulder, nearly knocking her off the chair. "

"Easy," Faith said, regaining her balance. She placed her feet on the floor, pointing and flexing, exercising her muscle memory, a wistful smile propped on her lips.

"And if everything is okay now," Hope said, "I'm just going to go to the corner and have this panic attack that's been looming."

Faith stood and wrapped Hope in a hug.

"Remember to breathe," Faith said. "Nice and slow."

Hope nodded into her shoulder and they both had a little cry.

"We could use Obsidian about now," Alessandra said.

The last time Matthew had seen him he'd been covered in the black moss.

"Whiskey-Tango-Foxtrot," Monty spoke into his useless walkie. "Enemy spotted."

Matthew rushed to the window. Darkness had descended quickly, and several pairs of glowing eyes shone from the forest. The black moss men. An entire army of them.

CHAPTER 27
MATTHEW

M ATTHEW PEERED THROUGH THE WINDOW, trying to count the moving dark shapes. There were so many pairs of winking, glowing eyes he couldn't keep track.

"What is it?" Robin asked at his shoulder.

"Your lurchers," Matthew replied. "We're surrounded."

"They're not mine, by any means," she said, pulling the elastic out of her ponytail and retying it, tighter, no nonsense. She rifled through her bag and loaded a new clip into her handgun. A loud click clanged as the hammer hit home.

"Can they get in?" Faith asked.

No more lies. He wasn't going to be that person anymore. He wasn't going to make false promises and burden himself with more guilt when the shit went to hell. "I don't know."

Matthew rummaged through drawers, looking for a way to block up the two windows. It was something to do. Then he didn't have to look at the glowing eyes focusing like laser beams on their dilapidated cabin.

When he pulled out the bottom drawer, it fell off its tracks and disintegrated on the floor. But there was a handful of loose nails rolling around. Matthew picked them up and located the hammer and the piece of wood Monty had torn off the wall earlier. He placed the plank diagonally across the broken front window and hammered the nails into it. They only just stuck into the main frame, and it wouldn't hold against any kind of force, but it made everyone feel better.

"What do we do now?" Faith whispered.

"We wait," Matthew replied. "And we sleep, if we can." He sat with his back against the backdoor, hammer in his right hand, knife in his left. Robin echoed his action by sitting against the front door. She thumbed the safety of the gun on and off, on and off, a rhythmic click, a metronome for them to fall asleep to. Monty stayed by the patched window, using the night-vision sight of his rifle to keep an eye on the glowing-eyed moss men. The rest of them huddled around the center of the cabin, around the bed and Luna, using hands and elbows and shoulders as pillows.

Matthew strained to listen. But only the occasional rustle of leaves whispered at them. Crickets chirped their mating calls, unaffected by the presence of the lurking moss men. There was no sound of a raven. He rested his head against the door and closed his eyes. Just a minute of sleep. When he woke, the others lay in various positions, asleep. He'd been asleep much longer than anticipated. Even Monty, who'd finally sat down, had his head on his sister's shoulder.

Matthew did a quick count, making sure they were all there, that none had been abducted during the night. Robin, Monty, Faith, Hope, Alessandra, Luna. *Luna*. Please Luna. And Kerry. Kerry had materialized during the night and snored softly at the foot of Luna's bed. Still no sign of Ariel or Obsidian. That left ten. They'd started with seventeen. Lost nine, gained two. He didn't like those odds.

Matthew stood and walked to the patched window. Against a backdrop of the deepest part of the night, the onyx eyes glowed menacingly. They hadn't moved. They hadn't attacked, but they were still there, an impenetrable wall of shifting blackness. He recalled how difficult it had been for Robin to dispatch the lurcher in the raspberry patch. What if they had grown stronger now?

"What do we do?" Alessandra whispered from behind, resting her chin on his shoulder so she could see through the window too. Daylight smudged the sky and birds called to one another. Matthew heard a raven. Shit.

"We arm ourselves with whatever we've got, and we go," Matthew said. "We don't have enough food and water to wait them out. I think they know that. If we wait too long, we'll be too weak to fight. So, we go, now. And we fight." It wasn't much of a pep talk, but it would have to do.

Alessandra nodded. She went to the others and began to rouse them.

"Kerry," Matthew said, sensing him at his back. "If you're here now, then be of some help. Keep your mouth shut and make yourself useful." He handed him the knife.

Kerry took it and stuck it in his boot. "We're going to fight our way through this blizzard, and take 'em all the way to fart's end."

"Whatever that means," Matthew muttered, then turned to the newest additions of the group. "Robin, Monty, we're going to need you at your best."

Monty offered a salute. "Mission Whiskey-Tango-Foxtrot. Operation *Save Luna* is a go!" He jumped to his feet. From his pack, he pulled an ammo belt and wound it over his shoulder. Robin checked her clip, nodded, and crept to the front door.

Matthew shoved the venison in Piper's bag and placed the strap over his shoulder. They could eat after the fight. Alessandra readied the others. Hope, Faith, Alessandra, and Luna stood in a loose clump behind the door.

"Give me something to fight with," Faith said. "I'm not going out there empty handed."

"You sure?" Matthew asked.

She nodded. Robin handed her the machete which was strapped to her belt. Faith tested the weight of it, swinging it in an arc, making Hope dive for cover.

"Easy with that!" Hope warned.

"That'll do," Faith said, running a finger along the blade and producing a bead of blood.

"Alessandra," Matthew turned to the older woman. "Stay on Luna."

She nodded, her eyes moistening, and squeezed his hand.

"We ready?" Matthew asked. When no one said otherwise, he used the hammer's claw to pry the nails out of the door. After placing the strap of Piper's bag over his head, he pulled the door and dashed out onto the porch. Robin and Monty flanked his sides.

Matthew scanned the woods. The eyes were waiting. Waiting for them to make the first move.

"Maybe they won't attack," Faith said, as she joined him on the porch.

Not likely.

"We need to move, and we need to move fast," Matthew said.

"Do you even know where you're going? Without Ulrich…" Hope said.

"I know." He'd done this route once before. He'd thought about it all last night, planning the path in his head while he'd stared at the glowing eyes. Grandmother's house wasn't much further. If they could just get through the moss men.

"Operation Whiskey-Tango-Foxtrot," Monty said, leaping from the porch.

That small action changed everything. All the moss men blinked as one, as if they were part of a collective mind. They moved. Fast. Hurling themselves over roots and bushes toward the unlikely group of heroes.

"Go!" Matthew yelled, holding his hammer high, reveling in the surge of adrenaline shooting through his limbs. "Go!"

He ran at the moss men. On his left, Robin fired with her two-handed grip, spraying the forest with bullets, scoring hits, but not stalling the progress of the moss men, now only ten yards away. Monty, on his right, gave up on the rifle's sight and fired at will. The vulnerable, the unarmed, cowered at Matthew's back. *Save Luna.* At all costs.

Monty screamed a war cry as he charged alongside Matthew.

Matthew raised his hammer, and when he pulled close enough, leaped at a shifting black moss man, bashing his hammer on its skull. With a satisfying crunching sound, the skull folded and the moss man dropped to the floor. Only two small glowing black eyes remained, which Matthew stomped on with his heavy boots. A swell of confidence bloomed in his chest.

"Come on!" Kerry yelled, stabbing another through with a knife. "Now we're having a craic!"

Matthew readied the hammer as another moss man came for him. He ducked. The moss man flew over his back and sailed at Faith. With a two-handed grip, as if she were wielding a tennis racket, she swung the machete upwards, slicing through its torso. She winced as the two halves separated and landed on either side of her, spraying her with a black liquid.

"Matthew!" Hope called a warning.

He turned to face a new assault. The moss men were too many to count, and the triumph over killing the first threatened to dissolve. But Monty and Robin continued to shoot, Kerry sliced with his knife, Faith advanced again with her machete. They were holding their own.

A moss man in front of Matthew attacked. He sliced with his hammer, shattering what he thought was a knee bone. The black moss man disintegrated into a thousand tiny black pieces, before snapping back together and looking more murderous than ever. A medley of curse words tumbled through Matthew's mind.

"*Ahhhhhh!*" Matthew yelled, bringing the hammer down again and again. More times than he could count. Until the shimmering black moss man dissipated for good.

Alessandra, with Luna, crept behind Kerry and Faith. Matthew joined them and hammered through the black and shifting undergrowth. Faith winced, her skin covered in black blood. Kerry thrust his knife into the belly of a moss man, revealing a pit of blackness that engulfed his hand.

Black moss swam over Kerry's hand and arm, then slithered onto his neck and face. Even as the moss man collapsed.

Kerry screamed, yanking his hand away, and his knife fell to the ground. Matthew hammered at the moss man's head. Kerry fell to his knees, the moss man on top of him, swallowing him in a black death. Kerry's mouth hung open and his eyes goggled. The black moss spread over his body, slithered into his orifices, suffocating him. Matthew had prayed for this. Wished for it. He felt sick to his stomach. No. Not this.

Robin's and Monty's bullets echoed around the forest, slammed into tree trunks, tore moss men apart, and sliced up the ground. Each time a moss man took a hit, they bucked and writhed and sometimes flew apart into a million microscopic pieces. But always came back together and resumed their advance with renewed strength. They'd gained a hundred yards. Maybe. But there was still a wall of black moss men to get through.

He plucked Kerry's knife from the black mess, wiping the weapon on the ground.

"We need to move!" Faith called.

They ran through the forest, sometimes slashing with their weapons, sometimes dodging the enemy. Alessandra pulled Luna along.

"A little help over here!" Robin called. A group of the moss men surrounded her. Her pot-shots kept them at bay, but there were ten of them. She wouldn't be able to hold them off for long.

Luna stood in the middle of it all. Motionless. With only Faith and Alessandra to guard her. But the moss men seemed to sidestep her, as though she wasn't worthy of their attention.

"Still need a little help over here!" Robin shouted, reloading her gun. Her hair had escaped her hair tie and hung loose around her shoulders. Black speckles covered her, head to foot.

Both Monty and Matthew hacked their way to her. Filled with a new anger, an uncontrollable rage, Matthew sliced and pounded at anything in his path. He reached Robin, pushing a moss man to the ground, and entered the surrounding circle. Monty made it to the other side of the circle, firing his shots inwards. Together, the three of them made a dent, systematically destroying one black mass after another. Until Monty ran out of bullets. The rifle was ripped from his grasp.

"Whiskey-Tango-Foxtrot!" he screamed. "Abort! Abort! Abort!"

A black hand rammed into Monty's mouth, gagging him, making him retch. His eyes turned black and soon black liquid seeped out of his pores.

"Monty!" Robin screamed.

"No more death!" Matthew charged at the moss man responsible, bringing down his hammer, shattering its malleable skull, spraying its black blood over the others, who quickly dived out the way.

Something white and fleeting jumped from a tree and toppled an ambushing attacker to his left. Ariel. She flattened the moss man to the ground, then removed the halo from above her head. Holding it in her hands it glowed brightly. She threw it at the moss man at her feet, decapitating it with one slice.

"Jesus H!" Matthew stared at the holy weapon.

A dozen moss men rushed at them. A black arm swept over Matthew's head, knocking him down. He turned, trying to get to his feet before the advancing moss man overwhelmed him. Faith screamed. Hope screamed. Everyone was screaming.

Ariel stood in the middle, spreading her arms wide. The glowing halo boomeranged back to her. She threw it again, decapitating ten moss men in one go. The halo continued to sail through the trees, its shining power setting leaves and branches alight until it was out of view.

The halo didn't come back this time.

A new fire ripped through the forest, burning moss men, advancing towards them. Heat flushed against Matthew's cheeks as he desperately looked for a way out.

Ariel tipped her head back and smiled at the heavens. The moss men gathered around her. Ariel glowed a brilliant white. The moss men tightened the circle. Matthew ran at them, swinging his hammer, but they pushed him out the way.

White light rolled off Ariel in shock waves of brilliance. Brightening. Blinding them all. It pulsed out from her hands and body. The moss men glanced briefly at each other, then as one, attacked her. Pressing closely around her, her white body turned black, writhing with shifting evilness. Her body vibrated, causing Matthew's head to throb. The moss men went flying, disintegrating in the air, permanently. Ariel's holy light pushed them away. But then her light winked out, flashing like the dying strobe in a dimly lit basement. She became no more than a dimming husk.

She had saved them. Or was it something more than her?

Ariel's light and the wall of fire created by her halo destroyed the moss men, burning them to a crisp in seconds. Burning them out of existence.

Caleb had been right. There was another fire. And it surrounded them.

He cast a quick glance at the others. "We have to run through it!"

They huddled together and held hands. Matthew roared and they leaped through the wall of flames, leaving the moss men to burn.

Matthew stood on the other side of the flames, smelling his singed hair, watching the growing fire. They weren't out of danger. For the breezeless day would allow the fire to go where it wanted. And already it had become a wall of crackling heat.

Luna stood. Oblivious. She blinked. Her head swiveled to Matthew. For a moment, a brief moment, Matthew thought he saw something in those dark pupils. Something conscious.

"Run!" Matthew yelled. He and Robin grabbed the others and yanked them away from the advancing flames. They ran. As a group. Only six of them left. They ran.

Take care of them, Matthew.

CHAPTER 28
MATTHEW

THEY RAN THROUGH THE FOREST, not really seeing or knowing where they were going, stumbling and holding on to each other, wiping the black blood from their exposed skin. Matthew guided them in the general direction he thought led to Grandmother's house. Smoke filled the air. Like the house fire all over again. His lungs quickly filled until he doubled over and coughed. He spat phlegm from his lungs. Black phlegm. Maybe he wasn't going to make it after all.

"We can't stop, Matthew," Robin said, her mouth and nose tucked into her jacket.

"You don't want to go back for Monty?"

Robin's eyes moistened. She brushed at her dry cheek. "There's nothing to go back for."

Matthew looked back. Orange light lit the forest. It was beautiful. And horrible. They'd lost so much, in such a short time. Going backward wouldn't achieve anything. They had to press on. A stag thundered by, its flank flaming.

"You're right," Matthew said.

He stood and reached for Luna's hand. As they walked, he spoke. "Please wake up, Luna." He'd asked her this before. Why did he think this time would be any different?

"We're dying," he told his best friend. "We're all dying. We need your help."

She didn't even look at him, just planted one foot in front of the other, methodically, as if she weren't barefoot and might be no more than a machine.

"We just need to get her to Grandmother's house," Robin said, taking his other hand.

"Is that what you want?"

"I want whatever you want, Matthew," Robin replied, giving his hand a fractional squeeze. "But I also want you to be happy."

The lump in Matthew's throat cut into his airway. "Luna makes me happy."

"I know that."

Matthew's thoughts raced. Memories of Luna. Memories of the others. Always together. Until now. "Do you?"

Robin patted his shoulder. "If you want to go to Grandmother's house, that's where we'll go."

He wanted to forget everything. Maybe find a private area where he could talk to Robin and pretend there had been no death. He knew it hadn't hit him yet, that he was probably in shock. There would be a toll to pay, perhaps worse than anything Luna had ever gone through. He wasn't sure he would make it out the other side when it came time to deal. So, for now, he didn't want to think about the blood and the death. He wanted to be numb. He didn't even want to run anymore. He was tired of running. The training whistle blew in his mind and made him feel like one of Pavlov's dogs and the thought of the starting gun made him think about bullets, and death, and moss men, and all the rest.

"Grandmother will make it all better," Matthew said.

"She will. She'll help Luna," Robin said. "But maybe not you."

How did she know? Had Robin met Grandmother before? With his thoughts vague and jumbled, Matthew shook his head. Ash floated around his face. Ash and something black. Something wasn't right, aside from the death, but he couldn't figure out what was niggling at him.

They trudged through the forest, coughing and spluttering, passing Robin's canteen back and forth.

"It will be nighttime soon." Hope wrapped her arms around her waist and threw a cautious glance at the canopy.

Had the day passed already? How long had they been walking? Matthew turned back to face the fire. Flames no longer streaked the forest at their backs. The smoke hovered, drifting around them like eerie, spectral fingers, but it was thinner. He could breathe again.

"We need to find a safe place," Robin said. "In case the fire comes this way."

When did she start taking charge? But Matthew was too tired to argue or make decisions. When Robin led him down the side of a ditch and under the umbrella of the roots of a large tree, he didn't argue. He performed a cursory look for patches of black moss, then plonked down next to Luna. The smell of soil filled his nostrils. And smoke. The smoke followed them everywhere.

Luna, Robin, Hope, Faith, Alessandra. It was only them who remained.

Maybe it was all a dream. Maybe he'd wake up back at the house, Luna snuggled next to him in his bed after one of her nightmares. They'd wake up, make pancakes for the kids, with blueberries, or chocolate chips, and go to school. She'd sit on the bleachers and watch him at track practice while she did her homework. Like they always did. Surely, they could get back to that, when he woke up in the morning?

But morning brought more devastation. Matthew was too tired to feel disappointed it wasn't all a dream. Instead, he slapped his cheeks a couple of times to dispel his sluggishness. The others woke, stretched stiff limbs and sipped water and ate slices of venison. Only Alessandra remained asleep. Matthew crawled to her. She'd used part of her long skirts as a pillow. He placed a hand on her shoulder, gently, so as not to startle her. But she remained asleep. He shook her. Still no response. Matthew lifted her hair away from her face.

She stared with wide eyes. At nothing. No, not staring. Never again. Her eyes were as clouded as the smoke-filled sky. He touched her cheek. She was colder than snow. He checked her body for injuries, but found none. Piper's cross hung from her neck. Matthew unclasped it and slid it into the canvas bag. Caleb had been right. There was another fire. He was too numb to feel anything. Death. So much death. It was becoming the norm. To be expected.

"How far is it now, Matthew?" Robin asked.

"I thought you knew," he replied, getting to his feet.

"I don't know everything."

"Alessandra is dead."

Faith blanched, dropping her machete.

Hope dropped to the ground, rocking on her haunches and took great heaving gulps of air.

"Breathe," Robin reminded her.

"I can't fucking breathe anymore," Hope screamed. "All my friends are dying."

Matthew crouched in front of her, pushed her hair back behind her ears. "I don't know what to say to you." He had nothing left.

Hope nodded, held her breath, let it out in a long shaky exhale. "I'll be alright in a minute."

Matthew got to his feet, stared at Alessandra's peaceful corpse. "She must have died early on in the night."

"Was she injured?" Faith asked.

"I assume it was smoke inhalation," he replied.

"We should go," Robin said. "Before the fire comes back."

"My feet." Faith hobbled around. They looked dark with dirt. On closer inspection, he realized they were dark red with her blood. Although Faith's toenails were normally wrecked and her toes misshapen from squeezing them into pointe shoes, the rest of her feet had been treated finer than the queen's ass. She wasn't equipped to walk barefoot through a forest. There would be scars.

Robin plucked leaves from nearby trees, those that hadn't been burned, and handed them to Faith along with a few strips of duct tape from her pack. Faith applied the leaves and tape to her feet to make temporary shoes.

"Are we going to make it?" Hope stood, clenching her sketchpad to her chest. How did she still have it? Her blonde hair trailed down the length of her borrowed black top. The black trousers hung over her bare toes. Unlike Faith, her feet weren't lacerated.

"We're going to make it," Matthew said. He wasn't making a promise. It was more of a prayer, for himself, because if he thought otherwise he might as well lay down here and call it a day. But he hadn't lost his friends for nothing. Their deaths had to mean something.

"But Alessandra just died in her sleep, for no reason," Hope said, then took a long draw from Robin's canteen.

"There was a reason. More than one," Matthew said. More than one. Something to do with Luna, but he couldn't grasp the truth. "It was her time." Now he sounded like Ariel. And then he felt guilty. The last time he'd spoken to Ariel he'd argued with her. Now she was dead. "There's nothing we can do about it." He walked over to Alessandra's body and shut her eyes.

"Let's go," Faith said. "Let's just go. And stop talking. You're scaring the hell out of me." She stood up, tested out her new shoes, and marched up the side of the ditch, pulling on exposed roots so she wouldn't fall. Matthew put a hand on her butt and shoved her up and over the lip, then climbed after her.

When they all reached the ridge, Matthew tucked Luna's hand in his and led her through the misty tendrils of smoke still visible in the air.

"What if the fire comes back?" Hope asked.

"Then it comes back," Matthew replied.

"But where will we go?" Hope persisted, picking a path alongside Matthew and trying to stay close.

"Away from the fire," Matthew said.

"But what if that's the wrong direction?"

Matthew held his breath for a moment, willing patience. "Then it's in the wrong direction."

"Matthew!"

"What do you want to hear? That it's all going to be okay?"

"For starters," Hope said.

"Well, it's already not okay. In case you haven't noticed, we've lost Kalisa, Caleb, Tyler, Joseph, Nell, Piper, Ulrich, Jasmine, Beacon, Ariel, Kerry, Monty, and Alessandra—" The names came back to him. But their meaning was elusive, like fog rolling off a coastal cliff. They'd been a family once, friends. They'd lived together in a large cabin on the edge of the woods. All of them. Caring for each other. But now the sense of belonging to a large group seemed unimportant. They were gone and already their memories were fading, their images hazy. Maybe it was better that way.

"I know who they are," Hope said, tears in her eyes. "They were my family too."

Matthew said nothing, just set his jaw and pulled Luna along. They walked abreast. They were only five, there was space. Robin held her gun out, loaded, safety off, ready.

"But seriously, Matthew, what do we do if the fire comes back?" Hope asked.

"Jesus Christ, Hope! I don't know!"

"Sorry," she muttered, taking a step away. "Just thought you might have a plan. You always have a plan. You're the oldest."

"I'm not the…" Matthew began to retort. He was almost eighteen. Luna was seventeen. Faith, sixteen, Hope fifteen. Robin, maybe his age. He probably was the oldest. The thought almost made him laugh. He was so used to Ariel being over four hundred years old, age had never entered his mind.

"Maybe I am the oldest. And the plan is to keep walking to Grandmother's house. If we run into more trouble, we'll deal with it. Okay?" He tried to inject some gentleness into his voice. She was only fifteen. Hell, he was only seventeen. A couple of weeks ago he'd felt like he was on the brink of manhood, as ridiculous as it sounded. But yeah, an adult, senior year, almost eighteen, scouts at the track meets. He could see his future so clearly. His *adult* future. It had all been pretty set. But now, he didn't feel quite so grown up anymore.

"I'm sorry about your brother," Faith said to Robin.

"My brother?" Robin questioned, a delicate frown wrinkling the skin between her eyebrows.

"Monty?" The name wavered on Faith's lips. She lowered her voice. "Back at the…you know…the lurchers."

"Oh! Monty! Yeah. Me too," Robin said. "He was…" she didn't finish her sentence and Matthew was left to ponder what she was thinking.

Matthew quickened his pace. It didn't take an expert to see the danger was far from over. Whether that danger came in the form of shifting black moss men, or lava-eyed beasts, or a fire, or an emotional state, didn't really matter. Life wasn't done with them yet.

Faith sauntered up to him. "Matthew?"

"Umm?" He kept his eyes on the way ahead. He thought he could detect a faint blush of orange. He checked the trees for birds. None that he could see. None. Zero. Zilch. Not even a raven. Maybe they'd all died along with Piper. But that didn't necessarily mean anything. He'd never noticed the birds much before. There'd been more immediate life-threatening obstacles to attend to than noticing a smattering of melodic birdsong. Their absence now didn't have to mean anything ominous, like the imminent presence of a switch-backing fire.

"How do you know Grandmother is going to help?" Faith scampered alongside, limping a little, choosing her footing carefully.

"Because she helped before," he replied automatically. He

thought about the question. Really thought about it. He couldn't remember the last time he'd seen Grandmother. Was she even still in the small house that sat between the forest and the rest of suburbia? What if she had moved? Died? He tried to remember exactly when he'd last been in her presence. But he came up blank.

Luna hadn't spoken about her in so long, as if doing so would be an admission that she'd lost her mother, and that Grandmother had lost her daughter. Too painful. In the early days, grandmother and granddaughter had shared their grief. When Luna had emerged from her first withdrawn state all those years ago, they'd cried together. Matthew had cried along with them. But as Luna had grown older and found new friends, she relied on Grandmother less. No more baking brownies on a Sunday afternoon. No more long walks to the cliff tops and gathering wildflowers. No more sitting on the old porch swing and watching the sun go down. No more. He couldn't remember the last time he'd caught a whiff of Grandmother's homemade hot chocolate. Maybe that had been the mistake, not seeing her, withdrawing. Maybe that's why Luna had withdrawn now, a second time.

He quickened his pace, seeing the mistakes so clearly. Grandmother was the key. They should never have stopped coming, even when Luna's father started working more. They could have found a way. They *should* have. Matthew hoped it wasn't too late to help her this time, that she wasn't too far lost inside.

"But, how did she help?" Faith asked. "What did she do *exactly*?"

"She's not magical, if that's what you're asking," Matthew replied, thinking of Ariel, Obsidian, Beacon, and Ulrich.

"She's not a doctor, is she?" Robin asked.

"No!" Doctors were the last thing Luna needed. Thanks to the 'helpful' doctors, Luna had spent a year away from them, in a special place, a place where she was supposed to get the rest she needed. Only Matthew had been permitted to visit. Not nearly as often as he'd wanted. The others had bitched and moaned, but never got to see her no matter how hard they tried. "No. Doctors can't help us. They can't help Luna. Truthfully, I don't remember what Grandmother did, but she helped. I know she can do it again."

"But you're not sure." Faith wouldn't look at him, just kept her eyes on her feet as she picked her way over the rough terrain.

"No, I'm not sure." Matthew narrowed his eyes. "Would you rather go back to the house and the fire?"

"That's not what I'm suggesting," Faith said.

"What are you suggesting?" Matthew held a slim branch out of her way.

Faith frowned. She stopped walking. "I don't freaking know. I just don't understand why we have to traipse through a burning forest. The authorities know about Luna's mother. They wouldn't stick her in a hospital for something that happened years ago."

"It's not about what happened to Luna," Matthew said. "It's about who she is. About who we all are." The truth of it flitted teasingly at the back of his mind. He remembered now. All of it. Why it was so important they stayed hidden. Why they were so inexplicably linked. *Shit*.

"Who we all are?"

He shook his hand at her. "Forget it."

"Forget *what*?"

Matthew hesitated a fraction too long.

"Matthew?"

The weight of her gaze made his skin prickle. Hope and Robin stood motionless, staring at him.

"What is it you're not telling us?" Faith crossed her arms over her chest. "Is there something else besides her mother's murder?"

Yes.

"I can't," Matthew replied, feeling the burden of Luna's hand on his arm. He looked into her midnight eyes. Dull. Blank. No recognition. "It's not my secret to tell."

Faith and Hope glared at him. Robin pinned him with a curious expression he couldn't define.

Faith stepped close to him and jutted her chin. "Neither was the story of Luna's mother. But you told us anyway."

The truth would devastate them. It would send them running. They wouldn't be able to deal. It was…incomprehensible. Ironically, it wasn't just Luna's secret. It belonged to all of them. He couldn't have them fall apart and scatter with the winds – for they would scatter, with the sheer magnitude of it all – Luna needed them. Without them, Luna would never recover.

"I can't. I know that's not what you want to hear." Matthew shifted his weight from foot to foot. His knuckles throbbed with an inner hurt. "Please trust that it's better this way."

Faith poked his chest. "For *who*? You? Luna?"

Matthew considered. Took a step back. "I'll make you a deal. We get to Grandmother's house, I'll tell you. If Grandmother says she can help, then we'll sit down in the living room, hell, I'll even give you two fingers of whiskey. And I'll tell you everything. But you have to wait until then. Agreed?"

He wasn't sure if it was the right thing to say, or if Luna would approve, but he had nothing else to make them stick together.

"Agreed," Robin said. "As long as that's what Matthew wants."

"Agreed," Hope echoed.

"No deal," Faith said, "as much as I want the whiskey after this little woodland adventure."

"Faith…"

"Seriously, Matthew. You're holding out on us. I want to know. Now." She jabbed her finger into his chest, her unicorn tattoo flashing.

"I'm sorry, Faith, I just can't right now." It wasn't that he didn't want to tell her. She deserved to know. But he wasn't sure he could do it. There weren't the words. He wasn't entirely sure of all the details himself. They were more like assumptions. Luna and he had never talked about it. He'd asked her one time on the roof, and she'd changed the subject.

Take care of them, Matthew.

He was smart enough not to press, and so he'd been left to think, for hours, what it all meant. That night, when she'd snuggled into bed and he'd carried on reading his abnormal psychology book, he'd read all night. Looking for answers. But that didn't mean he'd gotten it right or could pass down the concept with any degree of accuracy. Half of him didn't want to speak the words aloud, because he'd be confirming whatever existed only in his head. He wasn't ready for that. He did possess a sense of self-preservation after all.

"Fine, then I think I'll go on my own." She stomped off in a different direction, but she didn't get very far in her makeshift shoes.

"Well, have fun with the moss men, the yellow-eyed beasts, and whatever else is out there," Matthew called.

She stomped back, burned him with a scorching glare, but didn't wander away again.

"Fine," Faith replied. "For now. But I want answers. And I want them soon." She jabbed at his chest again. He let her. As long as she was coming, he'd let her jab away all she wanted.

They trudged over the uneven ground. He caught Faith giving him several sidelong glances. He ignored her. Robin and Hope remained quiet. Luna walked and said nothing.

Occasionally, Matthew detected a whiff of smoke. Then he'd check all around and try to determine the direction. But it was impossible. Tendrils as thin as Beacon's light in the day swirled from all directions. Maybe it was gone, just smoke hanging lazily as an afterthought. The sun cast every hue of the rainbow on the forest, glinting off rocks, highlighting craggy holes, illuminating healthy, green moss. No trace of the black stuff. Maybe the fire had burned it all. Maybe he should take his own advice and keep getting on until he couldn't anymore. *Stop thinking. Just do.* It was a surprisingly good plan, and it helped relieve the tension headache knocking at the base of his skull.

For lunch, they stopped and shared out the remaining slivers of venison. Matthew didn't trust the berry bushes in the woods, so this last meal would have to see them through. It wasn't far now. Not far at all. For the first time, he could see the metaphorical light at the end of the dingy, deadly, black moss-infested tunnel and entertained the idea that they might make it.

Faith sat cross-legged on the ground and inspected her duct tape shoes.

"Holding up okay?" Robin asked. "I have more duct tape if you need it."

"I'm good," Faith replied. "Just a little sore."

At the mention of the word 'sore' Matthew's knuckles pulsated with pain. Still swollen. Still raw and bloody. He offered the canteen to Luna and made her sip. The liquid dripped over her lips and down her chin.

"Luna?"

The mouthful of water pooled onto the collar of her blue pajama top. He parted her lips wider with a finger. In her mouth sat the three slivers of meat he'd given to her. Unchewed. He swept them out of her mouth and into his hand. His heart sank to the pit of his stomach.

"You have to eat, Luna. You have to drink."

She didn't even blink. There was no sign she'd heard him.

"Maybe she's not hungry," Hope said.

Faith raised a pierced eyebrow. "We're all hungry."

Hope shrugged. "Maybe it doesn't take as much energy when you're…like Luna is."

Matthew pressed the canteen against Luna's lips once more. Again, the water dripped uselessly out of her mouth. "Please, Luna." Desperation made his scalp prickle and his palms turn slick.

"Uh, Matthew." Robin nudged him with an elbow. Her gun clicked. Safety off.

He looked up.

"We've got trouble."

Faith crawled to him, crab-like. Stuck on the edge of the group, Hope froze, her eyes following Robin's gun.

As Matthew caught the water from Luna's mouth, he locked eyes with a lava-eyed beast. A menacing growl erupted from its throat. It pawed at the ground with an enormous foreleg and snorted a warning. Sparks and flames flew from its eyes, and steam billowed from its nostrils. It shook its shaggy mane and the smell of death filled the air.

"Shit," Matthew said, feeling for his knife.

CHAPTER 29
MATTHEW

THE BEAST PREPARED TO CHARGE.

"What do we do?" Faith asked, her hand closing around the hilt of the machete. Everyone stared at the deadly beast pawing the ground. It growled again. The trees bowed out of its way. The hair on the back of Matthew's neck electrified. A drop of sweat crept down his spine.

"We're going to die," Hope whispered, her body trembling. A small stream of liquid trickled from her crotch.

"We can take down one beast," Robin said, closing one eye to sight.

"Maybe, but how about five?" Faith asked.

Matthew turned his head. Identical beasts stood staring at them from all directions, tightening in a deathly circle. Flames poured from eye sockets, steam plumed from nostrils, feet pounded and pawed at the ground. He counted five and gave up. What was the point? They were outnumbered. This was it.

"Maybe," Matthew said. "Maybe we die. But we die fighting." He lunged at the closest beast. He ran up its outstretched leg and yanked on its mane to pull himself upwards. Shots echoed in the air and the smell of gunpowder filled his nostrils. Robin had the only gun. Was it enough? Faith swished the machete. It cut through air before landing on something solid with a satisfying *crunch*.

"Die, you sonofabitch!" Faith yelled and yanked with both arms on the machete buried in the skull of a beast. She planted her feet either side of the steaming nostrils and pulled the machete free. The beast roared.

The beast Matthew landed on bucked and writhed. He let go of the knife embedded in its shoulder. To stay on top of the beast, he grabbed hold of the mane.

Robin's bullets rained around them, whizzing and popping, like a box of fireworks. Hope collapsed on the ground, a trembling mess, crouching, rolling into a ball, her hands cradling the back of her neck. All the while Luna just sat there. Her arms folded over her knees, not seeing any of the carnage before her, as if staring at a painting. *Jesus*.

She could make this stop, if she wanted to. Luna alone held that power. What was she doing to them?

Hope stood frozen.

"Hope! Move it!" Matthew called as he gripped his knife, pulled it out of the beast's flesh, and stabbed again. He aimed for a lava eye. He scored a bull's-eye and pushed with all his strength. His fingers burned as the fiery liquid poured over his hand. But he continued to push. He would not let this beast harm Luna.

With his arm buried up to his wrist, the fiery lava advanced and burned away the fine hairs on his arm. He clenched his teeth. He pushed harder, deeper, with more strength than he knew he had. Finally, slowly, the beast's eyes dimmed. The remaining lava pooled out of its eye sockets and dribbled down its snout.

Matthew pulled out the knife. Blood gushed over him and streamed to the ground. The beast teetered and tipped to its side. Patting his scorched skin, Matthew leaped out of the way and turned to assess the others. Hope, still rooted to the spot, was speared by two long fangs of the largest beast.

"No!" Matthew yelled. "Hope!"

Robin's volley of shots followed him as he ran to Hope. Faith came at them from a different angle, covered in dirt and blood.

Hope's mouth fell open. A scream erupted from her throat.

"No!" Matthew leaped at the beast holding Hope captive on its fangs. He grabbed Hope's shoulders and pulled. Her sketchbook fell to the ground and opened in the middle. Matthew caught a glimpse of the drawing. A monster, a beast. The same one he was fighting now. How could she have known?

He pulled until she slipped off the ivory skewers. Faith sliced the beast's flank wide open.

Matthew fell backward, with Hope in his arms. Robin protected them with her bullets. He cradled Hope. Her black top camouflaged the dark red blood. But she'd been impaled through her guts with both fangs.

"Hope, I'm so sorry." Matthew trailed a hand over her blonde hair.

Her eyes rolled back into her head. She tried to reach up to him, but she had no strength.

"*Shhh*," she whispered, trying to comfort him.

"I'm so sorry," Matthew said again. Her body fell limp. Hope was dead.

Matthew threw his head skyward and roared. A roar full of the anguish and devastation of the last few days, and it reverberated through the woods for miles. He thumped the ground once. And it shook. The fight wasn't over. No time to grieve. He pushed himself to his feet and readied his knife.

Something flew down from the sky. Some new atrocity that would surely be the end of them all. Matthew waited for death. He waited for the imminent, bone-crunching end. Instead, he was swept off his feet and carried into the air.

When Matthew realized he'd closed his eyes, he snapped them open. He flew through the sky, fifty feet off the ground. Obsidian. Matthew lay nestled in his back paw, safe. They swooped back to the others. Matthew held his knife in one hand and stretched his other arm out, ready to pluck Luna from the ground.

"Matthew!" Robin called. "Get away while you can!"

"I'm coming back for you!" he called, averting his face as they flew over Hope's crumpled body.

As they dove in, Obsidian opened his jaw and shot a jet of burning fire at the beasts. They roared and retreated. But not far enough. As Matthew swept his hand toward Luna and grabbed her under the arm, Robin ran out of bullets. Robin ran to them. Matthew dropped the knife to lift her with his other hand. But Obsidian was already pulling into the sky for another loop.

"No!" he yelled, as he tugged Luna into the sky with him. "Run! Robin, run!"

Robin dropped the useless handgun, pumped her arms and legs, leaped for his outstretched hand. But a beast plowed into her side, knocking her into a ditch. Obsidian spewed another burst of fire. When the flames and smoke cleared, Matthew saw Robin's inert body in the ditch. Her legs lay at opposing angles, her neck twisted unnaturally. She wasn't coming back from this.

He pushed Luna onto Obsidian's back and encouraged her to hold on. As they circled once more, he wrapped his legs around the gryphon's rear paw and hung upside down, ready to rescue Faith.

Riding the back of a flaming beast like a cowgirl, Faith stabbed with her machete. But the creature bucked and stomped, refusing to go down.

"Faith!" Matthew called. She looked up. Took four quick steps along the beast's back and jumped. The beast caught her foot in its mouth. Faith grabbed Matthew's hands. They rose into the sky. And the beast came with them.

Obsidian ascended. He roared several streams of flames upon the remaining beasts, decimating them, but also starting a new raging forest fire.

"Matthew!" Faith screamed, her face contorted. "It's breaking my leg!"

The beast hung onto Faith's ankle. Blood dripped from the joint. She sliced at the clinging beast with her machete as Matthew held onto her one hand in both of his. He would not let go.

Take care of them, Matthew.

The beast wasn't slowed by the fire sweeping over its fur. The flames crept over its back, into its mane, and engulfed Faith's leg.

She looked at Matthew. "Let me go!"

"Never!" They were so high, way above the canopy of the highest trees. In the distance, Matthew could make out houses.

A town. Where Grandmother lived. They were so close. They could make it.

"Please, Matthew!" Faith tried to pull her hand free. "It hurts so much! It's going to rip off my leg. I understand now. I understand Luna's secret. Just let me go. Save Luna. She can dance for me."

He didn't have a choice. As he looked into her brown eyes, he recognized acceptance. His grip slipped. He couldn't hold her.

They flew for another mile, closer to the town, with just two tips of Faith's fingers in Matthew's hands. "Tell Luna I love her!" Faith called, and then she fell through the sky, the beast with its mouth clamped around her foot. She fell, but didn't scream or flail her arms. Matthew closed his eyes before she and the beast landed. He wouldn't be able to live with that image. He whispered a prayer for her. Just in case God was listening.

He hung upside down from Obsidian's paw for another moment. Then he pulled himself up, crawled up his back, and joined Luna at his neck. With their legs spread over the gryphon's body and his arms around Luna's waist, keeping her safe, they flew to the edge of the forest.

Matthew didn't speak, he just held onto Luna as they flew, as another night descended. As Obsidian touched down at the edge of the village, the sun fell over the tops of houses, and the forest darkened to shadows. There was no sign of a fire. Not a single tendril of smoke.

"Thanks, buddy," Matthew said, rubbing Obsidian's shoulder. He helped Luna down, making sure she was balanced. He scanned the houses for Grandmother's, trying to remember the correct one. When he turned back to the gryphon, Obsidian was no longer there. He'd just…vanished. And then there were two.

"We're almost there," he said and took Luna's hand in his. From the rolling grassy slope, rows of houses lead to the clifftops, which then tumbled into a distant ocean. The water sparkled as the sun descended. An old lighthouse stood in the distance, its beacon of light last used years ago. He squeezed Luna's hand. A glimmer of hope grew in him. Despite what they'd lost, they'd made it.

They walked down the gentle slope from the forest, along a sandy path that wound its way into the town. Grandmother's house was the first on the right. A flood of memories came back. Luna losing her first tooth in a piece of cake on her sixth birthday. Toasting mugs of hot chocolate one winter when they were eleven, on the night of the first snowfall. Grandmother's bedtime stories, his favorite was about a wolf and a girl with a red cape. The way she would pull the covers up and tuck them right under his chin. The fox that had come around one summer and refused to leave until autumn approached and with the first drop of an orange leaf, could no longer be found

He smiled. Remembering. He spoke the memories aloud to Luna.

"We should go." He tried to work up the nerve to knock on the solid oak door. "Grandmother will be able to help you now."

"Is she yours or mine?" Luna asked. Matthew jumped. After such a long spell of silence, her voice startled him. She squeezed his hand. A gentle pressure. The best feeling in the world.

He frowned, trying to remember. "I'm not sure."

"Will you come with me?" Her midnight eyes set on his, seeing him. Really seeing him.

Matthew willed his feet to move. "I'd like to." He paused, looking at the warm lights mantled by the newly-painted window frames. "I don't think I'm supposed to."

A single tear crept out of the corner of Luna's eye and trailed down the side of her cheek.

"I don't want you to leave," Luna said.

Matthew blew out his cheeks. "Why would I leave?"

"It's just a feeling."

They approached the back door of the house. A wrap-around porch encased the house and wooden steps ended in a grassy mound. The grass led to the forest and everything they'd left behind. Matthew stood before the bottom step. In the unfenced yard, he spied a rusted motorbike, mostly reduced to parts, an old helmet with a frayed leather strap hanging from a weather-eroded handlebar.

"Do you remember the day we rode that?" He pointed to the bike. It was a Volt, Matthew remembered, built in Ireland.

Luna nodded, smiled.

"You insisted on driving. The way you went around that corner." He shook his head. "It took off a good three layers of skin the length of my shin."

"Sorry about that," she said. "I felt so bad. But it was a good day, wasn't it?"

Matthew nodded. Any day with her was.

Luna took a step onto the porch. Then stopped.

"Aren't you coming?" she asked, tugging his hand. She swept her dark hair over her shoulder and bewitched him with her loveliest smile.

"I should wait here," Matthew said, though the light at the windows beckoned him. He shoved his hands in his pockets.

"I don't want to go in there alone." She came back down the step. "Let's sit on the swing for a while."

Matthew had forgotten about the swing. A wooden loveseat once painted white. It used to hang on the porch. Now it hung from an old oak tree, abandoned, in the corner of the yard, in need of a good sand job and fresh coat of paint. But it still worked. They could sit for a while.

Luna curled herself into one side of the seat, wrapping her feet over her knees, a contorted yoga position. She lifted a mess of twigs from the other side, creating room for Matthew, and held them in her lap. Matthew realized it was some sort of doll fashioned from twigs and wildflowers. A memory of another stick doll tugged at his mind. Lost to a river? As Luna flicked her hair over her shoulder, light from the last rays of the drooping sun illuminated a pendant at her neck. It was a fox, muzzle lifted to the sky. Ulrich? Wait a minute, who was Ulrich? The memory of a red fox slipped away. A different pendant hung at his neck. A medallion. A woman made of triangles. He had no memory of it.

"I started the fire," Luna said.

Matthew nodded. He knew, deep down.

"The candle in my bedroom. It was too close to the curtains."

Matthew swallowed and ran his tongue around the inside of his cheek. "It doesn't matter anymore."

"I couldn't have done it without you," she said. "Getting through the woods. You kept me safe." She patted the space next to her. "Thank you, Matthew."

She held his gaze. He couldn't stop the prickle of tears.

"You're welcome," he choked out. Matthew settled next to her, turned to look at her, placing one foot underneath him. With the other foot he nudged the ground so the swing rocked gently.

She shook her head. "I couldn't have done it without you. You were always there, from the very beginning. The first. My favorite."

"Why?" he managed to ask. "Why me?"

She cupped his cheek. "Because you're you, silly. My rock, my family, my soul."

"Luna…" he didn't know what to say. "I'll always be here for you."

"I know."

"Why did you ask me to look after them?"

She smiled. "Because you're the strongest. And you know me better than I know myself."

He leaned his head back against the pillar and let the last of the warmth from the sun caress his face.

"Jasmine," Luna said.

Something sad clenched his heart. Luna held a clump of flowers.

"Jasmine," she said again. She lifted a posy of fragrant white flowers to his nose. He inhaled the sweetness. "It's a beautiful flower. My mother…had it in her hair the day she married my father."

"I didn't know that."

She offered him the flowers and he took them. He threaded a couple of them through the stick doll, adding length to its hair. His gaze wandered over the darkening forest. There were no darting shadows. He couldn't make out a hint of the treacherous black moss. A cool breeze swept down the slope. The salty scent of the sea drifted inland. It was a perfect September evening.

"I think I need to go inside," Luna said.

He looked at his best friend. Her blue, men's pajamas were covered in footballs. He'd never noticed.

She caught him looking. "They were my father's. He almost threw them out. But I rescued them. They're so soft. He played football semi-professionally, won himself a scholarship to college."

"I remember that now," Matthew said.

"Do you remember the robin redbreast that lived in the oak in the garden last winter?"

Matthew nodded.

"You loved that bird, didn't you? Always bringing it food."

Matthew sifted through his memories of last winter. It had been a cold one. A couple feet of snow. "It had a mate. Caleb called it Monty."

Luna smiled. "That's right. Robin and Monty. They were your birds, Matthew. Just for you."

He took her hand. "I'm not sure I understand."

"I'm not sure I do, either." Luna pushed herself out of the swing, her gaze lingering over his face. "Won't you come?"

Matthew stood, took her hand, and laced his fingers through hers. That felt better. Now they were one. "I'll walk you to the door."

Silently, they walked to the porch steps once more.

"There's one thing I'd like to do before you go inside," Matthew said, gathering his courage.

Luna raised a playful eyebrow. "Only one?"

Matthew chuckled. "I want to kiss you, Luna Forester, if that's okay with you."

She smiled and tilted her face toward him.

Matthew's heart pounded and he pushed away the memories of their last kiss. He pressed his lips against hers to find them warm and welcoming. Her lips parted and he swept his tongue between them, probing, drinking her in. It was the best kiss of his life. Worth saving himself for. Worth everything.

The kiss ended naturally, and they parted.

Luna glanced at the house. "Matthew, I'm scared."

"Sometimes we have to do things we're afraid of. I'll wait here for you," he said, and sat on the step.

Luna crouched next to him and stared into his eyes. "I love you, you know."

His heart soared. That's all he'd ever wanted to hear. But a wave of despair washed over him. He had to tell her about the others. He opened his mouth to speak, but she laid a finger across his lips. "*Shhh.* Don't fret. Everything's okay now." Maybe she already knew. He glanced at the fox pendant hanging from her neck, the footballs on her pajamas, the clump of Jasmine wound through the head of the stick doll. She knew. She knew everything. And soon, it would be time for him to go. They couldn't inhabit the same body forever.

"Are you okay?" he asked. That's all he ever wanted. If she was ready to face life alone, then he wouldn't stand in her way.

Luna nodded. She leaned forward and pressed her lips against his once more. He took her hand and, with his thumb, circled the unicorn tattoo on her left wrist, remembering when she almost chickened out of it.

She stood and edged to the door. He watched her knock and wait. The door flew open and Grandmother stood in the frame. Matthew's heart warmed.

"Luna! Thank the dear, sweet Lord!" Grandmother said,

her accent thick. "I almost had forty-thousand canaries, worrying about you."

Matthew handed Luna the canvas bag. The one full of herbs and ointments.

"I'm okay," Luna said, staring down at her disheveled and dirty pajamas, perhaps only noticing the state she was in for the first time. She raised her right hand. Her knuckles were bloody and swollen. "Where did that come from?" she muttered.

Matthew's own hand was smooth and unblemished. He felt for the scar between his shoulder blades, the one he'd earned himself chopping wood before he was ready, without supervision. It, too, had disappeared.

"Luna!" Her father stood in the doorway. A tree trunk of a man, owed partly to a splash of native lineage. He wore a few days' worth of stubble and a set of crumpled clothing he must have been wearing for a week straight. He pulled her into a tight embrace. "I was so worried when I came back from work. The fire. You weren't there."

Luna glanced back at Matthew. "Thank you," she mouthed.

He stood up from the porch, watching the happy little reunion. He'd delivered her safe and sound. *Save Luna.*

"I've been dreaming again," Luna said. "About mother."

"I can help you with that," Grandmother said, drawing Luna into the house. "Are the others with you? Your…friends?"

Luna shook her head.

"It's okay, you know, if they are. They're part of you," Grandmother said.

"Are the police here?" Luna asked.

"No," her father said. "Thought it best not to, after last time. We didn't know what state we'd find you in."

"I'm okay," Luna said. "More than okay. I don't need them anymore."

"You're sure?" Grandmother asked. "Because it's okay if you do. It's who you are."

"I'm sure. They helped me. And then they left," Luna replied. Her bottom lip trembled, and her eyes moistened in the warm lights.

Grandmother shut the door.

Matthew stood in the night, shivering against the cold. There was nothing left for him to do now. He had saved Luna.

Saved Luna.

She didn't need him anymore.

CHAPTER 30
LUNA

THE SMELL of baking bread wafted from the kitchen and mingled with the lavender potpourri Grandmother kept above the fireplace. Old-fashioned lamps sat in the corners of the room and cast a comforting glow on the familiar knickknacks. A stack of my old, used sketchpads lay on the shelf under the coffee table. They were filled with light and dark. Unicorns and monsters. The beasts and the shadow men that haunted my nightmares. The black moss that suffocated my dreams. All of it was in there. All of it I had come to rely on. I couldn't have asked my friends to leave. I wasn't that strong. I'd had to show them. Light and dark.

"Luna?" Father took a step forward, blocking one of the lamps, and his face fell into shadow.

Grandmother's costume box was collecting dust in a darker corner of the room. I smiled at the beaded Rastafarian wig I'd been so infatuated with as a child. Inside, I knew she also kept my first pair of pointe shoes, the toes shredded with use. Grandmother could never throw anything away. Maybe I'd find my old running shoes in there too.

"Are you hungry?" Grandmother asked, wiping her hands on an immaculate apron.

Father stood a safe distance away. "Are you hurt? You look awful. There's blood on your pajamas."

I shook my head.

"Nothing a hot soak and a cycle in the washing machine won't clean up," Grandmother said, pulling my hair from the nape of my neck and tying it loosely with a beaded scrunchie.

Father stood with his hands on his hips, his brows knitted. "I can't believe you found your way through the woods."

"She wasn't alone." Grandmother let go of my hair and patted my shoulder. "She had her friends."

One of father's eyebrows rose higher. "Still."

Grandmother and Father asked question after question. Questions I didn't know how to answer. Questions I wasn't ready to contemplate. I could have healed them all. But then I wouldn't have healed. It hadn't been an easy decision. In fact, I don't think it was a decision. Something inside took over. A new part of me. An evolved part that no longer needed them. Even so, their absence left me hollow. The ache in my chest dulled any possible answers. And I needed to see Matthew. Only he remained. I stepped to the window and looked out into the darkening twilight.

In the middle of the front yard, still holding the posy of jasmine, he stood with his hand in his pocket, and the medallion around his neck glinted in the rising moonlight. He smiled at me. A sad, lopsided smile. His eyes glistened.

"Don't go," I whispered. I traced a heart in the condensation of the single-glazed window.

He shivered, uncontrollably, and I knew he would leave soon. The shiver turned to convulsions. Stumbling, he turned and walked up the grassy slope to the forest. On the edge of the trees, he turned and waved.

In the distance, a raven cawed.

I gripped the window ledge. I couldn't bear to watch. But I owed him that much. His outline blurred. He became transparent. Like Beacon. He shimmered and shook until his body was no more than a shifting shape of tiny colored spots. The smile was the last to go. Night swallowed the twilight and the shadows swallowed Matthew. Or maybe he'd returned to the woods. Maybe he wasn't gone forever.

Turning to face my family, I dug my finger into the chain of my fox necklace. But it wasn't the only pendant hanging there. A twisted metal woman made of triangles hung next to the howling fox.

I smiled and held the heavy pendant. It didn't matter if they were gone. I still held them in my heart. They would always be with me.

The End

If you enjoyed *The Unraveling of Luna Forester,* I'd be so grateful for a review. You can leave one here:
https://geni.us/UnravelingLuna

Read on for the first chapter of
The Shadow Keepers…

AUTHOR'S NOTE

Mental health is something I care about deeply, and it's at the heart of Luna's story. Though *The Unraveling of Luna Forester* explores themes of trauma, dissociation, and catatonia through a fictional lens, these experiences are very real for many people. If you or someone you know is struggling with Dissociative Identity Disorder (DID), catatonia, or any mental health concern, please know that you are not alone and that help is available. In the UK, you can contact **Mind** (mind.org.uk) or **Samaritans** at **116 123**. In the US, you can reach the **988 Suicide & Crisis Lifeline** by calling or texting **988**, or visit **988lifeline.org** for online chat and support. Wherever you are in the world, please reach out to a trusted friend, family member, or mental health professional—you deserve help, healing, and hope.

THANK YOU!

Thank you so much for making it all the way to the end. I hope you enjoyed reading Luna as much as I enjoyed writing her. If you did, leaving a review is the best possible present for an author! You can do it here:

https://geni.us/UnravelingLuna

Please sign up to my mailing list to get the latest news, free stories, novellas, as well as gain the opportunity to win some fantastic prizes.

www.MarisaNoelle.com

You will receive all eleven Unadjusteds prequel novellas, as well as a bonus scene from Wade's POV in Secrets of the Deep COMPLETELY FREE!!!

If you'd like to join my reading group where you can meet

other fans of my books, win giveaways, help me choose characters, covers and next books to write, you can sign up here:

https://www.facebook.com/groups/840324970233576

Read on for the first chapter of
The Shadow Keepers…

ACKNOWLEDGMENTS

Books cannot come into existence without a tremendous amount of support from other people. It really does take a team. With that in mind, there are two teams of people I want to thank, who I've also dedicated this book to. Firstly, my writing group, The Rebel Alliance – and yes, there is a Star Wars reference there - I couldn't have done this without your support. You've had my back for several years now and you've encouraged Luna at every step, from title changes to sensitivity suggestions. Secondly, Team Swag – you've been there while I negotiate the publishing waters. We hold each other's hands and share our knowledge. What a fantastic group of writers and friends.

Fay - the cover is gorgeous, and I couldn't be more pleased!

To my sensitivity readers – your knowledge and insight was spot on.

My husband, Neil, for all your cheerleading as I wrote draft after draft. You give me the space, time, and money to allow me to follow my dreams. I love you.

My kids, Riley, Lucas & Quinn, you have been so supportive and proud of me, as long as I don't turn up at your school fairs with a stack of books. You have encouraged me to keep going and stay strong. You are always my first port of call when I get stuck on a plot problem, and you always help!

My parents, Larry and Rita, who read everything I write and have always supported whatever path I chose to follow. Special thanks to Mom for being my eagle-eyed proofreader.

My early supporters who have given me advice and feedback along the way: Sasha Newell, Michelle Oliver, Nikki, Adrian, Darcy & Hetty Kane, and Rhia Mitchell.

The amazing writing community on Twitter. I've made a lot of friends there and you have all made my journey less lonely and the rejections easier to deal with. You know who you are. Thank you.

Booktok! What a fantastic community I've fallen into. You've made me buy crowns (several), and you've supported my journey, not just by engaging with me, but by buying my books too. I have found beta and ARC readers here and I know it is my new home. *"I could be brown, I could be blue, I could be violet sky..."*

My A-level English teacher, Michael Fox, who taught me to first think for myself and then to defend my ideas.

I'm saving this last one for the most special group of all - my readers. I wouldn't be here without you, and I hope you stick around to discover some of my other books.

www.marisanoelle.com

ABOUT THE AUTHOR

Marisa Noelle is the author behind a treasure trove of young adult and adult novels across multiple genres, but they all have running themes of mental health or the ocean. She tends to gravitate toward the speculative arena and loves to write science-fiction, fantasy, horror, dystopian, romance, romantasy, or a combination of them all.

Marisa's books include:

The Shadow Keepers—a spine-tingling tale to keep you up all night and semi-finalist of the BBNYA book awards.

The Unraveling of Luna Forester—a novel impossible to talk about because of its huge twist, but it snagged several awards, including: First Place Incipere Award, WriteBlend Finalist, BBYNA Semi-Finalist, Bookshelf Finalist.

Plastic—a powerful eco-thriller exploring grief, corporate corruption, and the fight to save our oceans. This contemporary YA novel blends activism with heartbreak as Sara Monroe battles her brother's death, a plastic-choked ocean, and the secrets of a billion-dollar beverage empire.

The Unadjusteds Trilogy delves into one of her favourite genres—dystopian. *The Unadjusteds, the Rise of the Altereds, and The Reckoning* make up the trilogy, but there are eleven further companion novellas that follow the secondary characters (FREE to subscribers). *The Unadjusteds* also placed as a semi-finalist in the BBNYA awards.

The Mermaid Chronicles is a seven book romantasy series that includes: *Secrets of the Deep, Quest for Atlantis, Fight for Freedom, Ghost Pirates, Vendetta, Denizens of Darkness, Vorago Returns*, as well as its own companion guide.

Marisa also writes steamy romance under the pen name Savannah Wilde.

When Marisa's not weaving literary spells, she's helping mold the future of MG and YA authors as a mentor for the Write Mentor program.

When not writing, Marisa likes to imagine herself as a mermaid, and can often be found in the local pool…or lake… or ocean. Despite her undeniable bookworm credentials since she was knee-high to a grasshopper, the author gig took Marisa by surprise. You see, she had a secret past as a bit of a science geek during her school days. But hey, science and storytelling make a surprisingly magical concoction! Currently, Marisa calls Woking, UK, her home sweet home, where she resides with her trusty squad, including her husband, three amazing kids, and a furry four-legged friend named Copper.

Marisa loves to hear from her readers. You can find and connect with her at the links below.

You can find her on TikTok @MarisaNoelle12,
or her website www.MarisaNoelle.com

Whatever you do,
don't look in the mirror

THE
SHADOW
KEEPERS

Marisa Noelle

THE SHADOW KEEPERS

Whatever you do, don't look in the mirror...

Sixteen year-old Georgia Boone knows the shadows are going to kill her. It's only a matter of time. They live in mirrors and look like humanoid crows. And stare at her with hungry red eyes. The insidious monsters have hunted her all her life, forcing her to drop out of school and driving her to the brink of insanity. But how can she prove their existence when no one else sees them? She is alone.

When Georgia is sent to the UK's most prestigious mental health centre, Brookwood Hospital, she is forced to face her fears and answer the question...

Are the shadows real, or is it all in her head?

THE SHADOW KEEPERS
CHAPTER 1

I STARE at the imposing front door of what is to be my prison for the foreseeable future. Solid wood. Oversized ornate door knocker of a lion with the ring through its mouth. How appropriate. The surrounding building is made from yellow bricks and the roof is grey slate. It matches my mood. Ivy crawls over the hospital, maybe a suggestion of cheerfulness. To me it looks like it's strangling my new home.

"Shall we go inside?" Bart shakes raindrops out of his hair as the smell of last night's vodka oozes out of him.

Something in my chest skitters. I don't want to be here. I don't want to go inside. But I don't have a choice.

I nudge the heavy front door with a wet trainer, testing its strength, hoping it's locked so I can remain in the world of the sane for just a little longer. It remains firmly closed—a small miracle—but I know this is only prolonging the inevitable. The court ordered me here, and here I must stay. I stand there, waiting for my parents, my anger pooling in my stomach, my skin prickling with indignation.

Bart throws an arm around me. I remain stiff, inconsolable.

I can no longer let my guard down. I can no longer give in to emotion. My mother and stepfather arrive, my stepfather dragging my suitcase through the puddles. Gee, thanks Dad.

They join me in the portico. My stepfather turns the stupid handle of the door. We go through the wide front doors and drip rainwater onto the wood floor of the yawning entrance foyer. I immediately lock my gaze on a large bird statue standing at the foot of the sweeping staircase.

It's a crow.

Not a crow.

My mouth goes dry.

The statue is taller than me. It wears its chip marks and dents with pride, as if to say nothing could ever destroy it, not even time. At some point in its life, it was kept outside; old bird stains mottle its surface. Its stone eyes keep vigil over the foyer. Its wings are half-erect, as if preparing to take flight. My heart picks up tempo, and my tongue becomes this weird, heavy object that doesn't fit in my mouth. The panic attack is coming, building. It will be here soon.

I scan the room for reflective surfaces. I find only the windows, but as it's morning, they are translucent. For now.

Grabbing my mother's sleeve, I plead with her silently. Tears form in her eyes.

"It's going to be okay, Georgia." She pats my hand.

I shake my head and grit my teeth. "I don't belong here."

"We don't have a choice. It's what the court decided," my mother replies. "It's only ninety days."

Three months. A quarter of a year. I'll miss Halloween. Out in time for Christmas, if I prove I have recovered.

"Why don't you believe me?" I shake her arm. If Mum, or the damn court, or anyone of my non-existent friends actually tried to believe me . . . they'd know the court order was bull-shit. "I'm not crazy!"

My mother and stepfather exchange a look. It's one I've seen a hundred times in the last few months. They've been here before. We've had this conversation before, but they've made up their minds.

"No one is saying that," Mum says softly. "But after the incident . . ."

Bart steps between us. "Give her a break, Mum. I'm sure she remembers."

I reach for his hand, and he squeezes it back. I can't bear to look at him. The pity in his eyes would break me. Who am I kidding? I'm broken already.

My mother takes a long yoga breath, then sets her face into an emotionless mask; guarded eyes, flat smile. "You're here to get better, and put this…bird stuff behind you once and for all."

"I won't make it," I mumble too quietly for anyone to hear. They'll make me look in the mirrors here. Mirrors I've avoided all my life. And then they'll come for me. The shadows.

"Georgia," Mum says with that flat smile again. "This place isn't what it used to be. They don't do electric shock therapy or hose patients with water. It's not like that anymore. There's no shame in it. The doctors and nurses here are the best suited to understanding and helping you."

I look around the foyer again. Brookwood Hospital. Or Lunacy Asylum for the Insane and Unreachable. It's the place people with money put their loved ones when they don't know what else to do with them.

"Why can't you help me?" I stare at Mum.

"We've tried, sweetheart. And we haven't been able to.

Now it's time to let others in. You heard what the judge said; it's here, or it's the NHS hospital. We no longer have a choice. And to be quite honest, Georgia, there's nothing else I can do for you."

Bart nudges my arm, and his wobbling smile crushes my resolve not to cry.

"Your father never got the help he needed," Mum says. "I don't want that for you. I watched him struggle every day until he died. He joined the army because he felt he had something to prove, that he was tough and could look after us all. He went off to Afghanistan and he died trying to prove it. You're so like him, Georgia, in many ways. You need to be here. You need to get better."

Two nurses and a doctor emerge from an office door I hadn't noticed. They stand in a line like teeth in a monster's mouth. Their Stepford smiles have me taking a step backward and looking over my shoulder.

"Georgia Boone?" One of the nurses asks, distracting me from my quickening pulse.

I turn towards the voice. According to her label, she is the head psychiatric nurse, and her name is Marion.

"Yes," Mum answers for me. "Yes, this is Georgia."

"We've been waiting for you," Marion says, looking down a puffy nose at me.

My heart thuds painfully in my chest again. It picks up speed, as if trying to gallop out of my body completely. I clutch my mother's sleeve again.

"I'm Nurse Marion," she says. "And this is Nurse Willow." She points to the other woman.

Deputy Psychiatric Nurse Willow, according to her name badge, is tall and skinny. Her eyes are blue, and I detect a flash of some intrinsic warning in them when she looks at me.

"Hello, sweetheart," Willow says, a warm smile propped on her lips.

"I'm Paul. I'm a psychologist here," the man says, stepping forward to offer his hand. My stepfather shakes it, and my mother smiles sadly at him. "Don't be alarmed. We'll take good care of Georgia. That's what we're here for after all."

"Yes, of course," Mum replies.

"We need you to sign some paperwork," Marion says to my parents. "Paul will show Georgia and her brother to a pot of tea."

She gestures to the office door. My parents follow the two nurses into the room and leave Bart and me standing in the large foyer with Paul under the penetrating gaze of an antique grandfather clock. It leans Pisa-like on the thick carpet, its gentle ticking the only audible noise in the hushed expectancy of the room. It strikes the hour, and I jump, grabbing onto Bart's arm.

"This way." Paul leads us around a corner to a small niche with a couple of floral sofas and polished coffee tables. A pot of steaming tea sits on a tray with a couple of cracked mugs and a plate of biscuits.

Paul pours two cups of tea and excuses himself to take my luggage to my room. I sip at the tea, but it scalds my throat.

"Easy," Bart says.

I point to the other cup. "You could do with some sobering up."

He gives me his sideways grin.

"Was it a big night?" I ask.

He winks. "It's always a big night."

I sigh as a tremble shoots through my legs. Bart notices and rests a heavy hand on my knee. "I wish I could go with you. I wish you could stay. I wish . . ." I close my eyes against the threatening tears.

Bart brings me in close and hugs me, smoothing the back of my head. "I wish all that too. But we can't get out of it. I've tried."

Bart is a junior lawyer for a swanky outfit in London. During my case, he was allowed to liaise with my defence attorney. But there's nothing to be done. I hurt another individual. The last straw in a string of offences.

I stare into the swirling tea. "I was with you when I first saw them, you know."

Bart pulls away. "Saw what?"

"The shadows."

Bart nods. Everyone knows about the creatures I see in mirrors. We just don't talk about it anymore.

To carry on reading, click here:
https://geni.us/ShadowKeepers